PRAISE FOR

Those We Love Most

"Lee Woodruff knows how to get to the heart
of the matter on every occasion."

—ALICE HOFFMAN

"Lee Woodruff has written a beautiful,
unflinching, and poignant page turner about the
complexities of love and marriage, tricky family
dynamics, and the power of the human heart.
Everything you want in a great read is here,
including wonderful storytelling that builds to a
satisfying ending. Loved it."

—ADRIANA TRIGIANI

"*Those We Love Most* is an engrossing story about
family fragility, rupture, and redemption.
Woodruff's beautiful and unflinching portrayal
of the grief, betrayal, guilt, tenacity, and love
that engulf this family in the aftermath of a
devastating tragedy will keep you turning pages
till the end."

—SUE MONK KIDD

"Flawless, breathtaking, and oh-so-real, *Those We Love Most* is a beautifully written book about family, love, betrayal, forgiveness, and how we pick up the pieces in the wake of unthinkable tragedy. When I turned the last page, I found myself missing the characters already. I can't recommend this book highly enough."

—HARLAN COBEN

"Those We Love Most is a poignant, heartwarming story that follows you beyond its pages. Woodruff skillfully makes the Corrigan family real—fallible and vulnerable, ultimately strengthened by the undeniable power of love. I grieved and cheered for them all, and finished the book with a big smile on my face."

—CATHERINE COULTER

"I opened *Those We Love Most* when my plane took off from Boston, and didn't look up again until I landed in Miami. In between, I cried and smiled and nodded, and turned pages faster and faster. It's one of those novels."

—ANN HOOD

Those We Love Most

Also by Lee Woodruff

In an Instant
Perfectly Imperfect

Those

We

Love

Most

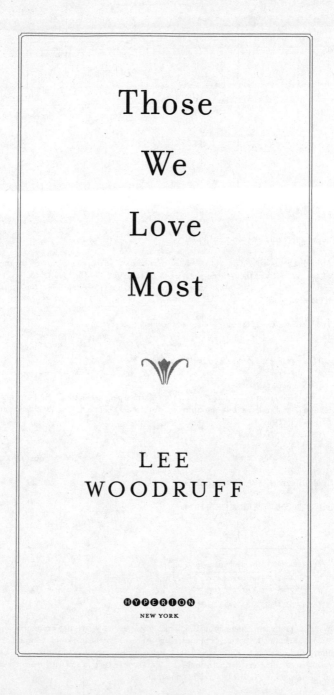

LEE
WOODRUFF

HYPERION

NEW YORK

The Library of Congress has catalogued the hardcover edition as:

Woodruff, Lee.
　　Those we love most / Lee Woodruff. — 1st ed.
　　　　p.　cm.
　　ISBN 978-1-4013-4178-7
　　1. Children—Death—Fiction. Fiction.　2. Married people—Fiction.　3. Betrayal—Fiction.　4. Family secrets—Fiction.　5. Forgiveness—Fiction.　6. Psychological fiction.　I. Title.
　　PS3623.0673T56　2012
　　813'.6—dc22

　　　　　　　　　　　　　　　　　　　　　　　　　　　　　　　　　　　2011049422

Trade paperback ISBN: 978-1-4013-4197-8

FIRST TRADE PAPERBACK EDITION

10　9　8　7　6　5　4　3　2　1

SUSTAINABLE FORESTRY INITIATIVE Certified Sourcing www.sfiprogram.org SFI-00993

THIS LABEL APPLIES TO TEXT STOCK

For Prince Liam,

who taught us more about how to live in

his six short years than most people

come to understand in a very long life

"Loss

is not

the end.

It's simply an

invitation

to change."

Those We Love Most

It *was only* the front edge of summer and the yard already looked overgrown, as if the squalls of May and early June had held a kind of magical elixir, a formula that put all of the plants on steroids. Standing on the perimeter of the flagstone patio with her coffee, Margaret studied the impatiens with their fat, red heads, nodding downward, and the fecund look of the peonies as they passed their peak, rotting from fuchsia and ballet slipper pink to a brown mush.

She began to walk out past the shed where the yard narrowed between two bent willows, toward her beloved vegetable garden. When the kids were little, she had carved out slivers of her day to be here, sacrificing so she could embrace the peace this plot of land afforded her. Morning was her favorite time to be out among her plants, when her energy and joy for the day were at their peak. "Your mistress," Roger had called her garden once, and she'd never forgotten it. The irony, she'd thought bitterly.

There was another one, she noticed, as her mouth curved downward with displeasure. Another chipmunk hole, or possibly a mole, next to the bright green shoots of her coreopsis. It had been burrowing down and feasting on the tender roots, and nothing enraged her more than having her flowers under attack. Rodents were where she drew the line, rodents and slugs. Summer was just beginning, and they were already declaring war.

Margaret could feel her agitation rising and fought to contain it. It was too early in the season to get worked up. In many ways, gardening was an exercise in patience, an endurance sport. She loved how it changed through the seasons. In July and August, she became an avid canner, preserving vegetables and then freezing sauces for winter. Autumn brought late-September raspberries, ropy vines with fat, lumpy pumpkins and squash. There was always enough zucchini to supply the neighbors, and she derived pleasure in baking bread and muffins. Her labors slowed in September until the first frost of October stopped the leggy fall dahlias, asters, and mums in their tracks. When it all hung brown and yellowed from the cold, she would cover the beds and perennials with dried leaves in a quiet funeral ritual, digging up the dahlia tubers to winter over in peat moss.

Weeding between the rows of beans, she thought she heard a distant sound from the house. Could that be the phone, or was the breeze playing tricks on her? There again, so faint from all the way out back. No matter. She'd be in soon enough. There was nothing that couldn't wait. It was probably Roger, calling from the road. This trip was Denver first and then Florida, if she remembered. It was hard to keep all the deals at his commercial real estate firm straight sometimes, and frankly she'd given up trying.

The members of her family were like lines intersecting at random points. Her two grown daughters close to home, Maura and Erin, and her son, Stu, in Milwaukee, flitted in and out of her weeks, as did her grandchildren, with their multiple school and sports activities. Roger was mostly consumed with his work and weekend golf at the club. These days, there were times she simply felt like an afterthought.

Margaret sighed and hauled herself up off the weeding pad and toward the shed. She would find a new sticky trap and then dig out the pack of Merits stashed behind the slug pellets on the top shelf. Although her kids thought she'd quit long ago, Margaret indulged

her secret vice once or twice a day, sometimes with her morning coffee and usually with a glass of pinot grigio before Roger came home.

Now there was the phone ringing again, just seconds after it had
stopped. Someone must need to reach her, or maybe it was just coincidence. There were so many of those automated callers now,
even on the off-hours, but it wasn't even nine in the morning. She
sighed and tucked the cigarettes back on the shelf in the shed.
Maybe it was Maura calling. Her daughter knew she would be alone
until late that night, perhaps she had an invitation for dinner. Margaret's spirits rose. She'd bring the rest of the blueberry banana
bread she had baked yesterday.

As she approached the house, Margaret heard the measured cadence of Roger's recorded voice on the answering machine asking
callers to repeat their phone number twice. There was the shrill
beep of the machine and then a woman's voice; it was impossible to
tell who was leaving a message. The words were indistinct but the
tone urgent, the voice muffled as it carried across the yard and out
to where she was walking. Margaret quickened her pace as she
headed in.

· · ·

Roger rolled over onto one elbow and squinted at the strip of white
light blazing through the slender gap in the curtains. The Florida
sun was low but already warming the manicured grass, and it
promised to be another hot, steamy day. A blanket of humidity lay
over the city, permeating even the air-conditioned room and its
muggy, damp smell. Outside, the low buzz of a leaf blower droned
and some kind of tropical bird squawked. The staccato, uneven-
ness of the noise was unsettling.

Julia's tanned toffee-colored back pressed against him with its
gentle curve. Her shoulders rose and fell softly with her breathing.
Roger's thoughts leapt ahead to the evening, when he would board a

plane home to Chicago. It would be at least a month or more before he would see her again, and he felt a melancholy about that, mingled with the comfort of heading home. He knew, from previous experience, that today would feel both eternal and swift.

Last night they had looked like any other older couple, swaying on the hotel veranda to the band. They'd ordered fruity drinks, and Julia had laughed at his jokes, almost too loudly, as the waiter delivered them with tiny paper parasols. He'd enjoyed that, her amusement at simple things. The way Julia clasped her hands in front of her chest in delight made him feel as if he were an all-powerful magician who could conjure up her happiness.

On his last day with her he would inevitably think of Margaret, despite his best intentions. She and the kids would intrude as he began the mental transition home. Roger forced himself to push those thoughts away. His children were grown now, with families and homes of their own, no longer in his daily orbit, yet he marveled at how the habit of that responsibility persisted.

As he had raised his glass the night before to toast Julia, an image had flickered briefly in his head of his wife scraping the remains of her dinner into the disposal and methodically lowering the plate onto the bottom rack of the dishwasher.

Julia rolled toward him on the bed, eyes fluttering open as a half sigh escaped her lips. This last day was always harder on her. She lived alone in this small stucco house in Tampa near the freeway, where she'd raised two sons and outlived her husband. For the past five years this had been their arrangement, and he had been careful never to promise her anything more.

"How long have you been awake?" Julia asked groggily.

"Not much before you." He shrugged.

"You have that look," she mused, rolling up on one elbow. "It's your leaving-day look."

"Then it must be leaving day." The words came out more harshly than he had intended, and he silently chided himself for beginning the distancing process this early in the morning. They had most of the day left, with plans to take a walk. Perhaps they'd grab some scrambled eggs at the beachfront diner first.

Julia looked down at the white blanket, picking at a snag in the weave. Roger closed his palm over her smaller, birdlike hands and tilted her chin up toward him, meeting her eyes with a reassuring smile. Her fine high "Puerto Rican cheekbones," as she called them, were burnished with a few freckles and deep crow's-feet around her eyes. Julia's hair was jet black, but a line of silver-gray roots growing in from her scalp jarred him. He appreciated the illusion of Julia's seemingly effortless beauty.

"I'm sorry," Roger offered quietly.

"No offense taken," Julia said breezily, though he knew he'd stung her.

"We've got one great day left, let's go down to that little coffee shop by the beach for some eggs."

Julia smiled weakly and rolled into his arms. Roger liked the way it felt to hold her. He enjoyed the heft of this woman, the fleshy fullness so substantial and weighty. Her shoulders were broad and her arms heavily freckled from the sun. Dozens of tiny white buttons swooped up the front of her lavender nightgown, ending in the soft cleave of her bosom. It was an ample bosom, seductive, womanly, anything but matronly. Roger began stroking her back slowly, and her foot moved across his leg in response.

The shrill ring of his cell phone pierced their silence, and Roger rolled onto his side, picking the phone up off the bedside table. He pressed IGNORE when he saw his home number and rolled back toward Julia.

It rang again, immediately afterward. Odd that it was Margaret calling him twice this early in the day. Without remark, he half-turned from Julia and swung his feet onto the wooden floor, reaching for his reading glasses to scroll through his e-mails, his brow furrowed. Julia studied the flecks of moles down by his lower back and the patchy hairiness up near his shoulders. She reached to smooth his hair at the nape of his neck, still full and only flecked with gray, and then she traced her finger down the length of his spine.

"Everything all right?" she asked casually.

"Fine. Fine. Just a call I need to return. Why don't you hop in the shower, and I'll follow," said Roger, with a more businesslike tone than he intended.

. . .

The sky was cobalt and cloudless as Maura headed out the door for the short walk to the elementary school. She was keenly aware of the scent of newly mown lawns and mulched flower beds, the summery lift of the breeze off Lake Michigan, as if all of her senses were heightened. A suburban serenity pervaded the neatly mani-cured yards of her neighborhood, and yet inside she felt unbound and provocative, the polar opposite of her surroundings.

Maura handed Sarah a lime green plastic sippy cup of juice, lift-ing her into the stroller as she called to James and Ryan to put on their backpacks. She bent to click the leash onto Rascal's collar and stood up as James shot one leg over his bike and coasted out the garage and down the driveway, straight-legged on the pedals, hel-met unbuckled and cocked to one side. Maura opened her mouth to admonish him and then closed it with a half smile. Today was not a day for nagging.

Inside she felt alive, glorious, and this bright mood and a sense of giddiness lent her a visual hyperawareness. She noted the cracks in the sidewalk where the tree root had split the cement, the bright red of a child's ball left on the grass, the way the morning sun cut sideways through the fence slats. Everything was in bas-relief. She reminded Ryan about the snack in his backpack pocket and then called ahead to James to slow down as his legs pumped wildly, pro-pelling the bike up the sidewalk toward the elementary school.

There was no response from James, and in her complete absorption, her mind replaying the events of the previous day, she let him ride on; he was too far ahead now.

Maura paused with the stroller as Rascal lifted his leg to pee against one of the giant oaks lining the shaded street. They were only three blocks away from the school now, and down the road she could see the traffic thicken around the brick building, a column of kids and multicolored backpacks bulging by the crossing guard in his neon orange vest. One week of school left. The high school was already out, and the elementary classes were down to half days, almost a waste of time in her mind. She was ready for a break in the routine, eager to loosen the reins on schedules and deadlines and the morning craziness of making breakfast and packing lunches while dressing Sarah for the walk. Some mornings her husband, Pete, was a help, other times it was easier to do it herself, even as she careened around the kitchen on overdrive.

Maura felt the vibration of the text in the pocket of her jeans and involuntarily smiled as she fished out her phone to check the screen. She stopped and stood for a moment, focusing on the display, her pulse quickening as she brought the letters into focus, and she smiled, a warmth spreading through her. Maura paused, gathering her thoughts for a clever response and waved absentmindedly at James, who was calling her name from up ahead. She began to type.

She heard the brakes before she saw the car: a sickening squeal, like a high-pitched whine, as tires slid on the pavement up ahead and then the sound of metal colliding. In an instant a stab of panic and fear exploded in her chest as she began running, instinctively, pushing the stroller aside, dropping the dog's leash and abandoning Ryan wordlessly.

Maura was sprinting now, screaming words that she would not remember later, primal and senseless. Every part of her was focused on getting to her eldest son. She hurtled forward on the sidewalk with a surge of adrenaline, and yet it all still felt like slow motion, as if her arms and legs were weighted. In the seconds before she got to James, she registered an eerie quiet, and then the scene was before her at once in a slash of vivid color and sounds.

In the tangle of bumper and bike, the bent front wheel and broken spokes protruded from the undercarriage of the car. And then she saw James, off to the left of the vehicle. She hesitated for a fraction of a second before she dove toward him on the road. She dropped to one knee next to his immobile body, afraid to touch, unsure of what to touch, as blood pooled onto the asphalt, soaking her jeans and then her hands. Why was there blood trickling out of his ear?

She was dimly aware of other figures around her now: a boy, older than James, moaning and muttering, perhaps the driver of the car, but Maura couldn't think about that now. Someone had a cell phone out, a woman urged her not to move her son, to wait for the ambulance. There was an adult restraining Ryan and Sarah, both of them crying and calling for her, and she looked up blindly to reassure them and yelled something about it being OK. Rascal was barking in the arms of someone she didn't recognize.

Don't think about them now, she told herself. Don't let the outside in. Everything on the periphery shrunk down to background noise. She had to focus on James. She was talking to him, cooing, reassuring him with her voice even though there was no reaction. He was so still, so quiet. And there was all that blood, thick and dark, darker than she would have expected, and her mind inexplicably conjured up the iron scent of beets or root vegetables. She had never seen so much blood.

And now there it was, finally, faint at first but growing in volume, the siren's wail. *That was good, fast,* Maura thought numbly. And then everything else, the warm feeling of the day, the sequence and the clarity of its events, coalesced into one horrible, terrifying blur.

2

W*hen Roger first* got to the hospital, directly from O'Hare airport, he took a moment in the lobby to compose himself before riding the elevator up to the ICU floor. Almost ten years earlier he had walked through those same sliding glass entry doors with a bouquet and a silver Mylar IT'S A BOY balloon to see his daughter Maura and meet his first grandchild.

Two years ago he had actually been the one to drive James here to have his arm x-rayed after he fell off the monkey bars. Maura had met them in the ER once she'd settled newborn Sarah with Margaret. She had been scared but purposeful. He remembered how impressed he'd been at his daughter's competency and focus then. She'd calmed her son, joked about how many people would sign his cast and what color would look best with his baseball uniform.

Maura had asked the doctors pointed questions, getting them to explain their medical jargon and then repeating what they said to James in a mother's words. But that had merely been a broken arm.

Now he was here under such unimaginable circumstances, and Roger blinked a moment in the fluorescent lights, taking in the institutional lobby with its forest green paint and maroon upholstery. A man in a corner chair was sedately holding a wad of gauze around his hand, and Roger could see rusty bloodstains on the front of his shirt. Two African American women were reading magazines, one older, with her purse clasped firmly on her lap. Behind the nurses' station, farther down the hall, people in brightly patterned hospital tunics with stethoscope necklaces moved purposefully around the desk, holding charts and paperwork.

"Touch and go" were the words Margaret had used to describe James's condition on the phone, her voice clipped and agonized. There was internal bleeding and a severe head injury. They had operated immediately, while Roger was still scrambling to get to the Tampa airport, Julia going well above the speed limit, dodging in and out of lanes to make the next flight.

James was sedated now; a "medically induced coma" they called it, and the surgeons had done all that they could for the moment. Brain injuries were so individual, they explained, the outcomes too unpredictable to offer any sort of accurate prognosis. So much depended on exactly where the person was injured and how severely. Age and level of intelligence could be factors in recovery too, they said. There were so many unknowns, Margaret had told him. But overall it was not good.

What happened next was up to James and whatever willpower was left in that little, broken body. The car, with the son of one of Maura's neighbors driving, had apparently struck him at a relatively slow speed. But it was the way that James had been hit, the angle of the impact, that had ruptured and bruised organs and the fact that he'd flown through the air and landed on his head. Roger hadn't thought until this moment about whether or not he'd been wearing his bike helmet, but the question flitted through his mind as he stood at the ground floor elevator bank. It wouldn't change the outcome now, he thought glumly. He exhaled, stepped into the elevator, and pressed the button for the fourth floor.

Roger set down his bag and briefcase and removed his blazer, feeling like a traveling salesman as he watched the floors click by in red digits. God, how the hell did anyone mentally gird themselves for something like this? You imagined it, experienced it occasionally with people your own age, but was anyone ever prepared to visit a critically injured grandson's hospital room?

He stepped out of the elevator and saw Margaret almost immediately, positioned by the ICU curtain down the hall. He met her eyes and saw something veiled and pleading in them, but then there was relief, a subtle unburdening played across her features relaxing her brows. He could tell instantly how upset she was from the tight coil of her body, but he knew that Margaret would refrain from showing Maura her raw fear. She would need to remain ramrod strong for her daughter, for all of them. That was her calling card. Signature Margaret. The artificial lighting in the ICU corridor gave a jaundiced hue to Roger's partially tanned forearms. He was aware of the smells of the hallway, antiseptic and ammonia mingled with what he imagined was the sweaty smell of human fear.

"Hi." Roger set his bag gratefully at his feet in the hallway and moved toward Margaret, arms outstretched. She placed both hands on his upper arms, rose on her toes, and offered her cheek, as she always did in public, something he'd grown accustomed to over the years. He felt a softening, a slump of her shoulders as one rogue sob escaped, and he drew her closer. Something about her vulnerability, her neediness of him, made Roger squeeze harder, and they stayed that way for a few moments until she pulled away to study him. She dabbed the wetness in her eyes, collected herself, and then assessed him, as if checking for damages.

"You OK?" Roger asked her softly, and Margaret nodded, looking inside the room toward the corner, where his daughter was leaning over the bed, obscuring the view.

"Hi, honey," Roger boomed, more brightly than he felt and too loudly for the circumstances.

"Daddy!" Maura jumped up and rose from the bed, out through the curtain and into her father's arms in one almost continuous motion. As they hugged, she began to cry, convulsively, her shoulders shaking, and he patted her back as if she were still a small girl.

"Oh, Dad." She lifted her head off his chest, and swirling across her face like a tempest, he saw terror and guilt, grief and pain. Roger recalled suddenly how easy it had been to comfort her when she was young. The wrongs and injustices in her life had been trifles then, bloodied knees and bruised hearts. He had thought, when they'd sent her out into the world, that they had prepared her for life. How did anyone prepare his or her child for this? he wondered.

"It'll be OK, honey, it's OK." In the absence of knowing what to say, Roger continued hugging and patting her in a reflexive response.

His eyes strayed through the wide opening in the curtain to study James on the bed behind Maura, and his first thought was how pale and small his grandson appeared, lying so immobile. There were tubes seemingly everywhere, and bruises and cuts on his arms and other parts of his body that were visible above the sheet. His scalp had been shaved on one side and a giant angry seam of scabbed skin ran across the one hemisphere, with what looked like oversize staples holding it all together. James's head swelled oddly outward like a balloon on one side, giving his face a lopsided look, and both of his eyes were bruised and blackened. A machine behind him made a *whoosh*ing sound, and Roger realized with a jolt that it was breathing for James, keeping time in exact intervals as his small rib cage rose and fell in a rhythmic shudder. Roger released Maura and moved to the bed, drawn by the fragility of his grandson, the sight of a life suspended in the balance so graphically.

"I'm here, James," he said thinly. "I'm here." He didn't know where to touch, what to touch; every inch of James seemed broken somehow or under siege.

"I'm sorry," said Maura. "About your business meeting. That all of this . . . pulled you away, I mean." She let out the last part in an almost inaudible voice. Now, standing apart from her, he took in her appearance. Her thick, dark hair was limp and unwashed, her blue eyes red rimmed. There was a smear of blood on her inner wrist, and Roger realized that the pressed jeans and clean cotton shirt she was wearing now had probably been brought to the hospital for her by Margaret or her husband, Pete. Whatever she'd had on at the time had most likely been covered with blood, he thought grimly. She looked defeated, determined, and terrified.

"Come, sit, Maura," Roger said, taking her arm and guiding her back into the padded chair next to James. "Have you had anything to eat?"

Maura looked up at him numbly, as if she hadn't understood the question. She nodded and reached for James's hand in the bed.

"I've been trying," said Margaret authoritatively. "She's managed a few bites." Roger nodded. He looked up as his son-in-law entered the small room with cups of coffee in a cardboard holder, and Pete's eyes met Roger's with a noticeable relief. He handed a Styrofoam cup to Margaret and then to Maura and turned to offer the third to Roger.

"Roger! Thank God, welcome. Coffee? I can get another one downstairs."

Roger shook his head and held up his hand.

"Take it, Roger," urged Pete. "You've been traveling."

He reached up to clasp the cup and studied Pete's sunken eyes, bluish around the sockets from shock and fatigue. His shoulders slumped slightly, his normal, more boisterous self diminished in the tiny space. Each of them in the room seemed older and sluggish, as if their life force had been extracted suddenly.

Roger watched Pete reach out to his daughter and stroke her back. Sipping his coffee in the austere hospital hallway, Roger let his thoughts drift toward a happier moment, Pete and Maura's late-September wedding day more than a decade before. The glorious Indian summer that surprised them all with its staying power had abruptly retreated, and there had been a bite in the air. Roger recalled how through the fuzzy edges of too many scotches at the country club reception, he'd walked out to the dock to study the crescent of white lights twinkling up the North Shore of Lake Michigan. He had wondered then about the prospects of his daughter's happiness. It occurred to him, with a sudden stab of sorrow, how you could know your child her whole life, and then she entered into marriage and a part of her was forever cloaked in shadow.

If Roger had harbored early misgivings about Pete Corrigan, he had come to view him as the antidote to balance out his daughter's sometimes selfish and willful streaks. Roger had liked Pete since Maura had first brought him home in her sophomore year of college. Two years older than his daughter, he'd attended high school a few towns away, and Roger had casually known Pete's parents, June and Stan. The Corrigans owned an insurance agency, which Pete had inherited, and coincidentally, maybe a decade before Maura had met Pete, Roger had purchased a homeowner's policy from Maura's father-in-law for the cottage in Door County.

On paper, he was great son-in-law material: dependable, a good provider with a built-in career in his family business, the solid ex-high-school-football type still in decent physical shape. Pete had an even temperament and no funny earrings or designer facial hair. Moreover, he was a practicing Catholic, something that had appealed to Roger after the string of Jewish and Protestant boys Maura had dated in high school and college. He was a straightforward, sturdy, uncomplicated person and by all appearances a decent father. Beyond that, it was hard to judge and certainly not his place.

Roger had to admit that he'd been somewhat surprised by the choices each of his three children had made in a spouse. Early on he had realized that the best course was to keep his own counsel. The qualities in particular mates that he'd thought suitable or unsuitable had no bearing on the way things ended up. And Roger certainly knew firsthand what a fickle and unpredictable institution marriage could be.

"The only people who know the real story are the people it involves," Margaret would always say when the kids would gossip or criticize someone at school, baiting her and trying unsuccessfully to bring her into the ring. They would laugh at her righteousness. But what she said was true, Roger reasoned. And marriage, especially, was a private entity. You could look in from the outside, see the lights in the windows, the beds made and the table set, and assume that there was order and contentment. But the truth was, as Roger himself knew after more than four decades of marriage, it was ultimately a fluid thing, a shape-shifter, holding different private characteristics at varying points in time.

Roger's reverie was interrupted by the arrival of the young neurosurgeon, Dr. Oberg, who bustled into the room, his surgical mask hanging limply on the side of his chest by one tie. He couldn't have been more than forty, but the fatigue in his face and his vague impatience lent him the appearance of someone much older. His eyes registered initial surprise at so many family members crammed into the small space in the ICU. Introductions were made all around, and the doctor, who seemed clearly pressed for time, began to give his pronouncement.

It hadn't yet been twenty-four hours and James's condition was unchanged, it hadn't worsened, which was good, Dr. Oberg said. But it was impossible to predict exactly what his life would look like after recovery. If he recovered. There was no way to know what he would be left with, but based on where he'd been injured, on the right side of his brain, he would probably have physical and cognitive issues. And all the rest of it—his speech, memory, and the extent of his mobility—would be revealed in time. The doctor's face was neutral, like a mask, and Roger wondered how many times a day he delivered speeches like this.

"First," Dr. Oberg went on to explain, "we need James to wake up. We need him to fight. And then when we see signs of him waking up or responding to our commands, we can begin to lower the medication and help him come out of the coma. He is still on the knife's edge." The doctor spoke in a quiet tone, averting his eyes from the respectful, anxious family members who felt the jab of each word, hanging on his sentences like worshipers.

Dr. Oberg looked almost uncomfortable behind his glasses, like he wanted to bolt. Roger imagined he was the sort of physician who felt more comfortable in the operating room than at the bedside. The ability to take action must be so much more preferable than standing amid this raw and palpable sea of grief and fervent expectation, parsing people's ability to hope.

"So what's our next milestone, what are we looking for him to do, doc?" Pete asked, and Roger noticed for the first time that Pete was graying slightly at the temples, little flecks just beginning right at the hairline, fine as a fishing line.

"It means we need your son to fight hard for these next seventy-two hours," the doctor replied. "They are going to be critical."

3

Four days had passed since the accident, and Maura felt as if she hadn't showered in weeks. Her tongue was thick, breath sour, her eyes dry and devoid of tears. There was a dull ache in her lower back from leaning over the bed rail to stroke James's hand, whisper to him and assure him, regardless of his lack of response, that she was there. All food tasted like cardboard, and she'd actually had to spit out the muffin her brother, Stu, had tried to force her to eat this morning. He and his wife, Jen, had traveled from Milwaukee the day after James's surgery and had toggled back and forth between the hospital and her children at home.

"Keep talking to him," the nurses had said. "He hears you somewhere in there, and that will help knit his brain back together." And so she talked. She told him the story of the day he was born; she read him the news from the *Chicago Tribune* sports section that Pete had found in the cafeteria. She'd described his room at home, his siblings, and how much his dog Rascal missed him, sleeping on top of James's pillow each night, waiting for him to return. And when Maura searched for new topics, just to keep the words coming, she began to name his friends at school and read their get-well cards aloud. The simplicity of their hand-scribbled messages comforted her. She'd even counted in Spanish, something she had been drilling her son on for an upcoming vocabulary test. When she had exhausted all of her energy and it was time to return to the house and pray for sleep, she would ask the nurses to make sure that his favorite CDs kept playing softly on the boom box her sister Erin had brought to his bedside.

The images of what Ryan and Sarah were doing now at home and exactly who was minding them at any given time intruded periodically, and she pushed those thoughts out of her head, as if shutting a door. Maura couldn't possibly think about anyone beside James right now. It would only tear at her, and there were so many needs outside this ICU that could splinter her focus if she let them. Every molecule of her energy needed to be wholly focused on her son, as if she could heal him through sheer will and the forcefulness of her maternal love.

The thought of ministering to her other children's simple needs, once the unremarkable but constant features of her day, now merely exhausted her. Contemplating the simplest actions, like reading a book to Sarah or organizing laundry, felt like summiting a mountain. But the hardest thing, the most difficult thing for Maura, was to cease replaying the accident over and over in her mind.

Anytime she stopped moving, when she collapsed in the hospital chair next to James with her legs tucked up under her, or when she paused at the porcelain drinking fountain in the long ICU corridor, she would see the images, as if a cinema were flickering through a private, internal screen. The bright flash of chrome, the abrupt swerve of the handlebars to the left, off the sidewalk, as if all of those admonishments, all of those warnings she had constantly made to all three of her children, all of the "be carefuls" and "look both ways," had never been uttered. In the film loop of her mind, she was inside James, looking out of his eyes. It was as if Maura actually *were* her son.

In her head, she could correct it. Maura would rewind to the exact moment when his bike fenders clattered noisily toward the curb. In her new, revised version of the day, she would be positioned vigilantly on his left, able to put a steadying arm on his bike, instead of yards behind, pushing Sarah's stroller. Maura would have waited until the car had passed, looked carefully in both directions with him, and then given him permission to cross as she eased the stroller's wheels over the curb behind him.

"Stop, honey," she imagined telling him as she instinctively caught him veering toward the road. She would have anticipated the pure childlike excitement that blurred caution and wiped thoughts of safety from his nine-year-old brain. The incident would have produced that surge of adrenaline and heart-thumping drama that pounded in your veins after a crisis had been averted and lingered momentarily as a physical reminder of the close call. Later that night at dinner, the example of James's carelessness, his forgetting to look both ways, might have gotten a mention, a parental reinforcement. And after he was safely tucked in bed, after she had brushed his bangs back from his forehead, the memory of his near miss, those few seconds of terror, might have returned to remind her how lucky they all were before it faded and then disappeared.

But that was magical thinking. There were no do-overs. And every time she let her mind wander, every time she gave herself the luxury of contemplating the "what if," of revising history, she was slapped in the face by the enormity of the fact that this was really happening.

Each day since the accident was a carbon of the one before. Doctors, nurses, and interns whisked in and out of the curtained area to study the machines, to take James's vitals, or to change his IV drip. When a nurse accidentally dropped a tray, causing them all to jump, Maura fought the irrational urge to yell at her, to scream at all of them to leave James alone. *She* would care for him. She was responsible for all of this and he was her baby, her very first baby. She would fix him, fix this.

When Maura was with James, physically beside her son in the hospital, there was a vestigial well of adrenaline within her that she could exist on for weeks if needed. She could feel it rising and propelling her forward as she questioned the doctors and nurses, followed his medications, checked on continuity at shift changes, and watched the monitors for the most minuscule changes. Maura would draw from her own body to nourish him, as she had done when she was pregnant, using the essential parts of herself to sustain a life. In those moments when she was by James's side, talking to him, stroking his skin, applying lotion to his feet, she didn't experience fatigue the way she would have imagined. In those moments it was as if all of her senses and nerve endings were standing alert, like shavings on a magnet.

Maura felt the presence of someone behind her and turned to see that Pete had walked into the hospital room, interrupting her circling thoughts, and she was momentarily confused. It was too soon. Was he coming from home? She glanced out the window and realized that the day had evaporated; time in the ICU existed like a black hole. How was it dusk already?

"Hey, babe, why don't you let me take over," Pete said quietly, moving toward her and touching the top of her head as she rose from the bedside. He circled his arm around her waist, steering her by the elbow for a minute, but she shook him off.

"I . . . can't," she said with more forcefulness than she'd intended.

"Sarah and Ryan are asking for you. I'll be here with James." Maura shut her eyes and put her palms over her face, raking her hair back through her fingertips and letting out her stale breath in a rush. Her temples throbbed, and she could smell herself through the cotton T-shirt, the sour smell of both sweat and inactivity. Maura had no desire to leave, couldn't leave. The thought of going home made her anxious. It felt terrifying.

"What if James wakes up while I'm gone? Who will comfort him?" she asked numbly.

"I'll be here, Maura."

"But I'm his mother, he'll need to see me." She blinked.

She imagined walking back into their house for the fourth night now since the accident. Her home and all of the objects in it were frozen like a diorama in the rituals of everyday life. Last night she had begun crying at the sight of her cardigan sweater thrown over her kitchen desk chair. The last time she had worn it James had been whole. The milk in the refrigerator had been purchased just the day before, when running errands was her most demanding task. How elusive that kind of simple contentment and routine normalcy seemed now. She was determined not to leave the hospital tonight. The house was now a frightening reminder of how quickly life had turned.

Pete remained silent, studying her, his arms folded and jaw set. Maura sensed something different in the way he looked at her since the accident. The quiet between them was weighty. She thought back to when he'd first arrived at the hospital the day of the accident, twenty minutes or so after she and James. "Where were you?" he'd blurted out in anguish, searching her face for an explanation. Between them lay their son, with tubes and IVs snaking from his tiny body. "How did this happen?" he had asked again, almost without thinking.

Maura felt stung by the naked, reflexive accusation of his blame. It wasn't as if she had pushed James or told him it was safe to cross. But she had been there. She was present as the watchful parent, and she had not been watching. She had been doing something else, entirely unplugged from the present. And this was the part, the awful dark part that she must continue to push back down.

"It just happened, Pete. An accident. I looked away for a second to get juice for Sarah . . ." But the lie burned, caught like a chicken bone in her throat, and Pete gave her an odd, ambiguous look. During their years together they had come to intuit each other's body language, to interpret the dead weight of unspoken subjects.

And since then, in the vortex of the eerie silence between them and the wide circumference Pete gave her, she felt something unnamed, steely and cold. A fissure. More than a fissure perhaps, a wide crack in their foundation that she was uncertain could be repaired, and that thought made her very tired. This whole thing—the accident, the circumstances—was a blow that would rock even the most solid marriage, which hers most definitely was not.

But for now, with her son suspended in this portal between life and death, she cared about nothing and no one else. The issues that had plagued her marriage, the stagnation and even the periods of apathy and distraction, were better left unexamined. Everything beyond the four walls of this hospital room was beside the point. All that mattered now was that James live. For this tender mercy, she would do or give anything.

4

The shrillness of the phone woke Margaret instantly, and Roger was by her side in the bed, struggling up from sleep at first and then immediately awake.

"Hello?" Margaret realized just how coiled she was, how braced for the call in the middle of the night since they had all been blind-sided less than a week earlier.

"Margaret." It was Pete's voice, hushed and defeated.

"Pete, we're here. What's happened? Is he awake?"

"He's . . . James . . ." His voice choked suddenly, crying, unable to speak.

"Pete?" Roger was listening now, his head up near hers by the receiver, temple to temple.

More silence. Pete struggled to form words.

"James is . . . gone. He . . . died," he said simply and then the strangled sounds of a person in anguish. Margaret was stunned. Her mind scuttled to make sense of the individual words he'd uttered. *Gone. Dead.* How was that possible? They'd just been there that day.

Roger rolled back on the bed with a groan. He covered his face with his hands and let out one long breath, and then she felt the bed moving. He was crying hard, shaking the mattress.

"Oh, Pete. No. How is she? Where's Maura?" she said softly. Silence on the line. "We'll come over now."

Pete made another sound, incomprehensible to her, and they both hung up. She should have told him she'd call Stu and Erin, save him from that, but she didn't want to call him back now. Margaret moved to comfort Roger wordlessly and then rose to dress. They could tend to their own grief later. Right now her family needed her, needed them both.

· · ·

Three days later it was the faces of the other boys at the funeral, the children from James's elementary school, that pierced Margaret's heart. They sat fidgeting in the dark mahogany pews, raising and lowering the kneelers, uncomfortable in small blazers and pressed collared shirts, as if they were perfect young replicas of their someday-older selves. Their lives would move forward, sports teams and report cards, orthodontists' appointments and growth spurts, first girlfriends and broken hearts. James would be forever nine to all of them. It seemed impossible, incomprehensible, as she sat here, looking between the sea of children and the enlarged photographs of James arranged on the altar, that her grandson would never grow another day older.

Margaret sat quietly as the pews filled behind her and closed her eyes to absorb the calming atmosphere of the church. She marveled at how quickly all of this had happened, like those flash floods in California that cascaded down a dry creek bed and suddenly swept cars and houses and whole families up in the current.

She opened her eyes and gazed upward at the vaulted ceilings, vaguely reassured by the familiar wood beams and the giant gold filigreed cross, which hung from the ceiling at the front of the church, suspended by almost undetectable wires. They had been coming to St. Thomas the Apostle since before her children were born, although she could never have fathomed that they would one day be here for a grandchild's funeral, such an inconceivably unnatural order of life, Margaret thought. She closed her eyes again, shutting out the noises of people settling themselves. The familiarity of this place, the rituals that had taken place here throughout the years—the baptisms, communions, and weddings—were a small comfort to her.

It was a hot, bright day outside, but the partial stone interior of the sanctuary was cool and removed from the world outside. Thick white candles flickered on long iron stands, and there was a profusion of flowers around the closed casket, the distinct waft of lilies, the flowers of death. Maura had been adamant about not having an open casket, and Margaret had been amazed by the clarity her daughter displayed during the funeral preparations and planning. She wanted to be involved in every single detail, choosing his clothes and the photographs, the songs, and even the catered dishes afterward. Her eyes had burned with the brightness that one sometimes associated with madness, but Margaret knew that such combustible energy, that superhuman overdrive, would not last. She was braced to catch her daughter when she crashed.

Margaret scanned the front pew containing the members of her family, all dressed in varying somber shades of clothing. She took in Roger's patrician profile next to her, his slightly hooked nose and round lips. At sixty-five, the almost full head of hair he proudly possessed was gray largely at the temples, his secret vanity. Their daughter Erin and her husband, Brad, sat to Roger's right, next to their two children, and beyond them was her son, Stu, and his wife, Jen, who had left their baby daughter at the house with a sitter. Next to them were Pete's parents, June and Stan, staring grimly ahead. They were good people, Margaret thought. June had been at the house or hospital almost as much as she had since the accident. On Margaret's opposite side, closest to the aisle, Maura sat stiffly as Ryan fidgeted uncomfortably between her and Pete on the faded red velvet seat cushion. Did her grandson even understand, at six, that his brother was gone forever? Little Sarah would only know of

James through stories. That thought abruptly sucked the air out of her, and she blinked back tears. The truly difficult days were yet to come, Margaret realized. The hardest part was being home after the rituals were complete, sitting angrily with grief and learning to accept it.

The organ music began mournfully, and the altar boys finished their preparations, heads respectfully bowed. Illuminated by the perfect projection of the summer sun, the elaborate jewel-toned stained-glass window at the front of the church glowed, each tiny fragment uniting into an image of Mary and the baby Jesus. The priest adjusted his vestments on the side of the altar, shifting his Bible to the other hand as he strode toward the center of the chancel. Margaret looked down the row at her family again. Underneath the current of grief, she felt pride in the way they had all pulled together. Stu and Erin had their own responsibilities, their own full lives. They had all simply stopped in the tracks of their respective days after that first phone call and manned the house, gently navigating well-meaning neighbors who wanted to linger off the front porch and stonewalling those who seemed bent on gleaning tidbits of information. In the days after the accident, they stood steadfastly in the doorframe of the Corrigan household with their own aching hearts, accepting the chicken casseroles and pans of lasagna with one foot protectively propping the screen, bracing against well-intentioned intrusion.

People always came out of the woodwork at a time like this, for good and bad. There was some need in human nature to insert yourself immediately, to take action, even if you knew the person only tangentially. The proximity to tragedy and sorrow caused an immediate evaluation of your own relative good fortune. The people who really understood, though, would hang back until the right moment, knowing that the real work began when all of the cars had left the driveway.

She and Roger had had little time for serious conversation since the accident and his sudden return from Florida. He was in shock, they all were, and he felt frustrated at how helpless he was to assist their child. The tragedy had seemed to turn him inward, sinking him further into his own thoughts and private grief. Yet there was a part of her, as she sat stiffly in the pew, that was hopeful. Perhaps their shared mourning might bring them closer, open channels between them that seemed to have been narrowing slowly over the years, like arteries.

The patterns and paths of their life together, especially in the past decade, had become more and more divergent. She had her set schedule: gardening, bridge, exercise, and the occasional lunch with friends. Being a devoted grandmother, a role of which she was immensely proud, also took up large portions of her time. She was a regular babysitter for Maura and Erin, especially when Roger traveled for work. But Roger still spent far too much time in the office at his stage in life, in her opinion. Some of their friends had begun to announce retirement plans, and although Roger pretended to find that idea attractive, she wondered how he would occupy himself without work. He was not a man given to introspection, not a reader or a crossword puzzle devotee, but a self-professed people person who brightened visibly in the company of others. She worried, privately, that retirement might shrink him, drain him of some of his vitality.

The priest gestured for them all to rise for a hymn, and the organ music swelled. Roger guided her up, cupping her elbow and leaving his arm entwined in the crook of hers. When they sat back down he suddenly clutched her hand, enclosing it in his palms, and brought it to his lap. Margaret raised her eyebrows gently in surprise and smoothed her black linen skirt with her free hand. She smiled inwardly despite herself and the circumstances. It was such a small act, but his spontaneity and their uncharacteristic display of physical affection pleased her. They would get through this together.

. . .

Maura stared straight ahead as the priest finished speaking. The pills her sister had forced her to take before the funeral had produced a floating sensation, as if she were a helium balloon above the pews. She looked down at her clasped hands, marveling that her body could sit so still while on the inside she was poised to scream. Next to her, sweating in his suit and tie, Pete grasped her hand so tightly that the slim bones curled toward one another. This discomfort was the only thing tethering her to the hard-backed bench, she thought. She would need to summon the energy to greet people after the funeral and then make it through the catered meal afterward at her parents' home. They would follow the hearse to the cemetery, but she couldn't think about that part right now. That would be unbearable, the physical letting go. Her eyes flicked to the small casket down in front of the altar and then back to Father Durkee's face.

Maura wondered suddenly if the neighbor boy, Alex Hulburd, the one who had hit James, had the nerve to come to the service. Her mother had told her that his parents would be there, but she could not look back behind her. They had stopped by the house the day after James had died, while Erin was manning the door, and enquired about their son visiting. Alex wanted to come meet with them, to apologize, they had explained. Her sister had told them firmly that it was not the right time.

There had been so much for Maura to focus on, first with the hospital routine and then with the funeral preparations, that the teenager who had killed her son had remained largely in the background. It was outrageous, though, to think that he imagined he could simply stop by and say, "Sorry." What could possibly come of that? His recklessness had brought them all to this place, she thought bitterly, but she would not contemplate that bitterness now. This was James's service, a tribute to his beautiful, too short life. Maura turned her head to the sides of the altar where vibrant enlarged photographs of her son in various poses were positioned—running on the beach as a toddler, grinning in his baseball uniform, his rounded baby face poking over the top of his crib. She recalled, suddenly, the way his baby fist had clutched and bunched the fabric of her shirt when he nursed, his eyes locked on hers in a way that fixed her at the center of his universe. A sob erupted in her throat, and her head lurched forward slightly. Maura brought her hand to her mouth. Her entire world had drained through a sieve and she could not imagine how it could be reconstituted.

"You OK?" Pete asked softly, leaning into her and then releasing her hand, smoothing it in her lap tenderly. She nodded slowly as he swiped his nose with his free hand, and Maura saw tears prick his eyes. There was a trace of alcohol on his breath, smothered by a breath mint and his heavy aftershave, but in Maura's strange, floating condition she felt neither the familiar reaction of disgust nor dismay.

Ryan was fidgeting in his seat, but she looked away, incapable of producing the desire to admonish him, and she noticed with gratitude that her mother was intervening, reaching across her father to put a hand on her son's arm. Sarah was in the back of the church with a babysitter. Thank God. She could not have dealt with that distraction during the service.

The disembodied, peaceful sensation created by the pills was pleasant, and when the priest signaled to their family that it was time to rise and walk up the aisle, she panicked for a moment. Her feet felt weighted like cinder blocks as she fought the overwhelming desire to stay exactly where she was, gazing at the images of her son's magnified face on the easels until darkness fell.

As the final hymn swelled on the organ, Maura followed the cranberry-colored runner toward the back of the church in slow motion. Darting her eyes on both sides of pews, she spotted the Hulburds. Maura was relieved to see that their son, Alex, was not with them. She momentarily caught the mother's gaze, and the woman abruptly looked down, flustered. Maura lifted her jaw, almost defiantly, directing her eyes back to her footfalls on the swirling textured carpet in front of her.

As she stood at the back of the church in the receiving line, Maura had to keep a hand on Pete's arm to steady herself. She felt as if her legs were about to buckle, and she couldn't remember when she'd last eaten. The almost pleasant detached feeling was dissipating, giving way to a gnawing anxiety. The combination of an empty stomach and the pills hit her suddenly, and she swayed for a moment, righting herself. Her feet hurt in the black heels. A few more minutes, though, and then she'd be outside the church in the fresh air, away from the pervasive and overpowering scent of white lilies.

5

"Can you hold Sarah?" Margaret asked, placing their granddaughter in Roger's lap. He nodded and began tickling her. "I'm going to heat up some soup and try to get Maura to eat something." Roger sighed. So much of the past week since the funeral had been spent indoors, staring at the four walls of Maura and Pete's home or trying to distract the grandchildren in their own house.

"Hello, beautiful." Roger bounced Sarah on his knee, and she let out a scream of delight.

"I'm glad Pete went back to the office," said Margaret. "Both of them moping around here was so hard to watch."

"I can't imagine he'll be able to concentrate."

"Everyone just needs a place to go," said Margaret. "People need to try to get back to a routine after something awful happens."

"I think I'm going to head back into the office this week as well."

Margaret nodded, as if she'd been waiting for this announcement. Roger avoided her eyes and began bouncing Sarah again, to her delight. "There's not much for me to do here, and the Crown deal has become a real mess. Too many cooks."

"Oh?" said Margaret, feigning interest. She lifted a spoonful of soup to her lips and began blowing on it before slurping loudly.

"Hot, hot, oh, Lord, I just burned my tongue." She abruptly turned off the flame under the pan and breathed in deeply.

Roger quickly poured a glass of water and offered it to her, but Margaret waved him away as if he were an annoyance. His inability to take any discernable or effective action left him feeling helpless in the Corrigan home. Roger could only bear witness as Maura's stoic resolve gradually began to crumple with each successive visit, like time-lapse photography. The bonfire of hope that had kept her spine straight and her adrenal glands pumping for that week in the hospital had been cruelly extinguished. In the lengthy stretches he sat, ate, or watched TV with his grandchildren, Maura looked more and more like a wax version of herself, her body limp, her eyes hollow and empty.

Roger took in his daughter's kitchen, the warm cherry cabinets and gleaming polished stone counters on the eating island, now under his wife's command. Soft lights below the cabinets gave the illusion of coziness, and he could see that Margaret had organized and cleaned every surface. Even the chrome appliances sparkled.

Out past the flagstone patio with the boxwood hedges, weeds sprouted in beds and in the potted geraniums. Roger thought momentarily about helping with the gardening and then dismissed the thought. Margaret always jokingly accused him of not knowing a weed from a flowering perennial; he'd better not disturb the wrong things out there. For the time being, he would have to grow accustomed to his ineffectiveness in his daughter's household.

Suddenly Roger remembered a colleague, a man he hadn't thought of in ages. Ed Schultz. He'd worked with Roger some fifteen years ago. They'd been on a prospective sales call with a burgeoning developer in Denver and had ended up at the bar together after dinner. Ed had been steadily downing one bourbon after the other, and as he'd moved from tipsy to drunk, he'd weepily confided in Roger that his high school—aged daughter had been raped at a rock concert in downtown Chicago. There was alcohol involved and

some rowdy boys, strangers who she had ended up with in the parking lot when she'd gotten separated from her friends.

As the father of two daughters, he found it impossible not to picture every parent's worst nightmare. The images of the drunken
boys holding her down in the back of the car and taking turns had
played out in his head. They had been laughing as they raped her,
Ed had told him, laughing, slapping one another and making
noises like rodeo cowboys. And at that point in the story Ed had
begun to sob, erupting over the highly varnished wood bar in the
hotel with a strangled, choking sound, almost inhuman, as he struggled to regain control.

He'd felt helpless, Ed told Roger. He'd been filled with a black
fury, and yet he was impotent. He raged, but his rage had no outlet.
He wanted to hurt someone, to punch something, to inflict physical
damage. The boys had never been identified, but he told Roger that
if he ever found them, he dreamed of what he would do to them.
Each night, he told Roger, he imagined something different, some
new, slow way to torture them, to make them physically pay.

"The hardest part," Ed told Roger, "was that I didn't protect my
little girl. I failed her. And I'm her father. " Ed had drained his
glass and wiped the snot running from his nose with his sleeve as
he moved unsteadily off the stool, his eyes tight and glassy. Roger
helped him to his room that night, opening the door with the key
and making sure he made it inside. The next morning, in the taxi to
the airport, neither one of them acknowledged the previous evening's raw confession. Ed sat woodenly in the cab, regretting, Roger
was sure, that he had spilled such intimate details to a coworker.
Within a year, the Schultz family had moved away from Chicago.

Roger remembered that comingled with the feelings of sadness
and outrage on Ed's behalf that night, he'd had a feeling of relief, of
feeling slightly sanctimonious and even superior regarding his
own good fortune. *Wasn't that something,* Roger thought, practically
snorting in disgust. He'd felt superior all those years ago that he

had been able to protect his girls. And now look at them. Life was a numbers game, a craps table. Apparently, it was his family's turn to slam head-on into tragedy.

As Roger continued to watch his wife flit around the kitchen with purpose, he realized his feelings of helplessness were exacerbated in direct proportion to her extreme competency with their children in the face of crisis. She was a cyclone of ceaseless activity, the centrifugal force that spoked out to sustain and nurture them all.

Roger was appreciative, even envious of the rote activities women engaged in that moved the family forward: washing dishes, folding clothes, stocking the fridge, and supervising all of the many containers of food that had been dropped off. The organization and sense of purpose required for these mundane activities eluded him. Yet those strengths, Margaret's capability and industriousness, were the very characteristics that had drawn him to her, he mused, sitting in the Corrigans' kitchen, holding Sarah and watching his wife ladle the steaming soup into a bowl.

His daughter's home was now a place of both stagnation and industry; of meals, laundry, and cleaning amid the reflective tide pools of pure grief. This was the kind of stage on which Margaret shone. She could turn her elbow grease on any problem and buff it up. Margaret's ability to "do" was a manifestation of grieving, a way of putting what had happened aside, of moving only ahead. Inertia, Roger knew firsthand, created a portal for the horrible thoughts and feelings to seep in.

"Can you take Sarah up for me so I can change her?" Margaret asked as she placed the soup bowl on a plastic floral tray.

Roger put Sarah up on his shoulders, which caused more giggling, and then he ducked slightly at the bottom of the stairs, following his wife to the second floor as Sarah reached out to touch the striped wallpaper on the landing. Margaret delivered soup to Maura, lying listlessly in bed in her darkened room, while he veered into Sarah's room. The cramped spaced smelled vaguely of baby powder, and a cache of stuffed animals was piled next to a wooden dollhouse in the corner. Margaret entered a few minutes later and lifted Sarah from his lap onto the changing table, then efficiently applied the cream and powder from the shelves while steadying his granddaughter with her other hand. *Have I ever done that?* Roger thought. Had he diapered his own children? He couldn't recall.

"You've still got it, Mother," Roger said, forcing a smile, and Margaret swiveled to meet his eyes, modestly pleased. She turned her attention back to Sarah.

"Oh, I did plenty of this in my day, didn't I, sweet princess?" Margaret was cooing at Sarah now, who was delighted with the attention from her grandmother and clapped her hands together with a squeal. "You're almost too big for these now, aren't you? Almost ready to give up your diapers at night and nap, hmmm?" Margaret lifted her granddaughter off the table and lowered her in the crib. "Do you want bunny with you?" Sarah nodded, her baby-fine sandy curls bobbing, and reached up to grab her favorite stuffed animal, flopping down on the mattress and popping her thumb into her mouth. She poked one chubby hand through the slats to sleepily wave good-bye.

"I just love babies' wrists," said Margaret. "I love the way there is a little fold right here where the arm meets the hand, and dimples by the knuckles and then . . . all that fat just goes away at some point." Her cadence slowed as they moved to exit Sarah's room.

They looked at each other for a second, each individually thinking about James, how he had been on the cusp of leaving boyhood at nine. "Double digits" he'd called his upcoming birthday. He had already been planning how he would celebrate.

Being in his granddaughter's small room, a large closet really, reminded Roger of the time right before Sarah was born. He had arrived unannounced at the Corrigan house one night on the way home from work and come across his very pregnant daughter stripping wallpaper and humming in a pair of ripped sweatpants. This third baby had been unexpected, a "what-a-surprise" baby, as Maura had called her. And yet, after they'd made the initial mental adjustment to becoming a family of five, Maura had embraced the idea of one more, especially when the sonogram revealed it was a girl.

"So, are you going to paint the walls a hot pink?" he had chided her.

"Maybe, Dad." She laughed, and then grew pensive. "It's funny, I always thought I'd just have boys."

"Aren't you glad James and Ryan will have a sister, like you do?" Roger had asked her.

"Of course. I can't wait to have a daughter. But I think boys are less complex. It's all right there on the surface. What you see is pretty much what you get. Then again, I get to paint a room pink." And she had smiled at him and patted her swollen belly with all the bright confidence of someone who was in the prime of giving life.

Roger reached out now and laid his palm against the blush-colored walls. He closed his eyes and ran his hand against the smooth plaster, ambushed for the moment by the past as tears welled up. Life back then, when the room was covered in wallpaper, had scrolled out before all of them with promise. James had been alive, and his eldest daughter, the one most like him, had been whole.

His cell phone rang in his shirt pocket. As Roger reached to pull it out, a slightly sour expression roiled over Margaret's face, and Sarah's head bolted up from the crib. They stepped into the hallway, and Margaret clicked the door shut. Roger studied the number. Julia. He'd spoken to her briefly a few times since the accident, assuring her he was OK. He had described how they were all consumed with the loss, the funeral arrangements, and taking care of his daughter's family. She had been understanding. But her contact had ratcheted up lately. She wanted more from him, wanted to see him, and to know when he would be in Florida next. He let out his breath slowly and let the call go into voice mail.

"Work again," he explained lamely and chided himself for using such a booming tone. "I'm going to have to get back to Tampa for the refinancing of that mall soon. The deal is dragging out forever."

"You'd think there would be other partners at a firm your size to help pick up the slack," said Margaret disapprovingly. "Younger partners who could fill in on some of these meetings and report back." They were padding down the hall toward the stairs, speaking in hushed tones. It was so still and quiet now, with Ryan at summer day camp, as if the entire house had been unplugged from its energy source, enervated.

"You know how clients are," whispered Roger. "People like to see the principals show their faces. This whole real estate deal should close in a few months, and then we can begin to draw up plans for the expansion and get some bids. Everyone just wants to feel important. Human nature." His phone beeped to let him know a message had been delivered to his voice mail. He blushed for a moment, surprising himself, and shot Margaret a veiled look. She was adjusting her permed hair with her fingers in the hall mirror, slightly sucking in her cheeks and gazing into the backyard from the second-floor landing. Out beyond the shade of the branches the grass looked slightly parched by the sun's glare, and Roger made a mental note to locate a sprinkler in the garage.

"I think I'll go back to the house and tackle some paperwork," he muttered to Margaret downstairs. "Should I look in on Maura?"

"Let's let her rest now. When I brought the soup in she was trying to sleep." She set a laundry basket on the mudroom floor and began straightening the family's shoes, tossing each pair into the assigned milk crates in a system Maura had installed after Ryan began walking.

"Roger?" Margaret suddenly cried out in a wounded pitch. She had stopped moving, poised in a bent position, and he noticed she was holding a small black Merrell shoe.

"Roger . . ." Margaret's voice cracked, as she stooped over the crate, holding the shoe. James's shoe. "What . . . what will we do with his milk crate?"

"I don't know . . . ," said Roger. He hadn't yet thought about the "things," all of the physical reminders of James, his possessions. On some level, he imagined that James would simply appear back in the house one day, as if some kind of magic was at work, or as if he had merely been at sleepaway camp.

"We can deal with that later, I imagine," Margaret said softly, but her voice was strong, and her face wore an expression of resigned determination. "We can't do this now." She tossed the shoe and its mate into the crate with James's flip-flops and baseball cleats and a good-as-new pair of winter boots.

"So, I'll go, then," Roger said again, leaning in the doorjamb of the mudroom now, suddenly desperate to get outside.

"OK," called Margaret, her back to him, bent at her task.

Roger hesitated for just a second and then turned toward the back screen door. He thought again of Maura. Hopefully she was napping, but more likely she was awake, sitting in the rocking chair, the same one in which she had nursed and comforted all three of her children. He had come upon her rocking yesterday, her body erect and perfectly still, only her feet gliding the rocker back and forth. Sarah was asleep on her chest, legs splayed out. She seemed to have Sarah in her arms all the time now, touching her, singing with her, drawing comfort from her physical nearness. "I want to freeze you, right here at this age," he had heard his daughter mumble to the child, and he had backed away, the plush hall carpeting absorbing his footfalls.

Outside Maura's house Roger let out a huge breath and climbed into the convertible. At the first stop sign, he steered the car off Maura's street, canopied by elms, and onto the wider avenue that eventually snaked along Lake Michigan. As he accelerated, the suburban Chicago houses in their North Shore town flicked by, growing larger as he headed east toward the water; white wooden columned structures, curving turn-of-the-century shingled edifices, and brick Georgian homes represented an earlier time of industrial affluence in the history of the North Shore. Here and there a flagpole accented a scallion green lawn, and planters bursting with boldly hued annuals graced porches and entryways. The residences became more expansive as he got closer to the water, the landscaping and flowers more magnificent. He loved summertime in Chicago, the large, evenly spaced oaks lining so many streets in their town, the way the merchants on the main street of Greenhaven all sported lush hanging baskets overflowing with orange-red geraniums, ferns, and purple petunias. The bright promise of the season and the cloudless indigo sky were in such stark contrast to everything his family was experiencing now.

The theme from *Mission: Impossible* began to play on his phone, something James had rigged on a lark only three weekends ago. He didn't have the expertise to deal with the technical functions of cell phones, but James had been a whiz at anything electronic. When his secretary had called, Roger realized that somehow James had programmed his phone with this silly personal ringtone, so incongruous with the seriousness of his office. James had gotten such glee out of the fact that Roger could never fix it. And so it had rung like that since, each call from his office now a painful reminder of his eldest grandson. His secretary had been holding calls and canceling meetings since the accident. The team at his commercial real estate firm had been working on pitching a big deal out of the San Francisco office, and things were now simmering in Dallas. Work would give him a purpose, something to focus on, maybe even a sense of measureable accomplishment.

"Roger Munson."

"Roger, it's Cristina."

"How are you? How is everyone at the office?"

"We're well, and all wondering how you are, and the family of course. I hope that Maura got the food basket we sent? The one with the ham?"

"Yes, thank you, that was very thoughtful," he said, although he had no recollection of such a basket. There had been so much food brought to the house, it was impossible to keep track of it all, though he had no doubt Margaret had already devised an efficient system for sending out thank-yous on her very best stationery. They'd actually had to throw a number of things out. Margaret had gone on about that, with a frustrated resolve. It always bothered her to waste food.

"We made a nice meal out of it," he added unnecessarily. "Very thoughtful."

"Well, I was just checking," Cristina said. "Checking to see if you needed anything. I saw your e-mail about Tampa and wanting to go down there in two weeks. Do you have a date in mind?"

"Let me check the calendar and get back to you. And, Cristina, I'm coming into the office tomorrow," Roger said, almost too abruptly.

"Oh. OK."

"There isn't much I can do here," Roger offered. "Maura . . . we . . . well, I guess time will just have to work its magic."

"I'm sure—" his secretary's voice began, and then a call-waiting interruption clicked, cutting off the end of her sentence. Roger removed the phone from his ear and glanced at the number. It was Julia, calling again from Florida.

"Do you need to get that?" asked Cristina.

"I'll call them back," he said abruptly.

Before James's accident, a call from Julia would have hastened him off the other line. He would have felt that slight lift, something hopeful at the sight of her number, and he would have ended his conversation hurriedly in order not to miss her. Now, as he drove past the corner diner in the heart of his town, the sight of her number filled him with competing emotions. It was hard to tease out the strands. It wasn't a dread, but her call carried a new weight of responsibility and complicity, as if she were somehow tied to what had happened to James.

Roger sighed and apologized to Cristina, asking her to repeat her question, the interruption of the call-waiting mercifully allowing him to change the topic back to some trivial issue, phone messages and an upcoming client meeting. For the second time that day, feeling vaguely guilty and unsettled, he let Julia's call go into voice mail.

6

Maura *had always* taken a secret pride that as a homemaker she hadn't resorted to those salads that came in a bag with the packet of dressing and the separately wrapped croutons. A month after the funeral, as she rummaged through the fridge, gathering ingredients to make dinner, she wondered why she hadn't saved herself the trouble all of those years. Why hadn't she done more takeout? Now she was staring into the refrigerator overflowing with casseroles and unfamiliar Tupperware. Her church, friends, the women in the PTA, had organized a schedule of dinners and grocery shopping and even rides to sports practices for Ryan, which made her feel immensely grateful. But this also highlighted her inability to perform these simple functions for her family. Tonight she was determined. It wouldn't be elaborate, but after weeks of reheating one of the unidentifiable dishes left by neighbors, Maura had decided it was time to cook a real meal for her family. They needed to all sit down together and reach for some semblance of normal. She would even try to get down a few bites herself, though her appetite had largely deserted her weeks ago. She thought of the stubborn ten pounds she had finally managed to lose. The jeans she was wearing now hung loosely on her hips, despite the belt she had dug out of the closet. The grief diet, her sister had called it.

Yet at odd times she would find herself ravenous, like an animal, and in those moments she'd eat an entire sleeve of Oreos or gobble up the remains of the kids' Day-Glo orange mac and cheese, right out of the saucepan. Last night she polished off a pint of chocolate Häagen-Dazs, almost as if she were in a trance, savoring each spoonful for the immediate gratification it provided and then feeling disgusted, and yet still empty, when it was consumed.

Her mother had been at her house almost every day, unloading the dishwasher, walking Rascal, folding laundry, and urging Maura to rest. In the first week after the funeral, when Ryan's summer camp had begun, she would hand Sarah over to Margaret and crawl back under the covers, to feel the weight of grief and guilt in shifting ratios.

Maura had been a morning exerciser, but now she could barely find the energy for a shower. Stopping for a loaf of bread or grabbing a roll of stamps had all fit seamlessly into her days before James's death. These trivial tasks outside of the house now overwhelmed her. It all seemed insurmountable, devoid of any importance. Her light blue eyes, always her favorite feature, were lifeless. She hadn't shaved her legs or plucked her brows since before the accident. She looked like that Muppet, which one had the unibrow? Bert? And there were new frown lines on her face, furrows between her brows that hadn't been so pronounced before. Grief had etched them there, she thought. Grief had disfigured and disemboweled her.

For all of her listlessness, though, Maura was rarely able to drift off during the day. She would lie in bed, willing herself to quiet her mind and sleep, rolling back and forth on the mattress as her trapped thoughts swirled like bats in a cave. She couldn't stop thinking of James. Sometimes images of him rushed into her mind at once, like a pixilated sensory overload. And then at other times she would panic when she was suddenly unable to recall the exact features of his face.

Maura moved toward the refrigerator door and fixed her eyes on the black-and-white photo of her son held in place by a magnet. She studied his wide, boyish smile, the splay of freckles across the bridge of his nose, and thought for the hundredth time how grateful she was that they had splurged for their first professional family photo shoot last November. The photographer had managed to capture the personalities of each child, including this one of James. How could anyone have known that some six months later, her favorite snapshot of her eldest child would be enlarged for his funeral?

She glanced at the photo of Sarah and Pete, laughing, from that same day, her daughter's head tossed back and giggling as her father tickled her. Pete. She sighed. Thinking about Pete was so complicated, laced with many competing emotions—guilt, anger, and anxiety. Their marriage, which had not been in a terrific place before the accident, was strained now, filled with long silences. While there was an affable varnish over the top of their parental duties, so much was left unsaid in the corridors between them. When they did talk, it seemed to be more about schedules and the children's needs and other perfunctory subjects.

Things had been operating on this half-speed for a while, Maura acknowledged, each of them heading down that easy slipstream in marriage where the valuable, intimate parts begin to erode in a tidal wave of banality. Maura had no doubt that she still loved her husband, but she no longer felt *in* love. How much was enough love? Funny how chemical attraction waned, how the things that made you fall in love with a person changed and the things required to stay in love were so different, deeper.

And then there was Pete's drinking. Pete had always been a drinker, but in the past, his boozy excess had mostly been contained to his weekly boys' nights out, although over the years this had become increasingly annoying to her. In college Maura had gravitated toward Pete's frat-boy, life-of-the-party personality. He had been so like her gregarious father in some ways, always ready to dazzle with a good story or make a self-deprecating remark followed by a perfectly timed punch line. She'd loved the raucousness of him, the spontaneous entertainer side, which was such a nice yin to her quieter yang. After James was born she had tried to lodge a firm protest, expressing her desire for more family time, more attention from him, and she'd even suggested they see a counselor, but Pete had bristled at that. Especially after the birth of Sarah, his simplicity, formulaic life, and unchanged adolescent drinking rituals seemed merely juvenile. Each time she had registered her need for him to change, she'd largely been met with a joking resistance or occasional lip service.

And in the years that followed, Maura had mostly held her tongue about the drinking and gradually about other things as well until she had submerged whole parts of herself from him. She and Pete had lost that easy access to each other's deeper thoughts and emotions. Part of her wondered if he had even noticed the growing gulf between them. Now in the wake of their son's death the pace of his drinking seemed to have lurched stealthily forward—a few fingers of vodka refilled at home, the beer bottles piling up in the recycling bin, the sound of a toppled stool as he entered the dark kitchen after his now more frequent evenings out.

It felt as if she and Pete had exhausted all there was to say during the weeklong period that they'd hovered over their son's hospital bed, taking turns holding his hands and talking to him. In those brief hours they were united by the logistics of fear and grief, alternately bucking the other one up, getting the cafeteria coffee, and quelling each other's tears with hopeful platitudes.

Maura thought again about Pete's spontaneous accusation at the hospital. Though he had never said anything more about it, had never raised those questions again in her presence, the guilt hung around her like a shroud.

She knew couples could and did survive losses on all scales, but could theirs? Could it continue when one person was holding back, harboring a secret? She pushed that thought away. She had no interest in rehashing that past or conversely in thinking that far ahead. It took all of her concentration just to stay here in the present. James's death was so recent, so fresh, right now it was an enormous effort to plant both feet on the floor each morning and haul her reluctant body out of bed. She couldn't begin to examine the fault lines in her marriage now.

Insomnia was taking its toll, making it difficult for her to focus on simple tasks, let alone think about the future. Lying in bed, Maura would will her mind to fill with imagined scenes of tranquility, empty stretches of beach in California, remote mountains in the Pacific Northwest, waterfalls in Hawaii, vistas both familiar and unvisited. She would force her mind to take refuge in those places. And then when the visual imagery exercises didn't work, exhausted by grief, Maura would pop a sleeping pill, which brought sweet and almost instant relief, a chloroformed curtain that silenced her mind and snuffed out all dreams. She worried that she was becoming reliant on them to sleep at all. Addicted. She'd begun to wake up at 3:00 A.M. and would often take another half pill just to drift back off.

Last night, Ryan had come into their bed in the middle of the night and she'd woken, groggy from the sleeping pills. She could hear the TV blaring downstairs and assumed Pete had fallen asleep on the couch. It was increasingly becoming a habit.

"I'm scared, Mommy," Ryan had said. And she could feel the slimness of him, his insubstantiality as he crawled next to her under the covers. His knobby boy knees and limbs were like a colt's on the verge of a growth spurt.

"What's scary, Ry?" she'd asked.

"That I'm gonna die. I don't want to die. I don't want you and Dad to die."

She'd become more alert, swimming up hard through the medication to tackle his fears. "You're not going to die, honey," she'd told him. "You are going to live for a long time and be very, very, old. Ancient. So am I. I'm going to be a good grandmother for your kids, and I'm going to get old and very, very gray and love you forever," and she had tickled him just above his belly button, and they both had giggled. They had lain like that for a few minutes, snuggling, and then Ryan had curled into her chest and let out a long, satisfied breath. As their bodies emanated warmth she focused on the memory of being pregnant, of carrying him for all those months.

She had thought him asleep, but then he piped up again, surprising her with his alertness. "I miss him, Mommy," he said. "I miss James."

This simple declaration had sideswiped her. She'd been focusing so much on cultivating a sense of normalcy in the house, stepping around the issue, that she had not spent enough time, she realized, probing the loss from her children's perspective.

"I miss him too, Ryan," she said, dry-eyed. And again she fought against the power of the medication as it tugged her back toward a dreamless sleep. "And it's OK to miss him. It's OK for us all to miss him forever. It hurts a lot." It must have been this admission that had freed Ryan to nod off in her arms. The next morning she couldn't recall when Pete had eventually come up and lifted their son back into his own bed. Such was the power of those pills.

Which was why today, Maura was determined to have a family meal. She had spent the last hour making a salad with her homemade dressing and creating a stir-fry of chicken and vegetables that her kids loved. It was 6:00 P.M. Pete should be home any minute. "Dinner," she called, lifting Sarah into the high chair. "Wash your hands, Ryan." Maura shook out the dry dog food for Rascal and lowered his metal bowl back onto the floor. "Sarah, here's your milk." Her daughter grabbed her sippy cup solemnly, turning it to study the cartoon image of the Little Mermaid on the exterior.

She finished cutting chicken bits for Sarah and spooning out white rice for Ryan as the phone rang. Maura could see from the caller ID that it was Pete.

"Hey," he said. There was the murmur of bar chatter in the background. The Depot, she thought, his favorite place to gather for a "pop." She'd been there a few times over the years, a darkened man cave next to the train station with the smell of tapped kegs and a sticky film on the highly varnished bar. Two giant TVs, held by chains, tilted from the ceiling at each end of the room, perpetually tuned to ESPN.

"Hey." They were quiet for a moment, and she could hear a loud baritone laugh spike over the conversation. How could he possibly sit in a bar, just four weeks after their son's funeral? She marveled for more than the hundredth time how differently men and women grieved.

"Billy just showed up and he's had a bad day. I think I'm gonna stick around here for a while longer," he said. Was he slurring slightly? How long had he been there? She had told him when he left that morning she wanted to have a family dinner, that they needed to reestablish some kind of normal routine for their kids.

"So I figured." Her voice was cool.

"Save me a plate, will ya? I'm just having one more pop with the guys. Just one. I'll be there. Billy just broke up with his latest. Or I guess she sort of blew him off. Remember her? Marjorie?"

"Uh-huh."

"He's been there for us through this thing, you know, Maura? For our family. I just want to support him. OK? Home in an hour." He practically hung up before she could reply.

On some level, Maura understood that this male camaraderie was Pete's therapy, his attempt to make sense of such a devastating loss. She wondered if Pete and his friends actually discussed James at all, if they ever even spoke about the accident directly or uttered his name. Either way, she knew it undoubtedly comforted Pete to sit, in communion with a beer, next to his longtime friends Michael, Chris, Thomas, or Billy. She could imagine her husband tamping down his grief, perhaps letting it defuse little by little as

he listened to comments about a score or a play, cheered his beloved White Sox, and motioned to the bartender for another round
for his pals. Those men had loved James too, she knew.

And yet as she sat down to eat with Sarah and Ryan, making an
excuse for Pete, she couldn't help nursing the old grudge. Pete was
cheating her and the kids with his absences. She had hoped that at
the very least James's death might cinch them tighter as a family,
draw them closer. If anything, Pete needed to redouble his efforts as
a father instead of burying his head in a beer with the boys. How
would they begin to rebuild their broken family if he didn't show up?

After reading to Sarah, she entered Ryan's room to kiss him good
night. Lowering the shade, she looked out the window, half-hoping
to see Pete's headlights sweeping the lawn as they turned up the
driveway. Maura was transfixed for a moment by the base of the giant maple tree in the center of the front lawn. The long fingers of
yellow light spilling out from the front room windows and onto the
grass touched the skirt of the trunk on one side; the other half was
shrouded in inky darkness. James had loved to climb that tree, and
he'd tried to convince Pete to build a fort there.

"Forts are for backyards, buddy," Pete would routinely answer.
"And we don't have a really good tree back there." How much of that
was true? Maura wondered ruefully, and how much of it was laziness
on Pete's part? Maura's eyes scanned the lawn again from Ryan's
window, and she gazed out onto the street where the lamplight pooled
in a neat elliptical shape. The soft whir of the air-conditioning
kicked on, and the blast from the vent furled the curtain slightly.

There it was again. Out of the corner of her eyes. A movement,
almost as if a figure were down there. Was someone under the tree?
Suddenly she wished Pete were home. It was Friday night in the
dead of summer. Maybe the neighborhood kids were getting into
some mischief now that school had been out for a while. The thought
made her uneasy, and Maura leaned over and kissed Ryan one last
time as she pulled her thin bathrobe around her, repositioning and

tightening the belt. She padded swiftly down the stairs and into the family room at the front of the house, moving over to the plate glass window and adjusting the curtain on the side. It was unmistakable now, the faint outline of someone lying under the maple. A tiny speck of orange glowed and then moved in an arc. Someone was smoking a cigarette on her front yard.

The unexpectedness, the pluck of it, banished her fear for a moment. Maura yanked open the heavier oak door and felt a rush of humid air *whoosh* through the screen door, as if the house had inhaled. The brightness of the interior lights made it difficult for her to distinguish shapes instantly, and as her pupils adjusted, she saw a blur of movement on the side of the tree. The figure had bolted upright and was running down the driveway and into the street with long, measured strides. It was definitely a boy, a teenager from the lankiness of his legs, and as the shape got smaller, disappearing and then reappearing at intervals under each streetlight, she thought she could make out longish dirty blond hair and a faded red T-shirt.

Maura was frozen for a moment on the front porch, her heart thumping wildly, and then gradually settling. It had all happened so fast that even as she closed and then locked the door behind her she was already beginning to doubt exactly what she'd seen.

7

One month after his death Maura felt the hollowed-out absence of James more acutely than she had during the funeral, or in the days immediately following, when she'd confined herself to her bedroom, shades drawn. Her mother was no longer coming daily, and Pete's parents too had cut back on their check-ins, which was both a relief and a loss. This "after" part was almost worse, her grief sharper and more intense during the empty stretch of hours in the house while Ryan was at summer camp and Sarah napped. In those moments of acute silence, Maura would visit James's room. She had created a ritual of lying on his bed, eyes closed, imagining him here.

She stood in the doorframe and took in the posters of her son's sports and music heroes on the pale blue walls, the worn stuffed animal frog above his desk that had been retired when he'd become "a big boy." Stepping over to the bookshelf, which she had sanded and painted with constellation stencils when he was four, Maura ran her fingertips across the books' spines. She brushed a light layer of dust off the volume of Greek mythology he had cherished, the encyclopedia of dinosaurs, the Harry Potter series that she had first started reading to him and then, with each passing install-ment, he had begun to read more quickly himself. There were the baseball trophies, the yellow dried palm frond in the shape of a cross from this past Easter, and the porcelain piggy bank that had been a baby gift from Erin with JAMES PATRICK CORRIGAN painted on the belly and under it his height and weight. Seven pounds, four ounces. Maura blinked, dry-eyed. She lifted the bank, and the coins slid into the pig's head. It was heavier than she'd expected. James had always been a saver.

Opening the closet door she drank in his boy scent on the baseball uniform and discarded pajamas from that very last morning. She had left his dirty clothes in the hamper so that she could retain this scent memory, and she felt him here, trace elements present in the objects of his room. But she could not yet fully admit that his smell was disappearing, being erased, the clothes in his drawers gradually assuming the generic scent of laundry detergent, mingled with the slight cedar odor of the round wooden air fresheners. With each passing week, little bits of James were slipping away and dissolving, thwarting her efforts at preservation.

There was always a point in her visitation of his room where the finality of his loss reared up and overwhelmed her. Life stopped at the edges of this room. Maura sat back down on the bed, holding her head as she let the sobs come, and then lay down, curling like a caterpillar on the thin SpongeBob bedspread.

Rascal, as if understanding her distress, moved over to nuzzle her ankles the way he did when he wanted a dog treat or to be lifted onto a lap. He yelped as she hoisted him up to James's bed, absent-mindedly forgetting to support his back with both hands. Rascal settled in the C-curve of her curled body and let out a sigh as Maura began to stroke his silky ears. The dog missed James too.

It had been James who had first noticed when Rascal seemed to struggle on the stairs last winter. Maura had guessed it might be something with his hips, or maybe his back. If only she'd known where that would lead, how something as innocuous as a visit to the veterinarian could be a catalyst for the fulcrum event in her life.

As the dog's mobility had steadily shrunk, Rascal began to drag his back foot slightly, and she'd called for an appointment. It was probably nothing, she'd told her son, old age. Dachshunds were notorious for back and disc problems, and he was at least eight years old.

Rascal had been James's more than any of theirs. He had begged for a dog practically since he could speak, and it had become part of the bedtime ritual. He began to step up his requests to include other times of the day, if they passed someone walking a dog or saw a movie where a dog was featured. It became clear to her that at some point having a dog was essential to her eldest son's childhood, like jumping in piles of raked leaves, playing flashlight tag, or learning how to ride a two-wheeler.

Pete had ultimately joined the chorus, arguing with her that they should do this for the kids. "Every kid deserves to have a dog," he'd said to her. "It's not like I won't be around to help too." But in her mind there had been no question it would be she who ended up with the dirty work, she who would be walking in the early hours with one of those little blue plastic bags in her hand as her dog crouched to poop with an embarrassed hunch. There were times when she'd felt her resolve slipping, and she would conjure up just this image to stick to her convictions.

But a part of her had always understood that all of this was just a slow process of erosion. Adding a dog to the family would simply be a matter of time. Once she was pregnant with Sarah, she and Pete had already determined that she would stay home with the kids full-time. She'd quit her job at the hotel's corporate offices and ceased commuting into Chicago. As she gradually adjusted to a new rhythm of life as a stay-at-home mom, she'd finally relented.

Maura could vividly remember how James was practically bouncing out of his seat with anticipation on the drive to the county animal shelter. They had all spent an hour looking over the dogs and holding them, but he had fallen in love with a dachshund mix, black for the most part with sand-colored markings around his eyes and ears, and a batonlike tail. The owner had died, explained the shelter worker, an older person, and they believed the dog was five or maybe six, but he was housebroken, loving, and most importantly, he needed a home.

Almost immediately James decided that the dog would be named Rascal. He'd been a fan of the old black-and-white "Our Gang" movies that her father had introduced him to, and he explained to Maura and Pete that the dog had a "rascally" look.

When Rascal's pain turned out to be a disc issue, Maura had entered the world of veterinarian visits and dog medications. While he had never been fully healed, they had all learned to handle Rascal more gingerly. Rascal let out a small whine, bringing her back to the present in the hush of the room. She lifted him carefully down onto the floor, and he moved toward James's small closet.

Maura could tell that the smell of the boy Rascal loved was present for him too as he circled the room, sniffing. She wondered what those scents told him and how a dog processed someone's prolonged absence. How long would Rascal remember? That dog had been the origin of so much happiness for James, and then after that one visit to the veterinarian, such an unexpected source of joy for her. But she wouldn't think about that part of her life now. That part, like mothering James, was over.

With what felt like enormous effort, Maura lifted her head off James's pillow, took in a deep breath, and let it out slowly, squaring her shoulders before rising and leaving the room. Rascal followed out into the hall, close at her heels. With one last longing look, Maura pulled the door shut and turned the handle with a soft click.

8

"I *want to* just look at you for a moment. I'm so relieved you are here." Julia was sipping a chardonnay at the hotel restaurant by the beach. Her deep purple silk sundress created a giant splash of color in the mostly white-toned vista of the patio. "It was so awful to leave you like that last time. You practically ran out of the car at the airport." She leaned toward him in her chair, looping her arm through his on the table. Her vivaciousness felt rehearsed and cloying.

"We just have the one night," Roger said, changing the subject. "It's a quick meeting, more information gathering, and then back to Chicago. We've gone through more financing scenarios with this client than I can ever remember. It's frustrating actually, the guy is just putting us through the paces. He's not very experienced." Roger tilted his head back slightly to sip his bourbon and soda.

Julia looked at him adoringly. There were times he felt he could be talking about deodorant soap, and she would still hang on his words. That quality about her, her rapt devotion, used to make him feel omnipotent. Tonight, after a delayed flight and thunderstorms over southern Florida, he simply felt impatient.

"Did you pack some things to stay at the hotel with me?"

"I did. It will feel like a minivacation." She smiled at him, the corners of her eyes rising pleasingly, and he relaxed. "We're going to order hot fudge sundaes from room service and eat them in bed. I don't care if we drip ice cream all over us!" She laughed wickedly. Tonight would feel good, Julia would feel good. He could unwind a little. Everything had been so tense and somber at home.

He had told her on the phone that he didn't want to talk about his grandson, didn't want to relive any of the details or discuss it. They were all moving on, or trying to anyway.

"We don't need to dwell on anything bad. Ever," Julia had purred. "Tonight is a celebration of us. So we need to get busy." Her laugh tinkled.

After Roger paid the bill, they headed down to the beach, Julia holding her sandals in one hand and wrapping her thin shawl around her shoulder. The cooler breeze near the shoreline was a relief in the wilting humidity. The tide was rising and, farther out toward the water, the spill of the floodlights from the hotel receded, and she leaned against him. He pulled her in for an embrace. Roger could still conjure up that old excitement, the newness of her, the lack of familiarity. And then a flash of conscience, a pang. Roger had always been an expert at compartmentalizing, and he'd never had much use for guilt, but an image of Margaret sitting at home alone loomed in his mind for a moment and then mercifully retreated.

"Let's go back to the room. It's so windy," Julia said. As if sensing his momentary mental absence, she tugged his arm toward the hotel. As they approached the stucco entryway, Roger observed an elderly man in a wheelchair with a younger woman, perhaps his wife or maybe a daughter, pushing him up the boardwalk from the beach. "Let's never get old," Julia proclaimed in a loud whisper. "I want to stay just the way we are . . . like this forever."

Roger was struck for the moment by the juxtaposition: the infirmity of the man and the dutiful caretaking of the more youthful woman. He could see her clearly now as she bent to speak to the gentleman at eye level and then offered assistance while he slowly raised himself up in the wheelchair to stand. "I'll bet that's his daughter," Roger said, still studying the couple, inexplicably drawn to their interaction. "I hope it is anyway."

"All I know is *that* will not be me," said Julia, matter-of-factly. "When Frank was diagnosed with pancreatic cancer, I became his full-time nursemaid. It was a labor of love, caring for him." Julia paused, softening her voice. "But I lost myself then. For three years. And it's taken me this long; it's taken me finding you, to feel alive again. I don't envy that woman, whoever she is."

Julia had mentioned her deceased husband before, but there was an uncharacteristic vehemence in her voice now that surprised him. She slid her arm down the length of his and grasped his hand firmly. They walked up the hotel beach ramp, now directly behind the couple as they peeled off to the lobby restaurant.

Back in the room, after two generous scotches and some wine, Julia pulled off Roger's loafers and made a show of undoing his tie. He felt himself relax into the night. The tensions of the travel had faded and he concentrated on the sheer pleasure of her, working the zipper on the back of her dress. But after a few minutes, after some writhing and repositioning, Roger found himself unable to focus, unable, to his horror and great shame, to become aroused. Each time his ardor would flag he would focus on it, will himself unsuccessfully to put his head in the moment, which only compounded his embarrassment and failure. "I . . . I'm sorry," Roger said finally, rolling off her with more than a little frustration. This had never happened with Julia. With Margaret, perhaps, there had been times he had excused himself with fatigue or mumbled something about one too many drinks. But this utter failure, this lack of control over his own body, panicked him. True, he was preoccupied with the deal and worn out from a day of travel. But Julia had always known how to soothe that part of him, to tease out the fun side and inflame his passion.

"I really am sorry," Roger said again and rolled on his back. He could read disappointment and maybe even mild alarm in Julia's eyes, but now she was on top of him, over him, rubbing his shoulders and cooing, unwilling to admit defeat. "Why don't we just lie here," she said, reaching for her sheer nightgown and pulling it back over her head. "Let's just lie here and talk . . . and cuddle. We don't have to do anything. I just want to be with you."

For the first time with Julia, Roger experienced the distinct sensation of not wanting to be touched. How ironic, he thought, all of those nights he and Margaret seemed to keep a football field between them on their king-size mattress, and now here he was, fighting the unfamiliar urge to fling Julia off, to wave her away abruptly and just fall asleep with his own thoughts. In his own bed.

As if sensing this, Julia rolled away from him and onto her back. She inched her right foot over to touch his calf, and when he didn't respond, she withdrew.

"Is it me?" she asked somewhat tentatively.

"You? No. Julia, it's me. I'm just having a hard time shutting off so many thoughts tonight, I guess. You know this never happens."

"Hmmmm."

"I'm thinking we get a little rest now and then in the morning, well, we have a whole new day. My meeting doesn't start until nine."

"I'd like that. Everything is always better in the morning." Julia's voice brightened and she rolled back toward him, laying her head on his chest and shoulder, her gardenia perfume overpowering. As he reached down to draw her closer with his free arm he felt a hopeful stirring, an increased sense of security and peace. Roger leaned to turn off the bedside lamp and pulled the covers up over them both. The air-conditioning was on too high, but neither one of them had the energy to get up and adjust it.

As he closed his eyes, he thought about being with Margaret on the night after the funeral. As they crawled into bed she had begun to softly weep, and he had drawn her to him. They had lain like that, wordlessly, for a long time, her head resting like a stone on his chest, and he had felt protective and united. Roger had savored the strength and satisfying heft of being integral to his whole family that night, of being deeply needed. Julia was asleep now. He could hear the growing sound of her almost cartoonish exhales of air. And before Roger drifted off he experienced a sense of warm anticipation about heading home. It was suddenly a place he very much wanted to be.

. . .

"Maura, you need to eat," Margaret urged.

"I am, Mom, I do eat." Maura was picking at the glops of tuna poking out of the sandwich. Next to her at the table Sarah's chubby fingers were grasping one buttered noodle at a time.

"You don't eat enough. Even Daddy was commenting that you look too thin."

"When is Dad coming home?" Maura asked.

"Dinner tonight. And then he'll head over to your house to see Ryan."

Roger had been spending more time at Maura's lately, taking Ryan into the city for a hot dog last weekend, and he had bought tickets to a Sox game this Sunday. The grandchildren seemed to be resurrecting themselves, recovering their old personalities and moving forward. Her daughter was a different story.

It was agonizing for Margaret to witness her child so transformed and in so much pain. What had happened to James was one thing, unspeakable and unimaginable. But to see your once vibrant daughter gutted like a fish, well, that was almost more than a mother could bear.

At least Margaret had succeeded in getting Maura to eat a little before she and Sarah headed home for naptime. She spent the rest of the afternoon in the garden, allowed herself one cigarette, and then wrote some thank-you notes at her desk. In the remaining hour before dinner, Margaret drew a bath. The late August day had been hot, and she'd gotten into some prickers near the shed that had left little red itchy bumps on her forearm. The soak would be soothing. She climbed in, sunk down to her shoulder blades, and closed her eyes, feeling the release of a long day as the setting sun projected a deep orange glow on the wall from the bathroom window.

She'd invited Maura over this afternoon for lunch, hoping to lure her out of the house a bit more, distract her with a change of scenery. There really were no words to help. Those old chestnuts about time healing all wounds or the folks who thoughtlessly said "thank goodness she has her two other kids" were simple fools. She would wait it out with Maura, that was what she'd do. Time could be whittled away with constant motion and momentum until one day the pain would release its tight pincer-hold on her daughter. It was all she had to offer, her ability to roll up her sleeves and help Maura white knuckle her way through the worst of the grief.

Margaret would wet mop the kitchen linoleum and then tackle the flecks of mold in the shower. She would read to Sarah and defrost the garage freezer, knocking the thick chunks of ice away with a screwdriver. The activity level in the Corrigan house, with just Ryan and Sarah, still seemed so chaotic. Ryan had multiple activities and sports, equipment for this and forms for that. Sarah was walking everywhere, language blooming at warp speed on her tongue.

The light toward dusk had begun to purple and soften the room. Running more hot water to warm up the bath, Margaret wondered if it had been just sheer will that had propelled her through it all back in her days as a younger mother. She came home now from the stretches of time spent at Maura's, the veins throbbing in her legs, steeping a cup of lemon tea, drawing the utter silence of the house around her like a cape.

And yet Margaret was satisfied that her presence was a comfort. Just being there to care for them all and usher them through the day gave her a sense of purpose, and creating some order out of the utter devastation in that household was satisfying. Order was what Margaret understood best.

It bothered her still, after all these years of marriage, the way Roger came into the house and threw his possessions around willy-nilly, shedding the responsibility of the workday at a dizzying speed. Glasses, loose change, wallet; his items claimed no particular place in the world and therefore he was constantly asking her, "Have you seen my car keys? Do you know where my watch is?"

Years ago she had hammered in little hooks for the keys and she'd found an old silver bowl, a wedding present from a fraternity brother of his, that she'd designated for the contents of his pockets when he walked in the door. "You can put your key chain and wallet here," she'd tried to coach him night after night, pointing to the bowl on the table by the front entrance. But he was unable to think like that, unable to remember something so methodical. She shook her head now, smiling in exasperation at the futility of her system. The bathwater rippled forward, the bubbles stilled to a weak foam at the edges of the tub.

That was during an earlier, somehow much simpler time in their marriage, when the current between them ran stronger. There was ease in the circumscription of their roles back then. She was the dedicated mother on the home front, he the gallant breadwinner, walking in the door just before cocktail hour with a huge smile, arms open wide for his excited children. Stu had still been in diapers, and Margaret's days were filled with completing the physically demanding tasks of a young mother—loads of laundry, grocery shopping and cooking, picking up the toys, soothing cuts and bruises, wrapping birthday gifts, and making doctors' appointments.

There had been plenty of good times, the rhythm of strongly connected stretches periodically followed by weaker ones, the feeling of moving in lockstep and then occasionally drifting, operating independently, like any marriage, she imagined. But it was when they were a team that she and Roger functioned best. And somehow, picking through the carnage after James's death, they had begun to feel like they were fitting back together after a long absence, returning to a kind of synchronized orbit. Margaret leaned back in the bath and closed her eyes in satisfaction at that thought.

When the water grew tepid she stood up, letting the rivulets drip off her body. Easing out of the tub, Margaret dried off with a thick towel, and thought about the fact that in a month it would have been James's tenth birthday. Then there would be Thanksgiving, Christmas, and looming ahead would be the anniversary of his death. All of these unwelcome firsts would be fresh cuts, she thought.

Margaret wiped the steam from the mirror, assessing the slackness of flesh, the still relatively muscular thighs at her advanced age, the droop of the puppet lines around her mouth. She sucked in her cheeks for a minute, watching the pucker lines gather around her lips, and she thought of cinching a kitchen trash bag and then, remarkably, of an anus. Now where had that come from? Good Lord, her pursed mouth in the shape of an anus. The outrageousness of this explicit thought made Margaret smile imperceptibly.

She plucked at the roots of her wet hair with her fingers, examining the areas where the larger streaks of gray were well hidden by the hairdresser. Although the skin on her arms was slack, the muscles underneath still held some definition from working in the garden and regular yoga classes at the YMCA. Her eyes flitted down to her stomach, soft and rounded, despite the exercises. The childbirths and the hysterectomy had finally, she supposed, simply worn those muscles out.

Looking between her legs made her think of Roger. He hadn't touched her body, really touched her, in a very long while. How long had it actually been? she wondered, and where did desire go? When was the moment physical desire first started to recede? When had his mind wandered? How silly, she chided herself. What was wrong with her today, all of these randomly ridiculous and serious thoughts?

Roger had never parted with his emotions freely or been prone to introspection, but then neither had she. It simply wasn't part of their generation, this need to talk about everything, to pick over each hangnail, slight, and feeling as if it were the center of the universe. People of their generation put up with things, they bucked up, they were disappointed at times and in turn would occasionally disappoint. They got on with life. If you spent all your time navel-gazing, you'd never accomplish anything, she reasoned. Besides, simply laying the very heavy things aside sometimes meant you could just plain get down to the business of living. Sometimes a person just needed to keep moving.

Margaret drew the terry-cloth bathrobe around her and tightened the soft belt. Moving downstairs and into the kitchen, she paused for a moment in the threshold of the sliding glass doors. The night was incredibly humid and still, and her skin remained pinkish from the bath. She poured a glass of wine and headed out into the garden to pick the last of the bolted lettuce for a dinner salad. She thought of the pack of cigarettes concealed in the shed and wondered how many were left. Perhaps she'd have another.

As she stood in the last pumpkin hue of the dusk, she saw it, one of the sticky traps she had laid under the broccoli plants just yesterday. Caught in the garish, yellow tar of the trap's base was a chipmunk. He must have recently stumbled onto the trap, she thought, as he was still full of fight. His tail writhed and twisted, as it lay beyond the outline of the rectangular trap. Most of the underside of his body and three of his paws were firmly embedded in the goo.

In the corner of the garden fence, where it was reinforced over the wood with chicken wire, a small spade stood upright. It occurred to Margaret that she could end the small animal's misery with one blow to the skull. She considered this distastefully for a moment and then rejected it. *Let him squirm*, she thought with a sudden fury, *let him suffer.* She pivoted abruptly, headed to the far corner of the plot where the last of the arugula sprouted. Perhaps she would tug out a scallion or two and poach an egg to accompany the salad. But first, she would have a cigarette.

9

"You *forgot to* bring in the mail yesterday." Pete was already dressed for work, and his leather soles clicked on the hardwood floor as he entered the kitchen, tossing the stack on the polished stone counter. The pile hit with a slap and fanned out. "Looks like the boy wrote us another letter," said Pete evenly. He didn't look at her. There was the usual collection of catalogs, bills, and postcards with sale offers, and a light blue envelope on heavier card stock that Pete was already ripping open. She finished loading the last glass into the dishwasher from the sink and turned to observe him, leaning against the edge of the counter.

"What boy?" Maura said, somewhat defiantly. But she knew. She knew it must be the Hulburd kid. Shortly after the funeral, he had sent a note asking if he could come over and meet with them. They had both ignored it at the time. Pete had already unfolded the stationery and was reading the letter, his face impassive. She fought the urge to grab it out of his hands. Maura could see the slanted penmanship on the blue notepaper, letters like tiny swords, the words hard to distinguish from her vantage point. Pete read for another moment in silence.

"Read it, Pete." He held up his hand, concentrating on the cramped penmanship. He handed it to her.

"You read it. It's standard stuff. He's sorry, wants to come over and meet us. Here." Pete thrust it at her, and she threw it on the counter as if it were scorching.

"Hey, he's trying, Maura," said Pete vituperatively. "He's trying something, right?" He ran his fingers through his hair with a sweeping motion and then tucked his pinstriped shirt tightly into the waistband of his suit pants. She noticed the gray was more prominent now on his temples, almost as if it had accumulated overnight. There was a smudge of shaving cream on the rim of his ear and his neck bulged slightly over the too-tight collar of his pale blue shirt, the slow softening of men in middle age.

"Imagine being him? One day you're on your way to work at the golf club, school just got out, and then, wham, a kid rolls in front of you . . ." His voice trailed off.

"What, are you defending him, Pete? The boy had been drinking." Maura looked directly at Pete and felt a hot flush rise up her neck. "You know it as well as I do, they found beer in his car."

"Maura. It was a single empty beer can. Eight-thirty in the morning. The police found tiny traces of alcohol from the night before. None of that was related to the accident. You know all of this." Pete moved in closer, but there was a reserve there now. They were both on dangerous territory.

"So you're defending his drinking, Pete? Why aren't I surprised? You can make excuses for anything. Even your son's death." Maura turned her back abruptly and opened the dishwasher, pulling out the top rack too quickly as all of the glasses rattled against one another, and she added her coffee cup, slamming the stainless steel door closed. She felt tears sting and wondered briefly if Ryan and Sarah were safely out of earshot.

"I think you need to get on top of your anger, Maura. It's not going to help anything, especially with the kids." Pete's eyes strayed toward the family room, where Ryan and Sarah were watching TV. She would need to get them moving and out the door for school soon.

"I *am* angry. That Hulburd kid . . . if he hadn't been—"

"Hadn't been what?" Pete's voice interrupting her was firm. "If he hadn't been driving, if James hadn't been on a bike, if you had been . . ." Pete's voice trailed off, and she glanced up sharply and then looked down, her face burning. She didn't want to meet his eyes, hadn't been able to fully search his face since James had passed away.

"I'm going to do the decent thing here, Maura. I'm going to put the kid out of some of his misery. The rest of it, he'll just have to learn to live with, I guess. But I'm not going to get any satisfaction out of making someone pay more than they already are." He looked up at her seething, almost disgusted. "Don't worry," he added, holding out a stilled hand, his voice dripping with sarcasm, "I wouldn't think of inviting him over here. I'll call up his parents and tell them I'll stop by their house. There's no reason that all of this crap has to take two lives." He stared at her a moment longer, and she still refused to meet his eyes. "I don't need a pound of flesh, Maura." Pete's tone was more even and in control. "None of this is going to bring him back." Without looking up, she heard his exasperated sigh and the sound of his footfalls on the hardwood floor, exiting the room.

Only after Pete had gone, when she'd heard the slam of the mud-room screen door and watched him navigate his car out of the garage and down the driveway, did Maura pick up the letter on the counter.

Dear Mr. and Mrs. Corrigan,

It's really hard for me to think about what I have done to your family. I am so sorry and I don't know exactly what to say. I want you to know that my life will never be the same because of this horrible event.

I understand that you don't want to see me now, and I get that. It must be hard to think about me being alive and your own son being gone. I want you to know that I did everything to try to stop the car as fast as I could. It all happened really fast and I will always blame myself.

Sometime I hope you will be able to see me and I can tell you how sorry I am in person. But I understand if you won't.

Alex Hulburd

Words, Maura thought dryly. His mother probably wrote the whole thing out for him first, and then he'd copied it. *His* life would never be the same? That was a joke. He was still walking around on this earth. With the passage of time the enormity of what he had done would no doubt begin to blur and recede. He would head off to college, join a fraternity, get stupid on beer, and graduate into the real world. James wasn't truly real to him, they had never met. He was just some nine-year-old boy, and Alex Hulburd had no concept of what it meant to be cracked open and hurting. He had no idea of the depths of despair one felt in losing a child, the complexity of the love that springs whole from your heart when you become a parent.

Let Pete go visit him. Perhaps it was better to get that part over with. Odds were they couldn't keep moving around in the orbit of their small suburban town and not ultimately run into the parents or the boy. Alicia and Ray Hulburd. By all accounts they were decent people, he was a banker and she was a stay-at-home mom. *Their lives must be a different kind of hell*, she thought. But they still had their son.

Pete could go over there and give the kid some kind of blessing, some symbolic gesture to relieve his guilt, if that's what needed to be done. That would let the air out for them all, her parents and Pete's included. She only knew that she would never go to see this boy, couldn't imagine doling out forgiveness or absolving him of his pain. Right now it was simpler and far more comfortable to make him the target of the rage, sorrow, and guilt she felt inside.

10

The *angry scene* in the kitchen with Pete and then reading Alex's letter had put them all behind schedule, especially for Sarah's new morning preschool. By the time Maura had cleared their cereal bowls from the den and hustled Ryan upstairs to brush his teeth, school was starting.

Both boys had attended the same church-run toddler program in town three mornings a week, and Maura hadn't hesitated to register her daughter last spring when life had looked completely different. Back then she had been excited at the prospect of unencumbered time, but when it was Sarah's turn this fall, Maura had hesitated. Her first instinct had been to keep her baby home. "Sarah needs the socialization just as much as the boys did," her mother had assured her when she waffled about her decision. "It's only a three-hour stretch, and you can take some time for yourself." But Maura suspected that some of her mother's firm stance on preschool was her concern about Sarah kicking around in a house with a grieving mother. She had to agree that a few playful hours outside the home with children her own age would be the best thing for Sarah.

The crossing guard was long gone by the time they zoomed up to the front entrance of the elementary school. Even though it was only six blocks away, Maura had begun the school year driving. It was easier all around. Inside the protection of her van, she wouldn't have to run into the other mothers, make small talk, or bear witness to their pitying looks. She had become accustomed to taking side streets to circumvent that stretch of Hawthorne Avenue where James had been hit. All these months later she still hadn't driven down that section of the road.

At the preschool, Maura handed Sarah over to Mrs. Fleet in the "Twos" room, and she wriggled her chubby legs excitedly to get down. Arms outstretched, her daughter ran back to the dress-up area in the corner where the small cribs of baby dolls and stuffed animals were already strewn around the linoleum floor. Two of the other little girls and one of the boys were chattering away by the miniature kitchen set. Clearly, Sarah had already made the transition to her new surroundings.

Pulling her keys out of her purse as she headed to the van, Maura felt the weight of free time pressing down on her. She thought about her carefree days before the accident, humming with engagements and to-dos. The old Maura would be in a hurry to attack a long list of errands, but now the chasm of an empty, unstructured morning yawned ahead. Erin was at work. Her mother was no doubt weary of seeing her in this state, dejected and quiet. She had become a sort of project for her extended family.

Although the refrigerator was empty, the thought of going to the grocery store exhausted her. Stepping off the isolated promontory of her own grief could have unexpected and unpleasant consequences. There was always the chance she'd run into people she knew and have to stammer out replies that she was well, moving through, feeling better, whatever platitudes were required of her for decorum's sake. Maura felt a sudden, spontaneous urge to go to the lake. Ten miles north of her commuter town, Gull's Bay was rockier and less frequented than some of the other beaches. The woods hugged the shore on stretches of the bay, giving the beach a protective, hushed feel. This had been the place where she'd go to center herself, reach for a few moments of calm and serenity as she focused on the infinite vastness of Lake Michigan. But that was before. Now with all of the complicated and trailing memories associated with that beach, she wondered if it would have the same restorative powers. Was she ready to face that part of the past? Despite her ambiguity, she felt herself turning left on Forrest Avenue and heading in that direction as if the car were on autopilot.

The flag furled in front of the post office on the corner, and a sandwich board sign in front of the local boutique, Wits End, advertised a sale. Maura tried to imagine the person she had been in June, strolling purposefully along the sidewalks of her North Shore town before all of this had happened. Her cares then had been so different, her outlook full of optimism and possibility. The bakery sported a new green-and-white-striped awning, and she noticed that the leaves at the tips of the oak trees near the butcher were already showing the first yellow streaks of fall, although the daytime temperatures were still warm. Tent caterpillars had spun giant webbed cocoons in some of the branches, and she recalled how James had once asked her if they were clumps of cotton candy.

Maura maneuvered the car off the main street and down toward the water. She slowed to bump over the train tracks beside the brick station that led into downtown Chicago. She thought of her father, who had paid for a parking spot here for more than thirty years. There were many gifts that came with settling down in the familiar surroundings of your childhood, and yet today, the confines of her hometown felt limiting and constrictive. As she drove toward the water, the closely spaced quaint houses near town began to give way to more expansive lots and bigger residences, a few with stone pillar entrances. A large bird, a hawk perhaps, was soaring in an air current high above the shore. She turned north, continuing to follow the road along Lake Michigan, past the stone water tower and then the lighthouse that lay beyond the rock shoal marking the end of the public beach.

Outside the town limits the bends in the road became more frequent and dramatic, and she realized she'd been gripping the

steering wheel with a sense of determination. She uncurled her
fingers and sat back in a more relaxed position. She was absorbed in
her memories, so the sign for Gull's Bay rose up suddenly, partially
obscured by a pine bough. She braked hard and set the blinker, her
tires making a sharp noise as they rolled off the asphalt and hit
gravel. Maura cut the engine and sat still in the parking area, fenced
by mature fir, beech, and scrubbier brush. To her right, beside a
stand of birches, was the sandy path leading to the shore. A break in
the bank of foliage gave her an unobstructed view of the lake, and
she sat mesmerized by the whitecapped waves, rolling forward at
regular, angry intervals.

The deciduous trees ringing the lake, with their large paint-
brush splashes of primary colors, had begun to make the internal
shift toward fall more quickly than the inland ones. With school
back in session, the September beach was sparsely occupied. A few
hundred yards down past the rock jetty, a couple perched on a blanket, and a lone figure walking a German shepherd bent into the
wind. Here and there the sand and rocks were littered with an occasional empty plastic bottle or food wrapper. The warmth of the
day, the bright sunlight, and the constant breeze offered a reminder
of what she had missed this past summer, largely confining her
grief to the four walls of their house. That one pivotal afternoon she
had spent here in June had been a warmer, more hopeful echo of
this one. Maura experienced a momentary sensation of time buckling and then, unsettled, she focused her attention on a rusty container ship at the lip of the horizon.

She sat down on the sand and pulled her knees up to her chest,
wrapping her arms around her legs. Maura untied the black fleece
at her waist and guided it over her head, where it snagged momentarily on her ponytail before she pulled it down and adjusted the
zipper at her neck. The waves lapped rhythmically against the shore,
and she drew a deep breath of freshwater air into her lungs, so distinct a smell and yet so much harder to articulate than the crisp

salty scent of the ocean. A lake was more complicated and individual. The Great Lakes to her had always smelled mineral clean, a combination of pine and loam as impossible to replicate as the smell of rain.

Maura closed her eyes and tried to imagine what it had felt like to sit here at a much simpler time in her life. The sharp contrast of those memories brought a flush to her face and neck. She could recall, with the shame of hindsight, her most recent visits here, so full of the reckless surety that all of the pieces of her life were neatly curated, held together in a fine balance. In that stretch of time she had believed that she had everything she wanted. That Maura had been an entirely different person from the one who sat here now, she thought. How was it she had crossed such a giant dividing line? How had she and Pete drifted to this point? They had let apathy and atrophy and a hundred little things grind them down into a couple simply going through the motions. Long before James's death they had begun to lose their language of intimacy, to adopt the varnished politeness one associated with acquaintances. Somewhere along the line, she wasn't sure where, they had simply stopped trying to make each other better. This morning's fight about Alex Hulburd was a perfect example, each of them clutching their intractable positions like pugilists in the corners of the kitchen.

Maura thought back to their fight this morning. Why wasn't Pete more angry? Their reactions about the Hulburd boy seemed to be equally opposite. The more outrage she unleashed, the more equanimity he displayed, and that infuriated her. Maura sighed. The thought suddenly occurred to her that it had probably been at least seven months since she and Pete had made love. Maybe more. At one point in time that would have been inconceivable. Back when they were dating they could hardly keep their hands off each other. And then kids, and duties, and work, and . . . it was all such a cliché. She let out a disgusted snort and shook her head as if to physically banish her thoughts.

Pete got a lot of "me" time as she called it, and Maura let her resentment at this inequality and his selfishness smolder. Throughout their marriage Pete had golfed, met the boys at the bar, and enjoyed lunchtime client meetings at some of the nicer Chicago restaurants. He knew how to take care of himself, but then again, he was the breadwinner, she'd always reasoned. That rationale had grown old. It was easier right now to catalog his faults, as that mitigated her guilt, her tremendous, suffocating guilt.

Fastening her eyes back out at the container ship on the lake's bleached horizon, she smiled at the memory of a cruise she and Pete had taken to Hawaii three years before Sarah was born. After a few frozen margaritas they had stumbled back to their cabin and captured some of the unfettered passion that conjures itself up when a married couple cuts ties to responsibility. The delicious alcoholic haze, the humidity in the air, and the gentle rocking of the boat worked like a balm. The cruise had been a little reminder of how and why she and Pete had fallen in love—their shared history, similar senses of humor—and what his attentiveness to her had felt like. They had danced to the ship's band and played cards, talked about topics other than children while gazing at the night sky on deck. That time together with Pete had made Maura hopeful. But that had been vacation. Sarah was born, and life had become even more full, Pete's parenting increasingly splintered at times. His drinking remained a constant, never to complete excess or total impairment, but more than she would have liked. The few times she had raised it, his defensiveness had immediately backed her down.

On a girls' weekend last fall, after too much wine, she had admitted to her college roommate that she'd married a simple man, an uncomplicated person. She had been looking for dependability, she'd confided, but instead had found a boy, the kind of person who would have a predictably complacent approach to life. He had proposed to the girl from the next town, stepped into his father's insurance business, and met his high school friends weekly at the same bar. In the early days of their marriage Maura had fit into Pete's life with ease, conforming herself to his lifestyle. But routine, complacency, and the lack of spontaneity had begun to chafe over the years. It was like wanting something more or somehow different but having no real idea quite what, she had told her college roommate.

Maura had regretted spilling this confidence to her friend the next morning, blushing at the thought of such naked honesty. But they had not discussed it again, and she told herself that the alcohol had probably blunted the memory of the conversation.

She lay back in the sand, turning her face toward the weak warmth of the sun. A few larger pebbles dug into her back, and she raised her eyes up to the cloudless sky. Even before Maura had completely put a finger on her growing restlessness, felt the daily routine sanding down and blurring her edges, she had understood how easily attentions could be diverted. In her early marriage, there had been a couple of temptations. Well, flirtations really, that had stayed with her all of these years later. When she was newly engaged to Pete, she and her girlfriend Beth Stevens had gone to a Sox game together. The first welcome tendrils of a spring breeze had begun to stir over the plains and off the Great Lakes, lending a recklessness to the premature warmth of the afternoon. Emboldened by the beers in the stands, they'd been stealing glances and giggling at the three boisterous guys seated next to them. Very quickly it had bloomed into playful flirting.

Tim was the name of the young man next to her, and he'd been more serious than his buddies, more animated and eager to talk. She'd let him rest his hand on her knee as they conversed, a small, harmless thing, she had told herself later, because she was, after all, only engaged and not married. They'd discussed music and politics and family. While they stole sidelong glances at the field, she had the feeling that the space around them on the bleachers had shrink-wrapped them both in, so that the sounds surrounding them, the cheering and the whooping it up, had begun to recede.

Beth poked her thigh at one point and gave her a strange, almost imploring look, which, she realized through her slightly beery haze, was meant to pull her back to earth. And it was only after both of them were back on the commuter train and headed out to the suburbs that she thought about how quickly she had attached herself to this person and had spoken so readily and intimately. It had struck her, later that night, that her conversations with Pete, even in the early days of their courtship, had a different feeling, not as earnest or intense.

During those two and a half hours at the baseball game a total stranger had lit her up and provoked an examination of the conventions and beliefs with which she'd been raised. He was Jewish, she recalled, and he had probed her feelings about her Catholicism as a woman and challenged her very orthodox decision to simply vote Republican because her parents did. Tim's sense of intellectual engagement in life had seemed electric, and that, in turn, had kindled a palpable mutual attraction, as if they'd both been illuminated from within.

And although she had never seen Tim again or even learned his last name, this one, vivid encounter had popped into her head at odd times over her yearlong engagement and very occasionally in the years to follow, on the heels of a fight with Pete or some small disappointment, like a forgotten anniversary.

There was another time a few years after she'd gotten married, on a train from Chicago to Indianapolis for her tenth college reunion. She'd been seated next to a tall, slim, serious man with piercing eyes, who was part Cherokee, which she had found inexplicably sexy. They had plunged into a deep and serious discussion in that anonymous way that strangers can adopt, secure in the knowledge that they would never see each other again. It was the first time since she had been married that she'd had the impulse to cover her left hand, obscuring her ring finger so that she could be just Maura and not somebody's wife.

She learned her seatmate was an underwater explosives expert for the navy, and he spoke briefly about depth charges and diving in a factual, not boastful, way that was authoritative and appealing. In this second memorable encounter with an attractive stranger, it had been less about what they said and more about something crackling in the air between them. Traveling solo to her college reunion to inhabit briefly that long ago carefree attitude, she felt his sloe-eyed gaze as it ignited her feeling of abandon.

There was a moment when the train slowed, approaching the station, and the ride together seemed to demand some kind of mutual ending. When the train lurched to a sudden halt, she fell toward him and made a joke as she moved awkwardly toward a half embrace, a sort of air kiss, while he simultaneously extended his hand, and they had both laughed. She understood then that so many of life's outcomes swung on a hinge; in that instant one made a choice. This was the moment she could press forward, get his number, or offer to grab a drink.

As he helped her with her luggage in the top compartment, she'd impulsively toyed with the thought of asking for his name and address, her heart like a wild creature in her chest. And then, as he turned to help retrieve an older woman's bags behind them, she lost her nerve and let the moment pass.

These encounters with strangers had been a sobering lesson about the human capacity to love and the laws of attraction. There was not just one right person out there in the world for you, there were many people, many directions, many couplings that you could make in life and be just as happy or possibly even more so than the random one you had chosen. This thought was at first disorienting and disquieting to her. And when she had returned from her reunion, she'd made love to Pete with a concentrated fierceness, as if to assure herself that she had made the right choice.

As she rose to her feet and brushed off the sand from her cloth-ing, Maura thought about how she had used that knowledge, the choices she had made since then and the unintended consequences of that path. She would barter almost anything she had to scroll back in time with the clarity and understanding she now pos-sessed.

· · ·

Returning from her trip to the beach, Maura pulled the car halfway up the driveway, and as she walked to the front porch, she observed the bushes and perennials that needed pruning and shaping. She'd inherited her love of growing things from her mother, and usually she enjoyed tidying the yard at the change of seasons. Now Maura tried to summon the enthusiasm required for such a task. They'd need to get pumpkins soon too and put out Halloween decorations.

Maura reached into the mailbox on the front porch and fished out the clump of envelopes, bills, and circulars. Flattened in front of the pile was a blue cardboard coffee cup, with the image of a Greek statue and the words WE ARE HAPPY TO SERVE YOU printed on opposing sides in the familiar diner font. Maura studied it with a puzzled ex-pression for just a moment and then her face sagged. The word *e-mail* was scrawled on the side in pencil, so faint that it would be easy to miss if one didn't understand the significance of the cup itself.

Maura slung the strap of her purse higher on her shoulder and dug back into the mailbox with both hands, checking to see if there was anything that she had missed in the recesses of the metal box. Heart pounding, she opened the front door and deposited her purse, keys, and the pile of mail on the front hall table. She walked swiftly into the kitchen to her computer on the small built-in desk and clicked on the symbol for her e-mail, something she'd rarely done since the accident. She groaned softly as the in-box rapidly filled with all the unanswered messages from well-meaning people, mass e-mails from the kids' schools, and spam. She had let all of this go for so long. Maura saw it there, delivered in the last hour. "Vet Check-Up Appt" the subject said, so innocuous that Pete or anyone else would most likely leave it unopened. She hesitated for a moment and clicked on the e-mail as the words filled the screen.

"We need to talk about Rascal's medical condition. Please call the office. Art" was all it said. She read it a second time and closed her eyes, letting her breath out in one thin stream. What an eerie coincidence that she'd just been to Gull's Day. Instinctively she reached toward the kitchen cordless phone and then stopped, moving her hand back to the desktop and rooting her feet to the floor. No, she told herself. Six months. She'd given herself at least six months. Although it would take every ounce of her self-command, she owed this to herself and Pete. Maura reread the message one last time, parsing it for clues, before she pressed delete.

11

"So I saw the kid today." Pete said it casually, crumpling his napkin on the empty dinner plate and sliding it toward the center of the table. Outside the kitchen window, darkness had begun to arrive early and a flock of geese, honking in a sloppy V formation, flew by above the trees. "I went to the Hulburds' house after work." He took a pull of his beer bottle and set it down on the table too hard, looking directly at Maura with a neutral expression. There was a speck of gravy on the front of his shirt.

"Yeah? How did it go?" She kept her voice even, relieved that Pete had waited until the kids were finished with dinner and glued to a video in the family room. The dishes and Sarah's bath could wait.

"Well, I think he was pretty scared. I gotta say, he seems like a good kid, but it was really awkward at first. Uncomfortable for all of us."

"Tell me about him." Maura realized she had been holding her breath and exhaled.

"I went over there after work, and they were all kinda sitting there, really stiff, like they'd been waiting for me. They had cheese and crackers, wine, stuff like that. The parents are decent people, nice. Alicia and Ray. Like us, I guess. And get this . . ." Pete smiled and looked down at his cuticles for a moment. "They have their homeowners' policy with us, with Corrigan Insurance. Dad wrote their first one years ago, when they bought on Chestnut." Pete shook his head with incredulity. "Life in a small town, right?"

"Mmmmm, go on," Maura urged him.

"Well, he said the stuff you'd imagine he'd say, how sorry he was, how this was an accident but he can't get it out of his head. He met my eyes when he spoke, you know? The kid is in a lot of pain, Maura. He looks . . . I don't know exactly, haunted, I guess. I mean this all has obviously taken a toll." Pete stopped to take a sip of his beer, and Maura sat still for a moment, imagining what it had cost Pete to knock on their door.

"The kid, Alex, is almost eighteen, and he goes to New Trier High School. He's a swimmer but when he went upstairs after we talked, his parents told me they're really worried about him. He quit the swim team, and his grades have tanked. He used to hang out with one set of guys who were athletes, and from what his mom can tell, now he's with more of a pothead crowd, and they're obviously concerned. I mean I guess he was never an ace student, but he was on some kind of college track before. His mother told me that she keeps trying to get him to fill out his applications to basically anywhere, and he just gives her lip service."

Maura lifted her arm on the table and rested her chin in her hand. "I'd give anything to have those problems with James, you know? To worry that his grades are slipping, to get bent out of shape about who he hangs out with . . ."

"I know."

"He's seventeen. How can he possibly understand what it means to lose a child? He'll go to senior prom and graduate and fall in love and . . ." Maura trailed off. The sound of her own voice was foreign, bitter and spiteful. Thinking about Alex Hulburd, she felt the incomprehensible injustice of their situation as if it were a sharp-toothed bite.

"Pete, I'm really glad you went over there, I am. But I'm just not there yet, I guess," said Maura tremulously. "I can't imagine what I would say to him, how it would feel to be with him and not want to trade everything I own to have James take his place." She winced and Pete moved toward her in his seat, reaching around to hug her as she covered her eyes with her other hand.

"Hey, babe"—Pete's voice softened an octave—"he's a decent kid, and this has wrecked his life too. That's just a fact." Her eyes were fixed on the floor, and she nodded without looking at him. "I think the key is going to be trying to make sure that both of us don't go down with the ship, right?"

Maura looked up, surprised by this unexpected declaration. She moved her hand over to the center of the table spontaneously. Pete reached out to grab it, and they sat that way for a few minutes, each lost in their own thoughts while a cartoon laugh track swelled at varying volumes from the family room TV.

"He's . . . he's hurting, Maura. And he'd love to see you at some point. When you're ready." She inclined her head slightly at this remark and began to move the remains of her baked potato around on her plate with her knife. She'd overcooked the pork chop and it was dry and leathery.

"I know it's only been a couple of months, but I'm just going to say this even though you'll probably get mad. I think you . . . you need to try to show the kids a little more happiness."

Maura's felt a flash of anger at the nerve of his comment, he who was so unyielding with his boys' nights out, ceremoniously calling from the bar to announce his "one last pop." Her eyes narrowed as she looked up. "I'm trying my best, Pete. I really am. I can't wave this away. You don't see me every minute of the day with them. You aren't here to witness my parenting, I'm not always walking around weeping, or whatever it is you think I'm doing."

"I'm just saying, maybe you ought to see somebody," Pete continued in a gentle tone. "I don't know, talk to somebody. Somebody other than your sister and the priest."

Maura sighed and poured Sarah's leftover milk in with Ryan's.

She pushed her chair back and rose from the table, scraping the dinner plates into the disposal and then stacking them, arranging the silverware in a pile on top. Her shoulders were slightly hunched, as if protecting her heart. The way she held herself now gave the appearance that carrying her grief had become a physical burden.

"I don't want to talk, Pete," she said quietly. "Not really. It won't change a thing. It doesn't make me feel any better to talk to Father Durkee. I go and light candles, I kneel and say prayers. All of this is just a temporary relief and Mass mostly feels like window dressing. I sit there and my heart isn't anywhere in that church. I'm angry. Angry at Alex Hulburd, angry at God and at the fact that no one can tell me why bad things happen. Why did it happen to us? Talking about it to some stranger or some therapist is only going to stir things back up. Father Durkee tells me to try to be grateful for what I have. But that puts a lot on Ryan and Sarah to fill that gap." She opened the refrigerator and put the leftover glass of milk inside before returning to the sink to load the dishwasher. "And it can't bring him back."

Pete sighed, and his chair made a scraping noise as he stood. He moved wordlessly to the refrigerator, grabbed a bottle of beer, and twisted the top off, skittering it over the counter. He stood in front of the door for a moment after it closed, studying the magnet decals and family photos. A laminated, typed list of useful phone numbers was taped in the center of the door, containing the numbers for family members, the babysitter, the doctor's offices, and poison control.

"You still haven't found your phone yet, huh?" Pete asked over his shoulder.

"No."

"We should get you a new cell phone this week." Maura was relieved by the change of subject, although they were still on slightly dangerous territory.

"I don't know, Pete. It's not at the top of my list. It's not like I'm out and about all day. I'm mostly here, and there's a machine. I don't really want to talk to anyone outside my family."

"What about me? Maybe I want to reach you sometimes, Maura. What if something is wrong with the kids? You can't be without a phone forever. It's not practical."

Maybe, thought Maura. But it was more comfortable this way. There were no surprises. Communication could happen on her terms.

"Let me look for it one more time," said Maura. "Maybe it's still around and it's just dead." Though it wasn't, she knew. She had made sure of that.

"Did you have it that morning?" Pete was glancing down at the morning paper now, still on the counter from breakfast. He was scrolling randomly through the sports page. She could see the bald patch beginning on the top of his head, the places where his newly shampooed scalp shone through.

"What?" Her heartbeat kicked up and she worked to keep her voice nonchalant.

"Your phone. You haven't had it since the accident. Were you talking on it that morning?" He was studying her now, his voice more steely, or was she just imagining it?

"A cell phone is the last thing on my mind right now, Pete. Honestly, there was so much confusion . . . when . . . when it all happened . . ." Maura stopped what she was saying, stared out the window over the sink, chewing on her bottom lip, and then turned back to observe him. The sky outside was ink black and moonless. Pete looked up at her quizzically for a moment, and then shrugged his shoulders in an exaggerated gesture of surrender before he took another swig of beer and left the room.

During other periods of their marriage, they had gone through rough patches, little fights, things that had gotten blown out of proportion, starting from some slight or transgression. They had lived for an entire day, once, barely speaking to each other. She could re-

THOSE WE LOVE MOST   85 —⁘•

member the first time they had ever gone to bed mad at each other, despite their newlywed pledge never to do so. It had started over something stupid, her telling him not to drag the porch chairs or blowing up at the condition in which he'd left the kitchen.

But this was different. This was a kind of corrosive apathy, a gentle disinterest in the bonds that had once held them together. And what made it scarier was that she suspected he felt this way too. They were two people adrift, had been for a few years now, and James's death had cleaved them further. It would take at least one of them to right the course, and she simply lacked the energy at present.

For a moment, Maura allowed herself to picture how she had broken her cell phone into pieces and slid it down the grate in the street on the corner, hearing the splash in the sewer water below. The records of the texts would be obliterated. There was so much about that day and the things that had happened leading up to it that she still couldn't bear to revisit. Maura slammed the window down on those thoughts as she removed Pete's empty beer bottle from the table, rinsed it, and dumped it in the kitchen recycling bin.

. . .

The next night, onions and bell peppers were simmering in butter on top of the stove, permeating the house with their distinctive odor. Maura heard the garage door begin to rattle open and was pleased to see that Pete was home early. He'd make another family dinner with the kids this evening, two in a row. He walked into the kitchen holding a plastic bag, pecked her on the cheek, and plunked a box on the counter.

"I got you a new phone . . . a nice one," he said cheerfully. "It's a better version of the one you had before."

"Thanks." Maura gave the contents of the frying pan a stir and punched the button on the stovetop hood fan up to a higher level before turning to observe Pete assembling the cell phone and its various accessories. It would feel strange to be available to anyone at any time again, she thought. There had been something wonderful about reentry on her own terms, with the safety of an answering machine to buffer her from the outside world. A mobile phone suddenly felt so immediate, so urgent.

"Now we can all reach you," joked Pete. "Even if you don't want to be found." She looked at him and made an expression that was both mocking and serious. Pete smiled, his eyes crinkling, and for a moment she glimpsed in his face the outlines of the boy-man she had fallen in love with.

"You're welcome," he said in a joking voice. "Dinner smells great," and he headed upstairs to change out of his suit.

12

Maura *was relieved* that the well-intentioned visits from friends had tapered off. More than three months after the accident she had grown tired of people hoping to "see how she was." They had begun to lose interest after her full-blown retreat. Everything had a life cycle.

She loved her friends and knew they meant well, yet each time they walked in the front door, she experienced a sudden, desperate urge to trade places with them. They could breeze into the wreckage of her household, trailing their visions of cheer or normalcy to comfort her. But then they would leave. And this was the part Maura resented. They would hug her and head out into the bright sunshine, off to the grocery store, to bring lemonade to the sidelines of a soccer game or pick up the family dry cleaning. They would walk off her front porch relieved, drawing fresh air into their lungs as they headed toward their cars, shedding the weight of her grief as effortlessly as a silk scarf.

The most persistent person had been Celia Murphy, the mother of James's best friend, Henry. Her dramatic kindness and overblown compassion often stuck in Maura's craw. Their friendship had largely been constructed around the kids, and they'd logged many hours together at playgrounds and sporting events. Celia was one of those striking faux-Scandinavian suburban wives who lorded their organizational superiority over less perfect mothers, the ones who didn't have the baseball schedule taped to the fridge or forgot the upcoming bake sale. She wore foundation and lip gloss when she exercised. And although Maura believed she meant well, Celia was a crisis rubbernecker, a kind of emotional tick, swelling with empathy as she feasted on calamities, inserting herself to extract the details. At the start of the school year, Celia had called the house on an afternoon when Erin was over, and Maura had seen the number on the caller ID. "Pick it up," urged Maura. "Please? If you talk to her maybe I won't have to call her back. She doesn't give up," Maura had pleaded, handing the cupped phone to her sister.

"Maura?" She could hear Celia's jaunty voice through the receiver up against Erin's ear.

"This is her sister, Erin."

"Oh, Erin, I'm so glad I got you. I haven't really had a chance to connect with Maura. I'd love to come over there and drag her out but I'm trying to be, you know, sensitive."

"She appreciates everyone being so respectful right now," said Erin evenly. "It's still very hard, as I'm sure you can imagine." Erin rolled her eyes at Maura, vamping.

"Absolutely. Well, actually I wanted to run something by the family, if that's OK."

"Sure," said Erin in a forced chipper voice, putting Celia on speakerphone so that Maura could listen in.

"Well, Henry had this idea. And I think it's a really good one, actually. I've shared it with some of the other families at the elementary school. It would be a way to honor James but also do some good too. You know how kids are so into that today, the community service thing and giving back."

"Uh-huh. Sure."

"We wanted to hold a fund-raiser in James's name this fall. A car wash and bake sale for our sister elementary school in downtown

Chicago," Celia explained. "It's in one of the 'less fortunate' areas,"
she added with emphasis. Erin made a motion of sticking her finger down her throat, and Maura smiled in response.

"That's a really lovely idea, Celia. I'm happy to run it by Maura
and Pete. I'm sure they will be touched."

"We were hoping all the Corrigans could come and be involved.
The tentative date will be early November and we've already gotten
approval to hold it at the elementary school." She had barely taken a
breath between sentences, Maura noted.

"Well that's a . . . nice way to honor James, Celia," began Erin
cheerily, "but I'm not sure the family will be up for that so soon.
Maybe you should plan on holding the one this year without us, and
we can see how everyone is doing when it gets closer." Maura nodded, her expression suddenly solemn.

"I'd love to bring some muffins over to the house, maybe just sit
with Maura for a little bit?" Undeterred, Celia tried a different tack.

"You know, Celia, I have to say that right now, my sister is just
kind of going one day at a time. I know you understand," Erin said
firmly. "It's still a very difficult period. I think everyone takes this
part of grieving at their own pace." An edge had crept into her voice.
She took her job as guardian of the gate seriously.

"Oh, I sooooo understand." Celia's unctuous voice was now abra-
sive to Maura and she rose with a livid industriousness to move
into the living room, plumping the red plaid cushions on the couch
and folding the throw blanket in an effort to keep herself occupied.
Erin added some pleasantries and assured her that she'd pass the
message on to Maura. "Maybe next year we can all be there."

"She's already working on her kid's résumé for college," Erin
had joked later that afternoon to Margaret, who had arrived to play
with Sarah. Erin had been reprising the conversation with her
mother, mimicking Celia's voice in an exaggerated southern twang.
"Oh, now that's cynical," Margaret had chided them both sternly.

"Ease up on Celia. Her heart's in the right place. You're going to need friends like her for the long haul." Maura and Erin had traded conspiratorial looks.

Maura hated the notion that she was now one of *those* people that others pitied, the ones for whom they held fund-raisers. Maura's family was now included in prayers at church or the subject of a cautionary example at the dinner table, about looking both ways or being careful. At least she had her family, Maura would think, when she needed to reach for some goodness in her life. Thank God she had Erin, her brother, Stu, and his wife, Jen, who was like a sister. Her parents and siblings were grieving as well, she acknowledged, although she had largely taken that for granted. But they had formed the webbing that had held her together. Although she hadn't spent much time alone with him since the funeral, her father had been a rock. His solid presence in the house was a form of protection, and of all three children, she was closest to him. Maura shared his same ski-sloped nose, the strong jawline with a slight underbite, and she could be forceful and stubborn like Roger as well, planting her feet like a mule at times. She and her father had always preferred being in the company of others to being alone, that is, until James's accident.

Through the years, she and Erin had spent hours dissecting inexhaustible topics, and they had never lost their ability to retrieve threads of conversations exactly where they'd stopped ten minutes earlier. As kids, they would rehash their worries and crushes or use their collective wisdom to try to solve some perceived slight with classmates or boyfriends. Tireless investigators of their parents' marriage, they'd had many a whispered bedtime conversation attempting to plumb the depths of what was said and decided behind the closed doors in their childhood home. As adults, they had grown even closer, confessing the weaker walls and broken places in their friendships and marriages, venting frustrations about husbands and the things they'd love to change if it were ever possible, which they'd agreed it wasn't.

Since James's death she and Erin hadn't had one of their customary heart-to-hearts. It was almost as if their natural sibling pecking order had reversed. Rather than being the oldest, Maura felt, at times, like the baby, with Stu and Erin watching over her and speaking in cheerful, patronizing tones. Still, she felt closer to and more grateful for her siblings than ever, united with them by this loss. So why didn't she have these same feelings of coming together with her own husband? If only she could experience this sense of joining seams with Pete, the restoration of tenderness to its natural axis.

. . .

She was sure of it this time. In fact she'd been waiting for him, on the lookout now in the evenings. It was Pete's regular Thursday out with his buddies, and it had occurred to Maura that the trespasser had been watching the house. He knew when Pete was gone, when the car was out of the driveway, and those were the nights he chose. She had spotted him two other times.

There was a sliver of moon and the stars looked embroidered on a black velvet sky. Her eyes adjusted to focus on the outdoors. The neighborhood was quiet, broken only by the occasional whisper of a car passing on the street. There it was, the outline of a figure. She would be more careful than the first time, she wouldn't open the door but would study him from the house. A sight line through the crotch of the tree allowed her a view of the lawn where he was lying, so still he resembled a corpse. A cold snap had turned the fall nights crisp, and Maura imagined the wet chill of the ground permeating his thin sweatshirt.

A spark flared, a lighter probably. He was flicking it randomly back and forth, toying with the striking mechanism until it caught. A thin blue flame suddenly jumped, and she could see his hooded head rise, almost vertically to his body, and he brought what looked like a cigarette, or possibly a joint, to his lips.

Maura shifted her weight onto her other leg and carefully pulled the shade back a few more inches. She didn't want to startle him before she had a chance to check out her hunch. She wanted to see his face, and she realized that the light spilling from the interior of her house on the first floor would afford her a better look at his features. She padded downstairs in the dark, entering the family room and stubbing her toe on the coffee table leg. Maura stifled an outburst and moved to the glass. He was younger and more vulnerable-looking than she imagined he'd be. In her mind she had pictured someone rougher perhaps, more hulking and imposing.

Alex Hulburd. She recognized him from Pete's description; who else could it possibly be? But what was he doing? Had he turned their house into a kind of shrine? His presence out on the lawn felt like a combination of both sentry and spy. There should have been something fundamentally creepy about him occupying their lawn at night, but in fact Maura found it oddly comforting, although she couldn't quite articulate why.

Her eyes fully adjusted now, she watched the boy as he lay back down on the grass and stretched out, releasing a lungful of smoke in a thin stream. He laced his hands behind his head, elbows jutting out as he studied the night sky. Observing him, Maura was surprised to recognize something spontaneous, almost combustible and singularly maternal loosen inside of her heart. She stayed glued to the window, perched on the arm of the sofa, as if studying a hummingbird that might startle at the slightest movement. When he had finished smoking, he rose, his storklike limbs curling into a cross-legged position before standing. He was thin and tall. Pete had told her Alex was a swimmer and he had a swimmer's body, lean and muscular, deceptively strong. He stretched his arms up to

the sky for a moment, arching his back, and then turned fully toward the house, staring directly at the plate glass window behind
which she stood perfectly still. Maura held her breath.

It appeared as if he were staring directly at her, and she shrank
back slightly, although she was confident that the curtain obscured
most of her. Now she could see his face more clearly, his deep-set
eyes and lighter longish hair, and the fullness in his cheeks gave
him a more boyish, vulnerable appearance. All at once Alex bent to
retrieve something from the grass, perhaps the cigarette butt, she
thought, and then he began to jog, at first a loping gait off the lawn
and then gaining speed as he hit the pavement and zigzagged under
a streetlamp before cutting off a side street toward the direction of
his house. For a few minutes after he had disappeared from sight,
Maura stood with a vacant distraction by the curtain, transfixed by
the spot where the boy had lain and the moon's soft glow. Then she
turned and went back upstairs to adjust her children's blankets
before climbing into bed.

13

S unlight *filtered through* the brocade cabbage rose drapes in their bedroom. It took Roger a few seconds to remember what city he was in. Chicago, not Florida. But it was Julia he'd been dreaming of and her town. He faltered at the recall for a moment. Tampa. There it was, he'd retrieved it. It still startled him when the rustiness happened in his head, at the oddest times, like an ambush. Of course he knew the name of that city. God knows he'd been there enough times for real estate deals.

Sometimes lately, especially when he was tired, conjuring up the exact name or word could be trying, almost as if there was a gumminess to his mental circuitry. "Cobwebs" he called it. He had been able to joke about it with Julia, and when it occasionally happened she would touch the back of his hand and smoothly insert the word. He'd been more reluctant to reveal the depths of this weakness with Margaret.

"Just old age," he'd explain it away to his wife. Except that at times it felt different. Words would swim in front of him like a stutter, eluding capture until he grasped them. But more than that, what scared Roger sometimes was the flat-out forgetting. And in those moments he would ask himself if it were real, the advance of something serious, or just the unreliability of short-term memory as people aged.

Roger looked at the digital clock on Margaret's side of the bed. The red numbers registered 6:37 A.M. and he noted his wife's rosary beads coiled like a snake on the small table next to a box of Kleenex. He was relieved that she found comfort in the rituals of prayer and religion. She had always been far more devout than he, although he attended Mass fairly regularly on late Saturday afternoons. Margaret lay immobile on her side, wearing the dramatic black satin eyeshade Erin had given to her for Christmas one year when she'd complained that her "change of life" left her unable to sleep past dawn. And now it had become a habit, the dark fabric erasing half of her face in a kind of Batman death mask. Her mouth hung partially open, and little gurgly sounds, too polite for a snore, emanated rhythmically from the back of her throat. She must have taken a sleeping pill, something she did more frequently to get a full night's sleep. Roger rolled over to his edge of the bed, taking care not to make any noise. He didn't want to wake his wife right now for any number of reasons. Saturday mornings were his cherished time, that first cup of coffee in the kitchen, padding out barefoot on the cool asphalt to grab the newspaper at the end of the driveway. He had planned to squeeze in nine holes of golf today. The course would close in two weeks.

The sun was rising in an iridescent burning ball that filled him with a sense of vigor. The October air had cooled markedly at the fringes of each day. Normally it was in the morning that he felt most like his old self, his thoughts firing efficiently, his brain crystal clear and not muddied by the day's complications. Halfway down the driveway, Roger stopped as a squirrel scampered in front of him, his tail seeming to float as he bounded. Roger could see the animal before him, he knew what it was, but he could not immediately retrieve the word. Other s words—*skunk, skull, skill*—swum around him murkily before *squirrel* emerged as a crisp, whole word with an attendant sense of relief. He remembered the Magic 8 Ball toy that had delighted Maura and Erin one Christmas as

proclamations of "Yes, Definitely," and "Very Doubtful," and "Outlook Great" floated up through the inky liquid when you turned it
upside down. Sometimes retrieving his words felt like that.

Roger had purposely kept these niggling worries about his
memory from Margaret. She might make too much of it, or fuss
over him with her high-strung nature. And of course then she'd
insist on him seeing a doctor and going through a battery of tests,
something for which he had little patience. As a husband and
father, he was careful not to erode or endanger his protective role,
and so it hadn't been difficult to keep these mental hiccups to
himself. Throughout the past decade he and Margaret had already
begun to fall into a pattern of avoidance in certain unintended
ways, bouncing off each other like amusement park bumper cars.
If he heard her in the kitchen, there were times he'd slip into the
den. Or if he knew she was in the bathroom washing up before bed,
he'd watch a few more minutes of the cable news before coming
upstairs. It wasn't completely calculated, he reasoned, not purposefully deliberate. Some nights avoiding his wife required less effort
after a taxing day at the office.

But in the growing light of day, a full weekend of activities and
visits planned with the grandchildren, Roger felt a sense of re-
newal concerning his marriage flare-up amid the backdrop of lin-
gering sorrow. James's death had caused their family to respond in
the ordinary ways that abrupt loss affects people, forcing them to
take stock of their own mortality and the fragility of life. But there
had been something more, something deeper, gradually opening
back up between him and Margaret that felt hopeful.

Memories of James and their moments together flitted through
his mind's eye at the oddest time, arresting all other thought. And
where he might not have remarked on these kinds of emotions before the accident, he had purposely mentioned this last night to
Margaret. They were picking over a dinner of plain grilled salmon

and broccoli, with some of her canned garden tomatoes over a mound of cottage cheese.

"Do you ever just think about James and stop everything you are doing? Do you ever feel so sad that you don't want to take another step?" His words rushed out in a jumble at the table with an intensity that surprised him.

Margaret had looked up at him thoughtfully, but coolly, her fork poised halfway to her mouth, her expression unchanged but for the arch of her brows. "I think about him all the time," she said in a measured tone. "But I don't let myself get overwhelmed. Not now. Not at this place in time. I can't see the point in letting yourself wallow in that kind of grief. I just keep going when I start to feel that way and I try to push out those thoughts. They're unproductive. " She cut a clump of broccoli in half and popped it in her mouth, chewing neatly, her jaws working rhythmically in a way that Roger had always found slightly annoying.

They ate for a few moments in silence, the clatter of their cutlery and the blaring TV news providing a background conversation. Margaret broke the silence. "I remember once reading something that Rose Kennedy said. It was in a magazine article, I think." Margaret set down her fork, and her eyes took on a faraway look. "I remember the interviewer asking her how she went on after all that tragedy—two sons assassinated, one killed in a plane crash, I think, along with another daughter. He was a war hero, remember? And there was that one, Rosemary, who was retarded." Margaret paused to take a bite of salmon before continuing. "She said, Rose Kennedy said, that she just made up her mind, years ago, that she wasn't going to let those events control her. That if she collapsed with grief it would have a very bad effect on everyone else in the family who had to go forward." Ennobled, Margaret picked up her fork and neatly cut a piece of fish with a sideways slice.

"Well, that's a pretty tall order," he had said softly. "Rose Kennedy was quite a lady. She came from an era where you learned to buck it all up. I guess it's nice to think we can control our emotions like that but . . . well, realistically, I don't think all of us can just flip a switch."

"I just think it's something to aspire to . . . is all. Sitting around sniveling and wringing your hands for weeks about something you can't change, that doesn't help the kids any, does it? There's Ryan and Sarah, and everything still needs to get done around the house. Someone just has to set an example is all I am saying. They can't see every adult close to them just incapacitated by grief. I think it's up to us to show those kids that life goes on. That we're here to love them too."

Roger had nodded. There was no point in countering her. Taking the path of least resistance when she got on what he referred to as her "high horse" was always the best course. But there was a ring of truth to what she said, and he found himself admiring her steeliness, the strength of her internal conviction. He frequently found himself on the brink of tears in the stretches of time he had spent alone with Maura after James died. In those moments he envied his wife's self-control, her centered fortitude. Maura and he jokingly referred to themselves as "the old softies" in the family.

They ate the rest of the meal listening to the network news echoing from the small kitchen TV, a welcome and legitimate distraction. Roger focused again on Margaret as she finished the last of her dinner. She was a handsome woman, had always been striking. Something sentimental unexpectedly hit him, a tingling of gratitude like an electric current, and for just a moment he felt as if his eyes would fill.

"Do you remember when we met?" he said suddenly, immediately feeling silly for the question.

"Of course." She laughed.

"Our blind date, at . . . uh . . ." There it was again, that tiny trip wire in his brain. "Wheaton College, of course. Wheaton. Good old

Phil Tracey set us up, and then he lent me his car to drive over to your campus from Northwestern. I took you out for ice cream, remember? Phil Tracey. When was the last time we saw him?" Roger smiled at the memory.

"Lord, we haven't seen Phil in at least two decades. I think it was at your reunion, sometime in the 1990s, and he was totally bald."

"I should call Phil . . ." He trailed off, lost in thought for a moment. "Think about those times, Margaret, the mid-1960s. We were so insulated from most of that mess, The Vietnam War and those hippie protesters. After Phil enlisted, I remember no one heard from him for a few years, and then he turned up in California. The guy was making a fortune in that early phone technology stuff." He shook his head, remembering. "It was automated switchboards or something."

"I almost didn't go out that night. But Phil kept bugging me that you were home from Northwestern. How could I forget? You had on that blue sweater that perfectly matched your eyes." Margaret's face softened at the memory, and they gazed at each other full in the face and then Margaret patted his hand maternally before pushing her chair back. Roger drained the last of his cocktail and crunched down on the slim remains of the ice.

"I'm glad I listened to Phil." Margaret rose with a coy smile and slid the remains of her food onto his plate as she began to clear the table.

Everything about Margaret had been mysterious back then. The way she held herself, the reserve, as if there were parts of her she was keeping back just for him. She had a quick staccato laugh, not an easy one like his sister, but one that took some work to coax out, making it feel like a reward. She was bright, and her dark looks and hazel eyes behind clumped lashes contributed to what he had referred to as her "unattainable beauty" when they had first begun to get serious.

All of the things about her appearance that had so drawn her to him in youth had now gelled in slightly sharper ways with age. But she was still attractive. Some of the qualities of her personality that had once felt alluring, like a challenge, were now occasional irritants and obstacles, varying in degree at different times. But he admired Margaret, he respected her, and of course, he still loved her. They had logged years, raised three children, and soldiered up the corporate career ladder together. There had been periods where their love had felt more dutiful. Yet, in the end, taking stock of Margaret, as if considering her with fresh eyes, he had to admit that they mostly fitted together with the satisfaction of a solved puzzle.

14

Sarah needed to nap today. Although she had mostly given them up this past summer, she'd grown tired of playing with the dollhouse, and she was rubbing her eyes between moving the plastic figurines from room to room.

"Hey, little beauty," Maura murmured as she whisked her off the floor and into her arms. "Whaddya say we go read?"

Thumping up the stairs with her daughter in her arms, Maura impulsively grabbed a book from the shelf and settled into the white painted rocking chair in which she'd nursed all three children.

"Sarah, sweetie," Maura began in a soft voice. "You read to Mommy." And as part of their little routine, her daughter pointed to an object in the book, and Maura launched into her version of the story.

"Big red bawl." Sarah pointed triumphantly.

"That's right Sarah, *b-a-l-l*," and Maura would repeat the word in that subtle nudging way a parent refines and corrects their child's speech. When they had finished the book, Maura began to softly brush her daughter's velvety belly skin with the tips of her fingers, as she grew more limp and pliant in her arms. They rocked a few minutes longer and then Sarah's head sagged. Maura rose from the chair in slow increments, skillfully lifting her over the rail of the crib and lowering her onto the mattress.

Down in the kitchen, the good feeling with Sarah sputtered, replaced by the strangled quiet of the house. The whir of the appliances was broken by the sporadic angry caw of black crows arguing in the branches outside. The old Maura would have had any number of things to accomplish during nap time, but now, she hung listlessly over the sink, staring out the window and into the side yard, fixated on the angry birds and the curled, dead leaves tumbling across the grass in a gathering wind.

Maura thought about the feelings of pure joy she'd experienced in mothering moments with Sarah and her boys, especially at seasonal times: ironing fall leaves between wax paper, choosing Halloween costumes, carving pumpkins. All of these moments were tinged now, sepia toned, the purity of them tinted by her overarching loss. And yet deep inside she had to admit she was feeling infinitesimally and incrementally stronger; there were spikes of her old self. She was more up to the challenge of being outside of the house for longer periods. She'd accepted a lunch invitation from Celia and was determined to go, although she was bringing Erin as a buffer. Pete was right. Her hiding from the world wasn't accomplishing anything other than to worry her two remaining children. She was trying hard to focus on placing one foot in front of the other.

Maura opened the front door and pulled her cardigan around her, bracing against the breezy October afternoon. She reached inside the front porch mailbox to grasp the day's delivery and a cardboard coffee cup flipped out with the magazines and fell onto the porch floor. Maura's heartbeat surged as she bent to inspect it. This time there was nothing written on the outside, but the meaning was clear.

Back at the kitchen computer, she found it sandwiched between some junk e-mails in her in-box. The subject heading read "Vet Appt Confirmation." Maura hesitated a moment before opening it and then clicked on it. She was surprised to see that this one was longer, an actual letter, the message no longer in ambiguous code. Her heart constricted as she began reading.

M—

I'm taking a huge chance writing this but I don't know what else to do. I figured you'd get the cup and check your e-mail right away and if you're reading this, I was right. It's been almost four months, and I'm going crazy. I gave you some big space at first because I assumed that I was probably the last person you needed to see or hear from. But then you didn't answer any of my calls or texts. I even called the house twice but didn't leave a message. I can only try to imagine what you are going through. It's an incomprehensible loss.

I was in the back of the church for the service, and then I left before you could see me. I had to steal in and just get a look at you. You turned around once and it was all I could do not to run to the front where you were sitting. I realized then, that I had never seen you sad, only happy. That's the way I want to picture you now, although I know that's not the case.

When I think back to how we happened, how simply it began over that appointment with Rascal and my growling stomach, it amazes me what followed. Our whole short history together makes me feel both foolish and still, oddly hopeful. Despite all of my promises to myself NOT to become involved with someone when I moved here, I ended up falling for a married woman at the practice. Great planning! (Joke)

Thankfully, you've spared me many of the insights into your relationship and it was certainly easier for us both to live in the present. But when I left Madison, I resolved never to make anyone else feel as miserable as I had by the slow crumbling of my relationship and my ex-wife's betrayal.

Your initial friendship while I was still very much a newcomer here was invaluable. But then I started to fall for you. Those walks on the beach, the sandwiches and coffee at the diner. I'm not sure either one of us could have predicted what that first lunch would lead to. I knew we were getting into dangerous territory and I know you did too. And yet when I think back to that day in the diner last spring, when I tried to break this off, you practically pleaded with me not to end it. You told me you thought this was what you wanted and that you felt we had a chance. And now I can't help but think that our decision only damaged you and damaged us.

After the funeral, I returned to our spot on the beach a few times at lunch, hoping to catch you there. All I wanted to do was see you and hold you. I wanted to look in your eyes and try to determine if there was anything there left for us.

I still hold on to those memories and when I want to really torture myself I sit back and think about how your skin smells, or your laugh, or the dozens of little things that made me fall for you against my better judgment.

I realize it's all complicated now, and that you are going through many things that I can't relate to. The only basis I have for comparison is losing my parents when I was in my twenties. But people say that still doesn't touch what it feels like to lose a child, and that must be true. All I know is that I have lost you. And with that the friendship, laughter, excitement, and so much more you brought to my life.

I've been biking a lot, and yes, in those tight, silly shorts with my bright orange helmet. Every time I start kicking around the apartment thinking about us and getting frustrated at the situation, I hop on my bike and go for a twenty-mile ride. Once or twice I've passed your house. Biking is the only way I can get you out of my head.

Maura, I understand where this is going. Or maybe I should
say, where it's not. You've made your intent pretty clear with your
total silence. I won't e-mail you again. I know I took a chance in
writing this, but I didn't have any other alternatives. I'd love to be
able to talk to you. You know where to find me.

Maura leaned back against her chair and let out her breath. She
had been frozen, statue-like, as she read, her hands clenched in
tight balls. She was incredulous and appalled at the giant risk he
had taken. Her heart was beating now as if she had shoplifted a
piece of jewelry or been pulled over for speeding. Pete might imagine someone had put an old coffee cup in the mailbox once as a
prank, but not twice. Maura felt competing emotions swirl inside
of her—confusion, guilt, anger at his calculated gamble to send such
an intimate e-mail. Then another feeling unexpectedly joined the
tumble . . . desire. Maura closed her eyes and sighed. This self-
control was far more difficult than she had imagined, but she would
not respond to his letter. She could not respond.

Maura focused on a photograph of their family pinned to the
bulletin board over her desk. It had been taken more than two years
ago at Six Flags amusement park and Sarah had been an infant.
The boys wore the satisfied expressions of a day of excess sun, sugar,
and excitement. She blinked back tears as she studied the snapshot. James's wide, freckled smile was directed right at the camera,
his bangs askew, and there were scarlet bands of sunburn under
his eyes where she'd neglected to apply sunscreen that day. Maura
pushed her chair back from the kitchen desk and rested her head in
her hands. No, she would not hit reply. It was the least she could do
for her marriage, the least she could do for James.

15

"So, *what are* your plans today?" Roger breezed into the kitchen, leather briefcase in hand. His suit was pressed and he had chosen a solid deep burgundy tie. Margaret always felt a sense of satisfaction at how his shirts started the day so crisp and white.

"Oh, some bridge at the club this morning. Then maybe over to Maura's later to play with Sarah." Roger kissed her cheek absent-mindedly and reached around her to pour a mug of coffee from the machine.

"I'm off again this week. I have to leave Thursday, probably just an overnight," he said casually, pouring the milk into his coffee and moving to sit at the table while she served him a bowl of hot oatmeal and bananas.

"Where to? Tampa?" Margaret drew the word out longer than necessary.

"Not this time. That may be inevitable next week, but this week it's Cincinnati. Something easy, I think." She relaxed her stance, slightly relieved it wasn't Florida.

"Oh?"

"We're looking at some new LEED commercial developments with Dan Hurwitz and his gang. Remember him? We need to beef up our expertise in that area."

She nodded. After he left the house, grabbing the newspaper for the train and whistling out the door, Margaret stood at the kitchen sink, thinking about how casually he had answered her when she had raised the subject of Tampa. Perhaps whatever transgressions he had committed there were long over. She could only hope so.

Yet she knew with absolute certainty that Roger had been unfaithful, she had proof. It was a boarding pass from an airline that she'd found three years ago. A moment of carelessness on Roger's part, emboldened, no doubt, by the foolish preening narcissism of a rooster in love.

She'd been searching for a smaller suitcase, needing to pack for a visit to Stu and Jen right after their engagement. As an assistant professor of technology at Milwaukee's city community college, Jen's teaching schedule permitted little time to plan a wedding, and Margaret had eagerly volunteered to help. She had located one of Roger's carry-on bags in the closet, and when she yanked it off the top shelf it had fallen open. A boarding pass stub from a flight to Tampa slipped out of the unzipped front pocket and onto the carpet. She had picked it up to throw it out until she noticed something scribbled on the back.

"Come back soon. Miss you already." It was signed "Love, J" with all the familiarity of a childhood sweetheart, and she studied the flight time and date to Florida, trying to imagine the hand that had written so breezily. Something thick had welled up and then clogged in Margaret's throat. A weak cry escaped, almost animal-like, which she'd suppressed with her fist despite being alone in the house.

On some level, she supposed, she had been bracing for this. It had been an unspoken thing, an intuition. Roger was a handsome man, patrician and charismatic. He traveled frequently, was exposed to all kinds of people in his business. Margaret had certainly been to enough of the annual meetings and some of the resort conventions to see the temptations, the eager supplicants and hussies who clustered in bars and at dinners, advertising their availability. She imagined them to be calculating and cunning about their conquests. But she'd always hoped, however blindly, that Roger was above that.

She thought about what she'd read somewhere, that the human heart can only sustain that kind of crazy, googly-eyed love for roughly a year. Twelve months. And then it became something else, something more familiar and at the same time more critical. It separated out those couples that were going to break apart from those that were going to go on ahead, to make the commitment and stand by each other. So what happened after thirty years? And then forty?

Margaret could still recall that moment of discovery with absolute clarity. She had let the sobs rise up in her throat and overtake her. There was no one to hear. She had sat pathetically on the carpet, legs splayed, as if she'd fallen, crying in great snuffling sounds. Oh what a sight she would make, she'd thought, if someone chanced to walk in and see her hoary, twisted face, the open suitcase and the note in her hand. How had she gotten to this place in her marriage?

Her mind shuttled back to their first blind date; it was odd that Roger had recently recalled it. It was uncharacteristic of him to be so nostalgic, but she had been touched. Sitting across from him in the ice cream parlor that first night, all those years ago, she was struck by his self-confidence. *Rakish* was the word one of her sorority sisters had used to describe him, but it didn't quite fit. He was too principled to be a rake, too full of regret when he inadvertently injured someone with a barbed or humorous comment. Tall, with chestnut-colored hair and a wide toothsome smile, Roger's most striking feature was the openness of his slate blue eyes. They held a kind of expectant promise, as if he assumed the world wouldn't dare let him down. It was as if he anticipated only good things. He'd come from a family of modest means in a small farming town in central Illinois, and he'd adopted the careful bearing and outward appearance of a man attempting to escape a penurious past while teaching himself to be invincible.

Margaret had wanted to be a teacher when she had met Roger. She had hoped to go on and get her degree after college so that she could teach high school English, but they had fallen in love and married. She had gotten pregnant with Maura soon after that, and Roger's first job had transferred him to Cleveland for a training program.

She and Roger had been born into the era of quiet decorum. They were raised by strict Catholic parents who had lived through the Depression. Her path to marriage and a family was clearly defined. Theirs had been a quick courtship, like many other couples in the mid-1960s, in the post-Kennedy years of gathering tumult. Margaret would understand, in retrospect, that their generation had stood on the cusp of great social overhaul set in motion by the war in Vietnam and the sexual revolution in the next decade. Insulated from the burgeoning unrest by their small-town and traditional midwestern roots, they had simply flowed from dating to their engagement and then the wedding. Roger was the only man Margaret had ever slept with.

He'd hungered for her early on in their marriage, locked eyes with her when they'd made love, spooned her at night in their sleep. But that desire seemed to thin after each child. Her fatigue, the predictability and routine of being a mother and homemaker, seemed increasingly in sharp contrast to his wheeler-dealer life on the road. It was the birth of their third child, Stu, which felt in some ways as if a string had snapped on a wonderfully rich old instrument. Juggling the demands of all three children, Margaret succumbed to the vortex of need, duty, and some days, exhaustion. Somehow she and Roger simply fell out of tune, and at some unknown point in time he had begun to share a bed with someone else. The naked betrayal of that fact hit her like the slap of an open palm as she'd sat helplessly on the rug that day three years ago.

Crying and keening in a ball had felt surprisingly good. A kind of wary, spent calm settled in afterward, and she'd swiped at her wet eyes with the backs of her hands, feeling an exhausted relief as she crawled to the side of her bed and tilted her head back against the mattress. Spying her rosary beads on the bedside table, she brought them to her lap, beginning to mumble the prayers with her eyes closed, the sanctuary of words centering her through the innate hardwiring of her faith. When Margaret was finished, she leaned her head back again and gazed upward, observing a single strand of a cobweb waving gently from the ceiling fan. It was that small detail that finally refocused and repurposed her.

She sighed heavily and struggled up to her feet. Bending over at the waist, she slammed the suitcase closed and lifted it onto the bed, sticking the note in the pocket of her slacks. Margaret hadn't consciously decided to keep it, she just didn't want it polluting her bedroom, didn't want it anywhere near them. And yet she couldn't bring herself to throw it out. She had stuffed it into the bottom drawer of the old rolltop desk in the living room, which housed an archive of kids' report cards and family medical records.

Margaret could still recall exactly where the old boarding pass was, although she had never felt the inclination to look at it again. There were moments she would think of it, comingled in that drawer with the history and documented achievements of her loved ones, and wonder if J was still in Roger's life. Or was there someone new? She had contemplated destroying the boarding pass, but in the end there was a twisted, inexplicable comfort, almost a security, in its secret possession. Roger had certainly forgotten it ever existed, and the carelessness of that, his disregard for her, was something best left unacknowledged.

16

R oger *looked at* his watch again in the crowded downtown restaurant. The associate he was meeting was now a half hour
late. Ten or even fifteen minutes was acceptable with traffic, but
this was ridiculous. Could the man have forgotten? He began to
dial his secretary when a younger couple brushed past him, following the maître d' clutching oversize menus, and the table jostled so
that his water glass spilled. His mild annoyance bubbled over into
open frustration. After this lunch meeting he had hoped to get over
to Maura's house, maybe take Ryan out to the backyard and play
catch before the weather completely turned. Work was in a lighter
phase between deals, and he was pleased to have the extra time to
focus on his grandson.

There was something so needy about Ryan now. At seven he was
intensely curious about the world, and yet his loss, his sorrow,
Roger sensed, was not always tended to by his parents, Pete in particular. Pete seemed to have retreated slightly since James's death—
there but not there, present but not actively so. He wondered idly if
Pete had even thrown a ball with Ryan in the months since the accident.

Roger had smelled alcohol on Pete's breath at odd times on more
than one recent occasion, but he had kept his comments to himself.
There had been one evening, after a family dinner, when he and

Margaret had observed Maura trying to wrestle the keys out of Pete's palm. Pete had grabbed her arm angrily. Roger had come close to intervening, but in the end he had exercised restraint. Everyone was hurting in different ways, he reasoned. Still, the urge to protect his daughter had flared, but the normally easy channels of their more intimate conversations had changed with the death of James. He would not raise the subject with her.

"I've been waiting here thirty minutes, Cristina," Roger sputtered into his cell phone in the restaurant, scanning the line of suits at the hostess stand in the front. "I'm about to leave."

"Tomorrow," his secretary said, after pausing to consult his schedule. "The lunch you set up with Mr. Pittman is tomorrow," and Roger swore under his breath.

"OK, my mistake," and he snapped the phone shut. He must have written it on the wrong day. He'd done that with one or two other appointments he'd arranged himself in the past few months, mixed up a few times or dates. He'd continued to write it off to stress, to the terrible crushing weight they had all endured, were still enduring really, in the wake of James's death. Roger waved the waiter over with a hurried gesture and requested the bill for his iced tea. He would grab a hot dog off the street cart and bring it back to the office. He'd had enough of the noise and the loud laughter inside the restaurant. The acoustics were terrible. It was one of those yuppie, hanging-fern-and-brass restaurants that seemed to come and go in downtown Chicago with regularity.

Pushing through the revolving door of the restaurant at the base of a glass and steel tower, Roger hitched up his trousers and adjusted, for a moment, to the early November temperatures outside.

He felt the buzzing of his cell phone and reached for it in his inside coat pocket. It was Julia. Images of her flooded into his head in muted colors. He could see the curve of her shoulder and the swell of her freckled breast. He envisioned the way her chin tilted upward, exposing the vulnerability of her neck when she laughed. Julia's kind of woman was the equivalent of instant gratification, immediate payoff. And then he felt unaccustomed shame for the moment, shame in his failure to please her when he was last in Tampa. He'd been tired, still very much grieving. The phone's insistent buzzing bloomed into a ring, and he was still for a moment, deciding whether or not to answer. With a sigh, he pushed the button.

"Hello?"

"Hi, Roger, it's me. Is this a good time?" Her words came out in a waterfall rush.

"It's fine. Yes. Julia, how are you, love?" Roger's voice softened imperceptibly, his features relaxed. Julia's voice still had a soothing effect on him, a tonic.

"Missing you. God, I'd love to see you."

"Me too. I've got to get back down there soon, but for now I'm grounded here in Chicago."

"You and your deals." She laughed in an attempt to be breezy, but a slice of bitterness edged in. She was working hard to contain it, he could tell. One of the things that had attracted him to Julia when they had met at a hotel beach bar five years ago was her complete absence of extracting promises and pressing demands. It was as if, submissive and compliant, she was grateful to take whatever scraps he could offer, counting herself fortunate simply to have someone in her bed from time to time.

Before meeting Julia, Roger had had only occasional one-night stands, to which he had never given much thought. The night he met Julia he imagined it would also be a single event, but something about her energy and vivaciousness had captivated him, and they had exchanged phone numbers. She offered the promise of spontaneity and joy, two things that had dimmed in Roger's marriage. And then she had been seductively persistent, calling him regularly after that first encounter, entertaining but never insistent. He had found himself more and more eager to see Julia and had begun inventing business reasons to return to Tampa more frequently than was probably necessary. Five years of secret liaisons and furtive phone calls had passed with very little effort on his part. But right now his relationship with Julia was suffocating, it felt sticky and weighted, as if he were carrying rocks on his back as he tried to retreat. He continued the phone conversation with some basic chatter, remembering to ask a few polite questions, always the gentleman, he thought impatiently, and then he rang off with some excuse about a meeting.

How could he possibly tell her, or did she already know, that somehow in that moment of their conjoined pleasure a stain had begun to spread over what they'd shared. He had felt it when he was last with her, as they lay together. It had grown and hardened like a small stone in the center of Roger's chest. In some way it was as if his being with Julia when James was hit had made them both complicit in the tragedy.

• • •

She was still three blocks from the upholsterer's house when an SUV pulled out of a spot in front of a redbrick church wedged in between the row houses on Chicago's northwestern margins. Recessed into the facade of the narrow parish church was a concrete statue of Mary, veiled head bowed with clasped hands. There were more than forty minutes left on the parking meter, a gift from the previous owner. Margaret needed the walk anyway; she'd been spotty about getting to her exercise class, and the sun was making an effort to poke through the slate gray November sky. As she strolled purposefully, she assessed the slight sense of decay and dilapidation in the once industrious neighborhood. When they had first moved to the area it had been largely Irish Catholic and now it appeared tired; it was hard to tell exactly who lived here.

The houses here were smaller with cement steps and aluminum

siding. They were working families' homes, and yet there was still neatness and pride of ownership in the majority of the orderly porches and small front lawns. Greengrocers and the occasional laundromat or shoe repair storefront were interspersed between the row houses. Window boxes on the facades had been emptied for the season, and the small patches of earth around the leafless trees in the sidewalk cement were barren, lending the streets an air of abandonment.

Margaret caught a quick glimpse of him, a flash of recognition as she rounded the corner on the upholsterer's street. Walking by the window of the neighborhood bar, at first she thought her mind was playing tricks on her, but something in the man's expression, his profile, made her catch her step and slow. Sure enough, it was Pete. She was certain of it now. In the middle of a workday, miles from his office.

Margaret shifted her purse and stepped just to the right of the window and pretended to busy herself looking for keys while surreptitiously studying her son-in-law. He was slumped over the wooden bar onto his elbows, ossified eyes staring ahead at the ESPN announcers. The position of the dartboard on the wall behind him made it appear that his head was framed in the bull's-eye.

From her vantage point at the side, his eyes held neither interest nor disinterest; they were numbly fixated on a pilsner glass of beer, the foam still frothy at the head. Above her, a noisy filtration system cranked smoky, stale air back into the street, and Margaret wrinkled her nose in distaste. It was a typical Chicago neighborhood bar, the kind of place you didn't look at twice, with sticky counters and dried ketchup on the tables. But this wasn't Pete's neighborhood, and moreover, the fact that he was alone in the middle of the day seemed pitiful and curious. She wondered if Maura had any idea where he was, and then the unsettling thought flitted in. Margaret wondered how much her daughter would care.

Margaret chided herself. These were tough times for the family, for the couple. They all needed to find ways to cope, and whatever was happening currently in Maura's marriage was not really any of her business. None of her business, that is, unless someone was getting hurt or the kids were involved. Right now, though, Pete was a man having a drink alone at a bar, and it was better left like this, without remark.

Margaret bent her head again and moved briskly past the building. The last thing she needed was to have Pete spot her. But the image of her son-in-law, alone on the barstool, dully worshipping a glass of beer in the middle of the day, was unsettling. Pete had always enjoyed his beer, he was definitely a party person, but Margaret had noted a marked increase in his consumption since her grandson's death, at least from her limited vantage point. There had been one disturbing night recently when she had observed Maura and Pete tussling over who would drive home after a family dinner, and she had busied herself elsewhere as the tenor of Maura's voice rose firmly. It had been painfully intimate, too uncomfortable to watch.

Margaret continued briskly on to the upholsterer, examined the pillows, and wrote her out a check for the work. What to leave in and what to leave out? Margaret wondered, her mind pivoting back to Pete as she stepped off the front stoop of the small beige house and walked toward the car, carrying two plastic bags with the newly covered couch accent pillows. As she opened the sedan's back door to place them inside, her eye lingered on the concrete Mary and the simple carved wooden doors of the church. On impulse she pressed the lock button on her key chain, heading purposefully up the front steps and into the darkness of the church's interior. It took her eyes a few moments to adjust, and she observed that this was a more simple church than their hometown parish, despite the glory days of the Catholic Church in Chicago. One large stained-glass window loomed above the altar with a depiction of Jesus, arms outstretched,

and tapestries hung on the whitewashed walls. The interior woodwork was dark-stained mahogany, lending the sanctuary a hushed,
somber feeling. A stone baptismal font stood in front, between the
rows of pews, and the stale air inside was redolent with incense,
ashes, and neglect that could be found in so many city churches
today, she thought with nostalgia. Margaret was relieved to find
the pews empty, and there was no sign of anyone, including a priest.
In the alcove halfway down the aisle, only a handful of low flames
flickered in the red glass votive holders, and above the bank of
candles was a small wooden statue of Jesus on the cross.

She reached in her wallet and located a twenty-dollar bill, stuffing it into the metal collection box, and took a taper, lighting it first
with a candle and then touching it to the wick of a new votive, solemnly observing the flame catch. Margaret bent her head and offered up a simple prayer, asking God to protect Maura and her family.
The familiarity of the ritual relaxed her, and when she opened her
eyes, she moved to the front of the church, kneeling slightly while
steadying herself with the back of the pew. "Father, Son, Holy
Spirit," she said under her breath, as she made the sign of the cross
before turning to walk to the back of the church and exit the front
doors.

As Margaret drove home she found herself questioning again
how much, if anything, to share with her daughter about seeing
Pete. It was still a fragile time. And it wasn't so much that Pete was
doing something illicit. She hadn't caught him with a woman or
trapped him in a lie. He was having a drink alone at a bar in the
middle of the day. But everything about it felt wrong and desperate.

She and Roger had actually only discussed Pete and Maura a few
times since James had died. Where once they spent much of their
dinner conversation dissecting, approving, or disapproving of
their children's choices, when it came to Pete and Maura, right now,
it was too painful to examine the collateral. But on one recent
weekend, when she'd been at Maura's and Pete had come home tipsy

and belligerent from a Bears game, Margaret confided to Roger that she worried about Pete's drinking. She was concerned, she said, that he was not being as supportive of Maura as he could in the wake of such a tremendous tragedy. Roger had admitted that he too had worries, but he argued that they all needed to give Pete space. The couple had a solid marriage, had logged enough years together to survive losing a child. They would recover, he assured her, and the surest way was for them both to butt out.

Margaret wasn't convinced. Her internal mechanisms, the interior sonar a mother has for her child, had been detecting some inchoate restlessness in Maura for the past few years, an unarticulated disengagement with her marriage. Margaret couldn't pinpoint exactly what it was or when it began, but somewhere along the way, she sensed Maura had ceased her diligence, become distracted. Margaret mostly chalked this up to the often overwhelming tasks of motherhood and running a household. She herself knew all too well how robotic and numb these activities could make one feel at times, how love could be diluted and thinned by domestic annoyances as mundane as routinely leaving a toilet seat up.

In her own early days with young children, Margaret had split herself into many little slivers, especially with a husband who traveled frequently. She had done the best she could, and she imagined her daughter was doing the same.

She knew from her own marriage that people spilled off the path, that sometimes couples wore blinders that rendered them unaware. For example, how satisfactory it would be, Margaret thought, to drop one zinger, to let one barbed comment fly to Roger that revealed what she knew about her husband's indiscretions. Many times over the years, she had come close. She'd articulated the words and accusations in her head so many times, lobbing a burning spear under her breath in the garden or muttering over the stove about Roger's secret life. But she understood that the release would be temporary. This kind of outburst would be a gamble. On the one hand it might be a catalyst that could bring him back fully into the marriage. And then again it also had the very real potential to drive them further away or even splinter them apart.

Over the years among their circle of friends in town and at the club, Margaret had witnessed the fragility of love and marriage firsthand. A couple that seemed to have weathered thirty-five years together could all of a sudden surprise you with an announcement of divorce. One pebble tossed on the lake rippled out to disturb the placid rhythm of an entire family. No, even after confirming her suspicions about Roger's infidelity, Margaret would not roll the dice and possibly lose it all. The rewarding family life they had constructed, their friends and home, their joy at being involved grandparents, everything she held most dear, would be in jeopardy.

Margaret's intuition about Maura's distraction was something she would never share with Roger. He would only disparage her about feelings and her lack of facts. Roger had a very large blind spot around his children, and all three of them, even Stu, had deftly and instinctively known how to manipulate him from an early age. He didn't like to see faults in his children, and they, in turn, viewed him in somewhat mythic proportions, the benevolent largesse often bestowed on the less involved, less present parent. Margaret wondered, smugly, if they could ever imagine their own father being unfaithful.

"I won't meddle, Roger," she had assured him when the topic of Maura and Pete's strained relationship came up in the aftermath of their grandson's death. "But I won't stand completely on the sidelines and watch a marriage dissolve while two people grieve side by side in silence."

"It's private, Margaret. What goes on with two people is private, and you and I can't honestly affect it one way or the other."

They had ended the conversation then. There were a hundred things Margaret had wanted to say to her husband, a dozen questions crowded her lips, but she had suppressed them all. She was not blameless in her own marriage, she knew, but the thin wall that had been constructed, quietly and deliberately, by Roger's infidelity had kept her from sharing all that was in her heart.

There were other things she wanted to discuss with Roger, things she had observed, memory issues, or his momentary disorientation, often infinitesimal, but they were aberrations only a wife would notice. Worry chafed at her, and yet she was wary of pointing out frailty. Roger wasn't comfortable in the face of disability, illness, or degeneration. In her experience, few men were. If she were to raise the subject, he would only call her paranoid and brush off her concerns.

And, of course, part of her job was to preserve his dignity, burnish the illusion of perfection and patriarchy for the children and for him. But she could see it, the spider veins fracturing his memory from time to time, the occasional blank spaces during conversation, as if he were two steps behind for a moment. Perhaps she would gently broach the subject in the months to come. She wanted him to see a neurologist. That was what her intern had suggested when she had confided in him, but the timing wasn't right yet. This was not the moment to force her husband to confront his deficits or even mortality. Her concern right now would be interpreted as criticism. And so much lately had begun to feel infinitesimally better, like the subtle shifting of radio waves when a satellite moves into position in the sky. She would not do anything to upset the fragile balance.

17

M aura turned the key in the door and slipped it in her purse. The sun was midway in a pale, egg-blue sky, and the temperature was well above freezing. The late afternoon light had begun to thin and wane early now, and Maura was dreading the winter. But it felt good to be heading out to run a few errands. Grief had shrunk her for too long now, it had circumscribed her life like the aperture of a camera. But she was feeling stronger. Maybe she would take a walk or possibly even head to a stretch class at the gym. No, actually not the gym, too many people. A locker room of familiar peppy faces in exercise clothes was still too much to bear. The thought arrested her for a moment that the last time she'd felt vibrantly alive was that final day, five months ago, the last week of walking the kids to school. The memory of her excitement then hit her like a punch.

Maura shook her head. She would not do this to herself today, would not marinate in her own sorrow and guilt and end up somewhere between the couch and the kitchen counter, dreamily lost in the tar pit of her own melancholy. She would go out. Get outside, maybe even to the beach. Her mother was happy for her to drop Sarah off at the house for a few hours after preschool, and Ryan was at school until 3:00 P.M.

Walking to her minivan she felt hesitation turn to a renewed burst of energy, almost as if the molecules of air outside the house propelled her forward. First, she would head to the post office to return a pair of running shoes Pete had ordered online, a package that had sat, neglected on the front hall table, for almost three weeks. She would bring Rascal with her too. They both needed a change of scenery.

In town, the storefronts had turned their focus from Halloween to Thanksgiving, and most of the branches were bare. She was not prepared for winter, not ready for the early arrival of darkness, the plummeting temperatures and the unrelenting wind off the lake. Her mother, the inveterate Weather Channel watcher, had told her they were predicting it would be an unusually harsh season this year.

The post office was crowded, clearly a busy time of morning to be here, but she had come this far. She could wait. Three counter windows were open, and the clerks seemed to be in no particular hurry, chatting with the customers as an occasional chuckle echoed in the marble interior. Standing obediently in line Maura observed a grandmother and a boy of perhaps eleven by the wall of individual mailboxes. He was small, dark hair falling in shaggy layers to his collar, with striking wide-set eyes that lent him the appearance of extra innocence.

The boy was flipping through the "FBI Wanted" pages, hole punched and bound together by a silver circular binder clip and attached to the bulletin board, next to the metal PO boxes with tiny combination locks. He seemed fascinated by the Xeroxed pictures, and as he turned each page he would stop at one that interested him and ask the older woman to pronounce the name, and then repeat it slowly after her. His grandmother, bent slightly at the waist to view the paper, read each word patiently in a tutorial tone, with the cadence of devotion. She patiently corrected him when his tongue stumbled over a syllable.

There was something wrong, Maura realized, something off or

slightly dull-witted about the boy, who was much more childlike for his age than his height or weight suggested. Perhaps it was a kind of autism or other disability. "What's this word, Grandma?" he asked flatly.

"Un-law-full . . . ," she said, pointing at the word with a gnarled finger and tracing each syllable. A starburst of gratitude, a guilty relief spilled out inside Maura that her children, despite all of their little idiosyncrasies, were healthy. And then the realization caught her ferociously in the throat, like a fishhook, yanking her to the surface of sudden remembrance, that her perfect family was not whole. Her eldest boy was gone.

She understood then just how lucky that grandmother was, because she, Maura, would resurrect her son under any condition, even if he were a silhouette of the boy that she knew. She would desire him under any circumstance, through any illness, difference, or disability and under any terms, so long as he was alive.

The earlier hopeful feeling of the day wobbled, and everything inside Maura's chest squeezed like a fist. It never ceased to amaze her how grief could suddenly bubble up like a spring or pack the wallop of a sucker punch. She tightened her grip on the package, shouldered her purse, and pushed through the heavy glass doors of the post office lobby and out into the late fall air. She would not cry, she told herself.

Back out in the car she paused, her sterling Tiffany-heart key chain in her hand, as she struggled to keep emotion in check. Each of us held things that weighed us down, to different degrees, she thought. No one was exempt. All of us whizzing by one another on a city street or highway, wearing our polite public masks, while the internal scars, the transgressions and the sadness of egregious loss, clung to us on the inside like trace elements.

As she was about to turn the key in the ignition, her cell phone rang, jolting her out of her reverie and back into the present, still such an unfamiliar sound. It was Pete's number, and she flipped open the phone and tried to add some enthusiasm to the tone of her voice.

"Hey!"

"Hey, Maura."

"I'm downtown right now. Just got out of a meeting."

Maura braced for the inevitable excuse, the backtracking to get a night out with the boys.

"I'm walking right by that indoor farmers' market. You need anything for dinner tonight? There's some amazing-looking fish and another stall with fresh bread."

Maura was stunned for a moment. This was not what she had expected.

"Uh. Sure. I haven't thought ahead to dinner yet. Fish would be great, fresh bread too, maybe a baguette? Thanks, Pete." She smiled for a moment, warmed by his uncharacteristic thoughtfulness.

She started the car and began the short drive home, feeling buoyed by Pete's call. She would return the package another time; it had already waited this long.

· · ·

"Why do they want O'Connor for the final part of the contract? I'm a senior partner." Roger's voice was rising despite his effort at control, and he felt suddenly frantic. The contract was almost inked, he had been the point of contact on the deal, and yet the client was requesting that additional team members fly to Tampa.

"I think they feel more comfortable with a big team," Bill Kindler offered reflexively. "They just want a few more of us represented in the final negotiation."

Roger understood instantly that this was a face-saving response from the way Kindler looked down, avoiding his eyes and focusing on meticulously straightening a pile of papers.

"Look, I'm not going to pretend I'm happy about this," Roger re-marked. "I've been putting these kinds of deals together since O'Connor had Johnson's baby soap in his ass crack. This is my ter-ritory. And let's not forget I brought this deal in. It was my original connection through Tom Hiltz."

"That was the father, Roger, and now his son Jay is running the business." Kindler smiled patronizingly and looked down again, letting Roger fume. The message was clear, and although it was ob-viously uncomfortable for both men, Roger felt no upper hand. He nodded slowly, regrouping, and softened his voice.

"I'm sorry, Bill. This isn't your fault," he said. "But it's tough to be a senior member of the team and have a client ask for a pinch hitter at the ninth hour."

"I think you're overreacting, Roger. They just want to be wooed, to see all we've got. The full complement of the team."

Roger nodded again, appearing thoughtful, as if this all made perfect sense. As he wandered down the hall and sat back in his own office, infuriated and humiliated, he absorbed the full impact of the insult. Was this what happened? What thirty years at the same company did to you? In the past decade he had been acutely aware of the thundering herd behind him, nipping at his heels. But this? It felt like being cut from the team or, at the very least, third string on the bench.

Roger knew that there was information below sea level, under-neath the tip of the firm's iceberg, to which he was no longer privy. In the heyday of commercial real estate, he had helped to build this firm, cutting deals and paving the midwestern suburbs with a se-ries of strip malls back when even village idiots could make money in the game.

But the market had changed; the commercial real estate busi-ness had been a roller coaster lately. And there were younger part-ners now, in bespoke suits with different connections to corporate bloodlines that fed the income stream. With their technological gadgets and savvy PowerPoint presentations, Roger understood it was a new playing field, with new rules.

The old ways of selling and of relationships and deals by hand-shake had given way to a cutthroat price-driven age. There were times Roger felt as if he were keeping current only by his finger-nails. Hell, he still quietly dictated things to Cristina, his secre-tary. He had never quite learned to type proficiently on a keyboard once they'd all made the leap to personal computers.

Unbelievable, he thought. Roger sat back in his chair and let out his breath. After all his preliminary work in Florida, he would not be the lead on the Crown deal. He set his face in an even expression and headed back out into the hallway and toward the lunchroom to get a cup of coffee. He felt his heartbeat ratchet up, driven by an internal suppression of rage like steam in an espresso machine. He was damned tempted to walk out the door right now, grab his brief-case, and leave for the day. But that would only give them more of a reason to nudge him further aside. He needed to mark his territory and hide any signs of weakness.

Kindler was spouting bullshit, the same crap that had come out of Roger's mouth when he himself had been subtly putting older colleagues out to pasture back in the day. Roger poured a styrofoam cup of coffee in the office kitchenette and noticed a brief unsteadi-ness in his hands, a quivering as a splash of brown liquid hit the Formica countertop. He leaned against the lunchroom table mo-mentarily and closed his eyes.

What had they seen at the firm? Were his memory lapses notice-able to his colleagues? he wondered nervously. Roger let himself panic for a minute as he scrolled through moments in internal and client meetings over the past few months. Had they been picking up on times when he might have forgotten something, missed in-formation, scrambled an issue or a detail? This self-consciousness and insecurity, to which he was largely unaccustomed, hit with a jolt. The thought that he had possibly been a topic of discussion in this manner had not occurred to him before, and it blunted his anger, suddenly humbling him. He worked to back himself away from this paranoid line of thought as he shuffled down the office hallway back to his desk.

Relax, he told himself, back in the confines of his office. This isn't personal. This isn't about anything other than the youth culture that's pervading all of corporate America. Companies in every sector were throwing away their greatest resource. Men his age, who knew where the skeletons were buried and how to make the clocks run, were in the process of being devalued after decades of loyal service for the younger, more cost-effective model.

Maybe it really was time to think about a retirement timetable. Hell, he was sixty-five, and although that still felt mentally young, he knew some of their friends were beginning to have health issues. God knows Margaret had been talking about trips she wanted to take. Images of tour buses, chirpy guides with flags, and pasty couples with cameras and bulging waists and buttocks filled his head, depressing him further.

Roger thought briefly of calling Julia. She would make him feel calm, powerful, and in control. In the past her voice had contained the power to reassure him, to disconnect him from the silly urgencies of his job that sometimes clouded his visual field with false importance. Or that had been how it used to work, anyway. Now, he realized, calling Julia would only conjure up complexities and emotions that he wasn't prepared to deal with. He lacked the energy. Roger only wanted to close his eyes in the privacy of his office, to reorganize his thoughts and regroup.

Clearing his throat, he drew a deep breath of air into his nose and let it out in one uninterrupted stream from his mouth. This simple relaxation technique Margaret had once taught him calmed him. Hell, work was important but it wasn't everything. Maybe he didn't have the lead on the Crown deal, but he'd had a long and successful career at the company, was a member of a country club, a scratch golfer, a friend, a loving father and grandfather. He'd been a steady provider as a husband, although he knew that on balance his role as a devoted spouse was perhaps less than stellar. Roger could feel his heart rate settling back down to normal as he worked this mantra like the stations of the cross. He tipped his head back against his chair and closed his eyes.

His cell phone's ringtone broke the momentary silence. It was Julia. Roger marveled, as he often had, at her uncanny ability to call just when he was thinking of her. A range of emotions competed with one another, from excitement to joy, and then trepidation as he pressed the answer button without thinking, an involuntary reaction.

"Hi there," he said with manufactured warmth, rubbing his temple.

"Hello, stranger." The tone of her voice reached for an easiness he knew she didn't feel. He understood how much it must have taken to call him yet again. It had been at least two weeks since he had initiated a call to her, probably since the middle of November.

"I have been a stranger." Roger sighed. "I'm sorry. Would you believe I was just thinking about you?" The words sounded hollow, and he felt stuck.

"I don't believe it. We haven't spoken in a week. But I'm ready to forgive you." She was Julia again, without any overt sense of petulance that he could detect.

"But can I forgive myself?" he said suddenly, as if the words had just slipped off his lips, unconnected to his brain. Perhaps she hadn't understood.

She was quiet for a moment and then she piped up, a trace of anxiety straining her voice. "What do you mean, Roger?"

"I just . . . don't . . . I don't know, Julia . . ." Roger blurted out unthinking. "I don't know where I am right now. The world is such a

different place for us than it used to be. There are people . . . people
here who need me."

"I need you too," she said simply, and let it fall flat. He pictured
the tanned backs of her hands, the long, talonlike nails, which were
always painted a bright pink or coral, so different from Margaret's
earth-chafed fingers.

"I know you do. And I need you too. I do. I'm just dealing with so
much here. Maura . . . her family, the other kids." There was an
apologetic smile in his voice and he was mindful not to throw his
wife's name into that litany.

"It's been months, Roger. Almost three months since I've seen
you, and that was only one night. Five months since everything
happened with your grandson. I have tried to give you space." Julia's
voice lacked patience now. It was rising slightly, generosity spent.
"Surely your daughter and your family are getting stronger, moving
down the road to recovery?"

Her innocently pat question made Roger bristle. It would be so
easy to flare up now, after the disastrous meeting he'd had with
Kindler. How simple it would be to erupt, to rise up and just smote
this connection from the center of his heart. Who were they exactly
to each other now? A fading affair? It had felt like something more
before the accident, something with interesting possibility. Now he
felt spent. For the moment Roger wrestled with an explanation for
how Julia fit into his life. She was not a mistake exactly, certainly
not something he regretted. But things had changed. What possible benefit could he provide in her life?

She had once told him that her romantic options were limited to
a stream of widowers looking for someone to care for them and men
in loud shirts who loved betting on the greyhounds at the track. This
parade of "factory seconds," as she called them, held no real interest
for her. Julia assured him she would never marry again. She liked
their arrangement just fine, she insisted, although he believed she

secretly desired more from him, even a commitment. But frankly, what she chose to do during the in-between time was none of his business, although he assumed she had been faithful.

The truth was, he still wanted her physically. Guilt, desire, spontaneity, and need were all bundled into one large cable connected straight to his heart and groin. Seeing Julia would be his consolation for getting screwed over at work, he rationalized. This was what all hardworking executives deserved after a lifetime of servitude. A little pleasure. And no one got hurt. He could so easily book a trip to Tampa, drum up a reason to drop in on the Santy/Gruber folks and solidify a few relationships.

"I can't come down to see you right now, Julia. I can't. But I've just gotten out of a meeting, and it looks like I'll be down in the next two weeks. "

"You can't come or won't come?" The pouty childish petulance had crept back into her tone. "You were always able to find some excuse to run down here in the past."

"There's a deal here in Chicago that needs me. A big deal," he lied. "And then the girls, Maura the most. And of course, Margaret." There. He'd said it; he'd uttered her name. "She needs my presence in a way that she didn't before the accident. She's more . . . fragile." He had searched for a word and found one that didn't fit Margaret precisely. But it sounded convincing to him. He hoped it would sound right to her too.

Julia sighed. "I understand. I really do."

"I hope you do," said Roger. "Because I love you." And he meant it.

"I love you too. I'm going to call you soon. Or maybe you call me. That would be nice. Can you call me?"

"I will," Roger promised. "I will."

"I love you," she said again with a tinge of pleading.

This sidewinder conversation made him feel just the tiniest bit conniving and dirty. Hanging up with Julia he felt a new sensation, as if he had done something in a subtle shade of wrong, like he'd

walked out of a convenience store inadvertently clutching the newspaper after only paying for the soda.

He couldn't fight the feeling of overall damage and impotence,
coming at him now on the heels of the meeting with Kindler. Did he
even have the desire to keep all of those balls in the air? Roger had
always been an expert at maintaining separate chambers in his
heart. But Julia, her unabashed expectations and all that she offered, were suddenly, inexplicably overwhelming to him. It was as
if at any moment, walking this tightrope wire of an act, he could fall
to one side without knowing if either Margaret or Julia would be
there to break his fall.

18

"H*ey, buddy, let's* go throw the ball while it's still light out," said Pete. He had unexpectedly come home in the middle of the afternoon, explaining he wanted to see the kids. "Yessss," yelled Ryan as he leapt instantly off the couch, pumping his fist in the air, eager and buoyant. It was heart wrenching for Maura to see how desperate her son was for this attention. In the months since James had died, the kids had sometimes functioned more like sidebars to their family life, objects that had needs, rather than the centers of their universe.

Although she was not included in the invitation, Maura knew it would feel good for all of them to get outside. The sky was gunmetal gray, but that wasn't enough to dampen her spirits. She watched through the window as one of the last stubborn leaves on the maple dislodged in the wind and gracefully spiraled to the ground. They had made it through Thanksgiving at Pete's sister's house, a place that held no real memories of past holidays with James. But Christmas, at her parents' this year, would be difficult.

"We're going to work on your arm," said Pete.

"OK, Dad," answered Ryan in a voice that sounded so plaintively grateful that Maura had to turn away for a second. He was already scrambling for his sneakers in the mudroom cubbies, the sounds of the Disney Channel distantly blaring from the family room.

Maura noted for the fiftieth time how their former firm rules and limits about TV viewing had devolved into a kind of path of least resistance, without either she or Pete seeming to care.

"You guys had better put on coats," Maura suggested cheerfully.

"Nah, we're tough guys, eh, bud?" Pete said with a conspiratorial shrug to Ryan. "A fleece is fine, go grab your mitt."

Maura stepped back to let them pass.

"We won't be out long," Pete said, and he brushed by her, squeezing her arm, and she felt warm gratitude for his spontaneity. Through the kitchen window she observed them both, Ryan running back and forth the length of the yard and Pete's long, lazy underhand throws. She heard the ball hitting the conditioned leather of the mitt interspersed with snippets of conversation about Ryan's "throwing arm" and the Sox. She warmed to the normalcy of the scene before her, something so lacking in their lives over the past few months.

A few nights earlier Maura had woken up next to Pete only to find that he was spooning her in a way that they hadn't in months, certainly since before James's death. Unable to fall back asleep, she had stayed that way for a while, absorbing the simple pleasure of the heat coming off his body. His breathing and the pores of his skin exuded the boozy fragrance she associated with holiday rum cakes, and yet she found that oddly comforting. And then Pete had stirred, half-woken, and moved away groggily.

At the window, Maura watched Pete tossing the ball to Ryan in a wide arc. Ryan missed the catch and ran with his glove held high across the almost frozen grass. She studied her husband objectively. Pete's frame was still the inverted pyramid outline of his football days. He was chubbier around the gut, like so many husbands their age now, thicker, paunchier, but not seriously overweight. His shoulders were broad, his hair mostly all there, not completely gray or thinning, the balding camouflaged by a close buzz cut like some of her friends' husbands had begun to do.

Observing Pete she felt a thawing of some of the harsher judgments that had congealed in the past few months in particular. There was a chance for them, thought Maura, a decent chance if they could tap into their shared history and trove of feelings. Perhaps they could each just keep moving slowly forward. Maybe that was a form of progress.

Sarah stirred upstairs; she had taken an impromptu nap once again, but her sleep had no doubt been interrupted by the animated calls and laughter outside. Sarah was so solemn, a quieter child than her two boys. How much of that was her personality and how much of it was living in a home absent of mirth? While mired in her grief she'd lost months of being her old attentive self with Sarah. And for the umpteenth time since James had died, she renewed her commitment to being more present as a mother, as present as she could be.

When she entered the bedroom, her daughter reached her arms up to her silently, and Maura stood, for a minute, holding her and rocking her back and forth as Sarah began to shed her grogginess. "Gimme Giraffy, Mama," said Sarah simply, pointing to her favorite stuffed animal. Maura set her on the floor and retrieved the giraffe, tickling her daughter with its long neck as she giggled.

"Gimme some more." Sarah clapped and Maura began to pull out all of the stuffed animals, the hand-me-downs, the ones worn and torn from her older brother's love and the rejects that had never really been loved, the stuffed bears with pristine clothes and hair ribbons. She and Sarah played for a few moments on the floor as Sarah gave a silly name to each one of the animals.

Sitting cross-legged on Sarah's rug, Maura picked at the knee of her jeans, wearing through to a light blue. She had always been somewhat meticulous about her clothing, and in her previous life these jeans would have found their way into the give-away pile. Maura reminded herself that she needed to make more of an effort. Sarah kissed one of the oversize bears with a pink cloth apron, and Maura leaned in to hug her. She would have to be careful, she reminded herself, not to pour everything into this child. Her sister-in-law, Jen, had tentatively asked her not long ago if she and Pete had considered having another baby. There were times Maura hovered on the perimeter of that possibility, and certainly the thought and desire had flitted in her mind at odd, guilty times. But did you replace a child? It felt somehow like creating a spare for the loss of James.

The phone rang, and she hopped up to answer it, pushing her hair back behind her ear as she picked up the receiver.

"Maura?" It was Erin.

"Hey."

"Just checking in. It's kind of a lazy day here and Sam is next door playing. I'm just here with Chloe. Want to come over before dinner?"

"Sarah and I are just hanging out, and Pete and Ryan are outside playing ball. Sure, I think I can come over. I'd love to, actually." Maura cradled the phone, scrunching her shoulder to lift her daughter up on her hip with both hands.

"Sounds good. Brad's working late tonight anyway. He has some big lawsuit that's going to trial next week. They've been all holed up preparing the documents."

"I guess I'm lucky nothing is ever quite that urgent in the insurance business," said Maura.

"Yeah, just be glad you didn't marry a lawyer." Erin laughed and they hung up.

Maura helped Sarah on with her winter jacket and they walked outside, car keys in hand. Pete and Ryan had tired of the game of catch. They were playing with Rascal now, throwing a faded, half-split tennis ball at him and waiting patiently for him to retrieve it. She could spot the limp in his hip, the way his gait swung laboriously, accommodating his weakened disc.

On the lawn, Pete squatted down and extended his arms as Sarah ran toward him, holding her arms out. He grabbed her in a graceful motion, burying his face in her belly, and then looked past her, eyebrows raised quizzically as he registered Maura's purse and jacket.

"We're going to Erin's for a little while. We'll be back before dinner. I'm cooking."

Pete's expression clouded slightly, and he shrugged, half turning away from her to throw the ball to Rascal in the far corner of the yard, higher and farther than before.

"Sick of us already?" he called over his shoulder with an attempt at sarcastic humor. "I came home early to see you guys."

She laughed lightly, for Ryan's sake, but she detected the annoyance in his voice. "Brad's got some big trial and Erin is alone tonight with the kids. She asked us to come just for an hour or so. Besides, you and Ryan are working on his arm. This is good father-son bonding." She smiled brightly.

"I thought we could have some family time." A bit of an edge curled in his voice, and she softened, moving toward him.

"This is important time for you and Ryan," she suggested firmly. "He needs more of you. And Sarah needs to get out of the house. We won't be long. I have a flank steak marinating."

Pete nodded slightly, and then his features softened. He threw the ball to Ryan, who in turn threw it for Rascal. For a moment Maura stood next to Pete, watching the dog lope away, Ryan encouraging him, running alongside.

"His back seems better," said Pete, and then they both silently watched their son's boundless energy. "James loved that dog," he said suddenly, moving imperceptibly closer. Maura could smell him, the complicated scent of Pete's aftershave mixed with sweat, his particular man-smell. For just a moment, something more intimate hung between them. All it would have taken was for one of them to gesture toward the other, to lean in, to lay a hand or a head or a finger on the other. She stepped away, averting her eyes, and simply nodded.

. . .

"How about a cup of tea?" Erin pulled the whistling kettle off the red-hot burner and grabbed two mugs from pegs over the stove.

"I'd love one." Maura was watching Sarah play happily on the floor with her cousin Chloe, their two heads bent over a jumble of multicolored ponies with synthetic hair tails. Next to them was a stacked Lego tower that they had built together. Erin lowered a bag of tea in each mug and filled them with steaming water. She set the milk and sugar in front of her sister. The interior of Erin's cozy kitchen was a warm yellow, and a series of blue and white Delft plates hung on the wall over the table where they sat. A matching set of china canisters was placed in descending order on the counter nearby.

"You OK?" Erin asked.

"Yeah, tired." Maura looked up at her gratefully. Her sister's home felt like one of the few sanctuaries in her life right now. Erin and Brad lived in a smaller Arts and Crafts–style house that was one town west but still part of their school system. Brad pulled long hours on the partner track at his downtown law firm, and Maura was envious of how handy he was around the house. On weekends he unwound with home improvement projects like painting and replacing the back deck, and he had even undertaken a renovation of their first-floor powder room. Over time they had both made the older house inviting and appealing.

"So how are you and Pete doing?" Erin glanced at Maura out of the corner of her eye, as if it were a casual question, but she understood the intent.

"I guess OK. Something feels slightly better lately. I can't explain it, and it's not coming from any one conversation we had or a fight. We just seem like maybe we're on a better track. You know?"

Erin nodded and blew on her tea before taking a sip. "How about his drinking? Did you guys talk about it yet? I mean really address it?"

"No," admitted Maura, steepling her fingers. "That's going to be

harder. I keep taking digs at him, and that's not the way to do it."
She let out an exasperated sigh. "I'm not even sure he sees that it's
become such a problem. There's a big part of Pete, well, you know,
the old Pete, the party guy. Booze has always been a part of his life,
his boys' nights out, all of that. You know."

"Yeah, but then you grow up. You back off or you deal with it.
Right? Listen, I know everything that happened last summer, with
James, well, that was more than any parents should ever have to live
through. No one could blame anyone for self-medicating, but you
can't keep sticking your head in the sand." Erin sat back against her
chair and tucked behind her ear a strand of hair that had fallen out
of her ponytail. Looking directly at her younger sister, Maura took
in the mirror image of some of her own strong features, the oval
shape of her eyes and the squared Munson jaw line. Erin's hair
was shorter than hers, lighter in color, and she envied her sister's
skin, complected like cream, almost free of wrinkles and freckles,
despite the intense sunbathing they had enjoyed during their
childhood summers in Wisconsin.

"We're working on it. We're getting there," said Maura quietly.
She stared out Erin's window at the trash cans neatly lined up outside the garage door, ready to be hauled out to the street.

"Sometimes I think I married my father," Maura said suddenly.

"Do you think we do that as daughters? Marry our fathers?" Erin
smiled.

"I think in some ways we probably do. Dad is the strong, head-of-
the-family type, brought home the bacon, and all of that. Mom was
a traditional mother. We didn't end up so differently from her. Dad
is kind of the life of the party too," said Maura more soberly. "He's
always pouring the drinks and making sure people are having a
good time. I suppose that part of him was attractive to me without
actually consciously choosing it. It was what I knew. People have
always gravitated toward Dad. When I met Pete back in college I
probably responded to that."

"You responded to other things too, Maura. Pete was loving and funny, and he came from a stable family. There were things there that made you guys work together. There still are." Maura nodded her head in assent.

"But I think I also responded to what was 'cool' back then in college. I was young. Pete was a challenge, that still-waters-run-deep kind of thing, mysterious. And I wanted to be the one who got under his skin." She paused, imagining herself back then. "I suppose that in the earlier years before kids, that whole package was really attractive. Life was so busy and full, so much was still happening, and we were evolving. There was all this possibility in that phase of our lives, you know? As time went on I think I started missing things, wanting things maybe down deep Pete wasn't really capable of providing. I wanted him to hang out and really talk to me, examine our feelings together, I guess. I didn't fully understand in my twenties how important that kind of intimacy was. This all sounds a little silly, right?"

"No, it doesn't," said Erin flatly.

"There are days I feel like I'm missing something," confided Maura. "Some deeper connection. But Pete is a simple guy. Kind of a meat-and-potatoes guy, you know? He doesn't really ask himself any tough questions. He isn't interested in things beyond work, family, and sports. He doesn't care about travel or learning about new ideas. He is . . . content. That's a lot like Dad too in some ways. Over the years that pattern has begun to feel, I don't know, limiting, and at times I want more. You can feel . . . overlooked. You can feel resentment."

"The fact is that you married a guy's guy," said Erin, sweeping crumbs off the table and into her open palm. "That part of Pete was appealing to you then. People go through different phases in life, and sometimes they need other things. They change. It doesn't mean that Pete can't change a little too. He is a really good man, and you know that. But you have to start the conversation, Maura." They were both silent for a moment.

"But honestly, I don't think you can change the fundamental nature of a human being. I think we're all born wired a certain way and you can only tinker with that to a degree. You can dress a pig up in a tutu but that doesn't mean he is a ballerina." They both laughed, letting some of the air out of the moment, and Maura shot Erin a grateful look. Sarah had tired of the games on the floor, and hearing her mother's outburst she walked over and put her hand on Maura's knee.

"Show me one marriage where the couple is always on the same page anyway, right?" scoffed Erin, rising from the table and grabbing a bag of pretzels on the counter for her niece. "That's not real life, and you know it. There are times I want to strangle Brad, just hang him up by his necktie in the garage," and they laughed again.

"But at least he brings out the trash cans and lines them up." Maura gestured out the window toward the neat row of cans in front of the garage.

"Brad?" Erin laughed. "That was me, who are you kidding?"

"Do you ever think about what it would have been like if you'd married someone other than Brad?" Maura asked nonchalantly, gathering her coat from the chair back and searching for where she'd set her purse and Sarah's coat.

"Sure. Who hasn't? But I haven't spent a lot of time thinking about who. If you married someone else then everything about your life now would be different, especially the fact that you'd have completely different kids, and I can't even imagine that." Erin looked down uncomfortably before glancing back at Maura. Her comment seemed not to have registered. "You're not thinking about that now, are you?" she asked. "Marrying someone else?"

For just a moment, the urge to confess her relationship with Art dangled enticingly in the forefront of Maura's brain. It would be so tempting, so relieving to tell the person in the world that knew her best all that had transpired. Everybody needed to tell at least one person a secret, was how the saying went. It would feel like a burden lifted. But something stopped her. What she had with Art was finished. No matter what Erin thought about Pete and his behavior, he was still her brother-in-law, and she loved him too. Nothing good could come from this admission, especially to her sister. This transgression was too close to home, and she let the moment pass.

19

Standing in snow boots and Roger's old down ski jacket, Margaret surveyed her frozen garden with the remains of the cigarette between her fingers. Fall had turned the corner abruptly into winter. The first frost had long ago come and gone, crinkling and browning the tips of the leaves and sagging the stalks. She had dug up the dahlia tubers and placed them in peat moss for the winter, storing them in the basement crawl space where the temperature was constant.

Chicagoland had already experienced its first snowfall, although it had since melted, and there was a storm predicted for this weekend. Somewhere down the street, she could smell a fire in the chimney, and it made her wistful. Margaret took another drag and tapped the ash into the stirring breeze. She exhaled the smoke in one long, thin stream and lifted the cuff of her coat to study her watch. 10:30 A.M. She took one last puff, crushed the cigarette under her heel, and carried the butt into the shed to dispose of it in the empty Altoid container by the weed killer. Shutting the garden shed door, she headed back toward the house. A breeze ruffled her hair and stirred the willow branch above her, creating a moaning sound that was almost human.

The rest of the day stretched before her with neatly filled time slots. Next, lunch and bridge, after that a visit at Maura's to watch

Sarah while she ran to the vet or to do some other errands. *They must have spent a fortune on that dog by now*, Margaret thought to herself. Her daughter had certainly headed to the vet's office numerous times over the past year with all that animal's ailments.

Margaret thought ahead to dinner tonight. She would defrost two chicken breasts and sauté them in a basil-lemon marinade with some Vidalia onions. She had a bunch of limp asparagus in the fridge that needed eating, and she would steam that with a little salt. Both she and Roger had to watch their high blood pressure and she'd been making an effort to cook more healthfully, with less butter and more olive oil, but Roger often complained her chicken was dry. Lately they had enjoyed more intimate dinner conversations, and she'd begun to relish mealtime, which no longer felt like an obstacle to be overcome.

Stepping indoors the change in temperature assailed her, and she stamped her feet in the back hall before reaching to remove her boots and the jacket. She could smell burned tobacco on her fingers, so she scrubbed her hands with coarse garden soap in the kitchen sink. As she pulled the plastic-wrapped chicken breasts from the freezer, she was struck by their resemblance to two pink hands, poised to pray. And then the phone trilled before she could unwrap them.

"Hello?"

"Margaret?" Roger's voice had an edge to it.

"Yes, Roger?"

"I'll be home a little early tonight. I just thought . . . I thought I'd let you know so we could eat together." Roger's voice had a halting quality to it. A low-level alarm went off. Maybe he didn't feel well. Roger was never one to admit it.

"That's fine. I've got chicken thawing." Something in his tone told her not to pry right now. She lowered the two breasts in a bowl of hot tap water to defrost. She had once read that you weren't supposed to freeze meat in its Styrofoam supermarket packaging. Apparently there was some kind of cancer-causing chemical that was released from the foamy container. Her kitchen freezer was a study in individual plastic- and foil-wrapped items, each carefully labeled with a Sharpie in portions of ones and twos.

Margaret thought about how you could spend your life trying to stay well, buckling your seat belt, eating organic food, wearing sunscreen, and then bad things could still rise up out of nowhere. Senseless things. She shook her head and pushed those thoughts away. She needed to make the marinade and get dressed for bridge.

By 4:30 P.M. Margaret was back in the kitchen, the chicken was already in the pan, and she diced the onions and pulled out the gold-rimmed fine china to set the table. They needed to use it more often, she thought. The kids had actually convinced her of this, arguing that it mostly collected dust. The sight of it might cheer Roger, Margaret mused. The sun was setting so early now, she noticed, there was so much less daylight in winter, no wonder more people suffered from depression in northern climates.

"Hello," Roger called out halfheartedly an hour later from the back hall. As he walked into the kitchen, setting down his briefcase, she detected a faint look of defeat, a stooped weariness.

Margaret smiled automatically, feigning diffidence. She had learned that the most effective way to extract information from her husband was to wait patiently, like a great white hunter in the Saharan grass. She had endured years of his distancing himself, and she knew better than to pounce now.

"Dinner can be ready soon," she said, measuring the rice.

"I'm going to make a drink first." Roger laid his suit jacket over the back of the chair and headed to the cupboard for a highball glass. She heard the freezer open and the rattle of the ice hit the bottom of the crystal.

"Well, the wild rice will take at least forty minutes," she said.

Roger ignored her and opened the door to the liquor cabinet. The ice crackled as the bourbon engulfed it.

"Good day?" she finally asked, breaking the silence.

"Not really." He set the glass down and loosened his tie at the neck.

"Oh?"

"I don't . . . I don't have the role I had hoped for on the Crown deal."

Margaret waited, drawing in her breath thinly, rather than risk making a noise. She wondered what direction this conversation would take, although she was slightly relieved that his darkened mood appeared only to be about some perceived slight in the workplace.

Margaret poked the chicken breasts with a fork to absorb the last of the marinade and flipped them over in the pan. Next she cut the ends off the asparagus spears, lowering them into the steamer while leaving the burner off. The kitchen began to fill with the moist smell of the rice, and she lowered the temperature under the pan. Margaret grazed her fingertips over the white napkins on the table, straightening them, waiting for him to say more. She was afraid Roger might grind to a halt if their eyes met.

"It may be time to think about retiring," he said simply.

"Really?" Margaret worked to keep her expression even. The remark didn't fully register at first. Did she feel surprise, shock, or even relief?

"Sometimes in your gut it's just time," he said, simply. "I've been doing this kind of work for almost forty years."

"Almost all of your professional life," she added more gently. Roger drained the last of his cocktail and set the glass down hard on the kitchen counter, causing Margaret to flinch. As he walked back to the liquor cabinet, his gait seemed unsteady, and he stilled himself against the counter with one hand. This had not been his first drink, she realized.

"Right now, Margaret, in corporate America"—he stumbled over this last word slightly—"there is nothing more obsolete than a white man over fifty."

"Come, sit," she urged softly, "while I finish cooking." Roger moved toward the table almost trancelike, his face projecting an emotion she couldn't quite fathom. This unstable Roger was unnerving. Whatever was troubling him was very close to the surface; the transparency of his emotions vexed her. If this had been about any other topic, anything but their future and his sense of security and position, she realized, it might have made her feel smug in an upside-down way. But something was wrong. Roger was off, somehow, and his unassailable confidence had been something she had always taken for granted. His position in the family and his career success had been a bedrock in their marriage. Margaret pulled a cork out of the remains of a bottle of pinot grigio and poured herself a glass, turning the heat down on the chicken. As she crossed the room to join him at the kitchen table, a slurry of fear fluttered in her chest.

They both sipped their drinks for a while in silence, and then she rose to turn the burner on under the asparagus. She could think of nothing else to say that would either calm him or provoke an elaboration. "You used the good china, Mother, what's the occasion?" he asked in a flat voice.

"I wanted to do something different and unexpected, I guess. We need to use it all more I've decided. The silver too."

"Very nice." He sat back appraising, head lowered slightly as he swirled the ice in his glass. She could tell his mind was elsewhere. "Let's see what's happening in the world." Roger grabbed the remote to click on the small TV under the kitchen counter, and Margaret rose to check the asparagus as the chicken simmered. Within ten minutes she had served up dinner and they watched the rest of the day's news, chewing in silence. The familiar patter of the local ABC anchor, Kathy, was a relief.

· · ·

Later that night, after she'd washed her face and run through her bedtime routine, Roger surprised her, reaching for her in bed with a boozy, sloppy kiss that she found largely distasteful. But she kept silent and returned his advances, both surprised and delighted by the unfamiliar forcefulness of Roger's passion. There was tenderness there too, and a probing softness to his touch; his murmurings ambushed her heart. Lying there next to him in the dark, after their lovemaking, she felt tears prick her eyes unexpectedly. She felt a sense of . . . was it gratitude? Yes, she was grateful for her husband's spontaneous display of love.

An hour later she awoke to a gargling in the back of Roger's throat, no doubt magnified by the alcohol he'd consumed. Margaret lay with her gyrating thoughts, contemplating Roger's words in the kitchen, his desperate, clutching ardor in bed, and the sudden possibility of a new future with retirement. How might her world be configured with Roger home every day?

She mentally ticked off the possibilities. There was golf and tennis in the warm weather. Perhaps he could be one of those husbands who played cards at the club. There was the YMCA for exercise equipment, and some of the men had a weekly movie club. He'd always talked about getting back to building things with his hands; he'd made birdhouses as gifts when they were first married. Years ago, when they'd lived in Ohio, he had even tried to build a model ship in a bottle, but the truth was, Roger wasn't a man who relished hobbies or volunteer work. The bulk of his life, like so many men of their era, had been devoted to his career.

And what was it now inside the company, or perhaps inside of Roger, that was crumbling? She knew that any business needed ultimately to make way for the next crop of leaders and go-getters. But Margaret had always imagined that Roger's departure from the office would be on his timetable. He'd been a part of the firm for so long, and they'd all ridden the real estate market through its many ups and downs, good times and bad. Roger had often joked grandiosely at parties that their company had been responsible for paving over half of the Midwest. Clients loved him, warmed to his self-assuredness, his ready knowledge of grandchildren's names or a wife's favorite variety of wine.

Roger's jocular, salesy personality, so in opposition to her own reserve, could at times appear fake and contrived, but she understood its value in his profession. Her husband's "gift of the gab," as one colleague had termed it, was a valuable asset that had put a roof over their head and helped to send three kids off to college and out into the world.

Roger's guttural snores irritated her now, and she rose, wide awake, grabbing her robe on the bedpost and padding downstairs. She turned on the lamp in the kitchen, and it cast a warm glow on the white painted cabinets. Margaret poured a glass of tap water and leaned over the kitchen sink, staring out beyond the crab apple branches and into the yard lit by a waxy moon.

They had more than enough saved for retirement; she supposed that wasn't the source of her anxiety. Roger had invested well, and they had never been big spenders, never reached beyond their means. They owned the cottage in Door County outright; the mortgage on the expansion there had been paid off for at least five years she knew. They usually took one good trip a year, with one or two other couples, always to warmer places with golf courses. Maybe they'd increase their travel in retirement and see more of the world together. Honestly, she felt slightly guilty and uneasy at how little she did know about the intricacies of their finances. She knew they had long-term disability, life insurance and policies on the houses, all of that through Pete's business, and their friend from the club, Hank Stabile, had managed their portfolio for years. Roger had always urged her to attend the annual financial meetings, to take more interest, and perhaps she'd need to in the future. She refilled the glass and then took a sip. Yes, there could be many upsides to his retiring.

She had once imagined retirement as a time of growing together, of shared activities, yet Roger had never spoken that language back to her. He'd roared more than once that they'd have to carry him away from his desk feet first. She'd hidden her disappointment at his theatrical chest-beating, and minimized her expectations. Work and golf were the things he enjoyed in his daylight hours, and she knew those activities kept him vigorous.

Margaret shifted her position to a chair at the kitchen table, leaning on her elbows and easing slowly down. She could feel the tightness in her back from carrying Sarah and she arched slowly, like a cat. Staring into the backyard, she began the process of teasing out what was really gnawing at her. It was the niggling feeling that there was more to this sudden talk of retirement. Something else was at work, a fumbling, an uncertainty in his actions. Absentmindedly she spun the lazy Susan in the center of the table that held the vitamins and the salt and pepper shakers, watching the objects rotate slowly.

It was weakness she detected, weakness in a man who had always prided himself on his vitality in almost every arena. Margaret sipped the water for a few minutes more, aware of the ticking hand of the kitchen wall clock. She rose and gently slid the chair back in place, automatically rinsing the glass before placing it in the dishwasher's top rack. If she had to be completely honest with herself, weakness was the one emotion in Roger she was not prepared to witness.

20

The temperatures had plummeted dramatically since the first of December, and none of them had a full set of their winter clothing—jackets, hats, or mittens. Somehow with a thief's stealth, the season had changed, and Maura, normally vigilant about rotating clothing, had left it to the last minute.

Rifling through the mangle of items in the front hall closet, she came across an old pair of navy blue winter boots, jammed in the back under a bag of ski hats. As she pulled out the first boot, her breath snagged in her chest. They had been James's, and she'd been saving them for Ryan to grow into. Somehow, like so many of her good intentions, they had gotten misplaced, shoved in the back and forgotten.

Maura slipped her hand reverently in the boot to feel the spot where his little boy foot had once fit. She put it up to her face, hoping to extract the scent of James, but it smelled only of the closet now. She wobbled onto her bottom as the first of a series of sobs hit. As they subsided, she realized ruefully how it was a form of progress that she could not specifically remember when she had last cried like that. And yet Maura was left with a vague sense of guilt, almost a feeling of betrayal at the diminishment of grief, no matter how incremental.

Later that afternoon, Sarah was coloring on the floor as Ryan sat huddled at the kitchen counter under the overhead light, working on his math homework. Maura sidled up to her son and ruffled his hair.

"Ready for me to quiz you on your spelling words?" she asked. Ryan beamed and the phone rang.

"Maura."

"Hey, Pete."

"I'm going to head out of work and meet up with Gil and Stevo tonight for a bit."

"OK," she said halfheartedly.

"We're just going to grab a burger and watch the Bears game at the bar. I won't be home late. But you don't need to wait up."

"Do I ever wait up anymore?" she joked, somewhat sarcastically. He snorted into the phone, a half-laugh.

"Up to you," he said in a somewhat jovial tone. "I can always slide into the spare room so I don't wake you." She noticed he didn't call it James's room.

"No need. I'll be OK. Have fun."

"Will do."

Maura pulled the lasagna out of the oven and cut it into neat squares, buttering the rolls she'd baked from a cardboard dough canister. Then they said the quick, simple family prayer that had been James's favorite, and they dug in.

"Mom, we gotta do my list for Santa," Ryan piped up. He reached toward her, and his glass of milk wobbled, almost tipping before Maura caught it. His bangs were so long they were falling into his eyes, and she made a mental note to take him to the barber this week.

"We have to do Sarah's list too," Maura said brightly, turning toward her daughter. "Right, Sarah? Santa is coming soon. He's going to bring you some toys."

"Yeah, lots of toys." Sarah picked up a carrot and popped it in her mouth.

"Do you guys know exactly what you want to ask for?" Maura

realized how unprepared she was for the holidays this year. She had previously been one of those women who'd had most of her Christmas list scratched off by Thanksgiving except for the stockings. The task of shopping for the entire extended family seemed enormous right now. Maybe she and Pete could go out together one night this week and purchase a bunch of items at one of those mega toy stores near the mall. That shared activity might make them feel more connected, she thought. At the very least they could put out some of the decorations together this week and hang the lights outside.

Two hours later the kids were upstairs, Ryan freshly showered and Sarah bathed, quiet in their own rooms, when her phone rang again. She was scrubbing the stubborn lasagna pan as the dishwasher hummed. She could see on the phone's caller ID that it was Pete again, calling from his cell.

"Hello?" No response from Pete, just noisy background chatter, probably from the bar.

"Hello?" Maura said again, but nothing. She could make out Pete talking as if into a tube. Maybe that was Gil's voice too, or Stevo, it was harder to hear them. She heard the strains of Journey's "Oh Sherrie" in the background. They had to be at the bar.

"Yeah . . . with her." It was Pete's voice now; she could distinguish some of the words more clearly. And then it dawned on her. Pete had pocket dialed her, inadvertently hitting the redial button that routed him to his last call.

"You guys . . . [unintelligible] better?" Stevo's voice now, she was able to pick up some of the words. Maura swallowed hard. She was both horrified and fascinated to be eavesdropping this way, but she continued listening. His voice was more distinct now, closer. Who were they talking about? What?

"It sucks," Pete said. "The whole thing sucks. We were good, well, maybe just OK, I guess. You know, normal. I mean we had issues, like every couple. But we were normal." There was a pause as the falsetto strains of Steve Perry warbled in the dead space. "And then . . . well, you guys know. James. Of all the goddamned shit to fall out of the sky."

There was a silence, and she couldn't make out what one of the men said. It sounded like a slap on the back, some kind of encouragement. Was Pete crying? She couldn't imagine that, not in front of these guys in a bar. Maybe he'd already had too much to drink? She bit her top lip.

"Here's the goddamned thing," Pete said loudly. She could clearly make out the words. "I still love her. But right now, we're nowhere." He paused for a moment, and she envisioned him taking a tug off a beer bottle. She could picture the overvarnished wooden counter, the TV tuned to a game but muted and captioned, the eyes in the bar trained to the screen like worshippers of a cult.

"You'll get it back, buddy." It was Stevo's voice, higher than the others, encouraging, but pitched at an unnatural cadence. Almost cajoling. "Everybody goes through shit."

There was something more, unintelligible, and then a collective shout went up in the bar, and she guessed that the Bears had scored. The rollicking cheers of the patrons obscured what was said next. Maura was frozen in one place, afraid to move, as if, ridiculously, she might be discovered. She was holding her breath.

"I dunno," responded Pete gruffly after the cheering subsided. "This is some big shit."

Another flurry of background noise and a new song came on the sound system with a thumping bass, and she couldn't make out the reply. A series of loud boos, no doubt brought on by an unpopular referee call, blocked what was said next. She considered hanging up, but something stopped her. She was both attracted and repelled.

"Sometimes . . . . . . if there's another guy." His voice was rising, slurred but distinct. Maura heard this clearly, and her veins froze for a second. She could hear Stevo now, laughing, they were goading Pete, talking him down from a ledge.

"Now you're overserved, buddy." It was Stevo again. ". . . good egg . . . loves you." She winced at the image of it, Pete, maudlin and spilling his worst fears. Thank God he was with boyhood friends, guys with whom he'd grown up, shared girlfriends, survived adolescence, if not necessarily fully left it behind.

A profound sorrow washed over Maura as she listened to the flecks of anguish in Pete's voice. His words softened her, as disgusted as she was by his drunkenness. Seemingly out of nowhere, something sputtered and flared like a match in her heart, a tiny thing, and she hung up the phone, unable to eavesdrop further.

Maura moved to the kitchen counter stool as a tangle of thoughts rushed in, relief that he did love her, gratitude that he had old friends with whom he could unburden, sadness that they were at such a place of attrition, that a sliver of uncrossable distance had crept between them. Later that night, as she stepped out of the shower, she studied her naked body in the fogged bathroom mirror. It had been too long since she had tried for any intimacy with Pete, long before James had died. Her marriage simply couldn't continue this way. She'd lost one person she loved already; she would not lose Pete as well.

At the window in James's room, Maura looked for Alex before turning in. She'd spotted him a few more times now since Halloween. And there were nights when the sky was moonless, and the darkness obscured vision, that she was left with the strong sense that he was out there, lying corpselike. Maura had become accustomed to looking for him, and she worried about him, now that the weather had turned so cold. Boys his age didn't like to bundle up or wear hats and gloves. One evening a week or so ago as she observed him, she was pleased to see he was at least wearing a down coat with some sort of hooded sweatshirt pulled up underneath.

The stretch of lawn on the other side of the maple was bare, and she was certain there was no one below the tree tonight, which left her with a vague feeling of disappointment. Maura was now fairly certain that he knew she was watching. There had been one time, around Thanksgiving, when he had looked directly at her inside the front room and met her gaze, even in the semi-cloud-covered night. At least Maura believed this was what had transpired through the glass. She had remained motionless, and whether it was a trick of the light or her imagination, the boy's eyes looked to her to be almost pleading, as if they were searching, but still she had stood immobile, unwilling to step toward the door and break the spell. This was her mutual secret with Alex, a complicit act.

For reasons she could not completely articulate, Maura had still not told Pete about Alex's visits. Rightly or wrongly, she sensed that Alex was sending some sort of message just for her. It was a wordless act of contrition. This was Alex's apology, his atonement if she would not come to him. And though it was perplexing and even a little creepy, it was also oddly and inexplicably comforting. No, thought Maura, this was between her and the boy right now.

Changing into her pajamas, Maura thought back to the conversation she had overheard from Pete's cell phone in the bar and grimaced. She imagined Pete would be back long after she was asleep. Impulsively, Maura grabbed her cell phone from the top of the bureau and texted Pete, SLEEP W ME TONITE. She studied it a moment before pressing SEND and then smiled to herself, turning off the phone and slipping under the covers and onto her side.

21

The *long aisles* of Lowe's were packed with people this time of year, but all of the holiday-related items and decorations seemed to be near the front of the store. It was mostly Christmas lights that they needed, the white outdoor kind for the bushes in front of the house. Maura had pulled everything out of the attic over the weekend, and half of the tiny bulbs didn't work. It was easier just to buy new ones, Pete had instructed, rather than search for the one culprit that was affecting the entire strand. While she was here she thought she might pick up a few items to put under the tree. Erin's husband, Brad, was such a Mr. Fixit she could probably find him some set of tools or nice work gloves; it was worth poking around. Maybe she'd locate some of those small LCD flashlights too, for Ryan's stocking.

Maura pushed the oversize shopping cart absentmindedly through the garden aisle. She had no real concept of exactly what she was looking for, perhaps a set of pruning shears for her mother, that expensive German brand with the red handles. Moving toward the next row, past the hoes and rakes, and into the lightbulb aisle, she saw a mother with a young boy in her cart. Next to them was a store employee with a blue apron. The worker was young, a kid, and something about the familiarity of his frame made Maura look

twice in the crowded store. It was the way the young man was leaning forward toward the cart and offering something to the child, a
toy or some small object perhaps from the shelves, as a look of shy
delight played across the little boy's face.

Maura realized, with a sudden ripple of alarm, that it was Alex
Hulburd in the Lowe's apron. He must have taken a part-time job
during the holidays. She stopped and then backed up the cart slowly,
keeping her eyes trained on him through the shelves to make sure
she was unobserved. Yes, she was sure of it now, the inverted triangle of his swimmer's frame, his fine features and sandy hair. She
panicked for a moment, wanting to be invisible, unable to tear herself away. His gentle interactions with the little boy fascinated her,
and she maneuvered the cart around to an angle in the next aisle
where she could better observe the interaction but remain unseen.

"What's your name?" she heard Alex say, his voice lower than
she had expected, more mature.

"Chris." The boy was shy but warming under Alex's coaxing. His
mother chatted brusquely into her cell phone, holding up various
sizes of lightbulbs and barking the numbers to the person on the
other end, clearly trying to determine what she needed. She could
see the object now; it was something on Alex's key chain that he was
using to distract the little boy, showing him how when you pushed
little buttons two eyes lit up. Another one made a silly noise like a
monkey call. It was the sweetness with which Alex treated the child
that fascinated Maura, and she found herself unwittingly mesmerized. An elderly customer with a cane ambled up to interrupt Alex
with a question, and he tousled the little boy's hair before offering
to lead her to the appropriate aisle.

Maura took a moment to compose herself, looking around the
store's cavernous interior, and found that the zeal to shop for gifts
had completely deserted her. She would grab four boxes of outdoor
Christmas lights at the end cap by the registers and check out. The

last thing she wanted to do was run into Alex Hulburd during the Christmas holiday.

On the way back home, Maura felt her previous energy plunge. Perhaps it was the surge of adrenaline and then the enervation she'd experienced in seeing Alex. His unexpected tenderness with the child in the cart had sideswiped her. Mostly, she assumed her fatigue was attributable to this hectic time of year, so fraught with memories and the high and low spikes of emotion. Maura had always heard people talk about how difficult the holidays were if you'd lost somebody, but now that this applied to her, she realized she had never given that trite saying much thought. Until this year the advance of the Christmas holidays had contained only the swell of joy and anticipation.

Maura felt the sudden desire to call Art, to talk to him and feel that supercharged sense of connection, the secret history of lovers. What she missed more, she understood, what she really wanted, was to reach back to a time in her life before the accident, when she had felt a fertile sense of happiness and fullness as a mother. She would not think about the guilt associated with Art now. She wanted a stretch of time in which to feel only good things.

The health food diner where she had occasionally met Art was two blocks away, and on impulse she turned the car into a fast-food parking lot and U-turned back in that direction. It would feel solid, maybe even uplifting, to be in a place she associated with past pleasure. That was where she had first commented on the bright blue cardboard coffee cups with the classical Greek-influenced logos. Coffee with a hint of cinnamon was one of the establishment's trademarks, and she would order a latte and let some of the good memories unspool in the bustling anonymity of the diner.

It was a place frequented by college students, with warm, pine paneling and butcher paper tablecloths with Ball jars of crayons.

The iconic framed poster of Farah Fawcett in a red bathing suit with her wide smile and winged hair greeted patrons as they entered. The walls were covered with pictures of customers and old posters and signed photos from the 1970s and 1980s. The first dollar earned was proudly displayed above the cash register, and next to the menu was a chalkboard explaining the day's specials.

There was an overwhelming smell of onions crackling on the open grill, and behind the Plexiglas barrier to the kitchen area, two cooks chopped fresh ingredients. Maura ordered her coffee at the counter and brought the mug to a booth by the window so that she could also observe the activity on the sidewalk. She welcomed the distraction of people-watching. Two tables to her left a young couple sat, heads bent in conversation; fingers laced, their body language telegraphed intimacy.

Not so long ago, that could have easily been her and Art. It seemed surreal to think of it now, but as she warmed her palms on the ceramic mug and observed the couple, she recalled the memories of their first meeting and subsequent visit to the diner.

Art's stomach had growled as he had bent to examine Rascal in his office and then again when he had taken a blood sample. He had looked up sheepishly and apologized. Learning that he had just moved to the area, she had half-jokingly suggested a bite to eat and had been surprised when he'd accepted. Although it had been the end of January, she recalled that the diner's Christmas decorations were still in the windows and the loud colored lights hung from the rafters. Art had been entertained by the chirpy student waitress from Northwestern with piercings and magenta hair, and although Maura had found him attractive that day, her mind had not been turning in that direction in the vet's office. She'd simply been focused on companionship and on introducing a newcomer to a decent restaurant not far from his apartment.

. . .

"Organic free-range chicken breast with hummus and mung bean sprouts." She had read the special out loud from the blackboard and laughed, looking over at Art, in line next to her at the counter.

"Be careful," he chuckled playfully, "those mung beans can get caught in your teeth." She had noticed the way his smile consumed his eyes, and the slight gap between his two front teeth, not at all unpleasant. They each took their sandwiches, on mismatched china plates, to a table for two by the window.

"How about a drink?" he urged and popped up again to grab two bottles of lemonade from the refrigerated cooler. What was she doing here? It was lunchtime. Rascal was in the car, no doubt sleeping off his anxiety from the visit. And she was sitting across from a handsome, divorced veterinarian. So what was this? Why was she here? Was it really a casual lunch or was she just pathetically lonely for attention, kindness, and for someone to focus solely on her for the moment? It felt recklessly good and flirtatious. It felt like adventure. Art slid back onto the chair and twisted the lid off the Snapple bottle.

"So, tell me about Maura," he had asked after some pleasant banter, and the question had confounded her for a minute.

"Well, right now I guess my life is largely focused on being a mom. And that's my choice. That's a pretty big job most days." She took a sip of her lemonade. "And there are times, I suppose, that it limits my world. But in the end it's my decision. This . . . right now . . . being out to eat like this . . . is different for me. It's very enjoyable actually." She had said more about herself than she had intended and was suddenly uncomfortable with his scrutiny.

"I hope that being here with me doesn't make you feel guilty," he probed, fixing her with his brown, almost pupilless eyes and holding her gaze. The exact nature of the question was unclear, yet he did not elaborate.

"Guilty? Do I feel guilty? Mostly because I told my mother I'd be home in an hour. But I deserve this, right? I deserve to go out and have lunch and do something totally spontaneous sometimes." And she had flashed him a smile, calculated to be full and radiant.

Observing him between bites, Maura realized there was nothing studied about him. He seemed to exude no outward predatory skills, no seeping, sexual lust, no telegraphed sense that this was anything more than a friendly lunch. And that ambiguity intrigued Maura. It deepened the focal point of her interest. She felt the power of the throttle in her hands in that moment, the ability to take this exchange into the next gear or ease it back toward earth. The headiness of this realization, the breadth of her power as a woman and a sensual being, felt so filling, it was intoxicating.

Uncomfortable for the moment with her assertiveness, Maura had set down the remains of her sandwich and stared out the window. A mother was pushing an umbrella stroller across the street, and the child looked to be about three, bundled up in a snowsuit and mittens. Dirty slush arced up behind the wheels, and Maura turned back to look at Art. She liked the directness of this person. She liked the fact that he asked her simple questions, faced things head on. His casualness seemed to have the effect of loosening her lips.

"Hey, everyone deserves happiness, a little time out. Why shouldn't you get a little bit? Mothers are the great unsung heroes of the world." There was a small smudge of mayonnaise on the side of his mouth, and she fought the urge to wipe it away with her fingertip. Maura looked back out into the street. The mother and stroller were gone now, the sunlight filtered through a gathering bank of clouds, dulling the bright edge of the sky. A torn newspaper page blew past the plate glass window, catching and fluttering for a moment on the base of a lamppost.

"So what about you? I feel like I'm doing all the talking." Maura laughed and looked down at her sandwich. "Tell me about you, you said you came here after a divorce?"

"Yup. Back in Madison. I'd say that after my divorce, well, I guess I was pretty bitter," he began. "We didn't have kids. Hadn't been able to. And I suppose, in retrospect, that helped contribute to some of what happened." He paused to take another bite of his sandwich, and she noticed a raised scar on his knuckle in the shape of a crescent.

"So what *did* happen?" She was grateful for the chance to turn the attention to him. She thought briefly about what she would say, what her story would be, if someone she knew walked into the restaurant.

"Nothing major. Not one big thing." He looked down and leaned forward on his elbows. "Just a series of little things, I guess, one slow slide. There were the years of infertility treatments, they kind of wear you down, you know? Disappointment after disappointment. You get your heart set on something and you keep thinking that luck is going to run your way." He was silent for a beat. "When it didn't, a kind of quiet blame set in, I guess." She nodded.

"How long were you married?"

"Ten years. Ten mostly good years, but somewhere in there we just began to grow apart. We stopped sharing, stopped finding things in each other that kept love growing. I guess you could say we stopped moving forward together. She wanted a clean break, and I didn't really want to be in Madison anymore. I spent more and more time at work to avoid all the bad stuff, the bucking her up, the her bucking me up. Hell, there wasn't a lot of bucking me up." He smiled sheepishly and shook his head, looking down at the remains of his sandwich.

"Eventually she met someone at work. Someone who, apparently, was more empathetic or interesting or more perfect for her than I was." Art lifted both hands onto the table and began absentmindedly rubbing the skin in between his thumb and forefinger.

"It should have felt like a relief when it happened, but instead it stung. Pretty bad. We fought over the little bit we had—the house, the joint account." He let out his breath in a long sigh.

"That's enough about me. Boring old sob story about some divorced guy." His mouth instantly upticked from a straight line into a bright, guileless smile, and he ran one hand through his hair on the side his head.

"Well, here I am, sitting in a diner when I should probably be home cleaning out closets or doing multiplication tables or something really exciting like that." The good feeling sputtered for just a second, replaced by the chill of guilt, the judgment of her inner compass. For a moment Maura fought back a voice that told her to simply bolt out of the place, to grab her coat and run. The meal finished, she drained the last of her lemonade and set the bottle down on the tabletop, screwing on the metal cap.

"So will Rascal be OK?" she asked. Art seemed grateful for the sure footing, the hairpin turn of the conversation away from the curve and back into familiar, navigable territory.

"I think so. Disc issues are pretty common in these little dogs. It's the long spine. Takes a lot of stress. Of course he isn't getting any younger, like the rest of us. It's never going to be perfect."

"James will be relieved."

"How old is he? Your son."

"Nine. And Rascal is really his dog. Or it was supposed to work that way anyway." She smiled and reached backward to grab her coat off her chair. "I end up doing all the work. But I guess I knew what I was in for."

"That's usually the way it happens. Mom is the pack leader." Art looked directly into her eyes for a second before he began stacking his napkin and bottle on the plate, arranging it carefully like a tower.

"I hope you don't think I do this with all my patients," he started, uncomfortable for the first time during their conversation. "It's, uh, nice to have someone to talk to." His voice fell off.

"It's nice for me too," she offered readily. "Nice to be with someone who doesn't know anything about me. I've lived around here my whole life, so there's no escaping my past. But with you I can just make it all up and you have no choice but to believe me."

He laughed. "Maybe we can do this again." He looked up, hopeful, as he tugged on his navy fleece. "I don't really have much of a social circle outside the practice. There hasn't really been time to work on that. I sometimes go out with my college buddy, and there are the guys I bike with on weekends, but most of them are married with kids." And in that moment his vulnerability snagged on something inside her, something loosening and unwinding that she had been working to contain.

. . .

It wasn't until she was driving home that day, winding across Lakeshore Drive, purposely taking the longer way, grateful for the stop and start of the lights and intersections in the towns on the way to her own, that she let herself admit how completely comfortable and even a little bit thrilling it was to feel that kind of companionship. She'd felt herself magnetized by him.

And in the months to come, it had been just that easy to continue the lunches, the harmless flirting, to pull the moments with Art up in her memory and review them like private flashcards while she sat folding laundry or unloading the dishwasher. She could reassure herself, honestly, that no physical lines had been crossed, that they hadn't kissed or touched and that she was, in fact, allowed to have male friends.

But in the good-girl part of her heart and mind—the smart voice that tried to interject from time to time and ask for clarification, point to the rule book—she had known that she and Art were hurtling toward something shapeless but with dangerous proportions. With each subsequent appointment for Rascal's treatment, followed by a lunch at the diner or walk by the lake, sometimes with Sarah in the stroller, she knew that she was becoming enmeshed. And yet because the steps were so seemingly harmless, subtle, and infinitesimal, it had been easy to assure herself that she was totally and completely in control.

22

"Y*ou're going to* get coal," Erin joked to Brad, swatting him dramatically as he opened the refrigerator and grabbed another beer.

"And you're going to get diamonds. Just wait until you see what's under the tree tomorrow," he answered, heading back into the den with the rest of the men.

"Somebody hand me the hot pads," barked Margaret, and the girls scrambled to oblige her. As she opened the oven, a blast of heat blew back her carefully coiffed hair, and she began to wrestle with the giant pan. The roast's savory aroma intensified in the kitchen as the fat crackled and snapped in the bloody juices. Piles of carrots and fingerling potatoes were arranged like a moat around the meat.

"Let me help you with that," Roger offered, and she stepped back so that he could do the heavy lifting. He'd come into the kitchen to get more ice and was taking in the pleasing sight of his wife and children working in unison on one of their elaborate holiday family meals.

"Eiiiiyaaaaaaaaahhh." Sam, Erin's oldest child, burst into the kitchen giggling. He was chasing Stu and Jen's daughter, Alice, and waving some kind of plastic light saber.

Conversation, laughter, and noise from the living room swirled into the kitchen, and the house throbbed with the cacophony of extended family gathered in one place. It was glorious chaos, but underneath the patina of mirth for all of them was the undeniable undercurrent of James's absence on this first Christmas. They would feel his loss at the heart of so many rituals tonight: the dinner prayer, the stockings, Roger's fireside reading of the Christmas story with the grandchildren after dinner.

Christmas eve. Here they were. They had made it through the last seven months without James, past Thanksgiving, when the cousins had been splintered at in-laws, and now they were at the doorstep of this next family milestone, and it looked like they were surviving it.

"Will you carve up the roast now, dear?" Margaret asked Roger brusquely. She was using her hostess voice, and he knew better than to interfere. Her territory was ruled with an iron fist.

Roger pulled the carving set out of its well-worn box on the counter. They'd gotten it as a wedding present, and he was pleased to remember that fact. Quite amazingly, Margaret could still reel off who had given them what. She had a cataloging knowledge of their possessions and exactly where things belonged.

It was somewhat of a relief to have a job to do amid all the bustling of children and grandchildren in his home. Now Ryan, on all fours, pushed open the swinging dining room door into the kitchen, chasing Sarah, who was waving a juice box. She rammed into a stool, almost toppling it, and then screamed in delight, heading for the den.

"Children, children," Margaret called testily, clapping her hands like a schoolteacher, her mouth tight. "Stay out of the kitchen while we get the food on the table. We're almost ready!" Erin, Jen, and Maura exchanged knowing glances. This was Margaret at full maternal tilt.

As he slit the knife through the meat's pink interior, Roger reflected that he felt largely back to his old self after that meeting with Kindler a few weeks before. For a time after that he'd been rattled, his confidence stooped and shaken. He should have stayed at the bar that night, driven around, anything but come home and worry Margaret by dumping his own personal crisis of faith in her lap. That had not been wise, yet the evening had ended wonderfully. They'd actually made love for the first time in a long time, and it had felt satisfying. More than satisfying. He had been surprised at Margaret's ardor, the way she succumbed so easily to his touch.

In the den, Pete, Stu, and Brad were subdued on the dark green couch, legs splayed in front of the coffee table before them, beers in hand, studying the flat-screen TV above the fireplace. The deep burgundy walls lent the room a cavelike atmosphere as they chatted, commenting from time to time on the basketball game and waiting for the final call to the table. Even on Christmas eve sports could be found all over cable, Roger marveled. The house that was mostly too big for just the two of them seemed suddenly to press in, and he felt the urge to escape the competing swirls of chaos and staccato bursts of conversation for a brief period. Perhaps he'd take a stroll outside after dinner. He should call Julia and wish her a Merry Christmas.

Roger's knife hit bone, and a thick bloodied slab of the beef curled down onto the cutting board. He could hear the women in the dining room, adjusting chafing dishes and bowls on the sideboard, pouring ice water and arranging the remaining condiments with the delicate silver serving utensils. He had placed every leaf in the mahogany dining room table, and Margaret had selected a forest green and silver tablecloth that set off the cream china and crystal wineglasses. The silver settings sparkled, and Roger warmed to the familiarity and festivity in the room.

"Do you want me to bring the roast out there?" Roger called. Above the bustle no one heard him, and he moved toward the swinging door of the dining room, opening it halfway with the serving fork pointed up in one hand. No answer. "Julia, do I bring in the meat?"

For an instant, Margaret stiffened, and an ugly, knowing look jammed on her face, as if she had just tasted something bitter. Roger, still unaware of the gaffe, was momentarily confused, as his daughters briefly stopped their preparations, wearing puzzled expressions.

Their grandson Sam burst into the dining room, hitting the table and causing the ice to tinkle against the crystal water glasses. Margaret turned back to look at Sam with controlled fury and then cut her gaze to the floor, wiping her hands on her apron. "Bring the roast in here, Roger," said Margaret curtly, after a strangled pause.

It took Roger one uncomfortable moment, as he backtracked along the guy wire of his utterance, to realize his mistake. Christ Almighty. Had he just called his wife Julia? Had he let that slip unconsciously? Roger set the roast platter on the sideboard and moved into the kitchen doorframe, lowering his eyes, grateful for Margaret's practical, unflappable nature. He was hopeful she wouldn't give it another thought. She had no idea of the significance of the name, couldn't possibly know who Julia was. It was a simple mistake, an honest mistake; he shouldn't place any more weight on it than the times he simply called up the wrong word. There was so much confusion in the house, so many boisterous people and kids colliding, it was disorienting. There was no reason for Margaret to suspect that there was any more to it than that. Reassured, Roger busied himself situating the silver platter on the trivet.

Minutes later Margaret was herding all of them into the dining room. The rolls were out of the oven, the mashed potatoes and the oysters and corn casserole steaming in sterling chafing dishes. In the center of the table, Margaret had artfully arranged little crèche figures interspersed with fir boughs and candles, giving off an evergreen scent. The long tapers in the candlesticks flickered, illuminating the room's metallic striped wallpaper. The grandchildren stomped their feet eagerly like ponies, entering the line one by one from the kitchen with newly washed hands. The fluffy piles of mashed potatoes their mothers had heaped on their plates were in disproportionate amount to the rest of the food.

Once they were all seated, Margaret reminded her grandchildren to put their napkins on their laps and turned to ask Ryan to say grace. For a small moment, everyone hesitated. This had been James's role for the past few years as the oldest grandchild, and he had relished it. There was a momentary awkwardness, largely unnoticed by the children, and a collective realization that it was not so much that they were recovering from the loss of James on this very first Christmas season without him, but that they were learning to live around the edges of his absence.

"Thank you, God, for our food and for family. Please take care of us and please tell James that I miss him." Ryan lifted his head but squeezed his eyes shut self-consciously.

Roger studied Maura as she smiled tentatively; the beginnings of tears swam in her eyes. He was pleased to see Pete reach for her hand. Margaret was also observing Maura, her mouth pursed.

"And may God protect those we love most," Roger added, his eyes darting back to Maura and then Pete, who looked stoic, glazed even, from multiple beers in the den.

"Amen," the table muttered in a staggered unison, and then there was the sudden scuttling of silverware on fine china as everyone dug into their heaped plates.

Later that night, after Stu and Jen had gone upstairs to settle Alice, and Erin's family had headed home to leave carrots for the reindeer, Ryan sidled up to Roger on the couch while Maura and Pete were gathering their things.

"Do you think Santa will find James in heaven?"

The simplicity of the question ambushed Roger, and he pulled his grandson in for a hug.

"I do," said Roger. "I think James is going to have a very good Christmas with God and all the angels up there. And you know, when you're in heaven, you get to watch down on everyone else. He'll be watching down on us too." Roger rubbed Ryan's shoulder for a moment and was struck by his marked resemblance to James, the same spray of freckles on the bridge of his nose, the clear blue wide-set eyes, a legacy from his side of the family. Ryan had recently gotten a haircut, and Roger smoothed the bristles at the nape of his neck where the barber had shaved him. As he hugged Ryan, Roger was struck by the slimness of his frame, the insubstantiality of a seven-year-old boy.

"Good," Ryan said simply, "because I miss him."

"Me too," choked Roger. "I miss him too."

23

B *ack home from* Christmas eve dinner, Pete read " 'Twas the Night before Christmas," and they'd put out cookies and a glass of milk for Santa. Maura and Pete took turns tucking in both kids, soothing their excitement and urging them to fall asleep soon. They wandered downstairs, settling on the couch, sipping glasses of wine until they were certain the kids were asleep before carrying the presents up from their hiding place in the basement. They tiptoed around, making noises and then shushing each other, and yet it had been hard not to focus on the fact that there was one less stocking, one less excited child. The previous year, James had figured out that there was no Santa, but he had sworn up and down to keep that secret from his siblings.

Maura hesitated when Pete opened another bottle of red wine, but she held her tongue. He was already partway in the bag, his eyes matte, head panning in that slow deliberate way of closed-circuit security cameras. He'd made a fire earlier in the night, scrounging old logs in the garage, as neither of them had thought to order wood this fall, one of the many details that had evaporated from their formerly ordered household.

After they'd organized the gifts under the boughs of the fir tree, they sat on the rug in silence, watching the blinking colored lights reflect on their faces. Pete put his arm around her first and then moved toward her with a look of naked hunger and need. Exhausted from the festivities and saturated with past family memories, this was not how she had imagined the night would end. Maura steeled herself as he lifted her sweater and fumbled with the button at her waistband. Struggling out of his pants with a sense of urgency, his hands grazed her stomach, moving up to her breast and finding the nipple between his thumb and forefinger. Pete bent his head and she squirmed out of her jeans, acutely aware of how her spine was pressed uncomfortably into the space where the rug dropped off to hardwood floor.

"I love you," he said, thick tongued, pressing his lips to the side of her cheek by her ear, making the little nibbling, blowing motion that had wooed her back in college when it had seemed sexy and not so canned.

"Love you too," she murmured, but she turned her head aside and squeezed her eyes shut. She was concentrating mightily on trying to relax her body from its involuntary, rigid stance. This was exactly what she should be doing now, she told herself, exactly where she should be, but she felt almost nothing; no desire, just a kind of vaporous rising panic. The wine at dinner made her a little fuzzy and now Pete was pawing at her, and she needed to pee. She shoved that thought aside.

"I've missed you," he moaned, and she wrapped her legs around him, clasping him closer. If she could do this right, she thought, it would mean so much. On one level, lying in his arms felt so simple and familiar, she momentarily believed it might save her life.

There was a noise upstairs, something like an object falling, or maybe it was just the creak of a pipe between the walls of the older house. She tensed for a moment, freezing, poised to listen, and they both stopped. Pete watched her carefully, never taking his eyes off her. He was drunk, she realized then, very drunk.

"What?" he said thickly. "What is it?"

"A noise. Did you hear that?"

"It's nothing, just the heat, those old radiators. Iss not the kids, they're sound asleep." His voice was groggy, his words slightly slurred.

"Are you sure?" Maura sat up, pushing him off of her and starting toward the steps.

"Yeah," said Pete, falling back down on the rug and letting out his breath in a frustrated *whoosh*. He rubbed both of his palms over his eye sockets in a hurried motion, as if to revive himself.

As she rose, Pete's arms suddenly shot out and looped around her ankles, pulling her back on the rug with a single-minded purpose, and her annoyance flared as he rolled to kiss her again. His merlot-soaked tongue called to her mind the textured underside of a portobello mushroom, fleshy and moist, and then her thoughts flicked briefly to Art. And as she fought the urge to push Pete's chest away, Maura once more willed herself to concentrate.

When they began again, their hips moving in unison, he entered her, somewhat rougher than she would have liked, and any trace of a spell that she had tried to conjure up had been broken. Her rhythm was off, her attention completely diverted. She could feel Pete's urgency but still felt no desire. Maura bit down on her bottom lip and closed her eyes. The floor cut awkwardly into her back, and she made an involuntary movement that somehow nudged Pete away, and he grasped her harder. As he moved inside of her, Pete seemed unaware of anything but his immediate pleasure, and because she could hold it in no longer, Maura began to cry, softly at first and then her shoulders shaking, her body rag doll limp. Pete suddenly slammed his hand down on the rug beside her head and rolled off of her body.

"I'm sorry," she whispered.

"I am too, Maura," he said between gritted teeth. "I wanted this. This one nice moment by the tree tonight. I wanted it to be like it used to be."

"So did I," she said, her voice barely a whisper. They lay there for a while, enervated, Pete's eyes closed, listening to the snaps and pops of the fire, the sudden collapse of a burned log with a shower of embers. She observed the neat row of the stockings on the mantel, the pinpricks of lights on the Christmas tree, throwing off the illusion of order and harmony.

"So where are we going with all of this?" Pete said suddenly, surprising her with how sober he sounded. She had thought him asleep and she paused to collect her thoughts.

"Pete. It hasn't even been a year. It's our first Christmas without him. The very first."

"But then will there be a second and a third? When does the black hole of James's death begin to fill in for us?" His voice was rising with anger, but there was an anguished edge that was almost pleading.

Maura was silent, and she fought the urge to get up and walk away, just crawl under the covers, but that would be too easy. "I don't know, Pete," she answered carefully. "Maybe we still need more time. It all feels brand-new some days, you know?" And she began to cry again softly, and Pete made no move to comfort her.

"You don't want to really talk, you don't want to try to move on, you don't want me in your bed. There's been something off for a while. You think I didn't see that? Even before we lost James, I was losing you." Pete rolled over and the back of his arm hit a wrapped present, which he fiercely shoved out of the way as it skittered on the rug.

"I don't know, Pete. I do want you. I want James back. I want that day back. I want to do it all over and change it, to make it right. And I want us to work too. I do. I want . . . I want . . . to not—" Maura stopped herself. Under the tree, in a moment of honesty, she had been about to confess, about to be swept up by some overwhelming need to confide in Pete all that had happened that day as their son had rolled off the curb. Something coldly rational swam up inside her and stifled the urge. This would do no good now. It wouldn't bring James back, wouldn't heal the breaks in their marriage.

"I wish," Maura had started and then continued boldly, "I wish you would drink less."

Pete rose, wordlessly, pulled his pants back on, belt unbuckled and flapping as he grabbed his shirt from the floor and padded upstairs without looking back. She could hear him fumbling, running water in their bathroom, and then he thudded down the hall. Maura understood then that he had gone into James's room to sleep. The thought occurred to her that she would have to make up a story the next morning, tell Ryan something about Pete when he flung open the door to their room on Christmas day and found only one parent.

Maura waited almost thirty minutes, until she knew Pete would be asleep. She unloaded the dishwasher, set out the bowls for cereal in the morning, and grabbed their wineglasses to rinse in the sink. She paused for a moment, absentmindedly gazing out the kitchen window, past the flagstone patio and into the indigo black of the yard beyond. She had always loved this time of night, when everyone was asleep upstairs and the still of the house was hers to inhabit. Before James's death, gliding through the rooms to plump pillows and straighten up had given her an immense satisfaction, a sense of restored order, that all was right with the world. Awake in a house of sleeping family, the view from her kitchen sink up into the vast night sky had made her feel, at times, like the captain of a ship, responsible for the cargo and the safe passage of all aboard. She felt none of that contentment now. Sighing, Maura grabbed the empty wine bottle and some of Pete's beer cans to take out to the garage recycling bins.

Pausing on the back porch, she looked up into the vast winter sky, clustered with tinseled stars. Maura inhaled the metallic scent of arctic air into her lungs. She leaned her head back farther to locate the outline of the Big Dipper, the brighter stars forming other constellations whose names she had once known. The North Star eclipsed all the others in brilliance, and she recalled how much James had loved anything to do with astronomy.

She could not remember the tribe; perhaps it was Eskimo, or maybe the Norsemen, who believed that when someone died, their spirit flew into the sky to become a star. Maybe that was where her son was, she thought with a weak smile, a steady ball of light fixed above in the prehistoric blackness, to forever keep watch. James had loved that idea when they had read the story. He had been fascinated with the constellations for months after that, pulling her outside with his little telescope and a map of the night sky for identification.

Maura headed nimbly down the porch steps in her slippers, mindful of the patch of ice Pete kept promising to chip away, and she moved toward the side door of the garage in the frosty night, holding the neck of the empty wine bottle in one hand and cradling the beer cans. Peering down the driveway she could see her neighbors' decorations, the strands of lights on bushes, the blow-up Frostys, steroidal candy canes, and the reindeers arranged on the snowy grass, motorized necks moving mechanically in the still, windless night. The Presslers had a crèche scene on their front lawn, the Dyalls had a giant grinning plastic Santa, lit from within. It hadn't snowed in two weeks and the crusty top of the old snow reflected the lights like a glaze.

Maura pulled the down parka tightly around her and tried hard to reach for anything resembling the holiday spirit. But the magic moment by the tree with the kids before bed had evaporated. The failed night of intimacy was clearly a turning point for both of them, and standing now under the night sky on Christmas eve, looking up at the glittering stars, Maura felt a sudden stab of clarity, a conviction about what she needed to do. She dumped the bottle and cans in the recycling bin and headed back indoors, watching her breath huff out in little cartoon gusts.

· · ·

Very early that Christmas morning, alone in their bed, Maura dreamed of James, one of those rare and haunting, intensely memorable experiences that obscures precisely where the dreamer ends and the dreamscape begins. She had been waiting for something like this to occur, wishing for her son to send her a message by dimming lights or knocking objects off shelves. She'd been hoping he would visit her in her sleep. Up to this point she assumed that the sleeping pills had mostly interfered. Yet even as she was dreaming, Maura knew that when she woke, she would remember elements of the experience for the rest of her life.

In the way that dreams take place in locations both specific and surreally distorted, she and her family were sitting in rows in a church that resembled St. Thomas the Apostle. A small white-and-gold-painted coffin sat in front of them on the altar, and Maura understood, with the internal clarity that dreams provide, that her son was not inside. Instead, she began to realize that the essence of him, his spirit, was somehow moving among and between her and Pete, Sarah and Ryan, his grandparents, aunts and uncles, and cousins. Softer than a whisper, he brushed against each of their hearts and wove between their hands and interlocked arms on the velvet cushioned pew, absorbing their breath and reassuring them imperceptibly with an unuttered comfort.

Although in her dream James couldn't speak, she knew that from the moment he had left himself in the hospital, floating briefly above his broken body, his job had been to stay close to them, a sentry watching over the ones he loved at the house, until the time was right. Maura understood that this new version of her son, ethereal and physically insubstantial, no longer fathomed what it was to be tired or heavy or bound by gravity. She could intuit, as a mother does, his growing anticipation for what would come next, a buoying sense that another warm place was waiting that

would feel as good and secure to him as living with his family had
felt.

In her dream, James was now entering their bedroom, although
Pete was there next to her, instead of lying in James's room as he
was in real time. Swirling around his father's sleeping form, James
dove down, burrowing himself in his chest. She watched Pete's
even breathing rise and fall, and then he stilled for a moment and
rolled serenely onto his back. James moved now to Sarah's room
and dipped down into her crib, tenderly caressing his sister's face,
her curls blowing back from her sleep-damp forehead as her hand
rose involuntarily, and relaxed its fist. James appeared to be zoom-
ing faster now, with a greater sense of urgency, moving into Ryan's
room, and Maura was inexplicably keeping pace, she was with him,
observing it all from the inside out. She watched as he circled the
room's perimeter once, past Ryan's books and games, the discarded
clothes on the floor, and moved to the bed to embrace him before
retreating.

Now James was increasing his speed, swirling like a mini-
cyclone toward Ryan's front bedroom window, and all at once they
were through the glass, outside by the big maple tree and up in its
leafless branches. In the night air Maura had the sensation of riding bareback, fused to a winged horse, and yet there was nothing
beneath her. James whorled once around the exterior of the house,
the white painted boards on the outside of the garage so close that
she reached out to touch them.

And then they began to pick up speed, rising swiftly over the
neighborhood, now the elementary school, the grid of their small
town telescoped beneath them. They soared above the dark turgid
waters of Lake Michigan, arcing over shores, lighthouses, and is-
lands, and then swooped across the Great Plains with their checker-
board farmlands and circular irrigation systems. Beneath them
in the dark, small towns with single intersections glowed like a
hundred lit crosses. Now she could make out the Upper Peninsula

above the mitten of Michigan, the shrinking comma shapes of the Great Lakes, and then she saw the whole continent, embedded in the ancient sapphire blue of the ocean. She and James flew past clouds luffing in the shapes of animals and physical things for which he no longer needed to remember the words. He continued up past stiff air currents and colliding weather patterns and up, up, up . . . and then all at once Maura's forward movement dissolved as a golden warmth infused her veins, a glow, and there was a sudden sensation of uncoupling, like the second firing of a rocket ship in space. She observed James continuing above her as one watches a meteor, with a consuming sense of wonder.

The force that was her son soared now at even greater speeds. Unencumbered by weight he accelerated beyond the planets' rotation, burning like a comet, compressed and focused into one tight pure glowing mass. And in Maura's dream, as her son broke through the byzantine darkness to join the universal light of a trillion twinkling stars, all that had once been James expanded and then burst into a million particles of explosive, refractive love.

24

With *Thanksgiving and* Christmas behind them, Maura felt the blues set in doubly hard this year. She had always hated January, that long stretch of a month with no festive holidays and nothing but gray, ice, and the deep suck of cold. She had rejoined her Tuesday tennis group and was playing in the bubble two towns away with her old gang. And twice, she and Pete had been out to dinner without the kids. Maura considered that a form of progress.

Yet still, Art danced through her thoughts. It had been almost eight months now, and unanswered questions percolated in the backdrop of her mind. She was becoming less effective at pushing them away. That relationship, which she had tried to will into mental storage, lingered as unfinished and undone. It was hard to fully put herself back into repairing her marriage with Pete until she had filled in those blanks.

Maura lifted the phone off its base in the kitchen and walked into the living room, sitting on the couch. Anxiety and excitement zipped around like bees in her diaphragm, and she took a deep breath to calm herself. She let her head fall back on the couch and studied the room for a moment, the soft mint green walls and geometric fabric of the armchairs. Above the TV was an oil painting she and Pete had purchased at a local art show on the

Navy Pier when they were first married. It was a view of Lake Michigan with the skyline of the city behind it. The giant Ferris wheel on the pier and the buildings were shaded in dusky violets and grays in the gloaming light that immediately chased sunset. How ironic that a painting purchased in her first year of marriage to Pete would be from the vantage point of a beach, similar to the one she had frequented with Art. Maura sighed and before she could reconsider, she furtively punched in the number she knew by heart. After four rings, he picked up.

"Hi, Art? It's Maura," she said cheerily.

"Maura? Hey. Wow. Maura." Art had drawn her name out softly the second time in a long vowel sound, as if working to reassemble his composure. She had surprised him.

"In the flesh," she had answered.

"Wow. I don't think I expected this . . . I . . . ahhh . . . I left you those messages and . . . when I didn't hear back . . ." His voice trailed off.

In those quick seconds, Maura tried desperately to determine what she detected in his words. She strained to process the nuance of his tone, his level of excitement. It was more difficult without the ability to study his face.

"I just wanted to . . . say hi," Maura began unsteadily. "I know I've been awful. It's . . . um . . . been hard. But I think of you, have thought of you so much. After everything that happened, all of it, and trying to not think about you . . . I can't. Couldn't. I'm calling because I need to see you, I guess. Maybe we could have lunch . . . if you want." The words had all came out in one jumbled but stilted rush. And despite everything Maura had rehearsed and polished in her daydreams, it sounded awkward, childish, and pleading.

There was an uncomfortable pause.

"Well, OK. But . . . why now?" he asked, and she hesitated for a moment.

"Because I needed to wait, Art. For lots of reasons." He seemed to accept that.

They planned to meet at the end of the week at the diner in Evanston, at twelve-thirty on Friday, although he would be coming from another direction, he explained.

Talking to Art on the phone after the abrupt curtain of silence for all those months had been harder than she'd imagined. They'd lost the ready intimacy, the easy back-and-forth banter. The distance between them now felt like a physical hurdle.

Imagining what it would be like to see him in person, she felt anxiety again rising up within her. She wanted desperately to feel nothing more than friendship, to experience the realization and relief that she had moved on, that her feelings for him had been an aberration. Maura imagined that some kind of logjam could loosen after she saw Art for this last time, which would obscure the past and dissolve the barriers to Pete.

Up until now, the great riptide of sorrow and guilt surrounding James's death had made the thought of seeing Art almost inconceivable. But everything that lay undone between them had remained a restless spirit, a haunting in her head. She had come to understand that this was the last piece that needed to fall into place if she was going to make some real progress in her marriage. A sense of finality, of choking off any remnant of what had transpired, might be illusory, but it was something she needed to at least attempt.

That was the rational part of Maura. But she was not completely surprised to discover that there was another, smaller part of her that hoped Art still wanted her on some level, as ridiculous and painful as that might be. This was the part she would tamp back down, a vestigial emotional impulse, the irrational part of the human heart, with chambers complex and sometimes treacherous. This sliver of desire had the potential to undo all of the progress she had made if she wasn't careful.

25

"*I don't understand* what you mean . . . what are you telling me, the check bounced?" Margaret was standing in line at the bank, staring at the teller as if she were from another planet. Well, she certainly seemed to be close enough, Margaret thought. The woman was a foreigner. She could barely pronounce the name on her tag—Rasheema? Was that it? The girl was obviously from another country, and she had one of those Arab head scarves to prove it. That was the explanation. There must be some mistake. Why couldn't the service industry hire people these days who understood, who spoke the native language clearly?

The young woman patiently enunciated each word, which only fueled Margaret's sense of frustration. *She*, Margaret, understood perfectly. It was this Muslim foreign person who was confused.

"As I explained, these series of checks were cashed over the last two weeks and there were insufficient funds to cover them."

"There should have been a paycheck deposited sometime last week . . ." Some of Margaret's anger began to diffuse, as a whisper of doubt crept in. A tiny interior voice allowed for the possibility that this might not be the bank's fault. What if it was their own error? Roger's error? The thought occurred to her to back down a trifle.

"There have been no deposits," the woman said in lilting English. "Not since a month ago."

"Thank you for your time." Margaret forced an inelastic smile and turned brusquely on her heel and out the bank's revolving door. The crisp winter air and sharp gusts caught her breath in her throat, and she pulled her gloved hand up to adjust the scarf around her neck. Temperatures had remained below freezing for almost a week, but the remnants after the most recent Chicago storm quickly tarnished into piles of blackened snow beyond the concrete strip of sidewalk. Margaret picked around a patch of ice that the merchant's efforts at salting had not affected.

The next stop was the dry cleaner for Roger's boxed starched shirts and then on to the butcher, where she purchased some organic sausages and a half pound of lamb chops, wrapped in waxed paper. During this time in and out of the local shops, Margaret scrolled through the possibilities of what might have happened to the check. What on earth could Roger have done with it?

There was really only one explanation. He had simply forgotten to deposit his paycheck. But in all the decades they'd been married, Roger had never forgotten to do something this basic. He had refused automatic deposit, in fact, because he was fond of saying he didn't necessarily trust the system. "Computers can make mistakes too," he routinely remarked to the kids. "And you can't argue with a machine." He liked to see his paycheck, make sure it was all there and the proper deductions accounted for. Roger had always been their financial maven, handling everything from the checking account to investment decisions, but she had to admit he had been distracted lately.

"Hello, Margaret." The conversation inside her head stopped as Nancy Palmer passed her on the sidewalk with an armload of bulging plastic shopping bags.

"Oh, hi, Nancy," she said, physically standing taller and forcing her expression to brighten.

"It's so good to see you. It's been ages."

"There's been a lot going on," said Margaret, tilting her head to the side, slightly annoyed at having her thoughts derailed.

"Are you going to bridge at the club tomorrow?"

"I plan to." Margaret shifted her purse to her other shoulder, trying not to look impatient. Her eyes narrowed and she turned her gaze down the street, toward the end of the block. "I haven't been quite as regular as I usually am these last few months. I've spent a lot of time at my daughter's house and with the grandkids."

"Well, that's just wonderful. I'm sure you've been such a help and comfort, but it's just so terribly sad too, I'm sure," said Nancy. "I can't really imagine what you've been through. All of you. But is she coming out of it now? Maura? At least a little?" Nancy shifted her packages to her free hand and leaned in ever so slightly.

"Of course," said Margaret. "As much as anyone can come out of something like that."

People had the most annoying responses to loss and death, Margaret had noticed, almost as if they expected you to be dancing in the streets after a few months. Nancy was a kind enough person, but like her body, doughy and soft, she had no edge. She was the type of woman who had skillfully perfected how to pan for gossip under the guise of concern. Margaret's guard was up, all right.

"And how is Roger?" she asked. "Teddy is just dying to hit golf balls. Honestly, this winter has already been so harsh. He's going on a weekend trip to Arizona soon with the boys and he's chomping at the bit." Nancy chuckled. "He just announced his retirement this coming June, and frankly, Margaret, I don't know what I'm going to do with him kicking around. I think I may have to go out and get a job." She smiled, rolling her eyes with a pleased but patronizing expression.

Margaret returned the smile flatly. Nancy could drone on so.

". . . certainly needs more interests. I keep telling him to get to the gym, he has put on about twenty pounds in the past year and he actually has one of those tires . . ." She gave a nervous titter and Margaret realized she had not been listening, her attention again drifting back to the bank account mix-up. She was bored by Nancy's ready cataloging of her husband's faults. Margaret believed it was a wife's job to keep the exterior facade spackled and impenetrable, to prevent the cracks from showing on the outside. In her mind, a classy woman never broke rank.

"Well, winter will end sooner than we think. If we can just make it to the end of April, the course will be open and he'll be out of your hair," Margaret said, setting her mouth in a conclusive way. Nancy nodded and Margaret made a step backward, as if to signify that they had reached the outer boundaries of the conversation.

But Nancy was not quite done rubbernecking, much to Margaret's dismay. "Now, Margaret, what about the boy. The Hulburd boy, was it? The one who was driving the car when your grandson was killed? Do you know what he's up to? He didn't go to jail as I recall . . ."

Margaret felt suddenly tired, exposed, and snappish. She tried to make her own face impassive. "No, no jail sentence. He was exonerated. Beyond that I wouldn't know anything about him," she said. "I wouldn't know about his family either, frankly. Maura and Pete haven't really had any contact." She made a deliberate shuffling motion with her feet, indicating the need to move on. "Perhaps I'll see you tomorrow then. At the club."

"That would be lovely," said Nancy, giving a little halfhearted queenly wave with her black leather glove as she began to wobble over the icy sidewalk toward her parked car. "I look forward to it," she called out over her shoulder and into a gust of wind.

As Margaret walked to the end of the block, Nancy glided past her in her giant white Cadillac sedan. Margaret noticed the CHOOSE LIFE! slogan on the license plate holder, and the corners of her mouth fanned up slightly. *That certainly fits*, she thought smugly.

Nancy was one of those people who wore their politics on their cars. That kind of advertisement of your beliefs just invited every crazy on the highway to weigh in with their opinions. No thank you. Margaret would make sure *not* to be in Nancy's foursome if she made it to bridge tomorrow. They'd both just exhausted all they had to say to each other.

Back at home it didn't take Margaret long to locate the check, balled up near Roger's cuff link box on his dresser. It was crumpled, as if he had mistaken it for an old receipt. She smoothed it out in one swift motion with her palm. What was it that Stu had been saying for years? That she should come into the twentieth century and get one of those ATM cards? She had resisted all of that for so long, while Roger had rattled on about bank error and how everything was paperless these days. And then you had no proof. A machine couldn't count cash in front of you and answer back if you were short by twenty dollars. Maybe her son Stu was right. He was a technology specialist at a Milwaukee software-consulting firm, and he knew a lot about these things. She'd give him a call this afternoon.

"I bounced a check today," Margaret casually remarked to Roger over a dinner of broiled lamb chop and a baked potato with low-fat sour cream. She kept her voice even. It wouldn't do to be accusatory.

"Oh?"

"It seems you may have forgotten to deposit your paycheck. Or that's what the bank teller told me."

Roger's face registered surprise and then a brief shadow of something else, was it fear?

"Well, that's a first," he said, reaching for humor. "I've, uh, been so busy at work lately I guess. Where was it?"

"I found it on your dresser," said Margaret. "It was all rolled up, like a piece of trash." She couldn't resist this last bit, driving in the knife and twisting it just a fraction. There was a part of her that still seethed at how casually he had called her by another name at Christmas. Julia. That had been a slap, but at the time she had stuffed it down and concealed the hurt. The sting of that memory would intrude at the oddest moments. And it had confirmed for her that the woman, Julia, was most likely still in his life. In the weeks since it had happened, Margaret had devised a dozen ways she would have liked to answer if the kids hadn't all been in the kitchen at the time.

"I am not that harlot, Julia!" she had wanted to scream at him then. But that kind of damage, that sort of honesty, would have unraveled so many things that had lain neatly coiled over the years in their marriage.

"Sometimes I worry about you, Roger." Margaret said this softly, in an innocuous tone, and as Roger looked up his expression made her think of a trout, on a hook somehow, his mouth jerked to one side.

"What about?" His voice was light and carefree. But Margaret knew better.

"You. Your memory and focus, I guess. I really want you to make that appointment for a total physical. You've had to cancel twice due to meetings. And honestly, sometimes your mind just seems to be somewhere else completely. You're not hiding some giant secret about our financial ruin, are you?" She smiled wryly.

It was relief she saw play over his face as his expression relaxed. He set down his fork and sighed for a moment, looking up at her sheepishly, like a sinner in the throes of forming his confession. If he truly had a concern over his health or his memory, a part of her wanted to hear none of it. She fought the sudden urge to clap her hands over her ears to block out what he might be about to tell her.

And then a sudden furrowing of his brow, an internal shoring up that rearranged his features back into the old capable Roger, the one who deposited checks and handled the finances, who held the door and slapped his buddies on the back over a Dewar's and soda at the club's putting green bar.

"Well, Margaret, I definitely have memory issues here and there," he said calmly. "Like a lot of us do at this age, I suppose. Certain names don't always fly to the tip of my tongue. Or yours either, for that matter, my love. But I guess the pressure of the deal in Florida is taking its toll," Roger explained, his voice more in control and confident now. "I'm going to have to head down there next week for the final set of meetings, and hopefully we'll come back with some signed contracts. This was all supposed to happen in December and it's been delay after delay."

Margaret met his eyes without expression at the mention of the word *Florida* and she continued to chew wordlessly, her mouth tight as a change purse.

. . .

"Oooooohhhhhh . . ." Roger had to hold the receiver away from his ear at Julia's high-pitched squeal. "I can't believe you are coming! I'm so excited, Roger."

"We'll probably only have one real night together," he said evenly. A horn honked behind him, and he swerved to avoid the car ahead, braking suddenly. He was almost on the highway, his attention fractured as he struggled to catch her exact words on the car speakerphone.

"Then I'll make it the best night ever. The whole works. We'll eat at my house and we can be more casual. I have the perfect meal, my frittata with artichoke hearts and lobster. I know just the cheese, the creamy one from that little bodega. And I'll make that sangria you love so much!"

"That sounds perfect." He could hear the measured cadence of his own voice and wondered if she had picked up on it with the weak cell connection.

"*You* are perfect, Roger. Perfect for me, and I can't wait to jump in your arms."

"I'll see you Wednesday then, Julia." Roger hung up the phone and creased his brow. He felt the weight of this trip, his reluctance to deliver the news to Julia that this would be his last visit. Keeping both Margaret and Julia happy had begun to feel like an impossible mathematical equation, an elusive balance.

Two days later, Roger placed starched shirts on top of his loafers and zipped the carry-on bag shut. It looked like the developers were finally ready to come to the table for the refinancing on the original deal. He had not needed a reason to drum up a trip to see Julia, and although he was not the lead partner, he would be part of the team. He had rented a car to head to Julia's bungalow for the extra night. This was all overdue.

Roger could hear Margaret downstairs in the kitchen, already assembling breakfast. He felt a slight dizziness for a moment, a need for caffeine, he imagined, and he sat back on the neatly made bed, bringing the top of his dresser into focus with its framed photographs cataloging a rewarding life of family spoils and leisure.

Roger's eyes settled on the professional shot of his foursome at the club's annual golf tournament a few years back, the silver trophy cup raised high among them. He'd gotten a hole in one that day and could still remember his incredulity and then the accolades, the rounds of drinks, the sense of being the envy of the room. He'd taken Margaret and his two daughters out to celebrate the next night; Stu, of course, lived too far away. Their husbands had stayed home with the grandkids and he'd looked around the table in the club dining room as if he were Lord of the Manor. He had built up a rich life, a solid life, Roger thought to himself as he rose off the bed and grabbed his suitcase. Jeopardizing that, at this stage, would come with too great a cost.

There was no question that Julia still excited him. She thrilled the part of his ego that required attention. And yet he understood that for the long haul, it was Margaret who was best kitted out to care for him. With their collective history she was better equipped to fill in a missing word in the conversation stream as smoothly as putty or cover a social weakness with riveted steel. As lovely and insouciant as Julia was, as inventive and eager in bed, she would not be the one to go the distance. Oh, she'd bridle at that conjecture if he ever said it out loud. She'd disagree and claim loyalty as tenacious as a hunting dog. But it was Margaret who shared his battle scars. And while passion and patience had evaporated between them over the decades like perfume, it was she who made him stronger, she who would hold him up like bones. Roger ultimately understood that their love was inextricably constructed of more solid, dependable qualities.

Yes, it was time for Roger to break it off with Julia on this trip. He had already made that decision, and he wanted to give them both the dignity of doing it in person. His business trips to Florida would be lessening now, and she deserved more than the crumbs of his occasional visits and the off-prime-time phone calls he parsed out. He would miss her—the quick infectious laugh, the comfort in her own body, the girlish spontaneity, and the sense of wonder that was lacking in his spouse. But maintaining all the rings in the circus of his life seemed infinitely more exhausting than it had eight months ago.

Roger did love Julia, but he had always known that he would never leave Margaret and the children for her. Where was that incentive? And live like an exile from his hearth and blood? Sex and mystery became familiar, he knew all too well. He was too old of a leopard to change his spots, and in the end, Margaret's loyalty, her sheer marital tenacity trumped everything. Admittedly, he had been enjoying the upsurge of togetherness he and Margaret were experiencing in the wake of all that they had endured as a family. They had settled into an easier pattern, tacitly familiar and comfortable. It was far from perfect, Roger admitted. But what was perfect in any of the marriages he knew that had gone around the track as long as theirs? They had their family and the grandkids, their friends and their social life centered around the club. Losing James had been the touchstone that had forced him to examine his own mortality in an unexpected and sobering way. It had been the knock on the side of the head that rearranged priorities, reminding him of how his own family was fixed firmly at the center.

So he'd go to Tampa and to Julia, for this last time. Roger would take his pleasure, and then he'd initiate the discussion with Julia, distasteful as that would be. It had been months since they'd spent any significant time together. She couldn't be happy with the situation as it was; Julia deserved more than this. Roger hoped she would see it his way if she didn't already.

26

Maura *pulled into* a parking spot on the mall's second-level structure and flipped down the visor mirror to study her face. The week had seemed both eternal and fleeting, but Friday had arrived. Was she really taking this much care to prepare for their lunch meeting? She felt like a schoolgirl. Two days ago she had bought a cashmere turtleneck at full price, spending far more than she ever had on a sweater. It seemed the perfect compromise between looking too put-together and her usual V-necked pullover standbys.

The periwinkle wool set off the bluish pigments in her eyes, but now she focused critically on her lashes. Too much mascara? Was the eye shadow too heavy? She snorted at the vanity of this exercise. When was the last time she had subjected herself to this kind of scrutiny? As much as she wanted to exude a nonchalant elegance, she cared very much how she looked today.

Maura had hoped maybe after the lunch she could convince Art to bundle up for a winter walk on the beach, figuring that the act of moving, of not having to look at each other directly in the face, meant that they could talk more freely than at the confines of a table. In the end, though, Art had called that morning to say he had limited time. It would be closer and easier to meet at the mall near his office, and he suggested one of those chain restaurants named after a day of the week. Maura's heart had sunk a little. It wasn't what she'd pictured, but then who was she to make demands of him?

It took a few seconds for her eyes to adjust to the low lighting on the walls full of fake antique road signs and vintage Hollywood poster replicas. When she spied Art, he was already in a booth, gazing at the laminated menu. Her step faltered briefly. She was struck by the enormity of seeing him in person. The luxury of spotting him first meant that she could examine him, take him in critically the way one studies a work of art.

Art seemed more "city" to her somehow, more sophisticated. His chin was down and his brow furrowed as he concentrated on the lunch options through his reading glasses. The goatee was new, she noted, and he was wearing some kind of stylish textured sweater, snappier than his previous post-college, lumberman look.

Maura made her way across the restaurant, clutching the straps of her purse and pressing it to her side. Navigating toward him around chair backs and tables, she saw Art glance at his watch before he looked up, searching the room briefly and then meeting her eyes.

Her pulse raced as she gave a small tethered wave. Snaking around the last of the obstacles, she was beside him. Art rose to hug her just as she bent to kiss, and they collided awkwardly, feigning comfortable laughter. She registered a guarded look in his eyes as she tossed her purse on the faux red leather banquette opposite him and slid in.

"I've only got an hour," he announced early in the conversation, already staking the parameters of this meeting, setting the boundaries before it had begun. Wounded, she accepted it with a nod and gradually relaxed her too-wide smile.

The Art she remembered was still there, the boyish earnest look, the slight gap between his front teeth that she found inexplicably attractive. His black hair was cut shorter, and she could tell from the rigid way he held himself that he was uncomfortable. This was awkward for him. Maura studied Art's hands before fully meeting his eyes. They had been one of the first things she had noticed during that initial meeting with him at the veterinarian's office. She remembered seeing the sure way they held Rascal, moving around the dog's body to diagnose the injury. They were large hands, "farm hands" he had called them, from growing up in rural Wisconsin.

"I like the goatee." Maura averted her eyes momentarily as Art reached up to stroke his chin, and she observed the filament of a scar under his right eyebrow, the legacy of a high school football injury.

"I think you are either a facial hair person or you're not," Art said. "I decided to give it a try. I have to add a little extra time now to stay in the lines when I'm shaving." He chuckled nervously. His smile fell short of his eyes. Today they looked cool, uncharacteristically impenetrable.

Snapshots of the times they'd been together flipped through her head—the beach walks, the diner, visiting Art's Evanston apartment, the picnic meals she had packed. The careful planning and subterfuge, her mother watching Sarah under the pretense of some meeting or appointment or another. *All of that unrecoverable time*, thought Maura.

The conversation was stilted at first; they were both uncertain of where to plunge in and so they initially skimmed over safe topics like Art's weekend biking and his further adjustment to Chicago. It was painfully polite, so different from their interaction eight months ago. Art hung back, listening more, letting her do the work, as if assessing her. Maura asked about his practice, and he enquired about Rascal. She got the distinct impression he was purposely avoiding the topic of James.

The waitress came up and Art ordered a cheeseburger while she chose a salad, although her appetite was nonexistent. Adrenaline had flooded her bloodstream and her brain and her heart revved like a hummingbird. Sitting across from him, Maura tried to gauge how she felt after so much time had passed. She was still attracted to him, but the entire landscape of her life had been reconfigured. She didn't want or crave him in the way she had before. A giant chasm had opened between them, and they were now two different people with very few common points of intersection. *How odd*, she thought, *that you could once be so close to someone and then feel completely removed, like a stranger.*

"So, you changed your vet? I saw the records transfer request." She could tell Art was reaching for a breezy tone.

Maura nodded and carefully examined her nails. "It's been hard."

"I'm sure," said Art with an elastic snap. And then he softened, his posture relaxed. "It's been hard for me too, Maura. That long silence from you. One day you were dangling the possibility of a future, sending signals to hang in there and the next . . . nothing at all? Not even a call to let me know you were OK? You owed me more than that. I wanted to be there for you in whatever way I could." His eyes were steely now, his face set in harder lines.

Maura watched his anger erupt, and she let it wash over her. She deserved this. He was injured and jilted, and she supposed that kind of emotion was easier to swallow than apathy. At least hurt meant he still cared.

"My son died," Maura began in a hushed tone, studying her nails. And she realized she had not had to utter those three final words directly to anyone she knew since it had happened. Everyone she had surrounded herself with, everything she had done, every person of consequence she had come in contact with since that day, had already known this fact or had no reason to. Maura's eyes glistened with tears and she silently cursed herself. She did not want to do this right now.

"And you associate me with that," he said softly. His hand moved over to tap hers, a gentle accusation as she played with the silverware. He darted it back to his lap.

She nodded glumly. "How could I not? After what we did, the timing of it and then . . . the next day."

"I think I finally pieced that together." Art was quiet, listening again, waiting for her to talk.

"I . . . I blamed you for part of it. I shouldn't have. But I felt so incredibly guilty"—Maura paused and her voice caught—"so guilty for everything I was feeling." She would not cry now. Not again at this lunch. She could climb back in her car afterward and let all of the mascara streak down her face in black ribbons, but she would not do this here in a mall restaurant.

"One moment I was walking down the sidewalk, and the the next thing I knew James was lying on the street." She paused for a moment. "I don't really remember anything else until I was at the hospital. I was out of my mind with fear and with . . . with guilt."

"I'm sorry," said Art, and his sense of wariness, of diffidence, was gone now, replaced by the old Art she knew, the compassionate, vulnerable person. "I really am. I think what happened, what you went through . . . well, that's hard for anyone to imagine."

They chewed in silence for a moment and the forkful of salad made Maura feel nauseated. She took a drink of iced tea and forced herself to swallow.

"I went into a tunnel after that." Maura paused for a moment. "He lived for almost a week in a coma and then his body just gave out. Massive internal injuries." Maura pinched her fingers over her lids for just a minute and seconds later she had the presence of mind to wonder if she had just smeared her makeup into raccoon eyes. "I suppose you see that all the time in your practice . . . things dying." He nodded solemnly, his eyes locked on her face.

"I understand your guilt, and your anger," said Art. "I understand you even blaming me to a degree. You are entitled to all of that. Completely. And that day . . . the day before, was perhaps more me than you, I'll take responsibility for that. But then you pulled the rug out. I was pretty tortured for a while there. You started something, and then you threw cold water on it. Your cell was disconnected, I drove by your house a hundred times . . . had to physically talk to myself not to get out and ring the bell. You know I actually called the house and left a message with your sister. Once I even spoke to your husband." Maura's head shot up. "I left a message as your vet. That's all," he said defensively. "Hey, I was worried sick about you. I finally came up with the coffee cup idea. I figured you'd know instantly what those cardboard cups meant, but no one else in your household would."

She nodded. She would not mention the e-mail he had sent, the risk he had taken with that and how frightened it had made her, how uncertain she was of what he might do at such a fragile time in her marriage.

"I was . . . I was doing the best that I could." Maura could see it all clearly from his perspective, a perch she had tried not to inhabit up until this point.

Art nodded and seemed to collect himself for a moment. "I guess that I thought we had something far more promising than we did. When I tried to break things off that one time . . . you basically begged me to come back. I . . . I suppose after that I allowed myself to think that we had some kind of a future." Art lowered his eyes to his plate, where he picked up a French fry and plunged it in a pool of ketchup before swallowing it in two bites.

Maura felt a sudden lurching of internal organs at the realization of how casually she had behaved. Her capriciousness had led him to make assumptions and plans. She leaned onto one hand to shift her position in the banquette. She saw now, with complete clarity, how careless she had been. Maura had led Art to believe she might leave her marriage. It was a sin of omission, in a sense, but it had resulted in so much collateral damage.

"Art. I don't know what to say."

"I didn't deserve to be treated as if . . . as if I were driving that car." His voice was softer now, as if he'd exhausted the energy to be angry.

They ate for a few moments in silence, Maura moving the food around on her plate as her mind grappled with where this was going. She had lost her enthusiasm for the charade of pleasantries involved in wrapping up this conversation and leaving. The leaving part, she knew, would feel like a vacuum seal, final and hard. She'd be left reviewing the one hundred things she should have said instead or done differently.

"So why are we here, Maura?" Art said more softly. "Why now?"

Maura looked down at her hands in her lap, the nails neatly manicured. How foolish that she had agonized over the right shade of ballet pink, as if that would carry a message, as if any of that mattered. How appalling that she had spent money on the new sweater to accent the color in her eyes. "I guess I wanted to tell you how sorry I was, although I'm not sure I could have done it any other way at the time. And . . . and I wanted to see you, to see if you were all right and that you had moved on or at least that you weren't stuck, like me. I've thought about you so much . . ."

"I liked you too much, Maura, and you weren't mine to like. As much as I wished you were." He stopped and took a sip of his iced tea. "I know what it feels like to be the person who gets left for someone else. I don't want to be that other person in anyone's marriage. I didn't even want to get near that line. And I did. I think that what happened to us in the end, the way it happened so abruptly, was the best thing for us." Art looked right at her, his expression softer but without its former intimacy.

She nodded, too close to tears to speak.

"It wasn't real," he said solemnly.

"What?" she asked automatically, before she could catch herself.

"Us."

"We're here right now," Maura said with a false bravado, as if to lighten the severity of the moment. "That's real." Her smile faded when she saw his grim expression, and she felt a little gnawing kick up in her gut.

He smiled halfheartedly and arranged his silverware in a parallel position on one side of the plate and then folded his cloth napkin on the table.

Maura paused for a moment before speaking. "I guess . . . although we never talked much about it, that you must know things weren't . . . aren't so great at home. That had nothing to do with you." Maura picked at the nail polish on her left hand, chipping it down by the cuticle. "My husband and I . . . well, I wonder sometimes if we were really meant to survive past college. Sometimes we feel like two different people connected by three kids." This was the most Maura had ever said out loud about her marriage to him.

He was studying her closely. Was he surprised by her candor? Their conversations had only ever grazed over the topic of Pete. It would have been so easy, she could see now with the perfect clarity of hindsight, to have let Art steer them toward a gentle end, as he had tried to do in the diner that day. It would have been excruciating in the short run, like ripping a scab. But when Maura pulled back the curtain on all that would happen after that day, she would have given anything to have made that one simple choice, to not have teased him on to satisfy her vanity and her own needs. The level of pain involved in ending it that day seemed inconsequential in the face of everything that would come later.

Maura reached out impulsively for Art's hand, resting on top of the table, a final act of apology and compassion, and he stiffened slightly.

"Maura," Art said, and the previous edge in his voice had crept back in. "We're not at that place anymore." She nodded instantly, stung, and retracted her hand. He'd misinterpreted her actions, but she would not correct him. Art sat back against the banquette and raised one arm, flagging the waitress and motioning for the check.

"I've got to get back to the practice," he said unapologetically. "There've been two emergencies today already. A black lab came in that ate a sock, and I have to do an extra abdominal surgery this afternoon."

They were both silent for a moment, and Maura felt the need to fill the air, to resurrect herself somehow.

"Pete and I . . . ," Maura began. "We're working on it . . ." Her voice trailed off. Sitting across from him now, trying to interpret his signals, was disorienting.

"I've met someone," Art said abruptly.

Maura worked to keep her face even, not to register dismay. She raised her eyebrows in a gesture of interest, and yet the effort involved in remaining outwardly calm was far greater than she might have imagined.

"Well, of course you have," she said slowly, measuring each word. "I would expect you would, would *want* that for you." He looked up with a bemused smile, a shadow of the good-humored man she had fallen for. But they were both playing roles now, and his total neutrality made her wonder if there were any fraction of him that was still attracted to her. It was difficult to imagine them as two people who'd once been deeply connected in an emotional vortex, who had shared such intimate moments.

"We both needed to move on, I guess," Art said as he signed the check and then rose, signaling his departure. Outside the restaurant, his hand on her shoulder felt fatherly, yet there was an undercurrent of leashed restraint. "You've been through a really huge thing. I'm not trying to minimize it. But you can't let it rule you, and you shouldn't let it destroy your family either. I don't know exactly what you want for your marriage, but I hope, for your sake, that you get to a better place. You deserve that. And I hope, most of all, that you'll be good to yourself." As he prepared to walk away, he leaned over toward her and pecked her on the cheek, a blessing and a dismissal.

Back in the parking garage, Maura flipped down the visor mirror and swiped at the ring of mascara under her eyes. She let out a deep breath before fastening her seat belt and starting the car. Whatever she had hoped to achieve, seeing him had only raked up odd, angular sentiments that were too sharp to hold or smooth back into place. She was exhausted. And yet she needed a moment to organize her ricocheting thoughts.

It was hard to recall how she had once fixated constantly on being in his presence, how the vast stretches when she was apart from Art could feel constricting and monotonous, when held against the startling thrill of being with him. And when they had been together, Maura could still remember the heightened sense of an electric current flowing through her, as if she were a fuller, more alive version of herself. All the incremental steps that had taken her and Art to a place of intimacy, so innocent when each encounter was individually examined, now felt selfish and wrong in the wake of their lunch. And yet at the time, each of these single acts of being with him had somehow saved her. It was both comforting and disconcerting to realize Art now felt just like any other person from her past who had once meant something more. He was flawed and self-absorbed in intervals, not vastly different from the man she'd married. Maybe her theory that all of life was a series of random couplings was correct, that there was not just one soul mate but in fact any number of possible prospects with whom you could end up. The key was that all of it took work. Oddly, she thought of her mother and her garden, each season a labor of love, requiring patience, sweat equity, and the need to constantly shore up the perimeter against intruders. Maura realized with certainty that all of the emotion she had invested in Art, all the good and desirable parts of herself she'd illuminated for him, had been pieces she'd denied Pete.

With a sigh, she plucked the parking garage ticket from the car's

cup holder and backed out of the spot to head home. Up in her bedroom, she pulled the turtleneck sweater over her head in one swift
motion and tossed it into a ball on the floor before climbing under
the sheets and closing her eyes. The anticipation, the knots of emotion, and then the inexorable emptiness had spent her.

27

The bolt slid in the lock as Roger's eyes flew open, and momentarily disoriented, he sat up on the couch. He must have dozed off. He'd arrived an hour early and used the hidden key to surprise Julia as she returned from work.

Surveying his surroundings, Roger blinked rapidly, his shoes propped on the glass coffee table, and he struggled to his feet, staggering as one knee gave out for a second and then caught.

The door swung open and a triangle of late afternoon sunlight knifed across the floor. Julia entered the room, a clump of grocery bags in each hand. For a moment Roger contemplated how to let her know he was there without startling her. He took a step forward, slightly, saying her name, and the movement registered in the corner of her eye.

"Aaiiiiiyah." She flinched, recoiled actually, and dropped her purse. When she recognized him, seconds later, she crumpled with relief and let out her breath.

"Roger!" Her voice was admonishing, but he could see behind the receding surprise and fear that she was pleased. More than pleased.

"Julia," he said simply, and he stepped forward toward her.

She was in his arms in seconds, practically launching herself toward him, and he fought the sensation to weep for some odd reason, a jumble of sentiments hitting him, from anticipation and joy to extreme sadness and apprehension. He was here to end it, and he felt like an assassin.

They embraced and kissed, her body rising up to meet his, readily.

"Why? What are you doing here so early . . . ? Never mind," she said slyly. "I don't want to know. I only care that you're *here* . . ." She flashed a brilliant smile and began to lead him toward the couch, tugging playfully on his arm. Something in his expression stopped her, and she slowed, her smile erasing as she detected reticence, a hesitation in his eyes.

"What?" she said more gently.

"I just want to . . . to look at you . . . ," he said. "For a moment." And her smile brightened again. There was a good ten years difference in their ages. It hadn't meant anything when they'd first met, but he could see the gap now. Her face was tanned from her time outdoors, and despite the Florida climate, her mocha skin, while not youthful, looked healthy. She was a woman who cared for herself, not in an overly meticulous fashion, but who kept herself up.

"You can look, but it's so much more fun to touch," she said impishly. Julia steered him toward the bedroom, now meeting little resistance.

A short time later, spent, they lay side by side, in the final yellowed varnish of the sunset through the sheer curtains. Julia rolled toward him and spooned his back, tracing his breastbone blindly with her fingers.

"So why are you here again? That old deal?"

"Business. You. The deal here is done. Almost. It doesn't really require much more corporate oversight."

"So, did you come for me?"

"And for me . . ." He laughed, rolling toward her, breaking out of the armlock she had created.

"You haven't made much of an effort to visit me."

"It wasn't that I didn't want to see you . . ." His voice trailed off, his ardor cooling. "It's just that it's all so complicated. There is so much . . . so much need at home."

Julia was silent.

"And your wife?"

"We don't need to talk about Margaret," Roger said evenly.

"You deserve—"

"I know." Roger cut her off. "But I have my life. And it's in Chicago. My children, the grandkids. My grandson's death . . . it changed things. You can imagine. And I think we need to talk about that a little bit this weekend. I haven't been what you've needed these last few months."

Julia sighed, moved away slightly, and then rolled back. She wore a new expression, as if she had made a split-second decision to bring in reinforcements. He recalled the early days of their relationship when she used to coyly feign a pout, but later she had always been the one to give in and forgive, to come back. Roger absentmindedly stroked her bare shoulder. The light had shifted, projecting low and blood orange on the wall at the foot of the bed. Roger was suddenly aware of the traffic noises outside, the distant sound of cars on the highway.

"But you came for me?" Julia asked expectantly.

"Yes. For you," he said, because it was simpler for now.

Julia lay on her back, smiling with satisfaction at the ceiling. For a moment Roger pictured his life back home and wondered briefly where in her schedule Margaret was. He would need to call her soon, perhaps when Julia was taking a shower. A small pang of guilt pierced his mood.

Julia's fingertips grazed his temples and strayed down his cheek. He could tell she was studying him, searching his features in a manner that felt pleasing and slightly suffocating. He turned his thoughts back to the present as she rose to shower. This would be the last time with Julia. It had to be. He could feel his resolve strengthening again. But he would wait until tomorrow to tell her. They would have this one last night, limbs entwined, her soft, purring snores partially muffled by the white noise machine she favored.

Roger lay for a few minutes in the disappearing light. He too would get up and take a shower. Julia had plans to cook for them here tonight. She emerged from the bathroom, her hair damp and rolled into a towel that always made him think of Carmen Miranda, and he turned on the bedside lamp. She adjusted her robe as she bent to peck him on the cheek and then moved toward the doorway.

"I have this fabulous antipasto and I'm so glad I went to the farmers' market early. I got some stinky cheese you will just die for." She rubbed both hands together in delight. "I've already cut the fruit for the sangria," she said over her shoulder. "And I'll put away those groceries while you're showering. Ooooh, that ice cream is probably soup by now," she trilled as her voice receded into the kitchen.

Roger felt a slight dizziness for a moment when he rose too fast, the result of lying down for so long. *Damned low blood pressure,* he thought. Who had that at his age? Weren't people supposed to be worried about sky-high numbers? Margaret was right. He needed to reschedule that physical. He felt momentarily unsure on his feet as he headed into the bathroom. The room righted itself and his face came into soft focus in the steamed-up mirror.

It was in the shower that he felt it, a burst of light, the explosive stab of an ice pick behind his right eye socket. He closed both eyes and pressed the palm of his hand over the spot, as if to physically block it out. The pain seemed to intensify and radiate through his brain, but still he felt frozen, moving sluggishly, not reacting or crying out. His left arm flopped jerkily to the side, and his other arm, which he had reached out to steady himself against the shower stall, refused to obey. The spray from the showerhead splashed over him, louder now, roaring like a waterfall, as if all of his auditory processing was on overload, his senses heightened in a dreamlike fugue state.

The lines between his physical body and his surroundings were beginning to blur. Propped against the shower wall, he could not feel precisely where his extremities ended and the tile began. As he tried to concentrate, Roger realized that his thoughts, his need to get help, were punctuated by periods of total silence in his brain—the hiccups of nothingness, as if his cognitive powers were shorting out and then blinking back on. Low-level alarm bells were being tripped in his mind.

And then he suddenly felt far away, sucked into a vacuum tube, as if he were watching it all through a telescope. He tried to make a sound that would bring help, but he was incapable, he was mute.

Roger's legs buckled and went numb. And then he was falling, hitting the shower caddy, sending Julia's soaps, shampoos, and razor tumbling to the shower floor. Summoning the last of his energy, Roger opened his mouth, and a low moan escaped his lips, its tenor indistinguishable between pleasure and pain. And in the matter of seconds during which all of this happened, the disconnected sense he'd felt was replaced with a bottomless terror and confusion. Before his head hit the tile wall, his right shoulder absorbed the first impact, and he crumpled to the tile floor in plush velvety unconsciousness. Roger Munson's final, unconnected observation was that the water drops fell in perfect orbs and then froze for an instant, like diamonds, before they hit his face.

28

Absorbed *by her* novel, the sudden interruption of the phone startled Margaret in the armchair by the bay window that framed her garden view. Her heartbeat spiked, and then slowed as she placed the bookmark in the spine and rose, making an irritated clucking sound. Why was it the phone always rang just as she had settled into a book, or sat down to watch her favorite news program? She never seemed to remember to bring it with her. It was probably one of the kids, or Roger.

His trip to Florida seemed to have come up so suddenly. She supposed she should be somewhat relieved after all of his griping about wanting more of a role in the corporate deals. He had been closer to home lately, she mused, on the road less than usual. But he was headed back to Chicago tomorrow, and frankly, as much as she had enjoyed the break, she was looking forward to seeing him. She'd heat up a can of soup tonight for dinner and dispense with all the culinary effort required when Roger was at home.

If she didn't get there in the next ring, it would click over to the answering machine. So what was the harm in that? She reached the receiver with seconds to spare.

"Hello?"

"Mrs. Munson? Uh, Margaret?" an uncertain voice began.

"Yes? That's me."

"I'm calling from Florida. It's . . . it's about your husband, Roger."

"Yes?" Margaret shifted her weight onto her left leg, feeling a rising panic. There was something about the nervousness in the woman's voice that alarmed her.

"He's in the hospital. Here in Florida. He fell. He might have had a stroke."

Margaret took a step backward and her hand rose involuntarily to cover her mouth. Her grip on the book gave way, and it clunked to the floor.

"He what? Roger? How is he?" Margaret battled for control. She needed to concentrate.

"He's in the ER now. That's all I know." The woman's voice sounded tired now and sad. "I, I thought I should call the family."

"And who are you? Are you a nurse?" Margaret demanded in a much sharper tone than she intended. Things were coming more clearly into focus. Something obdurate and flinty was coalescing inside of her. Good Lord, Florida, of all places.

"I'm a friend of Roger's," the woman said softly, and it was at that moment when Margaret's suspicions congealed with certainty, the click of a padlock giving way. She understood exactly who this woman was.

"Oh. I see," was all Margaret could muster, and she knew she would chide herself later, replay her missed opportunity with bolder and better responses. She felt her insides crumple, but she worked to keep her voice steady and strong. "Well, I'd like to speak to a doctor." She sat down.

By the time Margaret had hung up with Dr. Stangland, she was numb. It appeared Roger had suffered a stroke. And there might be a brain bleed, he'd intimated. It was not a life-and-death situation, the doctor had assured her right away in an effort to calm her. He was stable, but it was serious, and she needed to come to Tampa as soon as she was able. Roger was about to undergo all kinds of tests and scans, things that would give them more information. During the fall, or whatever had happened to him, God only really knew, he had also broken his collarbone, and so they were going to need to get that set and pinned.

How fast could she get down there? the doctor had asked her. Roger was not conscious, was in a coma, or had he said they had put him in a coma to keep him sedated? Something like that. Thank God she had had enough of her wits about her to take the number and the name of the hospital.

But it wasn't until after she hung up that she realized she had not gotten the full name of the woman who had called, or any information about how to reach her. She'd had a slight accent, Hispanic, Margaret thought. It had to be Julia, Roger's whore, the woman whose loopy, girlish handwriting had substituted a heart for the dot over an *I* in that long-ago note to her husband.

Margaret closed her eyes against images of what the two of them might have been doing when this happened. She realized how much a part of her had believed Roger's increasing presence at home, their recent intimacies, had allowed her to hope that his dalliances were in the past. Whatever they'd been doing, they'd most certainly been in each other's company when he'd had this stroke. This brazen woman had most likely brought him to the hospital. The guilt in her voice had been palpable.

For a moment Margaret felt the surge of a fighter and then she stifled the urge to laugh. The situation was so absurd, so ridiculous. This was like those late-night made-for-TV movies when the philandering husband is discovered in bed with his mistress. But this was real life, her life, and this was *her* husband. After all of her efforts to build a close-knit, stable family life, to protect and burnish Roger's respected image in the children's eyes, now she was left with this sloppiness on his part, this tawdriness. She might be able to look the other way at Roger's quiet out-of-town infidelities, but public humiliation was another story. She stiffened in the chair, seething, gripping the phone tightly as her thoughts collided.

Outside a breeze played through the blue spruce in the backyard, ruffling the branches like a skirt. Absentmindedly Margaret reached to rub her forehead. She had to call Stu and the girls, but for the moment this all seemed too complicated, too fraught with ugly details that might begin to unravel.

A stroke. Damn him. She knew enough to understand this wasn't good. People recovered in vastly different ways. A kernel of panic began to bloom in the pit of her stomach, and she beat it back. She needed to call the kids, the airlines. She would need much more information, but the key was to remain calm. Margaret took another minute to collect her thoughts, to regain her composure and get control of the fury and the fear she now felt. Yes, that was it—fury—at Roger's sexual avarice, his total disregard for all of them. And now, here she was, headed to Florida to assess the wrecked hull of his life. Of their life. He had done this to them all.

A small wren hung tightly to a branch in the crab apple tree. The bird riveted Margaret as it cocked its head, examining her with one eye and then the next. *Breathe in through the nose and out through the mouth*, she told herself. Calming breaths. When Margaret had regularly taken yoga at the YMCA, this is what she had learned. In . . . and out . . . she could feel some of her anxiety retreating as she exhaled. Slowly she bent at the waist to retrieve the dropped book, smoothing the pages where it had landed facedown. She sat for just one moment more, staring out the window and reaching for equanimity.

She was struck by the irrational thought that if she simply stayed in the chair, reopened the book on her lap, she could reverse time, pretend that none of this had ever happened. She could go back to life just the way it was before the phone call. Let Roger and his mistress figure this one out. In that moment, she was aware of being precisely in the center of a dividing line between her before and after.

When the girls were little, she had accompanied Roger on a business trip to London. One of the wives' junkets had been to the Greenwich Royal Observatory, where the official Greenwich mean time clock was located, and the imaginary line of demarcation, the prime meridian of the world, was engraved on a plaque in the ground.

They had visited the museum on a gray English day; the earth was muddy, and she recalled that the main street of the town had been lined with the intricately painted signs of cozy British pubs. At the maritime museum, she had waited for her turn with the other spouses and then straddled the actual line near the clock where the planet's hemispheres divide, posing for a picture. For those few moments in time, she'd had one foot in each half of the world. Although there'd been nothing physically special or magical about the plot on which she'd stood, she recalled the weight of the moment, the sensation of being in two worlds at once and the distinct but fleeting experience of time standing still.

Her life now hovered on the cusp of change. A terrible thing had happened to Roger, but at this precise intersection in time, contemplating both distant memories and the uncertainty of the future, she knew she was standing on the lip between past and future. She had not yet taken a step forward into her new unwritten life. Margaret let out her breath forcefully, and as if mirroring her, the wind outside her kitchen window blew a sharp staccato gust and the branch swung upward, startling the wren into flight. Margaret picked up the phone to call her son first. Next would be her travel agent.

29

Maura *could almost* feel the warm slant of the late afternoon sunlight in her dream. She was down at the beach, near Lake Michigan, not far from the Navy Pier, closer to the cramped apartment where she and Pete had lived when they were first married. James was little, toddling on unsteady legs, falling into the sand and then laughing and scrambling back up to his feet.

It was a Chicago summer day, a bold cobalt blue with a line of big, puffy clouds on the sill of the horizon where it met the lake. A steady breeze fluttered off the water, and the waves kept an even tempo in the humid midwestern air. Maura squatted in the sand. In the dream she could actually feel the granules between her toes, smell the almost iron, bracing tang of the Great Lake's water. She stretched out her arms as wide as they would go, and James began to run toward her with that wobbling gait that little children adopt on an uneven surface.

Just as she was about to grab James, to hold him, he had shapeshifted from a healthy, happy child into the older, broken, injured boy that she had held in her arms on the road. A part of her knew that she shouldn't move him, but still she had gone to comfort him. The mother part of her had responded instinctively, and now in her dream she was holding him up, supporting his head, as a dark stain spread over her jeans and onto her lap. Far in the background, she

could hear a siren approaching, but James was simultaneously disappearing from her grasp, melting and dissolving into nothingness.

Maura awoke rattled and sweaty. She rolled over and looked out
the window to clear her head. The dream had seemed so sharp featured, so real. And then the shocking news about her father invaded
her train of thought with a *whoosh*. A stroke. It was inconceivable.
Maura's eyes filled with tears thinking about what her father would
look like, unresponsive in a hospital bed. It was almost too much
to bear; memories of James in the ICU less than a year ago sent her
mind tumbling backward, the antiseptic smells, the bright lights
and beeping machines. *Too many hospitals*, she thought morosely. It
would take all of her strength to see her once vivacious and vital
father today. But she would need to be strong for her mother. There
was an infinite justice in being able to support her now, after the
many months Margaret had worked to ease her own grief.

Maura wiped her eyes, slid out of the bed, and ventured into
Ryan's room. She craved the manner of reassurance that only her
children could provide, and she bent to take in his sleeping smell,
pulling up and adjusting his blankets.

Heading toward the shower, hoping that Pete would keep sleeping, Maura was not ready to lose the very real feeling in the dream
of being close to her son, but the pictures were already a receding
vapor trail.

She stood under the hot spray of water and forced herself to look
ahead to the kids' schedules and the babysitters she had patched
together to get to Florida. Her mother-in-law and Erin had offered
to pick up the slack while Pete was at work. Absentmindedly she
rubbed her hands up her shins and reached for the razor to shave
her legs. Something about that simple act made her feel more polished, more complete on the outside. She lingered one more minute in the shower's stream, giving in to the heat, and tilting her
head back to feel the pressure on her shoulder muscles. Turning

the water off, she climbed out and twisted a towel deftly around her body.

Maura was spooning coffee into the filter when she heard the water from the shower upstairs splashing through the pipes in the kitchen wall, signaling that Pete was up. She was surprised Sarah was still asleep and took advantage of the time to quickly pack Ryan's lunch, pulling a juice box out of the freezer and cutting an apple into small pieces.

The February school break officially began tomorrow, but she would leave today for the hospital in Tampa. Last year, as a family, they had all gone to Disney World, but in the aftermath of James's death, neither she nor Pete had much enthusiasm for making vacation plans this year. In the end that had been a good thing. Her father's stroke and the severity of his condition had stunned them all, rocked the foundations of the extended family. It was hardest on their mother, who was still living out of a hotel in Tampa, hoping to take her husband home as soon as they'd allow. Gradually, Roger was gaining strength, although they had all pruned back their expectations. The hope was that he would be more lucid and mobile soon.

Pete had really chipped in to help once they'd received the awful news, urging her to go to Florida right after it had happened, to accompany her mother, but she'd staggered the trips with her siblings. He was taking time off work to watch the kids and would spend the first few days of the break with them at her family's cabin on Sister Bay in Door County. His parents would be joining them to help with the grandkids.

Maura wondered, for a second, if and how to raise the subject of Pete's drinking on this trip. The pace of it had more or less remained the same, and she was relieved it hadn't accelerated. She knew, or at least she was pretty sure, that he would never drive with the kids after a few beers, but Pete had never taken them both away alone before. And this was for three nights. But given the fragile peace between them, she was wary of bringing up the subject and insulting or demeaning him. He was being so responsive with the kids, so supportive of her need to get to her father's bedside.

Maura knew that a person had to want to stop drinking. They had to want it deep inside themselves. And alcohol assuaged that place of loss that had been punched out when James died. He was not a sloppy drunk, but she knew the booze for now had become a blunting mechanism, something to take the edge off. Pete drank to forget, to fall asleep, and to quiet his mind. And the muzzled responsibility she felt for James's death made it difficult to criticize him, yet she was worried for Ryan and Sarah too.

Erin had suggested they go to a therapist, which would at least provide them with a starting point, a way to acknowledge what was happening and throw a life preserver at the problem. But the effort required just to begin was enormous, hunting down the right person, talking Pete into it, making the appointment, sitting there, stiff limbed and noncommunicative at first. It seemed like a stretch. Pete didn't put much stock in baring his soul, and she had a hard time envisioning him in talk therapy. But perhaps the real reason she resisted, the honest reason, was that she was afraid of exactly what might bubble up. Therapy carried the risk of releasing all of the feelings and the secrets she had worked so hard to stuff down. Her unarticulated sorrow, guilt, and love had become a dam. And the thought of disturbing that, of dismantling it, felt absolutely terrifying and insurmountable. But she knew they didn't really have a choice at this point. Maura was determined to raise the subject of therapy when he returned from the camping trip.

Pete thumped down the stairs, reeking of aftershave, a drunk's camouflage, she thought cynically. "I've got the sleeping bags out in the basement with some of the other supplies," he called over his shoulder. "Would be great if you could deal with some of the food. You know, the basics that the kids need. I'm sure my mom will fill in the rest." He opened the freezer and grabbed the box of toaster waffles.

"The cooler is in the garage, I think," said Maura. "I can fill it with sodas and juice boxes for Sarah. And I'll set out some of the things like their vitamins and Ryan's favorite cereal."

"That would be great." Pete popped a frozen honeycombed waffle into the toaster.

"Pete?"

"Yeah."

"Will you leave the beer at home for this one?" Her heart thumped wildly, and she couldn't meet his eyes. She had gone out on a limb, but far too much was at stake. Did he even understand what a responsibility it would be to take two kids camping by himself, one of them only three? Pete looked at her for a moment, steely, and then his features softened.

"Pete," she began in a conciliatory tone. She was braced to backtrack, to mitigate the blow.

"Maura, I get it. I promise. No alcohol. I'd never do that with the kids. I was going to pack a few beers for the cabin, when we get to Sister Bay. But I won't if that makes you uncomfortable." He pulled her close and held her gaze. Maura softened, surprised at how effortless it had been. She'd been braced for an explosion that hadn't come.

For just a moment before Ryan bustled into the kitchen with his backpack, she laid her cheek against Pete's chest. Maura felt the regularity of his heartbeat through his rib cage, and he wrapped his arm around her back as their son joined them.

"Group hug," Ryan called out heartily, smiling, and they all laughed.

"Breakfast, Ry. I've got oatmeal," she said.

"I've got to go to work, buddy," said Pete. "Today is the big day, we leave for Door County after school. Special trip, just the kids and Daddy." Ryan nodded somberly, as if entrusted with a secret.

"And you, Mama." Pete turned to her playfully, animating his voice for his son's benefit. "I hope you get some rest in between helping with your dad. You need to give Grandma a break, but you need one too." She nodded.

"Erin's going to take you to O'Hare later this morning, right?"

"Yup. After I get the kids to school. My flight is at noon."

Pete filled a stainless steel travel mug with coffee and moved toward Maura, pulling her into his chest and then tilting her chin up toward his, studying her. He bent to kiss her and she relaxed into the embrace.

"I love you," he said, giving her one last peck on top of her head. "Take care of yourself. And your dad, he said solemnly. She reached to give him one last hug, suddenly unwilling to let the moment go.

That morning Maura gathered the kids' snowsuits and clothes, and began to pack a suitcase for her own trip. Locating the cooler out in the garage, she emptied the refrigerator ice bin into it and then set the whole thing on the back deck, where it was cold enough to remain frozen.

She stood for a moment staring at the bleak landscape of her backyard. It was almost surreal to think that by the end of the day she would be in Florida. The weather had been hovering around the seventies and was sunny, according to her brother. But the temperature was the only facet of her trip that would resemble a vacation. She knew she would spend most of her day inside the hospital with her parents. Hopefully she could truly relieve her mother and convince her to take a break and get outside the building.

Looking at the cooler, Maura thought again about Pete and the kids at the cottage, and she let out her breath, watching the puffs evaporate in the frigid air. Pete might drink, parents would get older and fall ill, children would grow up and make their own decisions, create more distant orbits. Life was teaching her that so much of everything was out of her control. And she would have to be all right with that if she wanted to keep moving forward, enjoying the passage of time. Otherwise, what kind of life did she stand to have?

30

Roger *was swimming* up from something. Everything around him felt dim and aquatic, as if he were underwater. Ahead of him was an extremely bright light, and now it seemed to be everywhere, bright, pure white incandescent light. Was he dead? Dreaming? What the hell had happened, and where was he? Roger stopped struggling for a moment and decided this must surely be a dream. Now he could feel things brightening, like sunlight as you moved toward the water's surface.

He began to register a hum, a drone, like an airplane off in the distance, and he realized it was people murmuring, more distinct, many voices, some talking at once, and now he could isolate them. He heard Margaret's voice, distinct but firm and then lower in tone, someone else, softer and farther away; someone unfamiliar spoke up next and the white light became more intense, the sheer celestial brilliance of it startled him. Someone was touching him now and he tried to groan, but he was uncertain a sound had escaped. Roger felt fuzzy and groggy, but with extreme effort he opened an eye.

That's right, he remembered. He was in a hospital. Each time he woke he was disoriented like this all over again, as if he couldn't fasten the thought that he was here. And now he remembered with crushing clarity that he'd had a stroke.

"Roger?" Margaret's disembodied voice floated toward him. "Roger can you hear us?" He tried to lift his arm or raise a brow, but he found that he was terribly weak. He could hear them, but why couldn't they hear him?

"He looks like he's in pain." Margaret's voice again now, more crisp and clear. The authority in her tone relieved him.

"He shouldn't be in pain," said an unfamiliar voice. "He is on so many meds, he isn't going to feel pain. But it's time for more sedation, if you'll let me move to his IV." And then Roger felt a rush, a cold fluid flush through his veins. The tsunami of fear that had continued to mount in his chest began to dissipate as the medication took hold and a syrupy warmth invaded, a gooey nothingness that tamped down his mounting panic. Roger surrendered to a feeling of serenity as he melted back into the bottomless twilight.

For an indeterminate amount of time there were the dreams, dreams that floated through his mind and dissolved like Technicolor movies, but which he would never remember later as he toggled between sleep and a sluggish wakefulness in the days following the stroke. It was impossible for him to distinguish between night and day. Voices flitted in and out of the room as he swam up and back down into unconsciousness. He was certain he had heard Maura once, possibly even Julia, but in his present state he was incapable of separating out what was real and what was dream state.

*   *   *

Seven days later, Roger was more fully awake but with no clear idea of what day it was or how long he had been here in the hospital. As he opened his eyes, he focused out the window. The harsh Florida sunlight was only partially muted by the louvered blinds, but the room was cold, over-air-conditioned. He shifted his eyes away from the glare and Margaret came into focus at eye level, in a chair next to his bed. She was sleeping, her head tilted back at an uncomfortable angle and her jaw hanging slack in a manner reserved for the very exhausted or drunk. Roger's thoughts felt clearer, and he was able to focus better than the previous day. He reminded himself of the facts, as he did each morning. He'd had a stroke and was still in the hospital and on lots of medication that made him feel fuzzy and floating. At times just moving his eyes around and concentrating on the conversation were exhausting. Draining. He remembered that his three children had all cycled through the hospital at one point or another and then returned to their families soon after he woke up. Margaret was here now, keeping vigil. He assumed she hadn't left Tampa since the stroke.

There was still an IV tube in his arm and the left side of his face was numb and drooped in an alarming manner. Margaret had told him tenderly that she wouldn't let him look in a mirror "just yet," but he had asked one of the night nurses to bring him a hand mirror and had been rendered speechless and heartsick by his own reflection. A dull ache throbbed in his collarbone, which had been broken in the fall. He felt as if he were a marionette, each limb and body part weighted and unresponsive, as if he were swimming through Jell-O. Roger's brain felt gummy; that was the only way he could describe it. Although he knew what he wanted to say in his head, the words didn't necessarily come out as he intended. He could hear them forming the way you could slow a 33-rpm record with your finger and distort the sound. Suddenly, he began to cough, a disturbing hacking noise, an irritation left over from the tube in his throat, the nurse had explained. The door to his room flew open suddenly, banging against the stopper, and a stocky nurse with overprocessed blond hair bustled in, pushing a cart with her equipment. Margaret bolted up at once, startled and momentarily confused, as she swiped the back of her hand across her mouth in slow motion.

"Time to check your vitals, Mr. Munson," the nurse called out in a loud voice.

"Roger, you're awake," said Margaret, pulling herself up higher in the chair with her elbows, her tongue still sock-thick in her mouth from sleep, her fingers working now to rake her hair back in place. There was a cautious look of delight in her eyes tempered by fatigue. He could see the lines around her mouth and eyes, deeper than he remembered. Something about her earnestness made him soften. Roger hovered on the verge of weeping and then he collected himself as his pride flared. He was ashamed at being such an invalid.

"Yessssshhhhh." Roger worked to form the words with his recalcitrant droop and he smiled at her, aware that only one side of his mouth lifted. When would the feeling return to the rest of his face? he wondered.

His thoughts flicked briefly to Julia and he recalled for the hundredth time, with a now familiar sinking feeling, that he'd been at her house when he'd fallen, but he was unable to remember any of the subsequent details. Julia must have called the ambulance, although he couldn't begin to sequence how the events had transpired from there. Who had called Margaret? When had all the kids come and gone? Did Margaret know about Julia? All of these tangled concerns and unanswered questions made him sleepy. It was too much to think about and so much easier to ignore. Trapped inside this shell of a body, he imagined that he might never see Julia again. She must be worried sick. Perhaps she had been there in person and visited at an off time when Margaret wasn't there. God, he hoped she hadn't.

At one point in his druggy haze, he was certain that he'd heard Julia. He had a distinct memory of her husky voice near his ear. Perhaps he was simply imagining her caress, the hurried declaration of love, and her touch on the side of his face that still had feeling. He'd experienced all sorts of hallucinations and strange dreams on the medication they were giving him, and he seemed to sleep for half the day. Perhaps Julia's visit had been conjured up by drugs in the end.

The nurse finished recording his blood pressure and ripped off the Velcro cuff, moving to check his IV line. Behind her another woman had entered the small room, holding a beige tray of hospital food, the condensation on the plastic wrap obscuring the food compartments underneath. She set the tray on Roger's rolling table and positioned it in front of him. He was incapable of bringing the utensils up to his own mouth deftly, and so Margaret began to rise and uncover the pudding-ish substance.

"How about some apple sauce, dear?" she asked with forced brightness, holding a spoonful of the brownish glop out toward him.

A part of him wanted to turn his head away, to spit it back out in defiance, but he knew it was futile to react that way, especially to Margaret. She looked so hopeful, her words and her voice overly peppy, almost patronizing. It was the same tone she'd adopted when the girls were small. He was as helpless as an infant, and the unfairness of that, the sudden injustice and the vast inequality between them now, temporarily overwhelmed his emotions.

Roger nodded his head, grateful for her forbearance. He had to focus so carefully on moving his lips and swallowing the food. Each sequence of those motions, which had once been as involuntary as breathing, now required immense effort.

Below the sheet, he knew, was a tube that ran into his penis, collecting his piss. He disgusted himself. How long would this be for? He couldn't quite grasp all the technical things the doctors had said. They spoke so rapidly and in such unintelligible medical terminology. And because Roger couldn't always make himself understood clearly, everyone spoke over him, talked to Margaret, looked at him as if he were a child or an imbecile, and then they were gone before he could form the words.

"Jhhhhhhrrrinnnkkk," Roger said with studied concentration,

and Margaret looked over, responding as if he had made perfect sense.

"You want a drink, dear?" She repeated it the way a nursery school teacher tried to model words, he thought disgustedly. But he nodded his head eagerly as she moved the Styrofoam cup and straw of ice water up toward his lips, and he raised his arm to take it.

"Here you go!" and he tried, unsuccessfully, to close his fingers. "Roger, let me do that," commanded Margaret, and she maneuvered closer to the bedside, offering him the angled straw once more.

Now Margaret was babbling something at him, chattering away, pushing those damned ice chips at him, placing the rubber reflex ball in the palm of his hand and pressing it together. A fuzzy-edged anger bubbled up as he emitted a strange, low growl, surprising them both. Margaret's eyes widened, and then her look narrowed quizzically as she fought to understand what he was saying, what he wanted.

"Are you hungry?" Margaret said, almost pleading for an answer, and her solicitousness sickened him. He sickened himself.

"Unnnnnnnhhhhfff," he managed and collapsed his head back against the pillow in frustration.

Later that night, with the moment behind him, Roger felt the kernel of determination begin to form. He would get better. He would work hard. He would devote all of his energy to his recovery, and he would walk again, talk again. This is not how it would end, a slow ebbing of all that was the essence of him. Another unintelligible sound escaped his lips as he held on to this thought, and then moving stealthily, Margaret was instantly beside him in the low fluorescent shadow of the room.

She leaned over him, misinterpreting his outburst as physical pain, and she brushed back his hair, caressed his cheek. The optimism and determination he had summoned deserted him almost as quickly as it had come. She had him, Roger realized. She had him completely and absolutely. Margaret would be his jailer and his captor, his gatekeeper and his interpreter. This is how it would be after all of those years that he was hers, but not hers. Gratitude, resentment, and self-loathing all clashed in his mind.

And now he was crying, he realized. He could feel hot, fat tears rolling down his cheek, almost involuntarily, and he was powerless to stop them. Without missing a beat, Margaret reached over to the window ledge by the hospital bed and pulled a tissue out of the box, dabbing his eyes before the tears could even fall on his chest.

31

"The world feels upside down, Pete." Maura was lying in bed next to him, her head resting on his shoulder. She had braided her body around him after they had unexpectedly and hurriedly made love while the kids were at Erin's for a Saturday afternoon. And while it hadn't set the world on fire, it had felt good and familiar.

"I know, baby, but it's good you were there for your father, even if he wasn't awake. Good you could help your mom through that period. She's been such a major help to us." Maura nodded in agreement.

"I'm really worried about her. She's trying to be strong for so many people. And she's exhausted."

"It's got to be hard," said Pete. "But I'm glad he's awake and making some progress."

"And I'm glad Erin will be in Florida for the transfer back up here."

"How do you think he is, really?"

"Pretty weak." Maura sighed deeply. "His speech is totally affected. Mom put the phone up to him today so he could hear me, but it was sort of hard to understand him. And his movements. They're so disjointed. Stu told me when he was down there that he's getting more mobility, slowly, but it's really shocking to see him so diminished. He can barely feed himself. I think he's depressed. I mean, anyone would be, right?"

"I'm glad he's coming back to the Chicago Rehab hospital," said Pete. He was absentmindedly rubbing her shoulder now with his forefinger, staring at the ceiling. It was beginning to feel uncomfortable, like he was wearing away a layer of skin, but she held her tongue. This felt like the old them, and she didn't want to disturb the pleasant sensation of equilibrium.

"All this sadness." Maura sighed. "So much for one family." Pete didn't answer but pulled her closer. They lay in silence for a moment, each cataloging their own thoughts.

"Thanks again for taking the kids camping," she said.

"Well, it wasn't really camping. We spent the whole week sleeping in the cottage. Just that one time we pitched the tent outside. Somewhere about one A.M. we got too cold and went in the house." Pete laughed. "Grandma June made bacon and eggs in the morning."

"Ryan told me," said Maura.

"But I told Ryan and Sarah that counted as winter camping. As long as you make it past midnight." Pete coughed, and her head, resting on his chest, rose gently up and down.

"Ryan told me you all tracked a bear in the woods."

"Yup, I had them both going. There were some tracks in the snow, a raccoon or who knows, some other small animal, and I told them it was a baby bear. Ryan's eyes got really big." He paused. "James—"

"You know that James—" began Maura simultaneously, and they both stopped. They'd had the same thought at the same time, she realized. They'd imagined their son's delight with the idea of off-season camping, his enthusiasm for the bear tales. He loved the night sky, loved animals and campfires. She watched sorrow flare up in Pete's face, and she battled back her own precarious emotions.

"Hey, come with me," Pete said suddenly, rising off the bed and slipping on his jeans. Maura looked at him quizzically and then threw on one of Pete's T-shirts on the chair by the bed. He led her down the hallway and turned the door handle into James's room. The afternoon sunlight cut strips across the floor where it filtered through the wooden blinds. This was less her son's place now and more of a shrine. It was a room where time and objects had suspended themselves in the life of a forever nine-year-old boy.

Pete led her over to the twin bed and they sat side by side on the SpongeBob comforter.

"I miss him so much," said Pete simply.

"I know," answered Maura. And she leaned her head on his shoulder. They sat for a moment, studying the trophies on the single shelf Pete had built around the perimeter of the room just under the dentil molding. She made a mental note of the fine layer of dust on his desk. They had picked it out together last year at Crate & Barrel, his own private place to do homework. He'd wanted to buy his own laptop too, and they'd all discussed what chores he could take on to earn money. Roger and Margaret had given him paying jobs around their house, like weeding the pachysandra beds and polishing silver so that he could achieve his goal.

Maura sighed heavily. "If I could have one wish . . ."

"Me too."

"Remember how James was scared about things under his bed?" Her brow creased, thinking about his night terrors and his certainty that something was lurking beneath him.

Pete smiled and nodded his head wordlessly.

"I guess there really was something under the bed, something bad waiting after all, huh, babe?" A tear spilled out of Maura's eye and ran down her cheek. She hadn't cried with Pete in a long time, and it felt strange at first, unpracticed. Pete was crying too, his shoulders rising and falling. And then he was holding her again, rocking her back and forth.

"Why did it happen to James? I let the bad thing happen to James." All at once the words were pouring out of her mouth, the horrible knowledge that she had been the parent in charge.

"Hey," said Pete, soothing her. "Hey now. I don't . . . I don't have any of the reasons why. Or the answers. I don't think there are any. Bad stuff just happens. It happens all around us every day. I know you're punishing yourself, Maura, but, whatever you were doing, looking away or not paying attention, you have to forgive yourself." Maura hiccupped a sob and then nodded.

They both stayed on the bed, rocking, as if afraid to break the spell. Something had dislodged and shifted between them this afternoon, a nestling together. Perhaps this was James's gift, she thought, guiding them back toward each other here in his room.

"I want us to work, Pete," Maura said softly, and it took a moment before she realized she was holding her breath.

"We're working," he said simply. "We're getting there."

They sat, each navigating their own thoughts, remembering James, transfixed by the pictures of him on the little bulletin board, the proof that he had been theirs. James standing next to Pluto in Disney World, James pitching, his fourth grade school portrait with the unnatural forced smile and fake blue cloud backdrop.

There was a bitter sweetness in sitting here together. Up to this point, their grief had manifested itself in such completely differ-ent ways. Today was one of the first times since the funeral they had sat together, comingling their respective sorrow. She was touched that Pete had taken her in here. It was a form of healing to lie on the bed together, the two people who had created James, shouldering their loss as a couple, in this sacred space.

32

"When *Maura and* Erin had sat with her in the hospital last month, they had repeatedly tried to get Margaret to go back to the hotel and nap, to read by the pool, to step away from the bedside. She wasn't ready yet, she'd told her daughters. She occupied the hotel just to shower and sleep. The rest of the time was spent by Roger's bedside, as if keeping constant vigil could improve his chances of recovery.

Although Roger had been awake for a month now and was participating in some basic therapies, there was no giant leap forward in his condition. It was hard to see him so incapacitated, and Margaret could intuit, beneath his intermittent thumbs-up and false bravado, the reek of anger and defeat. Where was the fight in him?

Margaret had to admit there was a kind of peace in being next to him like this, an abundance of unencumbered time together. It brought to mind the butterflies that she had trapped in a jar, as a girl, with a cotton ball of alcohol and then pinned to a bright felt background. Here was her husband, a perfect specimen, captured, but not present, not vitally alive.

Margaret reached out to touch his cheek while he slept. After four weeks in the hospital on a mostly liquid diet he had shed pounds, and his skin was sallow, hanging a bit from his face, muscles slack. The nurses had told him they were not allowed to shave him or cut his nails, hospital rules, and so Margaret had done it herself. She had been surprised by the emotions evinced during the act of grooming him. There was a gentle dignity in the simple tasks of physical caretaking that was hard to articulate. Lathering her husband's face and drawing the razor carefully along his jawline was such an intimate experience it almost made her blush. The way his eyes followed her studied gaze during these moments felt like a found purpose.

Occasionally Margaret had allowed herself to imagine what life might be like if Roger never fully recovered. There was only one incidence she could remember when they'd discussed end-of-life issues and it was at a dinner party, not many years ago. Someone had introduced the idea of a DNR, a do-not-resuscitate order, and they had all been bantering about what they would do or what their wishes would be in this situation, each person boisterously offering their opinion over multiple cocktails.

"I would never want to be a vegetable," she remembered Roger saying glibly. "If I couldn't live fully and move and talk, I'd never want to stick around." She could recall at that moment how confident he had looked, almost as if he couldn't fathom that age and infirmity would ever catch up with him.

"I want to go out like that governor, was it Rockefeller?" Roger had continued, raising his highball glass at the table in a jesting toast. "He died of a heart attack, didn't he, while having sex with a hooker? He sure went out with a bang!" That had elicited raucous laughter from the men at the table and some of the women. But to Margaret the joke was a razor nick too close to home, and she had masked the humiliation she felt with a polite smile.

"I don't want to linger," added their friend Richard. "If I end up like my dad, in a hospital and riddled with cancer, just take me out back and shoot me." The guests around the table had nodded knowingly, with the hypothetical mind-set that healthy, complacent people adopt at dinner parties to parse serious subjects.

They had moved on to the debate about which would be worse, to lose your mobility or your presence of mind. Although they were sixty-five, it was honestly the only time she ever remembered them both speaking about it. Margaret was keenly aware of Roger's aversion to frailty and aging. He'd been somewhat disgusted at his own mother's progressive senility and confusion, as if it were a communicable disease. Toward the end of her life, when she no longer recognized any of them, Roger had rarely visited her nursing home. He had been on a business trip to the West Coast when she had passed away, and it had been Margaret who had made the trek to Arizona to begin the arrangements.

Roger's mouth twitched slightly in his medicated sleep, his face uninhabited. The nurses had told her to keep talking to him, even now that he was awake, despite the fact that his words were muddled and he was hard to understand. He was processing all of this, they said, taking it in as his brain healed incrementally.

And so she had talked and read the paper to him, although she had felt foolish after the first few days as she babbled along in a one-sided conversation. Margaret was reminded numerous times of that precarious week in the hospital with James, when they had read to him from some of his favorite books. She recalled one time, coming upon Maura by the bedside, reading get-well cards from her grandson's class, the tone and messages innocently optimistic, as if he had merely had his tonsils out or his appendix removed. The juxtaposition between her grandson and her husband, hospitalized less than a year apart, was too much to wrap her mind around. It was an overload that threatened to short-circuit her, and she sealed those memories off in a separate mental compartment.

Margaret's talking and chattering had tapered off once Roger awoke. There was so much now that he was supposed to be doing to start the rehabilitation process, but overall he seemed to lack motivation. Sometimes, she thought, he feigned sleep to avoid her and the basic physical therapy exercises that had been prescribed.

By the end of the first week in Tampa, Margaret had settled into the rhythm of the hospital, the regular checks of the nurses as they bustled in the room. She had grown accustomed to their individual greetings as they checked Roger's vitals, changed his fluid bags, and emptied his waste. Once while he was in the coma, the trach tube had whooshed loose when the nurse was sponge bathing him. Margaret had been terrified by the sound of the air escaping, had yelped and jumped up as the nurse continued, calmly reattaching the breathing tube. In those moments she had realized how on edge she was, how close to unraveling from the yawning uncertainty.

Margaret had created a routine of going downstairs to the cafeteria and getting a cup of black coffee before lunch. She'd purchased a pack of cigarettes at the gift shop and allowed herself three each day, on breaks from the bedside. There was always a smattering of family members and the occasional nurse in scrubs clustered around the circular cement ashtrays in the designated outdoor smoking section. They made small talk and inquired politely about the progress of a loved one as they all stood flicking ashes in the fresh air and sunshine outside the hospital. Stepping back into the lobby after a cigarette, she always braced herself to feel the cool and over-air-conditioned interior.

Margaret became aware of a rustling behind her, presumably one of the nurses. But then it was too quiet. She felt the silent presence of someone and turned to look back. A woman stood rigid in Roger's doorframe. She was tall, tanned, full figured in navy pants and a ruffled hot pink blouse; she was younger than Margaret, but not by many years. She seemed nervous and out of place in the ICU. Perhaps she had entered the wrong room, but Margaret sensed that there was something more. It was the way the woman was clutching her purse to her chest, as if it contained all of her valued possessions.

"Mrs. Munson?" The woman asked tentatively, and Margaret rose quickly from the chair.

"Yes."

"I'm Julia Rolon."

Almost before she said her name, Margaret knew who she was, placed the slightly accented voice on the phone, and her breath quickened, each evolutionary animal instinct on alert. Margaret stood awkwardly as she smoothed her tan slacks, fluffing her hair with her fingers and working it into place at her temples. Her mind was a complete blank. She moved out into the hallway and motioned for the woman to do so as well. She didn't want to wake Roger, didn't want this woman to see her husband incapacitated, or for her to see him at all, in fact. Margaret had wondered idly if Julia had come to visit her husband when she was back at the hotel. But she had kept the query to herself. She would not ask the nurses, would not debase herself or Roger by asking such an embarassing question.

"I . . . I was the one who called the ambulance for . . . for your husband." Julia looked extremely ill at ease, and she halted, almost snapping her jaw shut. Margaret wanted the woman to feel this discomfort, to experience just a fraction of the displacement she had felt for years now.

"I know exactly who you are," Margaret said simply. "I suppose I should thank you for your actions." Margaret wished she had showered, wished she had applied some lipstick. She must look awful. How should one look when meeting one's husband's mistress for the first time? she thought ironically.

The woman nodded and bowed her head. "I assumed you did."

"You were with him," said Margaret. She tried to keep her gaze even, her voice aloof, but she felt everything inside her tight and coiled. What in God's name had this Julia person come for? To be alone with him? What had she hoped to achieve? The absolute gall of this woman. She would not avert her eyes.

Julia nodded her assent.

"What is your purpose in coming?" asked Margaret sharply, her eyes narrowed.

"I understand from the nurses that Roger is going home shortly . . . that he's being transferred to a hospital near your home," Julia continued nervously. Margaret blinked, said nothing.

"I just wanted . . . I guess I wanted to say good-bye. I'm sorry, I hoped to come when you weren't here." Julia looked over Margaret's shoulder and into the room at Roger. For just a moment she took in the scene, his diminishment, the serene way he lay. Her eyes revealed nothing. Margaret crossed her arms over her chest. She was surprised how much a part of her was enjoying this.

"I'm so sorry that this happened." Julia appeared to be fading, running out of steam. She seemed suddenly smaller, as if her spine had shrunk.

"I'm staying with him," said Margaret.

"Of course. Of course you are. I just . . ."

"You just what?"

"I just wanted to see him," said Julia softly. "Honestly, I thought you might not be here this late. I didn't want to intrude on you. But if you have any questions, if there is anything you want to know . . . it must be awful to just get a call. I know . . . myself that it's awful to just get a call out of the blue like that . . ." She seemed to wilt after this last sentence. The nerve of this woman, her assumptions. She was pleased to see that her earlier confidence and determination had abandoned her.

"I know all about you," Margaret spat out with controlled fury. "And I know that you were just a dalliance to Roger. Some . . . distraction. A body he could hop into bed with. Nothing more." Her heart was galloping.

The woman's face crumpled as she absorbed Margaret's well-placed barbs and backed away toward the nurses' station. "I'm so sorry to have bothered you at all. I'm . . . I'm so sorry for your family." Julia turned on her heel and strode briskly down the hall toward the elevator bank. Margaret heard the receding clack of her heels on the linoleum. The feeling of quicksilver and adrenaline

that had coursed triumphantly through her veins in front of Julia
had begun to retreat. She turned and reentered Roger's room, adjusting his blankets and tucking his sheet under the mattress.
Margaret felt compelled to touch his face. Thank God he had not
woken up while that woman was there. She would not have known
how to endure that or what to do. She could not have witnessed the
look on his face as he took in her presence. It would have told her
things she didn't need to know.

"I'm here, Roger," she whispered to him in a maternal voice that
evoked pleasant memories of talking, singing, and cooing to her
babies. In those years she could touch them and possess them when
they slept in a way you never could when a body was awake and in
motion. Then she sat back in the aqua lounger and felt the first of a
series of tight sobs hit her. Margaret reached for the small travel
pack of Kleenex she kept in her handbag, aware that the nurses
could enter at any time. She sat back in the lounger, crying silently,
rocking back and forth in the chair to calm herself with the repeti-
tive motion.

33

Maura *was determined* not to let him flee this time. It was a cool night in the fickle heart of March, and while there were small patches of snow here and there, it had mostly disappeared from the lawn. Alex was under the tree out front, his head leaning against the base of the trunk. She sucked in her breath and studied him once more from the window before moving to the front foyer. Impulsively Maura yanked open the front door, and with the reflexes of a deer, the boy crouched to run.

"Stop," she called, with more urgency than she intended. He continued to rise, headed toward the road.

"Alex, please stop." The boy froze like a statue at the sound of his name and turned slowly toward her. She noted his broad shoulders, the streamlined musculature of an athlete. She could just make out his features in the soft light from the house, the fair hair and darker brows, the frightened eyes. In her mind, Maura had built him up to be some kind of evil force, but the person in front of her now was just a kid, scared and tentative, nervously clenching and unclenching his hands. There was barely enough of a beard to shave on his face. What, exactly, would she say to him now that she had diverted him? Was she really ready for this? Maura had acted so spontaneously and now she felt momentarily unsure.

"Hey," she offered, coming down the front porch steps to meet him, tugging her sweater tighter around her. "It's freezing out here. Why don't you come in?" Alex looked up at her uncertainly and she could see the trepidation in his eyes, the look of a child on the verge of being punished. He had gotten this far and now his fortitude seemed to be deserting him. She softened her voice. "I know you've been out there some nights. I watch you. I . . . I like to think of you as protecting us. Come on in. I'll make some hot chocolate, but you've got to come in." Maura smiled warmly in the threshold of the door.

"OK,"•Alex said awkwardly, looking down at the porch floorboards. She wondered if he were fighting the urge to run.

"Um . . . I'm uh . . . Alex Hulburd." He thrust out his hand.

"I know who you are." She propped the door with her hip and gestured him in. She was afraid to make a sudden movement, that it might startle him.

"Come on in."

Alex shoved his hands in his parka pockets, and she caught a faint whiff of smoke mixed with a vague minty smell as he stepped past her. In the front hall foyer the warmth of the house snaked around them when she closed the door, and Alex leaned against the staircase bannister, bending to untie his sneakers.

"You can keep them on," Maura said quickly, but he had already removed them. "Why don't you come into the kitchen? My daughter is asleep upstairs and Ryan is at a Boy Scout event. My husband, Pete, is out. But I think you knew that." She smiled knowingly over her shoulder as she led him down the hall.

"How about that hot chocolate?" she offered. "It's colder out there than I thought."

Alex nodded. He stood next to a kitchen stool at the counter, hands still shoved in his pockets. He unzipped his coat and she saw his thin T-shirt with the words STOP GLOBAL WEIRDING stamped on it. His hair was long in front, almost swept over his forehead like a mushroom cap, and she had the urge to reach out and brush it back into place.

"Hand me your coat and, please, sit." She drew her bulky white cable cardigan around her middle and took the kettle off the stove, leaning against the sink as she filled it with water, and then turned on the burner, her slippers scuffling on the wood floor. Maura folded her arms across her body, leaning against the counter, and then sat down on a stool across from him. Her mind was suddenly empty.

"I imagine all of this has been very hard for you," Maura began somewhat formally.

"Probably not like you, " he murmured. She was afraid he was about to cry.

"What have you been doing? How are your parents?"

"They're good. I think they're pretty disappointed in me." Alex choked back a sarcastic laugh as he said this.

"Your parents? Why?"

Alex hesitated for a moment. "I just told them I'm not going to college next year. I'm working part-time."

"Yeah?" She waited for him to speak.

"College isn't for me. Not right now. I got a part-time job at Lowe's over in Skokie." He looked down at his hands. "I want to make some money right now." Maura nodded.

The teakettle began to whistle softly at first and then built to a crescendo. They both turned to look at the stove, grateful for the interruption, and Maura rose. She pulled two mugs out of the cupboard and shook out the hot chocolate packets, adding the hot water and a splash of milk to cool and thicken it.

"Will you go to college eventually?" She met his eyes.

"Maybe."

"Why don't you want to go?" she asked simply. She sponged up a milk spill on the stone counter.

"I just can't see it." He wrapped his hands around the mug of hot chocolate when she pushed it forward. "I can't see myself carrying books around on one of those tree-lined campuses. My mom keeps sticking all of these brochures in my room with pictures of these smiling, happy people who all know what they want to be when they grow up." He flashed a quick, wry smile. "I don't . . . I don't . . ." He bent down to blow into the mug, swirling the hot chocolate with the force of his breath.

"Deserve it?" she finished. And when he met her eyes, she was sitting down again, looking at him hard. He flicked his gaze back down to the mug, where his finger was absentmindedly tracing a raised logo on the ceramic exterior.

"Maybe. Maybe not."

"Look, Alex. This right now . . . is hard. It's as hard for me maybe as it is for you. I don't know exactly why you've been out on my lawn some nights. You scared me at first, and then I figured out who you were. I know that you wanted to talk to me after James died and I wasn't ready for a long time. I'm . . . I'm impressed that you came here . . . that you came inside. It was a very brave thing to do. But I don't know if you want my forgiveness or for me to say that it isn't your fault . . ." Her voice trailed off. "There are so many things I feel about that day."

"I guess I don't exactly know why I'm here either," he said, somewhat gruffly.

"Alex." She paused to select what to say next. "The truth is that you were driving the car. We can't change that. You can't change that. But you didn't set out to kill James. You weren't looking away or driving too fast or . . ." Her voice had dropped to little more than a whisper and she stopped.

"I'm sorry," he said simply.

"Bad things happen." She looked up at him, and her eyes were shining, tears collecting in the corners. "It was an accident. He dashed out. And you just couldn't stop in time. And I couldn't save him." One big fat tear rolled down her cheek and splashed onto the counter. She quickly wiped it with her fingertip and stood to move to the sink, running her hands under the faucet for a moment.

"James's death was the result of a series of circumstances. The wrong place at the wrong time, me turning my attention away for just a second, you being on that stretch of road, the way those cars were parked in the street." Her voice faltered and then she steadied herself. "A day doesn't go by, not one, when I don't think about if I'd done something differently, just one little tweak, one moment changed. If I'd left five minutes earlier, if I hadn't turned away, or been distracted by the baby in the stroller or . . ."

"I looked away for a second . . . ," Alex said abruptly, with knitted brows. He cut his gaze back to his mug. Maura's head shot up suddenly at the admission. "I was reaching for an empty beer can from the night before, trying to grab it so my mom wouldn't find it. I took my eyes off the road for a few seconds when I reached down . . . I haven't told anyone else that." A sob escaped out of Alex's throat, low and achy.

Maura bent her head, her shoulders sagged slightly, and she looked down at her nails, picking the cuticle, looked up at him again and nodded. "You know, I looked away too, Alex. I . . . wasn't watching him. Not the way I should have been." Maura's eyes were dry, but her voice quavered. "I was looking at a text." She looked up with a forced smile, her own admission an olive branch.

"I didn't know what to do. I wrote you that letter, and my family stopped by the house. It was really good that Mr. Corrigan came over that day. I think it helped me and my folks a lot. But then I didn't know what else to do after that. I figured I would always be the last person you wanted to see." He was quiet for a few beats. "I did something horrible, and I can't fix it. And I guess I wanted you to know how bad that hurts."

They passed the next few minutes in silence, neither one uncomfortable with the lack of conversation. She thought about James at Alex's age, what it might be like to sit in this kitchen with her own son instead of a stranger. Maura had once believed she might be capable of hating Alex Hulburd forever, and yet the passage of time and her growing acceptance of loss had declawed her. In such proximity to the boy who had killed her son, she was instead drawn to his vulnerability, her maternal compass stirred. They were each nursing a hurt in similar ways, she understood, and for different reasons. A shadow flitted darkly over them both.

The constant *click, click, click* of the kitchen wall clock seemed to expand in volume as they sipped their hot chocolate. It was Alex who broke the silence.

"Do you . . . do you believe in God?" He looked at her directly.

Maura sat still, forming her answer. "I do. I want to believe that somebody else is in charge, that there is an order to all this chaos." She looked up with a half laugh. "But I'm really pissed off at *HIM* right now." Alex grinned, visibly relieved.

"I read something once," she began. "About the Holocaust. Someone asked a rabbi how he could believe in God after what had happened to the people in the concentration camps. His answer was that God never promised that life wouldn't bring pain or suffering. He never told us life would be fair. He just promised to love us and walk beside us during the journey. I think about that sometimes when I get angry that this happened to my family. And I guess it makes me feel a little better on some days."

"So where do you think you go when you die?" Alex asked.

"I guess I'd like to think that a part of you sticks around. Watching. Protecting, like a guardian angel. I had a dream once that James was doing that. I'd like to believe in angels," said Maura softly.

Alex nodded but was silent.

"But I think you go somewhere really beautiful," offered Maura suddenly. "Somewhere very different from where we are now. I want it to be someplace so much better and easier and less weighed down than life here on earth."

"I'd like to believe in heaven, but I'm not sure I believe in God," said Alex in a measured voice. "I want to. But I don't."

"It's a hard concept to get your head around . . . believing in something you can't see." Maura nodded. "Especially when you witness so much evil in the world. There are no good reasons why babies die and moms get cancer and people go hungry. Some folks try to tell you that things happen for a reason, but I don't believe that." Maura was quiet for a moment, collecting herself. "There is no good reason why people you love get taken from you. No grand plan that I can see. I don't think anyone is up there moving the tiny chess pieces around." Alex nodded solemnly.

"But I do think just the everyday living is easier if you believe in something bigger than yourself." She opened her mouth and then shut it, taking a gulp of the cooled hot chocolate instead. Maura paused, considering her words, and suddenly looked up at Alex, brows furrowed.

"I've never really told anyone this except my family. But what I saw, what Pete and I saw, brings me the only real comfort I have. It makes it a tiny bit easier." Maura drew in a breath, and Alex sat perfectly still.

"At the end . . . in the hospital, James knew we were there. At least *I* believe he did. He would sometimes open his eyes or turn his head toward our voices. I know he heard us." Maura shot a quick look at Alex.

"And right before he passed from this world, he saw something so utterly amazing, so beautiful, that he was actually reaching toward it with his hands, like he was trying to grasp it or to catch something. And he was smiling. Even in all that pain and medication he was smiling." Tears brimmed in Maura's eyes as she kept speaking. Alex looked down, blinking. When his eyes surfaced, there were tears swimming in them.

"It was a pretty amazing thing to witness, but it was also sort of terrifying. A big part of me didn't want him to go to whatever it was he saw. I wanted him to stay right here with us. But as his mother, I also could see his excitement. There was so much broken inside my little boy that I knew his life here on earth would be . . .

different . . . painful. If he even recovered." Maura shifted on her stool and studied Alex's expression. He was completely absorbed with what she was saying.

"You know, I remember a few years ago when I was talking with James about heaven. He stopped me and told me to 'talk about something else.' When I asked him why, he said it made his heart sad to think that his dad and I would go someplace that he wouldn't be able to visit. He said, 'I don't want to think about when you die 'cause I never want to be without you.' Those were his exact words." Tears distorted Maura's vision as she smiled at Alex. "But that thing that he saw? I know it was more wonderful than any place or vision you or I can imagine. I know this because I saw it on his face. It was the very first time in his life he ever truly wanted to go somewhere without me. He had absolutely no fear at the end, almost like he knew the answer to a secret. That was where he wanted to go." Maura stopped, and a little moan left her throat. Two teardrops fell onto the counter, and she absentmindedly blotted them with a napkin.

Tears now filled Alex's eyes and spilled down his face. He let them come unabashedly at first and then swiped them off his cheeks with the sleeve of his faded blue sweatshirt.

"I miss him more than you can imagine," said Maura softly. "Some days I think I'll just simply implode. But if I have a tiny bit of peace, it's in remembering that moment. James saw where he was going next. And it was a good place."

Maura blew her nose into the napkin and brushed her hair back behind her ears. She leaned forward and reached out impulsively, closing both of her hands over the top of Alex's one as it lay cupped on the kitchen counter. Alex looked up gratefully and met her gaze. They sat in silence for a few moments, two people bound intrinsically together by a shared tragedy. Maura understood then that he too would never be the same. The loss of James had connected them in immutable ways, and yet she could not have fathomed the solace she felt in simply sitting here with Alex. It was an unexpected gift.

"Thanks. Thanks for telling me about that," he finally croaked in a gravelly voice. And he looked down as she pulled her hand away and stirred, rising to set her mug in the sink. Alex cleared his throat.

"So I guess I'd better start working on the God thing." Alex reached to lighten the moment for them both. And Maura laughed, clearing his mug and lowering it into the sink next to hers.

She turned to him with renewed energy in her voice. "Do you want to see his room?"

Alex looked up and blinked twice. "Yeah." He nodded. "Yeah, I'd like that."

Maura entered first at the top of the stairs. She observed Alex as he stepped into James's room and began examining the objects, the baseball trophies and medals on ribbons, the small rectangular bulletin board on the wall, an elementary school reading program certificate. The neatness of the room magnified its emptiness.

Alex picked up a toy rifle leaning against the bookshelf in the corner.

"I had an Airsoft gun just like this when I was his age."

"He loved playing with that around the neighborhood."

"You know, I'm thinking about joining the army," he blurted out suddenly.

"Really? That's a big deal. Wow. The army."

He nodded. "There's a guy I work with at Lowe's on the weekends. Dante. He was over in Iraq. He's, like, twenty-four and he's got this sick tattoo on his arm, this skull and snake symbol from intense stuff that happened over there. He's talked to me about what it's like, stuff he did. I don't know, it just sounds like it might be for me." He met her eyes, and she noticed that in between the hazel color were little flecks of gold.

"Do your folks know?"

"I haven't really told anyone yet. I just talked to the recruiter in Chicago last week. I'm still . . . I guess I'm still making the final decision." He set the rifle gently back down against the bookcase.

"Do you have family in the military?' Maura asked carefully.

"Nope," said Alex.

"What do you think your parents will say?"

Alex smiled ruefully for a moment. "They're probably going to freak out when I tell them. I don't think they have any idea." He was thoughtful for a moment. "But maybe they'll be glad to get me out of the house." Maura winced. She hadn't spent much time thinking about Alex's life. She considered what the Hulburd household must feel like, the tensions and disappointment, the ache his parents must feel and the stain that his actions had brought upon all of them in some way.

"Even though the wars are winding down it sure seems like it's a mess over there, in Afghanistan. Are you scared you might be sent there?" Maura said.

"A little. But I'll be ready," said Alex.

"And why the army?"

"The army?" Alex smiled. "My friend Dante says it's the best job you'll ever hate." He laughed nervously and then turned serious. "I guess I like what I hear about it being a brotherhood. You go through basic training with a bunch of people and you get deployed as a unit. You belong together, you watch their backs, and they watch yours. I like that, I guess." Maura inclined her head slightly, studying him.

"Dante talks about going back. He says being over there was the most alive he ever felt." Alex paused for a second. "Plus, he says that girls can't resist the uniform." Maura chuckled and Alex responded with a smile, lightening the energy of the room.

Downstairs Alex grabbed his parka and put on his yellow and blue running shoes. He stood awkwardly by the front door and thrust his hand out. Maura grabbed it with both of hers and pulled him closer, throwing one arm around him in an awkward half-hug. As she opened the front door, a blast of cool air flumed into the foyer.

"Do you worry about dying if you go over there? Do you think about that?" Maura said softly. The abruptness of the question halted him. The obvious fact that he was choosing to put himself in harm's way, whatever the motivation, hung between them.

Alex turned and looked her straight in the eye before he bent his head to zip up his parka. "All the time," he said, stepping over the threshold and out the door. "I think about dying all the time."

34

O ut of the corner of one eye, Margaret watched her husband bring the oversize plastic spoon to his lips, and as he opened his mouth, half of the cottage cheese fell off. Now that Roger was home from the rehab hospital, he was getting stronger, more capable, little by little. But it was painful to watch how slowly he moved, the times the spoon fell from his grip or the food plopped back onto the plate.

Roger followed her with his eyes, expectantly, as she moved from the kitchen sink to clear his plate. His look reminded her of a puppy that needed to go outside, the unconditional dependency and devotion that could feel, at inconvenient moments, like a millstone. She smiled back at him with the expression she had once reserved for children during mealtime, the maternal satisfaction of tending to your loved one's elementary needs.

The odd feeling of having Roger all to herself was both satisfying and frightening. He looked up at her in a dully expectant way that both fulfilled her and broke her heart. He was able to walk, slowly, with an uneven gait, but he was walking. It was more the fine motor coordination that was hard. She'd watched him try to write his name the other day, and she'd had to turn away. The stroke had impaired movement on the right side of his body, and he was right-handed. The therapist had told them it was hard going to teach yourself to eat with your left hand and retrain your body to use the nondominant side, but it was entirely possible. The corner of Roger's mouth still drooped, making it difficult for him to enunciate words crisply.

Margaret was bone tired. The adrenaline she'd felt initially in Florida by his bedside, the constant checking and waiting for him to come out of it, had evaporated. That heightened vigilance had taken its toll. She had been so relieved when Erin had arrived to help move him home, far away from that town and from anything that had to do with Julia Rolon. Margaret had done everything she could to protect the girls from learning the circumstances of Roger's stroke and the existence of that woman.

Maura had almost uncovered something when one of the nurses talked about the family member she had met when their dad was brought in, the same one who had visited at night once or twice. Her daughter had looked puzzled and questioned what the nurse meant, said she must have been mistaken, and Margaret had firmly interjected, claiming there had been no such family member.

"I think it was someone from the hotel who accompanied your father behind the ambulance," Margaret quickly corrected, giving the nurse a marble stare as she retreated.

No good could come from the children discovering Julia's existence. It would only crack the foundation of the pedestal they'd all placed him on. They'd had a good childhood, with two loving parents, and now they had their own lives, their own families. Seeing their father incapacitated like this was hard enough. Besides, thought Margaret, the connection to Julia had been effectively severed; at least she assumed it had. How would Roger even reach her? He could barely punch in the numbers for a phone call and certainly couldn't work a computer. No, presumably, all of that was behind them now. Still, the image of the overripe, tentative woman standing in her husband's hospital room left a dry coppery taste in her mouth. A Hispanic person no less. All that Latin blood, no wonder Roger had been bamboozled. Oh, she looked demure enough when she had introduced herself, but Margaret could smell the wantonness coming off her, the vulgarity in those full rouged lips. She probably had a drawer of frilly lingerie, all the window dressing that would appeal to Roger but none of the substance.

She thought of her old Roger, so full of himself and in command. She loved the way he entered public places—restaurants, the country club knowing that he cut a fine figure, understanding that people's eyes fell pleasingly on him. Margaret tortured herself, imagining him laughing with Julia, loudly preordering dessert soufflés before the meal, or the "top shelf" liquor. She envisioned him steering Julia through a room with his hand on the small of her back, the things he did with her.

What would the precious Julia think now? Would she have the fortitude to minister to this new Roger, this diminished person? Would she have wanted to stick around for this part of the bargain?

Now that Roger was home from the rehab hospital, Margaret was assuming multiple roles: wife, caregiver, cheerleader, coach, teacher, attendant, and yet she had been surprised by how the sheer tactile experience of touching him and going through the simple physical rehab exercises together could fulfill her, give her a renewed purpose. It was rewarding to be needed in sometimes physical ways that gladdened her husband's life. But on the other hand, his recovery was not the arc of a child learning. On other days she viewed it for what it was, the slow and often frustrating process of relearning and stumbling, measuring improvements in tiny increments. There were days when she could not help but feel that their world together had completely unraveled and collapsed around her.

When Roger had first come home, the girls and Stu had helped her move him into the downstairs guest bedroom so that he didn't have to tackle the steps. She'd changed the bedding and set up the first-floor bathroom with all of his toiletries. For now, Margaret still chose to sleep upstairs in their bed. It gave her a sense of comfort, and of course, sleep was everything if she were to maintain the strength to care for her husband. Erin had given her a set of baby monitors in case Roger needed her in the middle of the night, but the crackling noise they made had disturbed her, like a ghost in the machine, and so she'd left them unplugged.

There was a big part of her that desired to sleep next to Roger. But the exhausted part of her relished the nights she didn't have to push on his shoulder for snoring too loudly or shrink into one corner of the bed while he sprawled across the rest of it. She'd move him back upstairs eventually, but she'd have to see how it progressed. It would take time, they had all told her. But it had been almost four months since Roger's stroke. This was a process, a marathon, and not a sprint, all of the therapists constantly reminded her. She was sick of that glib phrase.

Margaret thought about her past ambitions for traveling in their retirement. Were they all out the window now? Years earlier, she had started a file of newspaper and magazine clips detailing places she'd like to see—sightseeing destinations, places of historical value. Occasionally she had flipped through the clippings, a roundup of the best Alaskan cruises, a tour of Venice, and an expensive African safari. Would Roger ever be able to manage that kind of active travel now? The doctors had told her that although recoveries inched along, many things were possible. But lately she'd been bumping up against the creeping reality of his limitations, her spirits and adrenaline flagging with the recalibration of her expectations.

Margaret still had a few more changes to make around the house. Pete had installed a bar in the shower for Roger, and he knew a man who could build a ramp in the back if his balance didn't improve. She might have to get to that too. The thought of overseeing those details exhausted her.

Roger had finished the pudding and set his head back in the den chair, dozing off. They had worked him hard in rehab today. She liked his young physical therapist, Shane, who wore a silver hoop earring in one ear and some kind of shaggy haircut. Stu had explained to her that this was called a mullet. The kids had told her that earrings in men no longer meant you were gay when she'd commented about that. They were just a statement, Erin had said. She smiled, remembering how both of her daughters had worked to convince her to get her own ears pierced.

"Over my dead body" is what she had always told them. "Putting holes in your skin is for savages," she had joked. But in the end, she had let them take her to the jewelry store in town where the salesclerk used a gun to pierce her ears with two tiny gold studs. Margaret groped at her own lobes now involuntarily, fondling her small flower-shaped diamond and pearl earrings. Lately, she'd been so tired that she'd often forgotten those little touches she always took pride in—bracelets, a scarf, some of the accessories she knew made the difference between letting yourself go and presenting your best self.

This morning Margaret had simply picked up her clothes from the chair where she'd tossed them the night before. She'd had every intention of going to a stretch class at the Y, but her own inertia had kept her in the kitchen too long, and when she glanced up at the clock it was 9:35. She had already missed the beginning of class. She felt snappish and spent, although it wasn't yet noon. For the last week there had been faint bluish smudges under her eyes. Instead of exercising, Margaret longed to smoke a cigarette, to walk back behind her fallow garden into the early spring air and locate the pack in the garden shed. She'd ratcheted up the number she allowed herself these days, and Maura had commented that she smelled smoke on her recently when she leaned in to hug her good-bye. Margaret had felt compelled to make up some line about being in a gas station, and her daughter had looked at her knowingly.

"Mmmmmmfffffpphhhhh." Sitting upright in the lounger, Roger

let out a gasp of air in his sleep that was part snore, part unintelligible, and she sighed, studying him. He had spontaneously clasped her fingers yesterday and held them, and Margaret had been surprised at how soft his hands were now, like a woman's. The previous roughness, the natural calluses from simply being out in the world, had been smoothed away to a delicate peach flesh in his captivity.

"Maaaaargaret . . ." He was calling her ten minutes later, after his catnap. His yowling voice, with the slight slur, the inability to fully form the words with his lips, was grating at times. You never really thought about the cadence of speech or the crispness of language until that was tinkered with. Now the sound of his voice was a heartbreak to her, harsh and imperfect.

Margaret sighed and dried her hands on the tea towel by the sink. She was not herself today, something was off, and she was bristling at the sainted role of caregiver. Pouring a glass of juice for Roger, she headed toward the den, pausing in the threshold to view him. Even with all of these months of coming to terms with his stroke, she was still brought up short by the sight of his diminishment. A part of her half expected to see his old, robust self each time she rounded the corner. Despite his facial droop, the outline of his profile from this good side was still so handsome, his jaw strong and his eyes bright. Tears welled suddenly in the corners of her eyes. What if she had lost him the way they had lost James? That would have been more than one family could bear. What if Roger weren't here right now? She'd had those thoughts so often lately, twinned with the cavernous sadness of James's death. They bubbled up and intertwined at the oddest moments.

And then the opposite feeling. A backlash of bitterness; anger that this had happened to him, to them, the randomness of the stroke and the accident that caused her grandson's death. Margaret felt an overall sensation of blackness and despair tug her down. She thought about all of the time Roger had squandered with Julia, how many days and nights he had chosen a stranger's company instead.

But it was larger that that. She had been harboring the growing feeling of being defeated, cheated out of this promised rich phase of life with Roger. She hated when these ugly feelings welled up inside of her and abnegated all of her mental progress and positive thoughts. And yet today, fatigued and churlish, she felt powerless to stop them.

Margaret entered the den to hand the juice cup to Roger, who brought it slowly and deliberately to his lips with both hands. He removed the straw to drink directly from the cup, and as he took a long sip, a dribble ran down his chin. The numbness on his face prevented him from feeling it, and Margaret moved to dab at his wet chin with the tea towel over her shoulder, swooping down to grab the almost empty glass.

"There you go," said Margaret with forced gaiety.

"Thankssss." Roger looked up at her standing beside him. "But I'm not done. You donnn't have to wait."

"You dropped two yesterday, Roger." She could hear her schoolmarm tone.

"I cannn take care of myssself." His expression was a combination of wounded and rebellious. Something stretched and brittle, deep inside of Margaret, shattered.

"Maybe you'd rather Julia do this for you," she uttered with a sudden fury. "Julia Rolon." The words were out of her mouth with an elastic snap before she could snatch them back.

Roger sat back slowly in his chair, stung. His face roiled with various emotions from surprise to fear before fixing into a glum glare. He dropped his head, which made the slack side of his face hang loosely. She had injured him, and she had certainly ambushed him. Still, he said nothing.

"I'm . . . I'm . . . sssorry. I'm sorry." His tone was deferential and when he finally looked back up, his eyes were wet and pleading.

Margaret's stance softened. She uncrossed her arms and moved to sit in the stuffed chair next to him.

"You thought I had no idea," she said flatly. "That woman came to the hospital one night early on. Julia. She's attractive, Roger. I'll give you that. I understand what you saw in her." Roger remained quiet, contrite. "She told me she was coming to say good-bye. She was obviously hoping to find you awake, and I told her to leave. You didn't need anyone else."

"I nnnever . . ."

"Roger." Margaret raised her hand to silence him and closed her eyes. The bracelet with the engraved birthdate silhouette charms, representing each of her children and grandchildren, jangled at her wrist.

"I don't want to rehash this. I don't want to know right now how you met or how many times. The last thing I need is to torture myself with images and information. Maybe I'll ask you to tell me everything at some point, but right now I take comfort in the fact that it's over. I told Julia that you were through with her—that you won't be contacting her again." He nodded, and tears zigzagged through the stubble on his lower face. "I love you, Roger. I know I'm not perfect, not by any means. But we've built a life together and it's supporting you now. We are all supporting you, everyone who loves you."

"I looove you, Marrrhgret," he choked, his upper body heaving now in irregular convulsions, and then he gradually calmed, as if something inside had broken and annealed. He looked up in anguish, and she bent to kiss him. Roger reached to cradle her head, and they stayed that way, not speaking or moving for a few moments. Then Margaret pulled away, patted his hand, and grabbed the juice glass, carrying it back to the kitchen wordlessly, as an almost imperceptible smile flitted across her lips.

35

The movie had been only mediocre. There were so many special effects and quick camera shots, some of the dialogue felt rushed and the jokes fell flat. But Maura had chosen an action adventure for Pete. In the multiplex lobby, Pete took her hand, and they filed out into the parking lot past the line of people waiting to purchase tickets. She thought for a moment about checking in with the sitter, but she figured no news was good news. They deserved this night out, and they'd be home soon enough. She was still adjusting to the unencumbered feeling of being alone with her husband without the kids. This was an official date.

"Where to for dinner?"

"How about some place easy? Pizza or a salad, something like that," she answered.

After they'd ordered and discussed the movie's convoluted thriller plot for all of five minutes, they settled into the usual patter of reviewing work, news, and the kids. Maura was pleased to see Pete taking his time nursing a single beer.

"So tell me more about the kid coming over. Alex. You only gave me the big details yesterday and I want to know more."

"Well, I saw him out on the porch, maybe working up his nerve, and I just invited him in. I didn't have any warning." Maura took a sip of her wine. "I think I shocked myself. I had no idea what I was going to say, and for a few moments I couldn't think of anything intelligent at all." She still couldn't bring herself to tell Pete about Alex's previous visits to the lawn, his unofficial role for months as night watchman on the evenings she was home alone.

"What *did* you say?" asked Pete. "What did he want? The timing seems a little weird that he would wait all these months."

"I'm not sure exactly. To meet me I guess. We talked for a while, I asked him why he had come."

"And what did he tell you?"

"He wanted to make it right, something like that. He wanted to tell me how badly he felt that this had happened. He'd said he had been wanting to do this for a while." She paused. "I . . . I really liked him, Pete. I was so prepared to hate him, and I didn't." They both sat for a second, watching the votive candle flicker in the center of the table.

"Took some guts," said Pete.

"Yeah."

"So, it was good that he came? Were you OK after he left?" Pete tenderly probed.

"Obviously, I've thought about him over the months. But I didn't ever want to think about how this affected him, you know? How it all wrecked his life too. I was relieved when you went over to meet him and his parents for both of us. Back then, that was enough for me, for us. In my mind he was just plain guilty, or evil, and he had hurt us.

"The last thing I wanted to think about was forgiveness or any of that. We were going through too much as a family. And then when he showed up on the door, it really hit me how much he was hurting too, that he was just a boy. I know that sounds silly, but you were right. He's just a kid."

Pete nodded and Maura slipped her foot out of her pump and hooked it around her husband's ankle as he looked up in surprise. The remains of their pizza were cold, and the restaurant was thinning out. There were one or two tables left on their side of the room.

"He even looks young for his age," said Maura. "Did I tell you he said he's not going to college? He said he wants to enlist in the military."

Pete looked up, his eyebrows raised. "That's a big move. How old is he?"

"Eighteen. Nineteen maybe? I guess he doesn't need his parents' permission. I got the sense that he was trying it out on me. Sounds like he hasn't made a final decision, I don't know. There's some guy where he works at Lowe's who's a veteran, and he's been telling Alex stories, maybe giving him encouragement."

"Hey, maybe it will be the best thing for him. I can't imagine being him right now in a town like this, everyone talking about college and the future. And he's had a rough year, all the neighbors staring at him, judging him for the accident. Maybe he just needs a clean break. He needs a shot at a place to define himself away from everything that he's grown up with," said Pete. "It might put his head back on straight."

"I can't imagine what his parents must feel. I wonder if they have any idea."

"Not a lot of kids from this town enlist, that's for sure," said Pete. He raised his glass and drained the remains of his beer, signaling the waiter for the check.

"Do you think he's punishing himself?" Maura asked.

Pete cocked his head, considering this. "He's been through a lot," said Pete. "Maybe this is how he feels he can pay some kind of debt, make it right. I don't know all the psychological mumbo jumbo." The check arrived and he pulled out his credit card, squinting at the figures on the bill and hastily scribbling a tip.

"Would you let Ryan go to war if he told you he wanted to be a soldier?" she asked idly.

"If he were an adult, I guess there wouldn't be much we could really say, right?" Pete set the billfold back down on the table with the pen and pushed his chair back. "I imagine a parent has a choice to either get on board with your kid's decision, and, if you chose not to, maybe you risk losing them twice." They were both quiet, gathering their coats and her purse.

"Still, I can't imagine," said Maura. "All those years you raise a child and try to keep them safe, and then they volunteer to walk into a war zone. That's hard stuff for any parent, no matter how patriotic you are." Pete took her arm without comment as they stepped out into the street and toward their parked car.

The children were asleep when they returned home, and after Pete came back from driving the sitter, they made love in an unhurried, familiar way. Lying next to her husband before they drifted off, Maura had the satisfying sensation of a loop being drawn in, the sense of something gradually inching back together.

. . .

"Mom, you should try the crab cakes here," Erin urged. "And then, of course, I can have a bite."

"I was thinking about the pasta primavera," mused Jen, studying the list of specials clipped to the Spartan menu. "Any good?"

"At a place called Caprice?" Maura joked. "You'd better be able to make pasta," and they had all laughed. Looking around the table at her daughters and daughter-in-law, Margaret could almost believe for a moment that nothing had changed, as if they were enjoying a meal out on a random day in the time before their worlds had upended.

The girls in the family were treating her to lunch for her birthday at a trendy downtown restaurant. It was one of those austere foodie places that Margaret assumed Roger had regularly taken clients to, all chrome, glass, and muted grays. The walls held only black-and-white photographs, minimalist close-ups of industrial-looking machinery. Looking at the oversize white ceramic plates of the other diners, she was amused to note that the portions of the appetizers were the size of her thumb.

Margaret was touched that Jen had taken a day off teaching and driven over from Milwaukee. This was a day off in Erin's part-time schedule and Maura had gotten a babysitter in the middle of the week, all to pry her out of the house. She had taken care with her appearance, choosing one of her bright silk shirtdresses, upgrading her handbag, and selecting a lipstick to match her red leather belt. At the last minute Margaret had impulsively plucked the ruby and gold bracelet Roger had given her for their twenty-fifth wedding anniversary from her jewelry box. She'd even put in hot rollers this morning, and Roger had joked that she must be "looking for a new husband." They had both laughed at that. Today, surrounded by the cheerful, attentive faces of her family, Margaret felt festive and loved.

She had to admit that her children were right. Getting out of the house more was the tonic she needed, a welcome break. It was good to see the girls' smiling faces, especially Maura. She had gained back some of the weight, and there was color in her cheeks. She'd gotten a haircut recently, and Margaret admired how her thick dark hair fell in a blunt cut just below the collar of her white wool blazer. Two gold-knotted studs gleamed from her ears. She was making an effort again, caring enough to rifle through her closet for something other than jeans. The restaurant was on the top floor of one of the city's skyscrapers, and the view of downtown Chicago and out across the Gold Coast and Lake Michigan in late spring was magnificent. Each of their eyes strayed continually to the window.

"I feel like I'm on top of the world," said Erin, raising her glass for a toast. "Happy birthday, Mom."

"Happy birthday," they all echoed, and Margaret beamed, dipping her head modestly in acknowledgment.

"Next time you all need to come to Milwaukee for brats and beer," joked Jen, with a sweeping gesture around her and out at the lake. "This is a little bit fancier than where I usually go with my girlfriends for birthday lunches," and they had all laughed. Talk turned to the kids and summer vacation plans and then the waitress interrupted with the appetizers, refilling wineglasses all around.

"Dad seems better," Maura offered tentatively, digging into a seafood salad. "Don't you think, Mom?"

"I do. I really do think so," Margaret answered somewhat tentatively. "It's slow but gradual. You can probably track it better than me. I see him every day." She wiped a smear of tartar sauce off her lips with her cloth napkin and then took a sip of her chardonnay. Grasping the long graceful stem of the wineglass made her feel elegant. Margaret thought to herself how much Roger would enjoy this restaurant, how little they had socialized since he had been home.

"What do his therapists say?" asked Erin. "About how he is doing?"

"Well. Just that, pretty much," said Margaret. "They tell you that it's slow but that progress is being made. The brain has the ability to rewire itself and find new routes for the parts that were damaged by the stroke. "

"He was walking pretty well without the cane when I was over the other day," said Maura.

"Oh, I'm very proud of your father. There's no doubt he's coming along. But he's much more sure of himself inside the house than outside." She cut the crab cake with the tines of her fork, her expression guarded.

"How is his state of mind?" asked Erin. "How's his mood?"

"Well, it's all gradually improving, I guess. There was a while there I was a little worried about his spirits," said Margaret with a forced lilt in her voice that belied her true emotion. She was aware of how important it was to be positive for the sake of her daughters. They were grown women, and yet she wondered if her instinct would forever be to protect them, to soften truths.

"What about his job?" asked Jen. Her skin was almost translucent, and she kept her chestnut hair short, almost boyish. Jen rarely wore makeup and favored large chunky jewelry.

"Well, you know they've given him a six-month leave. That happened instantly. And actually many of the partners have been over to visit since we've been back from Florida. But you know, your father had begun to talk about retirement before the stroke. He had been saying this deal in Tampa might be his last big one."

"Really?" said Maura, arching her brows in surprise. "I thought Dad never wanted to retire. Wasn't he the one always going on about how they would have to drag him out of there kicking and screaming?"

"Well, people's perspectives change," Margaret said demurely. "There are lots of other things your father wants to do in life." She reached for a pumpernickel roll in the basket at the center of the table and then passed it to Jen.

They all nodded politely, each of them intrinsically understanding that Roger would likely never return to work, never be able to assume the career he'd held before. Margaret only hoped he would be capable of swinging a golf club and hitting the ball again. Without that, she knew, his life would be even more circumscribed.

36

Maura had anticipated the arrival of this day with dread. The one-year anniversary of James's death. Pete had no interest in creating some formality or ceremony that would highlight the loss to Sarah and Ryan all over again. In the end they had chosen to mark the day quietly and in their separate ways. She would visit the gravesite. But Pete hated the cemetery and had been there only twice in the year since James had died. He had told her he planned to go to early Mass at the church near his office and light a candle before work. They would have a family dinner at home, maybe share their memories of James and open some photo albums. One year. It was a minute and it was a vast chasm. Maura could still mostly conjure up her son's voice in her head. She could imagine his hug. But other things were fading, and that made her panicky. She had walked into his room this morning before anyone else was up and stood, still as stone, as if calling up a spell to bring him back.

After she dropped Ryan off at school, Maura took Sarah to the classroom and headed straight to the cemetery. At the entrance, wilting horse chestnut blossoms swirled up from the black asphalt like flakes of snow as the car passed. Inside the grounds, the shoots and buds flexed their June muscles in verdant greens, and the whorling pattern of recently cut grass swirled between the headstones.

When she opened the car door, Rascal jumped out immediately

before she could leash him. His foot had only a slight drag now when he was tired, traces of his former disc issue. He stayed fairly close off the leash, sniffing at the clumps of wild onion that had pushed up near the hedges and borders of the grounds. Maura had no idea if dogs were allowed, but Rascal had just as much right as anyone else to be here at the cemetery today. When she reached James's plot, she placed the small bouquet of backyard lilacs to the side of the stone and dropped to her knees, murmuring a prayer. Rascal sidled up quietly and nosed her hand, as if looking for a treat.

Closing her eyes, Maura could see the sunlight through her lids, and she concentrated with all of her focus on talking to James, to God, to anyone up there who might be listening in this hushed expanse on the fringe of summer. Her visits here had decreased in the last few months. Early on it was as if she'd been drawn to this plot, tugged by an elemental need. But in the past six months she had come less frequently.

She cried less easily than she had a year ago. All of the emotion was still present, still palpable, but it had tunneled down deeper inside her to find its own quieter place to reside. That was progress, she thought wryly. She could tap into the pain instantly, but it didn't reside on the surface as much, didn't linger in every pore and follicle.

Maura's thoughts settled briefly on her parents, the extreme stress and heartache they had been through. But her father's stroke and subsequent health struggles were at least a part of the natural order of the universe. She had always assumed that her parents' deaths would be the first difficult milestone of loss in her life. It was so out of sequence to bury a child. Maura knew she would never really come to terms with that.

Of her two parents, Maura had always been closest to her father. As a teenager she had regularly sought his advice and even selectively confided in him about boyfriends and broken hearts. When she had tried her first cigarette and later, in college, smoked her first joint, Maura had ultimately felt compelled to tell him, despite her fear of his judgment. She couldn't articulate why. But he had only nodded, listening. When she had finished recounting her experiences or pouring out her heart, Roger would say, "Some things in life you have to find out firsthand. Just as long as you stay true to yourself. Don't ever let anyone else tell you what you have to do. You know in here." And he would always thump his heart with his fist.

Her father had been a rudder, especially after James's death. To see his life force bifurcated, his speech slurred and his movements still jerky, pained her. Her mother was the lodestar, ceaselessly moving forward, caring for her, caring for them all. Maura understood that her sense of duty and devotion was perhaps the greatest form of love.

She recalled the afternoon at her father's bedside, two days after his stroke. He had still been comatose, but the tubes and the monitors, the abject familiarity of her time in the hospital with James, had put her in a kind of anxious dream state, as if she were stepping out of her own body. It was as if her father, lying completely still, eyes closed, were an older effigy of James.

Up to this point, neither she nor her siblings had spent any time thinking about the inevitable period in midlife when the roles of children and parent begin to slowly reverse. That aspect of the future, which had seemed light-years ahead, had suddenly jumped out and spooked them all. In such a short span, she, Erin, and Stu had gone from nurtured to protectors, from children to advocates. Maura understood now with clarity that was how life worked; the fulcrum of responsibility ultimately tipped.

She wondered, the way anyone who has ever swallowed loss wonders, if she would again experience pure joy, or if those unadulterated moments of happiness that were so abundant in her younger years would now always carry an echo of sadness and nostalgia. And yet she marveled how with time the absolutely unbearable had slithered into shock and then mellowed in to a commingling of sorrow and even poignancy. They had all been crawling forward somehow.

Incongruously, the bezeled edge of a whitewashed ghost moon was set in the daytime sky like a hologram. Maura studied it for a few minutes and then closed her eyes, ending her visit to the cemetery as she always did, head bowed, lips mouthing the Lord's Prayer. She added the Apostle's Creed for her parents and conjured up an image of Roger, before the stroke, robust and full of life.

Maura reached her palm out to steady herself against the cool granite of the gravestone before rising to go. The early summer leaves were just shy of their peak. Spring had taken so long to arrive, and she thought about what she had been doing at this exact time last year. This had been the turning point, the day that marked her before and after. One moment she had been walking along a sidewalk, with three beautiful children, and two healthy parents, giddy with the flush of lust. All the Corrigans had been whole, complete. And the next moment everything had crumbled, in an instant.

A whole year. Maura kissed her fingertips and reached to touch his headstone one last time. They'd marked progress in this past year, all of them. There was laughter in the house again, a sense of family reorganized, reconfigured. And she and Pete were making strides too, she thought warmly. They'd need to keep working the rough parts, but their shared history and longevity had counted for something. There were so many different kinds of love, she thought, so many mutations.

Headed back toward the car, through a set of iron gates, Rascal followed dutifully behind her, and Maura pulled out the short grocery list in her pocket and studied it, stuffing it away again. Perhaps she would shop later on with Sarah in tow. This time alone right now on such a sacred day would be spent on her terms.

She had a feeling, as she always did when she pulled out of the cemetery and merged with traffic on the double-lane road, of leaving something important behind. It was an incompletion, the sense of missing a piece of her, of leaving a place that comforted you and broke your heart all at once.

Maura drove by the supermarket and through the center of town and then, on the spur of the moment, emboldened by the significance of the day, she turned down Hawthorne Street, headed toward the very spot where James had been hit. Over the past year she had done everything possible to avoid the spring-loaded memories on this stretch of the neighborhood, but on the one-year anniversary of his death, it seemed important to face down this last demon.

There was nothing remarkable about the spot, nothing to distinguish exactly where it had happened, although of course she remembered. And now here she was, in front of the Carlinos' house, where everything terrible had unfolded in a split second. Maura slowed and drew in her breath. She pulled the car to the curb and turned off the engine, closing her eyes to let the memories of that day come. She had pushed the exact sequence of events out of her mind for so long and built a berm around the truth. In the wake of all the horrible things that had transpired, she had almost convinced herself of a different and more benign version of what had really happened.

· · ·

It had all begun with a picnic. Art had packed the lunch, buying prepared foods from a specialty market near his apartment, and he'd iced a few beers in a small plastic cooler. As Maura began her drive to the beach to meet him, she could taste the elation that accompanies sharp anticipation and the desire to savor it.

Maura could picture exactly what she had been wearing that day. She had chosen it carefully, a floral sundress and a white cotton cardigan to buffer the winds from the lake. The sun was warm, and they had spread a blanket on the edges of the beach right before the grass ledge precipice hit rocks. She was aware that Art could see the outlines of her body through the thin material of her dress as she lay back. She'd allowed herself two beers, more than she ever had during the day, and she could picture the way the breeze played with the hem of her skirt and the cowlick of hair at the top of Art's forehead, fanning it up endearingly like a fringe. They lay together talking, then bodies inching closer as the sun peaked in the sky.

The warmth and the beers had loosened them, and all at once, laughing at something he'd said, she'd curled into his body in a familiar way. And then when Art bent his head and kissed her, fully on the lips, she had momentarily panicked that someone might spy them. But the beach was largely deserted; the spot they had picked was far from the parking area.

Reliving it now, she recalled how her insides turned over and jellied with his kiss. And although they had been leading up to this for months, had danced around serious physical intimacy, she remembered her sense of surprise as he had pulled her tightly to his chest, the appley sour taste of fermentation on his breath from the beer, which called to mind kissing boys in high school. There was no stab of guilt, no moment of hesitation, Maura remembered, because she deserved this. It was possible to be here as long as she didn't think about what it stood for. This type of happiness was a part of her that could live independently from her family, in a chamber she had built for herself. In this way she would remain Maura, regardless of the many roles she played for everyone else.

She and Art had rolled up the blanket, laughing like teenagers on the walk back to the car. The thought now of that giddy, adolescent mirth, in the sobriety of the present, made her flush with shame. His kiss had been the flint spark. And as they stuffed the remains of the picnic into the trunk and climbed into his car, their cheeks pink from the sun, something volatile and combustible had begun that Maura felt incapable of stopping.

Art pulled her forward, decisively, and kissed the top of her head hard. He had made a joke about being at a drive-in movie and then he was upon her, almost without warning. She couldn't remember, if ever, a time when she and Pete had contorted their bodies like that in a car. She tasted salt above Art's upper lip, and all at once her body was a new and unexplored continent where everything became incredibly simple.

The rest was a tangle: her sundress, up over her hips and the strap ripped loose. They pressed their bones and hips together until they felt like one person, until there was no difference between them. And when he began to spasm and buck beneath her, her hands on the muscles of his lower back, she thought oddly of death throes, the way the body of an animal goes on moving long after its head is gone.

And in the intense wrinkling of time within the confines of the car, she had no longer been somebody's mother or wife or daughter or sister, but one giant nerve ending of feelings and pleasure, completely and wholly herself, burning outward from the core.

• • •

That night, home from the beach, she had been unable to sleep. Luckily it had been one of Pete's regular boys' nights out. When he had finally crawled under the covers, Maura had feigned sleep so that she wouldn't have to talk to him. In this way, the electrifying moments she'd experienced with Art could remain intact and sacrosanct.

Rising early that next morning, Maura had been bursting with secrecy and excitement, a part of her terrified at what had been loosed and set in motion. She had the acute feeling that every sense was heightened, her love for her kids, her enjoyment of the day, and the nurturing capabilities inside of her. All of Maura simply felt more alive, tingling. They had planned to see each other that weekend, and she was already cooking up a plausible excuse to get away from the house, however briefly.

Daydreaming through the routine of making breakfast, packing lunches, and finding the kids' backpacks that morning, she was in a gauzy mental haze. The last week of school was down to half days, and the high schoolers were already finished with exams. She had worried that with the kids home now, their summer schedules more erratic, it would be trickier to fit Art into the spaces between her mothering. As she lifted Sarah into the stroller for the short walk to the elementary school, Maura had smiled to herself, replaying the private scenes with Art from the day before.

James kept riding ahead of her and then circling back on his bike, smiling and making faces at Sarah in the stroller as she sucked down her juice cup. He'd put his helmet on, but he'd always been lazy about buckling the straps. She could recall how it was askew that day, tilting at an odd angle off his face, the chin strap dangling at the sides. Maura winced now at the thought that she'd been too preoccupied that morning to remind him to snap it closed. Walking along the sidewalk, she had felt the vibrating buzz of her cell phone through her pants pocket. It was a text message, and she understood intrinsically who it was from. Pete was not a big texter. Her pulse quickened. She pictured Art walking around his apartment, dressed now, most likely, and ready to head out the door to the clinic. She felt the secret thrill of two separate people moving through the same day in tandem, connected by thought and desire. Maura slowed the stroller and fumbled for the cell phone in her pocket. She had giggled as she read it, bringing her fingertips to her mouth like a schoolgirl to mask her delight.

LUST YOU it said, and a vision of the previous afternoon washed over her, accompanied by a physical ache in her groin. Maura had stopped all forward motion then, consumed by the need to respond, focused on creating something short and yet clever that would let him know she was craving him too.

And somewhere ahead of her—exactly a year later now, she could barely bring herself to think of it—her son had already biked far beyond her and down the sidewalk toward the school. Maura closed her eyes for a second in the parked car and lowered her head to rest on the steering wheel. She replayed the screech of tires, felt the blade of fear catch in her throat as she had jerked up from her phone that day and understood in a split second what had happened. She had begun to run then, yelling James's name in a rising pitch, the sick feeling spreading as she rocketed the stroller forward on the uneven concrete sidewalk slabs.

Maura felt the hot flush of what she had done wash over her now. She had told Pete and everyone else that James had been in her sightline when the car had struck him. She had described to her family, almost convinced herself, that she had stopped the stroller to give Sarah juice. No one had any reason to disbelieve that. It could happen to anyone, was what her sister and brother, her friends, had all assured her. And she had worked hard to believe all of that, to carefully edit the story of how she had lost James.

"Kids are impulsive, no child looks both ways, you can't watch them every second." She had heard all of the pat phrases intended to assuage her own feelings of parental inadequacy. But in the end her guilt was an iceberg with only the tip showing. The truth of that morning's events was submerged somewhere beneath the surface.

As she had climbed into the ambulance with James on the way to the hospital, passing Sarah to a virtual stranger, calling her mother, unaware of the blood on her shirt and jeans, she understood the enormous price of her momentary happiness at the beach the previous day.

No good could come from admitting all of this to Pete or to anyone else. It wouldn't change the course of events or bring James back. The knowledge of what she and Art had done had been her own private self-flagellation. But it had become increasingly hard, with the passage of time, to carry it all neatly inside. She burned with the occasional, inexplicable need to tell, to unburden herself. There were times she would feel it bubbling up, like a bottomless spring.

Two days after the accident, back at home between hospital visits, she had smashed her cell phone with a hammer and pushed it through the sewer grate to remove the evidence of Art's texts. She made the decision then to tell no one. And in the early months, when she had felt an urge to confess, there was a place on the inside of her arm where she applied pressure, physically digging in her nails to stop the desire. She had read about teenagers who cut themselves to feel something, to rise above their numbness, and she wondered if her ritual in the early days after James's death was akin to that. She had felt absolutely nothing then, hollowed like a gourd, empty of anything other than total self-loathing and the deep yawning chasm of loss. But the dull ache of the truth kneaded and worked on her. Keeping the secret felt increasingly cumbersome, as if she were trying to swim with lead manacles.

37

"G*ood work, Roger*," called the therapist in his cheerleader voice as he punched up the speed of the treadmill. "We're going to try for another quarter mile. Think you can do that?"

"Yeeesssss." Roger gave thumbs-up, taking one hand off the treadmill and then wobbling slightly.

Christ but this was hard. He could feel beads of sweat pricking his forehead, and he'd only just gotten on the machine. Walking . . . holy hell. Who could have imagined that was something he would have to learn again. But Roger could feel himself getting stronger in tiny increments. He was still worried about his speech. He could hear how garbled he sounded, how inarticulate at times.

Now that he was living back at home, he didn't feel quite so much like an invalid. He had hated being in the rehab hospital in Chicago. That was no place to get well, those pushy, zippy nurses always waking him to check vital signs, the goddamned tube in the back of his hand like some marionette. All of that had almost leached the spirit right out of him. He had felt, for a while there, as if he had lost the will to live.

There were periods of acute frustration when he couldn't accomplish simple tasks, like get the knife and fork to behave the way he wanted, and Margaret would cut his baked potato or slice his meat.

In those moments, he had felt shame and anger, hair-trigger rage.

"Come on now, just a few more laps," the physical therapist called out. "You're killing it!" Roger's smile was more of a grimace. Truth was, he felt like he was going to collapse right on the treadmill. But he was not going to show any of what he felt to this young kid with the earring. He was going to make the distance, despite the grating tone. He was going to get better. He had so many things to get better for.

At home, Margaret had set him up in the first-floor bedroom so he didn't have to tackle the stairs. But he was getting better at stairs. Better, but not great. He loved it when he could sit in his kitchen chair and take meals because he could summon up his previous feelings of being master of his own domain. Despite his herky-jerky movements, he could walk out in the garden, hike to the end of the driveway, and get the paper in the morning. Some of the old routine was returning in thin slices.

This week marked the end of his leave of absence from work, though no one had formally addressed it yet from the firm. He'd known early on that returning to work was a fiction. He was finished. And frankly, he didn't have the desire to go back to that old life. He knew a call would have to be made, to make it all official, and he supposed Margaret and the partners were being generous by waiting for him to raise the subject.

Friends and even some of his colleagues had visited him, and it had been uncomfortable, even painful. Everyone acted so solicitous, speaking to him slowly and loudly, as if he were the village idiot. He'd take the retirement. He'd been a smart and cautious investor over the years, and they had enough put away, even if his pension wasn't fully vested.

When he had imagined retiring it had always been with a big party, lots of lunches and a speech or two that reprised his career achievements. But the stroke had robbed him of all of that. It was anticlimactic, no, downright depressing for Roger to think about ending his work life by filling out forms from human resources. It was humiliating.

Roger glanced up at the large numbers on the wall clock. Margaret would be picking him up in another hour. Margaret. He sighed and tried to focus on his breathing. There were times he couldn't stand the look in her eyes. One minute it was loving and protective, watching him like a hawk, and other times cipher-like—it was hooded and then pitying. Occasionally, when she didn't know he was looking, he saw naked fear lodged there.

He was shocked at how, when she patronized him, used that pedantic tone, the occasional desire passed through his head to physically reach out and hit her with his fists. In those moments of vengeful rage, he imagined the satisfaction of connecting with her jawbone. Roger could envision the surprised look as she registered the fact that he wanted her to stop hovering, stop being so concerned, so damned good and saintly all of the time. At times her kindly smile resembled the knowing smirk of a jailer. Those feelings would be followed by extreme shame and self-loathing. He had done this to her, he thought bitterly. The desire to lash out was irrational, especially with Margaret waiting on him hand and foot. And then, Roger winced shamefully, what she'd told him about Julia. That she had run her off at the hospital and that, incredibly, his wife had known all this time and never uttered a word. He shook his head, causing his pace to momentarily falter on the treadmill. Another lap subtracted itself from the red numbers on the machine's digital display, and he looked over at his therapist as he consulted a clipboard in front of a younger patient on the stationary bicycle.

The boredom of the treadmill allowed his thoughts to wander further, and he was momentarily overwhelmed by an image of all the parts of his life colliding. He and Margaret had still not spoken in any detail about the exact circumstances of his stroke. He knew that Julia had called 911 and then driven to the hospital. Of all the times and places for this to happen. He had managed successfully, for all of these years, to keep that part of his life separate. Wasn't it ironic that this would happen on an overnight to Florida?

It was difficult to think about Julia and Margaret having met. They were such contrasts. He hadn't contacted Julia himself. He couldn't easily punch a number in the phone, and even if he did get her on the line, his speech was slurred. He didn't want her to hear him like this or to effect a false bravado. It was better for them both to remember the way they had been together before the stroke.

Though Roger had contemplated sending Julia an e-mail, he couldn't determine what to write or where he would begin. Nothing he could put into words seemed adequate. Hell, he couldn't really work a computer keyboard. He'd have to labor to hit the keys one by one.

His cell phone was on the dresser, and in the first few weeks he was home, he had studied it hopefully, checking for a message or call from her. She had not reached out either, as far as he knew. It was best to let Julia go, neglect her like an atrophying limb that diminished in stature over time. Perhaps somewhere down the line, when his penmanship was better and his speech more crisp, he would contact her, put a final conclusion on it all. For now, they both needed to get on with life.

Rivulets of sweat poured down Roger's forehead, and his T-shirt was soaked. A few more laps; he could see the red illuminated picture on the console of the treadmill that told him where he was on the imaginary track.

But here was the truth. And Roger knew it. He was never going to get back to who he was, the same person he had been. He was never going to be the Roger Munson who walked out on the putting green at the club and just sunk the ball, or who could shoot a few hoops with his grandkids on the driveway.

He could recover many parts of his old self, the rehab doctor and the occupational therapist had explained patiently, but he should not expect to resume all of his previous activities. Life would be different. "The new normal" they all called it. The new goddamned normal. What was that? Well, he hadn't wanted new. He liked the old Roger.

One of the things he had thought long and hard about, especially in the hospital, was his Plan B. It gave him a measure of reassurance to know that he had something to fall back on. A man needed a backup plan, was what his father had always told him. And so he had secreted away some of the sleeping pills he had been given when he was discharged from the hospital. It hadn't been easy because getting the tops off some of the bottles was a struggle. He'd once asked the cleaning lady to help him when Margaret was out, and she'd opened it readily without even glancing at the label.

It felt good just to know the pills were there, stuffed in his golf socks in the top dresser drawer. Plan B made him feel both calmer and illicit. It gave him control. Margaret would have a fit if she knew, but really, what was the big deal? They did this kind of thing all the time in those progressive countries like Sweden. He was pretty sure even here some states had laws that allowed it. Whether or not he would really ever swallow the pills, his stash made him feel as if he had a say in his own destiny, a choice about whether or not his diminishment was an acceptable burden to his loved ones. Autonomy was one of those necessities, like oxygen or water, the very minimum a man needed to possess to keep his dignity.

Roger finished the last lap on the treadmill and the speed of the belt began to gradually slow. The therapist was back by his side, bracing his arm now for the cool down, urging him on. *One step at a time*, he thought. That was how he would beat this back. *But a man ought to have control over how he lived and when he died*, he thought. No one could take that away from him.

38

P*ete was taking* Ryan to Saturday baseball practice and bringing Sarah along. Maura needed to do some shopping, and then she had offered to stay with her father while Margaret got her hair done and ran some errands. Ryan needed a pair of new khakis and some jeans, and she wanted to find some elastic waist pants for her dad at the mall. He was still getting the hang of the buttons and zippers, his fine motor coordination coming back slowly. She had been teasing her parents that the series of old track suits he wore made him look like a mobster on *The Sopranos*. Maura was determined to find him something more dignified to wear now that he was getting out of the house more frequently.

As she locked the minivan in the parking lot, it was the distinctive laugh, infectious and boyish, magnified and reverberating in the walls of the underground lot, that caused her to freeze. Without looking up she knew it was Art. Maura paused on the side of the vehicle, positioning her body so she could see but not be seen between the rows. Headed in her direction, Art came into view with his springy, up-on-the-toes walk. He was holding hands with a woman, maybe a little younger than she, and they moved briskly through the knot of people slowly exiting the movie theater. The woman was blond and fit, her body poured into fluorescent-colored athletic wear. Maura observed how she was looking at him, absorbing what he was saying without seeming to hang on every word. Studying Art's profile she noticed that the goatee was gone, but the expression on his face was one of total ease and engagement. He looked as if he were telling her a story. And then suddenly, before reaching the row where she crouched, the couple doglegged at a right angle, and dropped out of sight.

Maura felt rattled as she stood from her hunched position. The brief encounter left her with neither an acute sense of desire nor longing. It was such a strange feeling to have been spying on Art, resisting the opportunity for contact. It felt like studying an exotic animal through glass.

Inside the mall she sped through her errands and found some respectable pants at a men's chain in the sportswear section. By the time she pulled into her parents' driveway, it had all taken barely two hours.

"Dad," she called out, entering the house. No answer.

"Daaaad." Maura's concern grew slightly. Margaret had said he'd be home alone for a stretch, and she liked to make sure there was someone there when her absence was greater than three hours.

Maura set the shopping bag on the kitchen table, and glancing out into the backyard, relieved, she spotted her father, standing over a golf ball with one of his putters; a look of determination gripped his face.

"Get any hole-in-ones?" She breezed out the back porch door, startling him for a second, and then his expression relaxed into a half-grin. She was still adjusting to the way that one side of his mouth drooped slightly.

"Maurrra. Hi, honey."

"Come inside, Dad, I got you some pants and I wanted to see if they fit right. I can take them back if they don't work." Roger nodded his head in assent and walked slowly to the patio table, leaning his golf club against one of the metal lawn chairs. He stretched out his arms to embrace her and she leaned in for a hug. Her father's shape was changing in the wake of the stroke, his limbs thinner and his waist more thick. The contours of his face had filled back out, thankfully. He had been so gaunt when he'd first come home from the rehab hospital.

Maura poured them each a Diet Pepsi, and she made him try on one of the pairs of pants to her satisfaction. Roger joked about how stylish he appeared, turning around in a circle in the kitchen to display the slacks, mugging like a model. His motions and facial expressions were slightly overexaggerated, as if he were determined to emphasize his present happiness and well-being.

Her mother would be back any minute and Maura knew at this juncture she could easily leave and return home, but she relished her time alone in her father's company. She could see how it cheered him as well. They moved into the den and settled comfortably into the overstuffed chairs. Maura observed the indent in her father's cushion, the spot where he now spent so much time. On the side table next to him was a half-read newspaper, an empty glass on its side, and a granola bar wrapper. If her mother were present, the trash would already be whisked away. This mess was her father's unspoken form of insurrection.

There had been so many things tinkered with in the aftermath of the stroke. Their relationship, which once held such defined roles, had shifted in almost imperceptible but painful ways. His omnipotence had dimmed. They were both renegotiating their new positions, trying to gauge the boundaries and possibilities in the face of his diminishment. It was this confusion and vulnerability now that gave her the opening, and without much forethought, she began to speak, the question spilling from her.

"Did you ever do something you totally regretted, Daddy, something you wished you could take back?" His head recoiled slightly, and she could tell that her question had surprised him. He leaned back against the blue and white floral upholstery of the chair with a thoughtful warniess.

"Sure. There are thingsss we've all done that we aren't proud of," he said, slurring slightly. Maura nodded. "Why? What isss troubling you?"

Maura sighed and cast her eyes up at the ceiling, unable for the moment to meet his gaze. Tears began to burn in her eyes and she let them come, her voice cracking. All at once she was the small girl again, looking for her father's absolution.

"When James got hit . . . I was doing something else. I was focused on other things." She was crying openly now, and she could feel Roger studying her carefully, allowing her the release while working to intuit the hidden message in her words. He remained quiet as she lowered her face in her hands, her back heaving with the sobs.

"Oh God, Daddy. I did this." She moved from the chair and down onto her knees on the floor in front of him, crumpling her upper body into his lap as he reached over to rub her back in a rhythmic motion. "I can't believe that this happened. I should have been right there . . . and not . . ." She sobbed harder, and he kept patting.

"It'ssss OK, Maura. OK." They sat that way, slightly rocking, as her outburst subsided. "You didn't do thisss, honey. It's OK."

"But, Daddy, I did something I'm not proud of," Maura started and then stopped, drawing in a deep breath with a shudder. She could not see her father's face, only the side of the chair, and this position gave her the feeling of a disembodied church confessional.

"There was somebody I met. And for a little while that felt exciting and good." Maura exhumed the facts and let them lie there. "I was . . . thinking about him, texting him, when the car hit James." It was harder than she had thought it would be to form the words out loud, but she also felt a burgeoning sense of catharsis, a levity that she hadn't totally anticipated. Maura adjusted her position and lifted her head, rubbing her eyes with balled hands. She teetered on her knees and then moved up to sit in the chair next to him, looking him full in the face with a weary smile. A spent calm began to settle over her, the clarity that could follow a tempest.

"You're going to have to move passst the guilt." Roger smiled at her tenderly. They sat for a long stretch without speaking. She thought momentarily about the woman, Julia, whom she had met unexpectedly in the hospital in Tampa. She had practically run into her in the doorway one night as she was leaving her father's room, headed back to her mother at the hotel. The woman had hastily introduced herself as a friend, but then she had hesitated nervously. Maura had gotten the distinct sense that she was something more, that she was omitting something important.

"I know you've seen things with me and Pete over the years that aren't all good, especially since James died," Maura began. "We haven't always been our best selves." It was refreshing to be sitting here alone with her father, without her mother's constant presence at his elbow. Maura now felt their relationship seesaw back to her being the child again, and he the wiser parent. There was a goodness connected to confiding in the one person she knew might understand the complexity of the secrets with which she lived.

"Life isss fuller than we sometimesss imagine, hmmm?" said Roger pensively. "Sssome people see life asss black and white, and they live it that way. But most of usss live in the gray areass. I think the older you get, the harder it iss to see absolutessss." Roger drew out this last word, and a piece of saliva hung in the corner of his crooked mouth. "It takess an awful lot of energy to do that."

She nodded. "I wasn't focusing my attention where it should have been, Dad. I sort of lost myself."

Roger shot her a look of understanding. "Honey, you need to ssstop beating yourself up. We all take our eye off the ball at sssome point in life. It doesn't mean you are a bad person. And if you looked to other thingsss for a time, whatss important is that you are ssstill in the ring. Are you ssstill there, Maura? Innn the ring?" Roger wiped the spittle in the corner of his mouth with a handkerchief from his shirt pocket, and Maura looked at him quizzically. His eyes burned bright.

"What do you mean, Dad?"

"I mean as long as you are ssstill in there slogging it out every day, still showing up to give it your best shot with Pete, then you're still in the game. Don't spennnd time in the past, on what you should have done." He paused for a moment, collecting himself. "It only hurtsss."

"You and Mom seem pretty good now," Maura offered, ready to deflect the conversation. He looked up at her gratefully.

"Your mom and I arrre doing great. She's terrific, she really iss."

Roger tilted his head to smile at her with genuine warmth. As she reached to take her father's hand in an unspoken thank-you, they both heard the sudden rattle of the garage door opening and exchanged the tacit look of accomplices. Margaret was home.

39

Maura *pulled into* one of the car pickup lanes at the elementary school and was startled by a rap at the driver's side window. Celia Murphy's straightened blond mane and melon lip gloss smiled at her from outside the glass, and Maura rolled down the window.

"Hi, Celia."

"Maura. I'm so happy to catch you. I was going to call you this afternoon." Celia leaned into the car, her pink form-fitting yoga top and air-freshener-strength perfume invading the interior. Sarah rhythmically kicked the back of Maura's seat from behind, and she glanced in the rear-view mirror, scanning for Ryan. Maybe Celia would get the message that she was in a hurry, but the dismissal bell still hadn't rung yet. She was trapped until the line began to move.

"I . . . I know this month is the one-year anniversary . . . of . . . James." Celia was struggling for the right tone, and Maura decided to let her finish.

"Yes, thank you. It was last week."

"Well, our thoughts and prayers are with you all, I wanted you to know that," said Celia, inserting herself even farther into the window. "And I thought this might be a good time to circle back, since we're all thinking about James. Last year, you know, we held that fund-raiser at the elementary school. Henry had wanted to do something after the . . . tragedy, he was so devastated. I think I spoke to your mother back then on the phone, or maybe it was your sister? Anyhow, I know you weren't in a frame of mind to attend. We are planning to hold it again this year in the fall. It was such a success, and kids these days all want to do something to give back, you know? You may have seen the flyer that just went home in the backpacks for people to save the date. Anyhooo, we were hoping that your family would come. So I wanted to get to you ahead of time so you could put it on the calendar." She stepped back from her perch in the window and straightened, narrowing her eyes at Maura, her head cocked. "We'd love to have the Corrigans there."

"Well, I . . ." Maura felt blindsided. She heard the bell ring loudly on the outside of the brick school building, relieved that the kids would come pouring out soon. Ryan had a dental appointment in fifteen minutes, and it was at least a ten-minute drive.

Celia didn't give her an inch. "I saw Ryan the other day after school, and he told me how much he wanted to be there. It's a car wash and bake sale. And we are collecting old bikes and used helmets for inner-city kids. The money we raise goes to—"

"Sure, Celia," Maura blurted out. She was annoyed at her use of Ryan as a kind of collateral. "Of course we'll be there. It's wonderful that Henry wants to remember his friend. I'll get the details from the flyer and talk to you a little later. I've got to get the kids to the dentist, OK?"

"That's terrific, I'll speak with you soon." Celia pulled away with a toodle-loo wave, and Maura studied her aerobic walk, her tight butt in slim dark jeans and the ballet slipper flats that easily cost triple digits. She loathed and loved this woman in ever-shifting ratios.

They would all go to the fund-raiser, thought Maura decisively. The whole family would wash cars and sell cookies. If nothing else it would be a good activity for Sarah and Ryan to honor their brother

and witness how sometimes good things could blossom out of hor-
rific tragedies.

· · ·

"Your turn, Daddy," said Sarah. She was already in her pajamas,
flopped on the rug, studying Maura's hand of cards. Pete had been
the one to bathe her and get the bedtime routine going. This was
ordinarily a boy's night out for him, but he had elected to stay in.
And now here they were after a roast chicken dinner and homemade apple pie, playing cards as a family. Maura took it all in and
allowed herself a secret smile.

"Do you have any fours?" Pete asked Ryan.

"Go fish," said Ryan as Sarah peered over his shoulder.

"Pick up a card for Daddy," urged Maura, pointing at the pile.

Although it was only early fall, the last two nights had grown
cool, and this evening Pete had built a fire at Ryan's request. The
wood crackled and popped loudly. It was cheap pine, too green and
full of sap, but she had bought it from a man with a truckload going
door to door.

After the children were in bed, they sat together by the fire. Pete
was sipping a glass of orange juice, and Maura realized suddenly
that he hadn't had a drink all night. In fact she tried to remember
now if he'd even had a beer last night.

"I was thinking about the Hulburd kid today. Have you heard
anything about him?" Pete asked drowsily.

"Not since he called that one time," said Maura.

"Right before he went to basic training?

"Yup, and he told me he wouldn't be allowed any contact there.
He can write a letter but he doesn't get e-mail or a cell phone. They
take all that stuff away."

"Sounds like heaven," chuckled Pete, and she laughed.

"I'm worried about him," mused Maura. "I hope he makes it. That picture he gave us, with his uniform and his shaved head, something about it breaks my heart. It makes him look so young."

"He is young. All these guys are young. But you know, he looks really proud," said Pete. She agreed. As scary as it was that he was headed overseas, she wanted him to find a place somewhere, his own sense of peace. The picture in uniform made it feel as if he had. Maura had tacked his photo on the kitchen bulletin board and explained to Ryan it was the boy who had hit James by accident. Her son had solemnly studied the portrait, asking a few questions, and then had seemed to accept it all.

A log suddenly burned through and the two pieces fell, one rolling toward the fireplace screen. Pete jumped up to push it back with the poker.

"Hey, I've got something to tell you," he said with forced casualness. She knew this tone, and she braced herself for the moment, not sure which way it would break.

"Yeah? Am I going to hate this?" She tried to keep her voice light and quizzical.

"I went to a meeting today with Billy." He paused. "An AA meeting." Pete's voice was soft, and Maura felt her heart flip-flop and balloon out again. She took a breath and weighed her response. Her heart rate rocketed as she waited for him to continue.

"I've been going this week, but I was afraid to say anything to you too soon. I just, I guess I just wanted to make sure it was going to be for me."

Maura couldn't move and then all at once she pushed her face into Pete's chest, feeling warm tears springing up, unbidden. This was fragile territory. He was offering her the potential for a huge transformation, and she hadn't been in that position for many months.

"Hey," he said. "I'm going to try. I'm going to give it my best shot, not going to be easy every day. You OK? I figured you'd be thrilled."

"Yeah . . . I'm . . . just . . . happy," Maura said simply. Pete was quiet for a while, and they fitted easily into the silence. She was afraid to interrupt, to probe further or meet his eyes, as if that kind of directness would drive him in the opposite direction.

"I scared myself."

"Yeah?"

"Last week, on Monday, remember I met some of the guys to watch the game in the city? Well, I was driving home after a few beers. Corner of Hubbard and State. There was a streetlight out, bad visibility, but it was me. I blamed it on the light. But I'd had more than my limit, and some old guy, a bum, probably homeless, just shot out of the dark." Pete's voice was clipped. "Maybe he was on the crosswalk and I just didn't see him . . . it happened so fast, and—" Pete stopped for a moment, remembering it afresh. "I sort of wasn't there in that car and then all of a sudden I was, my reflexes kicked in. It was all OK, but I freaked myself out. I kept thinking, what if I'd really hurt him, you know?" Pete paused for a moment and let out a long breath, bringing his hands to his hair and running them through it in a quick scalp-scrubbing motion that she had always found endearing.

"The guy ended up with his hands on my hood, screaming and slamming his fists, cursing the hell out of me. He was fine. I mean, he was pretty loaded. His hands were cut, I guess, from hitting the ground. So the blood made it look worse than it really was. I got out and he shook me off, pushed me away. Didn't want me to take him to the hospital, didn't want to give me his name." Pete picked up Maura's hand and laid it in his lap.

"I was so goddamned scared, Maura. It could have ended so different." He paused for a second and his composure broke.

She sat there for a moment, lying on his shoulder in the flicker of the firelight, taking in what he was saying. Here was this new Pete, hurting over his loss and his mistakes, this vulnerable, confessing, intimate Pete whom she had craved for so long.

"I thought about . . . well . . . I thought about . . ." And then he was silent. She ran her hands over the sides of his head, smoothing his hair by the temples, feeling for the tears in the dark and gently wiping them away. "You thought about James," she finished in a whisper.

These early days of working on Pete's sobriety would be tenuous, Maura knew, too tentative to expect a sudden happy ending. But in the absence of anything else in the quicksand world that had been reshaped after their son's death, Maura figured hope was at least something. As they fell asleep that night, like spoons, she could feel Pete's strong heartbeat through the back of her ribs, overpowering the vibration of her own. For the first time in a long time, Maura felt an emberlike sense of hope flare higher.

• • •

"Mom, look at all of this money." Ryan held up a fist of dollar bills.

"Wow, honey, that's amazing," said Maura.

"Look, Mom, one man gave us a hundred-dollar bill!" Ryan waved the money excitedly over his head and then placed it reverentially back in the cash box.

"That's a big tip," she called.

"James would love this," said Ryan breathlessly, waving the stack of bills and then fanning them out to organize into piles of tens, fives, and ones.

In the days leading up to the car wash and bake sale, they had all trekked around town to staple photocopied signs in the local stores and on telephone poles.

The school had turned over the front parking lot, and people had donated hoses and brought buckets and brushes. Teams descended on the cars, scrubbing in a furious mass of bubbles, punctuated by screams of delight when the hoses were sprayed. There was no one present who wasn't wet to some degree, and Maura was touched by how many of her friends and acquaintances had shown up. One of the volunteers had told her they'd washed well over a hundred cars.

"You keep counting, sweetie. I'm going to get a drink of water." Maura headed for the entryway of the elementary school.

It was a sunny day, and the season had doubled back for a rare stretch of Indian summer. Some of the baked goods on the table in the school parking lot were beginning to wilt. Chocolate chips bled onto the cellophane of the individually wrapped cookies. The supply of brownies and cupcakes was dwindling.

Pete had been spraying and soaping the cars with Ryan, and they were both completely soaked, giggling and laughing when the water from the hose inadvertently hit them. Even Sarah had gotten into the act, sponging cars and floating back and forth between her parents. Ryan had a palpable sense of pride in being connected to the event, and Henry, Celia's son, was especially solicitous of him in a way that made Maura's heart ache. It was hard to see how much her son's best friend had shot up in a year and a half, hard to believe this would have been James's eleventh birthday, his first year at the middle school.

Henry and the other sixth-grade boys who had turned out to work the fund-raiser seemed so mature, so much older in such a relatively short span. Observing them working the event, Maura beat back a complex mixture of longing and jealousy. Her mouth was dry and she was deep in thought as she entered the front of the school to find the restroom.

As she washed her hands and splashed water on her face, Maura heard the bathroom door creak open and saw Celia Murphy in the reflection from the sink mirror.

"What a day," Celia said, smiling broadly. She had little patches of sweat under the arms of her tangerine shirt, and she appeared to have been sprayed from the back.

"A big success," said Maura. "Ryan couldn't wait to count the money. I really am so touched that Henry started all of this. It's . . . it's . . . a very generous thing to do."

"Well, it really was Henry's idea. Truly. I mean, I think all of the kids were so stunned, so shocked, really that one of their friends could . . . that something like that could happen to their friend. Just crossing the street."

Maura nodded. When was the last time she had taken a sip of water? She felt dehydrated all of a sudden, light-headed.

"I mean it really could have been any of us, right?" said Celia, nattering on. "After it happened I decided I had to be more vigilant, and I made a real rule with myself. It's so easy for me to get distracted, to get caught up on my cell phone or whatever. We can't be watching every second."

Maura moved back toward the sink to try to cup some water into her hands.

"Our worst fears as a mother," Celia added more softly.

"I guess it could happen to anyone," offered Maura. "It was so fast, you know? I just glanced down for a second."

Celia trained a sympathetic expression on Maura, and Maura fought the urge that sometimes overtook her in public places to run out the bathroom door, gather up her family, and go. "Well, I mean, and the texting thing has just gotten out of control too, hasn't it? I'm on my kids about it all the time. Maura? Are you OK? I didn't mean to bring all this up. I hope I didn't upset you talking about James."

"I'm fine. I should probably get back to Sarah," Maura offered weakly, and she swung the door open and turned the corner in the cool stone corridor of the elementary school, leaning her back against the wall for relief, out of Celia's sight. Maura could hear the door of the girls' bathroom close with a slam and the brisk *clickety clack* of Celia's sandals receding. When she walked back out to the bright sunlight and the remains of the car wash, she was amused to see Henry turning the hose on his mother. Celia's dark jeans were completely soaked and the seams of her lacey bra showed through her wet V-necked T-shirt. As Celia shrieked good-naturedly, her blond hair shellacked to her head by the spray, Maura smiled and then tried to suppress a giggle, and because it was impossible not to, she erupted into peals of outright laughter.

40

They'd watched the local 6:00 P.M. news in the kitchen over dinner and now they were in the family room with bowls of sherbet, taking in the national broadcast. There had been a school shooting in California, and heavy rains had overflowed riverbanks in the South, upending homes and wreaking havoc. Margaret was sick of the carnage on the news. Where were the positive stories?

"Those poor families," said Margaret. Roger nodded. She took a spoonful of raspberry sherbet and then bent to wipe a small trickle of it from Roger's mouth, almost without thinking. He waved her away.

"Economy's comin baaack," said Roger, catching on the final word. He pored over the *Wall Street Journal* daily, and Margaret had grown accustomed to bringing him his coffee and papers in the den each morning. More often now, he walked out and retrieved them himself. They had found a comfortable routine, and although he was still unable to drive, Roger had been more interested in getting out with her, accompanying her on errands sometimes. His mobility with the cane had improved, and he hadn't used the walker in months.

"How about a movie?" Margaret offered. "There are a couple on cable that I've heard the kids talk about." She scrolled through the TV guide section of the *Sun-Times*, squinting through her reading glasses.

Their children had been so attentive through all of this, she thought, coming over to help with meals, playing cards, and staying with him when she had to run out. Maura and Erin had even run through some of the speech therapies with their father in the earlier days. They were blessed to have such a close-knit family. It was difficult times that let you understand good fortune; you could take an accounting of what you had in a way you weren't able to when life ran smoothly. Margaret had reminded Roger of that fact when he needed to be bucked up.

A few months after the stroke, Roger had gone through plenty of days when he seemed in despair, and Margaret had been concerned. She'd mentioned it to Father Durkee, and he'd come by to visit Roger. She wasn't privy to anything they'd discussed, and she had made a point of not probing Roger afterward. She was merely thrilled that he'd been receptive to the idea. But there were days, she knew, when the realization of his disabilities coalesced into a terrible sadness and frustration.

Rummaging through drawers in the bedroom around that time, Margaret had come across an old prescription bottle of sleeping pills, stuffed in a sock, of all strange things. The disturbing thought occurred to her that maybe he had been hoarding them, that perhaps he was contemplating taking his own life, and then she dismissed that as foolhardy. Looking at the label, she could see they were left over from the days when Roger had traveled more extensively for work. And they were three years old, past their expiration date by months. If anything, Roger slept too much, nodding off in the chair in front of the TV and passing out nightly almost the minute his head touched the pillow. She had pitched the prescription bottle into the trash.

One afternoon, exhausted and short-fused, Margaret grew tired of his moping around, his taciturn moods and unwillingness to say much, and she'd really let him have it, just unleashed her frustration on him like a drill sergeant. Margaret told him he was being a sad sack when he had all of this family under his nose, Maura, Erin, and Stu. All those beloved grandkids. Most people didn't get that lucky in a lifetime. He was a survivor, she had screamed at him, a blessed survivor. After that, he had seemed to make more of an effort and it had pleased her. He was still working hard to come to terms with the person he was now. Maybe he would always be in some way, she reasoned, and she'd have to accept that.

"Make peace with who you are," his physical therapist had said. "That's one of the greatest gifts you can give yourself. People are constantly changing in life no matter what. No one stays the same." And while it had felt like mumbo jumbo at the time, she and Roger had both moved closer together as a couple. He was really working at his recovery now, determined to get back to the mostly positive and energetic person he had been, or at least as close as he could. And he seemed committed to their marriage in a way she hadn't felt in years. Their children had really supported him, and of course the grandkids were a constant source of cheer. She could see his spirits lift when they were around.

Even her disconcerting thoughts and images of Julia had receded lately. In the first few weeks after Roger had been transferred to the rehab hospital in Chicago, she had checked his cell phone daily. There had been two calls from a number in Florida, but no voice mail message. She had deleted each one. When she saw evidence of the third call, Margaret had pressed redial almost without thinking, and thankfully, she had gotten Julia's voice mail. Her heart had thumped like a snare drum, rage singing through her veins, and yet when the phone clicked to the sugary message asking callers to "leave your number for Julia," she had become focused and cool.

"This is Roger's wife. Margaret Munson. And I wanted to tell you that he is not interested in taking your calls or talking to you at all. Whatever you thought you had with my husband is over. Don't ever call here again." Margaret had pressed the end button with a flourish, and she was amazed, even thrilled, at how good it had all felt.

Of course, she would never confide any of this to Roger. Better for him to think Julia had never tried to contact him again. Margaret could keep secrets too, especially when there was a higher purpose.

"What do you think about the movie *When Harry Met Sally*?" Margaret asked, studying the guide again. "Remember that one? It's a comedy and a love story. Looks like it's on at eight. That gives us a little time."

Roger nodded and seamlessly maneuvered another spoonful of sherbet up to his mouth, smacking his lips. "Sounnnss good." Margaret turned off the news in the kitchen and rose to clear their bowls. Roger stood, deliberately, and headed into the powder room. When she joined him back in the den, she reached to pat his arm as she rounded his lounge chair, and he impulsively grabbed her hand back, drew it to his lips, and kissed it as she came to a full stop in front of his chair. Margaret smiled, momentarily off-kilter at the unexpected act. He tilted his head up, bright eyed and hopeful, and studied her. The expression on his face was that of the man she had fallen in love with all those years ago in college, handsome and confident. Roger suddenly tugged her arm impishly and then pulled her into his lap as she laughed out loud.

. . .

"Moooooom . . . *we got you* a present . . ." Ryan burst through the door, and tiny clumps of dirty ice fell off his boots and onto the mudroom floor.

"Whoa, buddy," said Pete, shutting the door behind them with Sarah in his arms. He beamed and set his daughter down as she ran toward Maura excitedly.

"Don't tell Mom what we got her, Ry. We need to wrap it before we put it under the tree. Go find some wrapping paper, OK? Christmas stuff." Ryan was off like a shot.

Pete bent to pick up the kids' coats from where they had shed them on the mudroom floor and hung them on the wall hooks. He let out his breath in one long *whoosh*, rubbing his hands, and then moved toward her for a hug.

They stood in comfortable silence for a moment in the middle of the kitchen, and Maura circled her arms around his torso. Outside in the waning dusk, two squirrels chased each other in the frozen grass, punctuated by piles of snow, and then cut sharply into the neighbor's yard. "I need some scissors!!!!" Ryan's singsongy voice called from the family room, and she smiled up at Pete before breaking away to oblige.

Teeth brushed, books read, the chaos of laundry still spread on the floral chaise in the bedroom corner, Maura headed back down the stairs to make sure all of the lights were off. Pete was already snoring, and he and Sarah had both fallen asleep in their bed. She had decided to leave her daughter there for the night. The days of wanting to sleep in Mommy's bed were numbered and precious, she understood.

In the kitchen, the artificial light from her computer illuminated the small built-in desk. As she moved to switch off the machine, she impulsively jiggled the mouse to check her e-mail one last time. There were three new messages. One of them was from school, something from the recent PTA meeting, and the second was an Evite to a jewelry sale for charity. The third was an unfamiliar e-mail address, and she hesitated for a moment before clicking on it.

Hey Mrs. C—

I know I haven't been in contact for a while but they barely give us a chance to breathe here. I'm still getting used to military life, but I'm adjusting faster than I thought. Now that basic is over we can at least talk to the outside world! My parents are coming down

*to Kentucky to see me before we head out. They're pretty much
still having a tough time with all of this and I know my mom is
going to cry.*

*The last time I e-mailed I wasn't sure exactly where we were going,
but it looks like we'll be headed to Marjeh, in the Helmand
Province in southern Afghanistan. That's about all I know right
now. But I've met a bunch of great guys and they're all from
different parts of the country.*

*One of my really good buddies is a guy named Jimmy. He's from
Brownsville, Texas, and he's always going on about BBQ and
southern girls and all kinds of crap about his truck, but he makes
us all laugh. His real name is James. I thought that might make
you smile.*

*I'll try to send another e-mail when I get settled. Sometimes it's a
little hard to think about home, especially at night. I do miss it,
probably more than I thought I would. I'd love to see the lake about
now and I'm craving a hot dog with the works from Frank's. Say hi
to Mr. Corrigan and send him my best. I'm going to crash right now
but I just wanted to send this off.*

   Alex

Maura reread the e-mail one more time. She would respond tomorrow instead of dashing off something now while she was tired.
She was touched that Alex wanted to stay in contact; she hadn't expected that. Maybe she and Sarah would bake some cookies or
brownies and send them to him. Everyone loved to get mail.

Back upstairs Maura sighed as she lifted the covers around her
and slipped her legs under the blankets. She moved toward Pete's
arm to absorb the warmth of his chest, and he stirred in his sleep

as she reached to smooth her palm against his cheek. Outside under the streetlamp's trajectory, she could see a few large flakes beginning to fall. They had predicted a few inches tonight, and maybe it would stick. Snow for Christmas would be good.

Sarah had moved toward Maura's side of the bed in her sleep. The third child, Maura thought. She had the keys to their kingdom, and she had her daddy twisted around her little finger. Maura looked over at her daughter's chest as it rose and fell, a tendril of hair flipped across her forehead, her mouth partially opened, face angelic. She was already beginning to lose her baby fat. Maura felt her heart swell with a fierce love for her family. All of them.

A truck rumbled outside the window, breaking the still, winter air. There were no other night sounds, no wildlife, no birdcalls. The world was in hibernation.

As she waited to succumb to sleep, Maura felt the touch of Pete's foot, gently, probing, moving toward her like an outstretched hand. Her own foot met his and moved up his ankle, and she left it there for a moment longer than was physically comfortable.

For a few minutes before she surrendered to sleep, she let her thoughts focus on her marriage. She and Pete were connected by the years, the kids, and their shared experiences, and yet she could still feel the outlines of herself as a wholly separate being apart from him. Maybe that was all right, Maura reflected. Perhaps that was exactly the way it was supposed to be. There were boundaries, even in the best marriages, and they'd bumped up against them. And maybe there wasn't just one person in the world whom you were meant to fit into with the surety of a jigsaw puzzle. In the end, the rough patches and the harder things you endured were far more useful and valuable to have survived than the long stretches of calm and peace. Mastering the turbulence was how you achieved longevity, by simply making it through, by outlasting the bad.

Trust took such a long time to earn. And yet it could all come unmoored in an instant. She was smart enough to know at least that.

People kept secrets. People built walls. It didn't mean they couldn't and didn't love with all their hearts.

And so this was what she would have to make peace with; this was what she would have to hold close. Like the cross section of a tree, the bad period would be marked in interior rings, the years of drought, the blunt force trauma to the heart, all of it only visible after death. Maybe silence was a price we sometimes paid for loving so completely, the price we sometimes paid to protect those wo loved most.

Maura could only hope that they had already survived the worst of it, that loss had, in the end, become their terrible unifier, the thing that had strengthened and cauterized them. As she scrunched her body closer to Pete and reached out to touch her daughter, a satisfied smile creased her face. One last contented sigh escaped her lips, and she rolled drowsily onto her side. She could feel them all turning toward one another again, moving in unison as subtle as a gravitational pull.

ACKNOWLEDGMENTS

In the three years it took to complete this book, I stopped and started numerous times, and shelved it once for almost a year. Initially, I thought it was a story about loss, the club to which we all eventually belong. But as I began to flesh out the different generations, I came to understand it is a book about resilience. It's about the best parts of us; the secrets we choose to keep and how the ones who love us can move us past the hard places and orient us in the right direction.

While I enjoy just about every genre of literature, I find richness in the stories that deal with real-life issues and surmounting hardships. Those are humbling moments that force us to reconstitute ourselves, sometimes in surprising ways. That was the genesis of this story.

But any novel, especially a first work of fiction, takes a village. And I had an exceptional one. Forgive me if I don't mention you by name.

Undying gratitude to my family for allowing me to write outside my day job and in the shadows of my life. To my children, especially, for understanding when I needed you to hush up at times. For Bob, who has always championed me as a writer and encouraged me back when I was writing kitty litter and bunion-prevention press kits to pay the bills.

To all the folks at Hyperion with whom I've had the pleasure of working. Thanks and blessings to the indomitable Ellen Archer, who saw the manuscript's bone structure and believed that with plastic surgery it could become this book. To my exceptional editor, Christine Pride, who just kept making it better. Your attention to every line and determination to challenge me like a personal trainer is what every author prays for.

For Kiki Koroshetz and her ability to keep all balls in the air effortlessly. Thank you to Beth Gebhard, who cared for this book and delivered a baby in the middle of it. And to Kristina Miller, publicist extraordinaire, who forgave my poor typing skills and type-A organization. Thanks to Marie Coolman and Bryan Christian for getting the word out.

To my agent, Richard Pine, whose sage advice and partnership has been invaluable.

A bazillion hugs to social media/literary expert Susie Stangland and her amazing family. Your friendship, enthusiasm, generosity, and innovation are legion. To Kathy Twietmeyer, another exceptional mother who has technical skills I can only hope to possess. Thanks for keeping it all straight.

To my dedicated and thoughtful early readers, Susan Baker, Jenn Brandt, Cristina Carlino, Carrie Cook, Lisa Gruber, Catherine Kroll, Megan Lucier, Vicki McHugh, Nancy McLoughlin, Nancy Palmer, Mindy Pressler, Jan Stabile, Susie Stangland, and Andrea Weiswasser.

To Melina Bodor, for an unexpected phone call that became the seed of this book, and to Kerri Ratcliffe, Elizabeth Arnot, and Laura Tarrish for their input and for listening to me ramble on about plot one long weekend.

Undying love to Gretchen Holt Witt and her husband, Larry, for sharing Liam and their journey with us. You can learn more and help at http://www.cookiesforkidscancer.org.

To Father Edward L. Beck for ensuring that this non-Catholic had her facts straight. Wet kisses to Harlan Coben, Catherine Coulter, and Adriana Trigiani for encouraging me after they read the manuscript and for all of the other writers and authors who make up the webbing of mutual support and encouragement in this often lonely and sometimes painful process. You know who you are.

To the people who helped me get my facts straight—my de facto military advisors Sheila Casey and Anne Marie and Capt. Kevin Dougherty, USMC, for making sure it rang true. For O. Alton Barron, MD, and Col. Rocco A. Armonda, MD, for medical scrutiny. To the Rye police for teenage DUI background and to our family veterinarian, Dr. Gina Antiaris at Miller-Clark Animal Hospital.

For all the book bloggers, bookstore employees, and beloved indie bookstores who cleared me a space on their shelves, suggested this read, tweeted a kind word, or put a bottle of water on the podium, thanks for your dedication to the writing life.

My admiration goes to the caregivers, parents, spouses, siblings, and loved ones who endlessly give of themselves to make life easier for those they love most. Respect and gratitude for our military families who serve on behalf of our country. You are all my heroes.

And last but never least, to my parents, Terry and David McConaughy, who set me on a course of knowing I was loved unconditionally. And that has made all the difference in how I move through the world.

READING GROUP GUIDE

INTRODUCTION

Those We Love Most is a sensitive, emotionally complex window into what happens when a family is cracked open and must learn to heal. The story explores the seasons of marriage and the surprising effects of grief on our bonds with the people we love most dearly. When Maura and Pete Corrigan's oldest son, James, is killed by a distracted teen driver, the fissures in their relationship are revealed. In the wake of James's death, the ugly sides of marriage, the secrets long kept tucked away, and the allure of a break from reality—from a tryst in Florida to another beer at the local pub—all come to light and threaten to shatter the struggling family. But slowly, over time and with brave first steps, James's death forces everyone left behind to fight their way to a new normal and to create revised reasons to believe in life beyond loss.

DISCUSSION QUESTIONS

1. *Those We Love Most* has moments that are dark and painful. Why do you think the author chose to write something that examines this side of life so intricately?

2. Lee Woodruff has personal experience dealing with critically injured family members. Her husband, Bob, was struck by

a roadside bomb in Iraq while reporting on the war, and he suffered critical injuries and spent a year in speech and physical therapy. How much of Lee's life did you feel coming through in this story?

3. How guilty do you think Maura was in James's accident and death? Must some party always be guilty, even if their actions were unintended? Is there such a thing as a guilt-free accident?

4. How did Maura's own feelings of guilt grow and change throughout the book?

5. How did each character process and work through their grief? Who handled the grief in a healthy way, and who handled it destructively? Lee writes, "[Maura] marveled for more than the hundredth time how differently men and women grieved." How did men and women grieve differently in *Those We Love Most*?

6. An ongoing theme in *Those We Love Most* is the ebb and flow of loving relationships and the changing currents of affection between people. How did James's death alter the currents of love between couples (both married and illicit)?

7. Another theme this book explores is secrets. Do you think it's possible to have a good marriage and still keep secrets? Do you have a secret (or secrets) from your spouse and has it had an effect on your marriage? Would you ever confess?

8. Along those lines, is there one person to whom you confess your secrets? If it's not a partner or spouse, who is it? Does every person need one confidante?

9. Lee writes that before James's death, Maura and Pete were "heading down that easy slipstream in marriage where the valuable, intimate parts begin to erode in a tidal wave of banality. . . . How much was enough love?" How much love do you think is enough in a marriage? Why do you think Maura and Pete's marriage survived James's death?

10. Do you think Alex will be able to overcome the trauma of killing James? Was going into the military a good choice for Alex?

11. Margaret's characterization as a stoic, firm, emotionally controlled matriarch is written with reverence and respect. Do you agree with Margaret's emotional choices? What flaws, if any, did you find with the characterization of Margaret?

12. What roles are sainted in the book? What roles are scorned? Do you agree with these value judgments?

13. How did Roger's stroke alter the trajectories of the central relationships in the book? What were the positive effects, if any, of the stroke?

14. The entire Corrigan family is extremely privileged: none of the women currently has a full-time job, and money is never an issue. In what ways, if at all, did the Corrigans' privilege affect their healing processes after James's accident? How would the grieving process have played out differently if the women (Maura, Erin, and Margaret) had needed to return to full-time jobs? Do you think privilege can ever ease grief?

15. How do you think the book's central relationships would have played out differently if James had survived the accident? Consider the triangles of Maura, Pete, and Art and Roger, Julia, and Margaret.

16. Toward the end of the book, Margaret thinks, "It was difficult times that let you understand good fortune; you could take an accounting of what you had in a way you weren't able to when life ran smoothly." Do you think people need to go through hard times in order to appreciate other aspects of life and family?

17. How were Roger's and Maura's motivations to be unfaithful and their entanglements the same or different?

A CONVERSATION WITH LEE WOODRUFF

What was your writing process like? How much of the plot did you plan out in advance, and how much came to you as you wrote? Were there any twists or revelations that you surprised yourself with?

This novel grew out of a real-life experience. I was out of town and a friend called me in a panic. A seventeen-year-old driver in her town had struck a child, and all these years later I can still picture the hotel room where the phone conversation took place. The child had suffered a brain injury, and my friend wanted to know if I would talk to the parents and provide some hope based on my own family's experiences. After I hung up, I kept thinking about that one pivotal "in-an-instant" moment and all the lives that had been affected by a split-second action.

That call formed the basis for a fictional story about how one pebble dropped in a pond ripples out in many directions. Although I never ended up talking to the real-life parents, and thankfully the real-life boy recovered, the seeds for this novel evolved from that one phone call.

I didn't start the book with a definitive idea of what was going to happen to each of the characters. I began by finding each of them a voice and giving them some secrets, and then the story kind of took over. About midway through, I began to plot out exactly how events would begin tying together. My biggest challenge was figuring out what would happen to Alex, where he would intersect with Maura, and then how his actions and subsequent decisions would change the course of his future.

I think the biggest surprise was what happened to Roger. I didn't originally conceive of his crisis, and once I had begun writing him, I realized it was the starting point for Margaret and him to forge a solid path back to each other.

This is your first novel, but not your first book. How was writing fiction different for you from writing nonfiction? Which do you prefer?

To me, fiction is so much harder to get right than nonfiction. With my first two books, *In an Instant* and *Perfectly Imperfect*, the facts of my life were, well, the facts, and so the art form is in figuring out how to tell the tale or present and edit it in an interesting way.

With fiction, it's like starting from modeling clay. You can make your characters do or feel or say anything that you want, and so you have a big responsibility to end up with something plausible that hangs together. That also means that the sky is the limit, so it's more about narrowing choices.

***Those We Love Most* is an emotionally complex book. Why did you choose to write about such a difficult topic and such a difficult time in the Corrigan family? Was the book emotionally draining to write?**

I read and love all kinds of genres, but the books that have stayed with me over time tend to be those that deal with the emotional complexities of real human issues. I am fascinated by the moments when we are tested and forced to reach down to find out exactly what stuff we are made of. People respond to tragedy in heroic and sometimes not so heroic ways. I wanted to examine the process of life coming unglued and then look at all the strengths and the wonderful qualities that lie within us to do the right thing for the ones we love most.

The business of living is chock-full of so many extremes, and while there are parts of this book that deal with sadness, real life is a complete stew of love, loss, joy and sorrow, betrayal, triumph, and achievement.

I think the intricacies within families—the secrets people hold, the love that ebbs and flows in marriages and relationships, and the bond between a parent and child—are all interesting themes we can relate to.

I also liked the idea of looking at multigenerational and cross-sectional layers of the family: fathers and daughters, mothers, sisters, and grandchildren. The father's and daughter's decisions about what to do with the choices their infidelities present were an extra layer. Each had the power to destroy what they had built or knit it back together.

There are definitely little aspects of my own real-life journey. For example, I drew upon my husband Bob's own experience being injured in a roadside bomb in Iraq to write some of the emotions required in the hospital and rehabilitation scenes.

You write, "It was difficult times that let you understand good fortune; you could take an accounting of what you had in a way you weren't able to when life ran smoothly." Do you feel this is true, from a personal perspective?

Absolutely. We all get sick of trite phrases about taking life for granted, but the truth is that the contours in life, the good days chased by a bad day, all allow us to get a perspective on what really matters. If there was a blue sky every single day, you would lose the perspective to fully appreciate it. Likewise, having a few challenges makes the happier, peaceful times all the sweeter. It reminds us to be more in the moment.

The most interesting people I know, the ones I want to talk to at a dinner party, are the people who have faced some kind of adversity, in whatever form that may take.

You say on your Web site that in college you dreamed of writing novels one day but were waylaid by the reality of needing a job right away. What does it feel like to finally achieve your novel-writing dream? Do you have any advice for aspiring authors who need a paying job but still hope to write for a living?

It feels amazing to be a published author. I'd tell any aspiring author to just keep finding those moments to write. Dedicated writers say to write three hours a day, but I've always worn many hats and have never been able to carve that out as a working mother. Three hours ain't gonna happen in my life right now! But I write whenever I can, on planes, in hotel rooms, sometimes early weekend mornings. I say to anyone who wants to write a book that you can do it. Just keep plugging. There is no one right formula.

Which character would you most like to take out to dinner? What would you want to ask him or her?

I'd want to take out Margaret. But I'd need to be able to ply her with wine and loosen her lips. I'm fascinated by women of my mother's era who were taught to keep up appearances: the 1950s–60s housewife who was supposed to burnish the family's public image to perfection and not demonstrate weakness, sadness, or fear.

There is so much going on inside Margaret that she has stuffed down, including her knowledge of her husband's affair. She grew out of someone I knew in real life who confided to me that she would never have mentioned her husband's indiscretions to him, for it would have opened up the door for him to leave, and she had no idea how she would live if that happened. That generation of women who were taught forbearance formed the basis for a really complicated and interesting character.

© Cathrine White Photography

LEE WOODRUFF is the coauthor with her husband, Bob Woodruff, of the number one *New York Times* bestseller *In an Instant*, and the author of the essay collection *Perfectly Imperfect*. She is a contributing editor to *CBS This Morning* and has written articles on family and parenting for numerous magazines and Web sites. She and Bob founded the Bob Woodruff Foundation (remind.org) to assist wounded service members and their families. Woodruff has four children and lives in Westchester County, New York.